DARLINGTON CIRCUS
THE ETERNAL ACT

Published by Darlington Publishing
ISBN: 979-8-9908912-8-9

Printed in USA

Second Edition July 2025

DARLINGTON CIRCUS

THE ETERNAL ACT

SK HINKLEY

CONTENT WARNING

This series contains mature themes, explicit content, and sensitive subjects, including:

- BDSM and DOM/SUB relationships
- Scenes of rape and kidnapping

Reader discretion is advised.

This book is lovingly dedicated to my husband, my soul-mate and forever companion. Your unwavering support and unrelenting belief in me have been a constant source of inspiration.

You would traverse the farthest reaches of the universe to find me, and I am eternally grateful for your love and encouragement.

Thank you for embracing the crazy, wonderful journey that is our life together. I love you and our family more than words can express.

OPAL SEA
EMBERLYNN FOREST
Cemetery
VELAR'S COTTAGE
BLACKWOOD'S COTTAGE
LIBRARY
TOWN SQUARE
Casmira
Eve's Home
MISS POPPET'S BAKESHOP
GUILDED GOBLET
JUBILEE

PROLOGUE

As the day drew to a close it was time for everyone to gather at the cemetery on the highest hill in Jubilee. I hesitated, unwilling to accept that she was truly gone. Our lives had changed in an instant, and I was consumed by anger and grief. It felt like a cruel joke from God himself.

My fellow circus performers and crew members walked up the hill, but I couldn't join them. I felt weak, despite my strong appearance. She had been taken from me again, just when I thought I had her back. The pain was unbearable.

I surely can't be the only one feeling lost and depressed, I just want to crawl in the ground and die with her, but I cannot die, none of us can. Only the one I love gets to face that fate, again.

My friend Eve approached me, her voice barely above a whisper. "They're waiting for you." I couldn't meet her gaze, fearing I'd break down if I saw her tears. I forced myself to start walking, feeling like I was being dragged against my will.

When I finally reached the top, the entire community of Jubilee had gathered, respectfully waiting for me to arrive. They parted to let me pass, and I made my way to the coffin beside a six-foot hole in the ground.

Nearby, her other graves stood. I stared at them, feeling an ache in my empty chest. We used to joke about having her own cemetery, but now it wasn't funny. I walked towards the white coffin adorned with white roses, her favorite. The witches of Jubilee had written "Revertere Ad Nos" - "Come back to us" - on the coffin, just as they did at every funeral before. I placed my hand on the coffin, feeling the weight of her absence. Scarlet tears fell like rain as I prepared to deliver her eulogy.

I took a deep breath and turned to face my immortal family, who were mourning alongside me. I noticed who wasn't there, but I knew he wouldn't show his face. Eve nodded encouragement, and I began, my voice raspy with emotion.

"Today, we gather to honor Nicole Darlington. Though her time in this life with us was brief, her impact on our lives will be everlasting. She brought joy and love into our world, and her inner beauty is what we'll miss the most."

I paused, fighting back tears. "When we see her again, we'll be grateful for the chance to share her mortal life once more. I know she'd want us to keep traveling with the Circus, carrying on until it's time to be with her again." My still heart ached as I concluded, "It won't be easy, but we'll find her..."

CHAPTER
ONE

I blinked repeatedly, wondering if I was still dreaming. "Darlington Circus is the most famous and oldest traveling circus in the world! Can you believe it's here?" *Did they say Darlington Circus?* Looking up at the TV mounted on my bedroom wall quickly realizing I had left it on from the night before and it was now airing the morning news.

I sat up in bed, rubbing my eyes. Darlington Circus was in my hometown? Nothing exciting ever happened in this small farm town in PA. I stared at the TV, mouth agape, as the camera panned over the crowd gathered at the entrance gate.

The reporter's voice continued, "If you want to experience a once-in-a-lifetime event, you'd better hurry. Tickets are selling fast!" I jumped out of bed, my heart racing. I had to go. I stared at the coverage in complete shock. A tall and skinny female reporter was standing in the swarm of people. "Just look at this crowd lining up behind me..."

Then the camera panned slowly, capturing the lengthy line of people standing at the entrance gate. "We are going to move locations now because the rain clouds are moving right on top of us. Reporting live from WGAL, this is Mony Tendez, back to you in the studio."

When a commercial aired, I quickly switched the channel to another news outlet. There it was, Darlington Circus was in big bold letters on the TV banner. I realized the location, It's right across town from me. This was the most amazing news I had ever heard in my life.

This must be the biggest event that's ever happened in this Podunk town. I could see past a different reporter that was now speaking about the mysterious circus, behind them stood the famous black and white tents peeking out from the entrance gate.

Since I was a young girl, I had dreamed of going to Darling-ton Circus. It is believed to hold real magic inside the circus gates. I'm not sure I believe in such things myself, but it sure is intriguing to fantasize about. I walked over to my dresser and picked up an old picture of the circus I had found years ago inside a library book.

The picture must have been from the early eighteen hundreds as it was sepia and had been torn around its brown edges. I stared at the picture admiring the beautiful outside. Black and white tents of varied sizes, but the black pattern was in a wave shaped pattern cascading down getting bigger towards the bottom. How whimsical! If I designed a circus I would have picked the exact same design.

A reporter's serious tone caught my attention, and I turned back to the TV. "It comes to your city in the deepest and darkest part of the night while the whole town is fast asleep and quite magically greets the rising sun with open arms the next day."

I listened to every word. "That's what made this particular circus so alluring, no one ever knew when it would show up or leave. You never know how long it's going to be there, they don't have any social media, no website, no phone number. Nothing. It's the biggest magic trick of all."

That was it, I had to go! I grabbed my cell phone and checked my bank account, and of course, broke as fuck. I thought about asking my parents, but knowing they could barely afford to put me through art school, I would not be asking them for money.

Another commercial aired, I quickly turned the channel again desperate to keep watching the coverage. "The smells coming from the circus are making our mouths water, cinnamon and sugar, sausages, and kettle corn. It smells so delicious from outside the gate already." A male reporter explained.

I wondered why they came to this small town, not much of a crowd and most of the people who live here including me probably couldn't afford to go. *Why would Darlington Circus show up here of all places?*

The reporters were now discussing the storm that is coming in and how that may put a damper on things at the circus. Still listening to my TV I walked to my bedroom window and looked up at the dark cloudy sky. *It wouldn't be fun in the rain anyway,* I told myself. It looked like the heavens were going to open at any second.

I usually love the fall weather, but it has been extra rainy October which has made all the fields muddy. What a mess that would be! I wrapped myself in my soft comfortable white robe without taking my eyes off of the screen. I picked up the remote control and switched to a different station that was also covering the infamous Darlington Circus. I heard the reporter say that ticket prices are astronomical. Sighing aloud and accepting my fate as I turned off my TV. I stepped into my well-worn slippers and headed to the living room.

I share an apartment with my roommate Eve, whom I have known for just three months, but we instantly clicked and became close friends. I responded to her online ad seeking a roommate, eager to escape my parents' house and gain some independence. While I told them it was to shorten my commute to school, the truth was, at nineteen, I was ready to break free and start my own journey.

Most of my high school friends had either moved away, gotten married, or even started families, leaving me feeling left behind. Meanwhile, my parents were focused on raising my ten-year-old brother Lucca, and I felt it was time for me to spread my wings.

In the small living room, I turned on the TV, more coverage of Darlington Circus popped up on the screen. No sign of Eve, who was probably still asleep. Small drops of rain appeared on the window, and I felt bad for the people standing in line. I wondered if they were going to shut the circus down. I was admiring the dark sky when all of a sudden, the front door swung open, startling me.

My roommate Eve burst through the front door, startling me with her sudden arrival. "Nicole!" she exclaimed, her voice vibrating with excitement. Her petite frame and shoulder-length light brown hair seem to radiate energy as she hurried towards me. Her big brown eyes were telling that she was about to overflow with excitement.

I gestured towards the TV, eager to share my excitement. "I've been watching the coverage all morning, Eve! I know all about the circus coming to town!" Without a word, she grasped my hands and started bouncing up and down, her infectious enthusiasm drawing me in. I couldn't resist joining in, and soon we were both jumping and laughing together, our smiles mirroring each other's joy. The thrill of Darlington Circus's arrival had us both elated, and in that moment, nothing else mattered but the magic of the circus.

It wasn't long before reality set in. I stopped jumping and shook my head, my voice laced with disappointment. "Eve, we can't go. Tickets are too expensive, and we have rent to pay and bills to cover." But Eve's face remained set in determination, her eyes sparkling with a fierce resolve. She whispered under her breath, "Today's the day!" A phrase that seemed to hold a secret meaning for her.

I had never seen Eve this enraptured before, I thought to myself, *maybe this has been a dream of Eve's just like it was for me.* I started talking to myself aloud. "Maybe we can put all our money together and see what we have, I could also try and pick up more shifts waitressing to cover rent..."

Thoughts raced through my mind trying to figure out some way we could attend this once in a lifetime experience.

Since I have known Eve, she wasn't one to take no for an answer. She always seemed to get what she wanted. I think part of the reason I wanted to be her friend was because of the way she carries herself. For such a young woman she was oddly wise beyond her years. An old soul, she just smiles whenever I call her that.

As I paced back and forth in the living room, mentally calculating how I could possibly scrounge up enough money for a ticket, Eve approached me with a mysterious smile. I assumed she was handing me my mail, but instead, she pressed a sleek black envelope into my hands. I turned it over, and my heart skipped a beat as I noticed a white wax seal emblazoned with the words 'Darlington Circus' in elegant script. The seal seemed to shimmer in the light, radiating an air of exclusivity and wonder.

My jaw dropped as I stared at the envelope in disbelief, my eyes fixed on the intricate wax seal. I glanced up at Eve, who was watching me with a mischievous grin, her eyes sparkling with excitement. "Oh My God" was all I could say. I carefully broke the seal and opened the envelope, my heart racing with anticipation. And then, I saw them, two tickets, nestled inside, beckoning me to a once in a lifetime adventure.

I was left speechless, as Eve burst into an enthusiastic explanation. "I was out running this morning and I stumbled upon the circus! I rushed over and, luck of luck, I was the first person in line! And, can you believe it, they gave me two passes!" Her excitement took over and she broke into a little song and twirled around the room like a little girl.

Overcome with excitement I grabbed her hands and started jumping up and down again. "This is the best day ever!" I shouted. Eve smiled and she whispered under her breath, "Just you wait." I hugged and thanked her profusely. "This has been a dream of mine." Eve's knowing smile hinted that she had more to tell me.

After we celebrated, Eve suggested we get ready quickly so we could make the most of our day at the circus. I wholeheartedly agreed, already envisioning the wonders we would soon experience. As I turned to head to my bedroom to get ready, Eve suddenly grasped my arm, halting me in my tracks. I turned back to face her, and she beamed a radiant smile at me. "This is for you as well," she said, her eyes sparkling with mystery.

She handed me a smaller ticket, which I took with growing curiosity. As I read the words printed on it: Side Show at 1pm in the Little Black Tent. Eve skipped off to her bedroom, leaving me wondering what secrets the Little Black Tent held, and what surprises lay in store for me.

As I reached my bedroom, I was tingling with so much excitement. I carefully placed the tickets on my bed. I was thrilled, but also curious about the mysterious ticket. I did not even care that it was teeming outside. This weather was not going to keep us away, I just hoped that they wouldn't close the circus because of it.

I quickly took a shower, blow dried my hair and got dressed in jeans and a black sweater. Not my usual look, but I didn't want to be in a dress walking through a muddy corn field where the circus was set up. As I got ready, I flipped the TV back on, and the screen showed a sea of rain-soaked faces at the circus entrance, their determination to enjoy the show despite the weather mirroring my own excitement and anticipation.

In the hall closet I rummaged through to get to my black raincoat and to dig out my old ugly rain boots that were buried somewhere in the back. I yelled for Eve, but she didn't respond. Finally, I found my boots and pulled them on quickly. I wondered if she was soon ready because I was beyond ready to go and growing antsy waiting for her.

I grabbed an apple from the kitchen counter and started snacking on it while I patiently waited for my roommate. A few minutes passed and my impatience grew, I walked to her bedroom and knocked a couple times. "Eve, are you ready yet? Do you think they will close the circus because of the rain?" No response.

I opened the door to her bedroom slowly, "Eve?" No answer. I opened the door wider, but she wasn't there. I scanned her room without leaving the doorway, it was bare for having lived here longer than me. The walls were bare white. No pictures or posters. Just a small dresser and a full-size bed. That's when I saw a note lying in the middle of her bed. It read: I'll meet you at the circus, I have to run an errand first. See you soon!

Ugh, I was a bit irritated at her, I wish I found this out sooner. I picked up my phone to call her, but it went straight to voicemail. Eve was always doing last minute things like this. Her behavior was not unusual.

She was always running off somewhere or meeting someone at the drop of a hat. I have noticed in the past three months living with her she could be a little mysterious, maybe she was dating someone and wanted to keep it private. I shrugged it off and ordered an Uber.

While I waited for my ride, I watched more of the news coverage and checked the weather. A meteorologist on the local news predicted that the storm would last well into the night. I was too excited to care about the storm, even if I got to go for an hour or two, I would be grateful to say that I had been to Darlington Circus.

A few minutes later my Uber arrived. I put on my raincoat and grabbed an umbrella that I found while I was digging out my boots from the hall closet. Once outside the rain was coming down hard and the wind was blowing which made it feel like it was raining sideways. *Why did I even bother drying my hair?*

I hopped in the back seat of a blue sedan just as thunder rumbled loudly above. "Darlington Circus please." I eagerly said to the driver. "Wow, you are so lucky! I have been dropping people off there all morning, I sure hope the weather gets better for ya!"

I informed him that it is most likely going to storm all day and night according to the news report. Every few minutes the dark cloudy sky would light up with lightning. We drove about a mile towards the circus and soon I started seeing crowds of people heading in the same direction. The car wipers would clear the windshield for a brief second as rain continuously fell on us. From the distance I could see the pointy tops of the black and white circus tents.

"Will this do?" The Uber driver asked as he pulled over. Since the crowd was so thick he couldn't get any closer. I was only a couple of blocks away, so I grabbed my umbrella to face the storm and said "Yes, thank you."

I stepped out into thick, slippery wet mud and followed the fence that enclosed the circus all the way to the entrance. The howling wind was blowing so strong that my umbrella was useless and by the time I got to the entrance gate I was completely soaked.

I was extremely glad that I wore my rainboots, the mud had completely covered them, but at least my feet were dry, for now. I looked up when I got to the gate and there it was emblazoned with big bold black letters: DARLINGTON CIRCUS. I stood there for a moment taking it in letting the rain wash the makeup from my face.

When I got in line I waited patiently alongside the other guests, but to our collective surprise, the line progressed at a brisk pace. I scanned around for Eve, but it was pointless. The endless sea of people made the search impossible. I pulled out my phone and tried calling her again, but it went straight to voicemail, just like before. I shrugged it off, thinking maybe she was already inside, and I made a mental note to try calling her again once I was under the dry cover of one of the big top tents. I looked forward to escaping the rain and finding some respite from the downpour.

Before I knew it, I had reached the front of the line at the entrance gate. An older gentleman with a distinguished salt-and- pepper hair cut was manning the ticket booth, his imposing figure commanding attention. As I approached him, I couldn't help but notice his massive, muscular arms, decorated with vibrant tattoo sleeves that seemed to tell a story of their own. His rugged appearance was a stark contrast to the whimsical atmosphere of the circus, and I found myself wondering what his story was, and how he had come to be the guardian of the gate.

When I was caught staring, I swiftly averted my gaze, but not before catching a glimpse of his warm closed lip smile. I tried to play it cool, pretending to focus on something else, but my curiosity got the better of me, and I sneaked another glance at the ticket man. To my surprise, he was still looking at me, his eyes crinkling at the corners as he smiled. My face began to flush, and I wondered if he had noticed me admiring his tattoos. As the line inched closer, I tried to compose myself. *Be cool.*

As I drew closer, it became increasingly clear that he was indeed staring at me, his gaze fixed on me with an intensity that made me feel both curious and uncomfortable. Confused, I glanced over my shoulder to see if there was someone behind me who had caught his attention, but no one was looking in his direction. When I turned back around, he was still looking at me almost as if he was struggling to contain a laugh. My gaze was drawn to his arm, where a vibrant pirate ship tattoo seemed to leap off his skin, its colors and details so vivid that I found myself mesmerized.

When it was finally my turn, he remained silent, his snicker suggesting he was amused by my soiled appearance. I must have looked like a drowned rat, judging by the way he was struggling to contain his laughter. I handed him my ticket, but he didn't even glance at it, his piercing emerald eyes fixed intently on me instead. His gaze was so intense that I felt my face flush bright red once again, as if his eyes were burning into my very soul.

His eyes were mesmerizing, and I felt like he was gazing deep into my very essence. The moment stretched out, and I was frozen in place, unable to look away. Finally, he broke the spell with a sweeping hand gesture, motioning me to enter. As I walked past him, I felt goosebumps, sensing his eyes still fixed on me. Though I didn't dare turn around, his gaze lingered like a gentle caress on my skin.

As I trailed behind the crowd, my attention was drawn to a solitary door standing freely. The door itself was unassuming, painted a crisp white and sized like any ordinary door. Circus security stood on both sides of the door making sure all the guests entered through it. I felt an overwhelming urge to explore what lay beyond, and so I joined in the line leading to the doorway. What happened next was pure magic, if you believe in that sort of thing.

CHAPTER
TWO

As I stepped through the mysterious doorway, the atmosphere transformed instantly, like a veil of magic had been lifted. The dark, rain-cloud-covered sky gave way to a bright, sunny day with a warm, golden light that enveloped me. I felt the sudden absence of raindrops on my skin, and my long brown hair, once wet and limp, was styled perfectly, better than I had done it before leaving the apartment.

I continued to inspect myself and quickly noticed I was wearing a flowing black and white dress with matching sandals in the same distinctive pattern of the adorning circus tents. I felt special, noticing I was the only one dressed in this magical attire making me feel like a part of the mystical world.

As I looked around, I saw that everyone else shared the same look of wonder and shock as they entered through the mysterious door. They were all met with the same wave of realization that this entire experience was magic. Guests stood with their mouths wide open in surprise and utter shock, taking in the breathtaking views of the circus. Many of them stood frozen, like statues, trying to process the surreal beauty around them. I, too, stood in awe, taking in the sights and sounds of the circus.

A cobblestone path beneath my feet led me through a beautiful circus, with not a trace of mud in sight. Which was fascinating, considering the circus was set up right in the middle of a cornfield. Well-manicured gardens with vibrant wildflowers lined the different paths within the circus, creating a symphony of hues. And instead of just one big top tent, I saw at least ten, each one more magnificent than the last.

I was taken aback for a moment, because of a majestic weeping willow tree at the center. I knew there was not one before, certainly not in the middle of a corn field. I marveled at the endless surprises of this enchanting place. *Have I been transported?*

I had been standing in the same place taking in all the magical scenes when I remembered my quest to find Eve. I reached inside my pocket and grabbed my phone to call her, but my phone was dead, despite being fully charged earlier. I slipped it back in my pocket and when I did, I felt something else inside.

I found the side show ticket in my pocket. I had almost forgotten about it. I read it again, Sideshow 1pm in the Little black tent. I couldn't see the tent from where I stood, so I continued walking, taking in the vibrant atmosphere.

The sound of laughter and music filled the air, and I could hear the distant roar of lions and the chatter of excited voices. The smell of popcorn and sugary treats wafted through the air, making my stomach growl with hunger. I felt like a kid again, full of wonder and excitement, ready to explore this magical world.

As I walked through the circus, I noticed that each tent was themed differently, with its own unique decorations and attractions. One tent was filled with acrobats and aerialists, their bodies bending and twisting in impossible ways. Another tent was home to a magnificent menagerie of animals, with lions, tigers, and bears oh my! And yet another tent was dedicated to magic and illusions, with a mysterious sorcerer performing tricks that left me speechless.

I forced myself to keep walking because I still wanted to find Eve and I also didn't want to miss the side show, whatever it was. I followed the winding cobblestone path that weaved around the circus tents. I came across an elephant eating peanuts from visitors' hands. Being my favorite animal, I couldn't resist petting the magnificent creature.

I walked up and started to pet the gentle giant. To my surprise, it wrapped its trunk around me and gently lifted me off the ground. I was startled but not at all frightened. He was so friendly he put me down gently after a few moments.

As soon as my feet touched the ground, I heard a voice from behind me, "Attaboy, Orlow!" A young man, Clove, introduced himself and explained he cared for Orlow, the friendly elephant. That was just one of his jobs at the circus. He wore a pair of blue worn out overalls. He looked like a sweet scruffy young man.

He gave me some peanuts and I started feeding Orlow. We were laughing together for a little while about the beautiful creature just picking me up the way that he had. The young man explained that Orlow must really like me because he never does that to just anyone, that made me smile. After a delightful encounter, I continued my search for Eve and the Little Black Tent.

A mesmerizing Cyr wheel performer quickly caught my eye. Right in the middle of the main path I had been walking on. A young woman, and from a distance it looked just like Eve, and started spinning. Everyone gathered around creating a circle around the performer.

She spun faster and faster until I couldn't see her at all. When the spinning slowed, she was gone, vanished right out of thin air. The spinning wheel stopped and instead of falling over which I expected it to, it simply rolled down the path and disappeared between a slit into one of the tents. Marvelous. Cheers and applause erupted from the audience.

Once the crowd dispersed, I continued down the path to a split right in front of a weeping willow tree. I assumed I had reached the middle of the Circus. I was figuring out which way to attempt when I noticed a young girl sitting under the willow tree. She was wearing a dazzling blue dance outfit, no doubt a performer.

I walked over towards the young girl, "Excuse me," I said to get her attention. The young girl swiftly bounced up to look at me. "Poppy!" She abruptly yelled. I must have startled her. Just as I approached another young girl appeared from behind the tree now startling me.

The two girls look identical. They were twins and even wore the exact same matching sparkling outfits. They both had shoulder length blonde hair and blue eyes. They looked to be about 10 years old like my little brother Lucca. They were giggling now, and I wasn't sure why, but I smiled back waiting for their help.

"Do you know where I can find the little black tent?" I asked hopefully. The twins looked at each other and started giggling even more. I smiled at them, but I didn't really understand what was so funny.

Eventually the two girls started speaking. "I'm Pixie," "and I'm Poppy." Then they giggled some more. I asked again "Do you know where I can find the Side Show at 1pm? One of them said, "Poppy will tell you" Pixie interrupted and said, "No! Pixie will tell you!" Poppy laughed. I was getting frustrated and decided to move on, they were no help at all.

I was about to walk away from the twins when they started to block my way. Soon they were circling around me. Poppy said giggling, "It's over that way!" Pointing me to the left of the tree. "No, it's that way" Pixie said as she pointed to the right path.

The twins were once again giggling and I kept walking away from them, knowing they were not going to help me, and I was running out of time. From a distance I could hear one of them say to the other, "It's about time." I didn't know nor care what they were talking about.

Frustrated but determined, I followed the path to the left passing through beautiful gardens of lavender and mint. It was beautiful and smelled even better than it looked. I thought about Eve and wondered if she had arrived at the circus yet.

People ahead of me seemed to be heading in the same direction, perhaps to the side show so I followed the crowd.

The cobblestone path I had been following abruptly ended at a huge field with green fluffy grass. A sign read: HEALING GRASS.

I took off my sandals and stepped on the grass. In the distance a thick forest lined where the fence around the circus should be, but there wasn't a fence, only trees. It was so mind trippy to think I was still in Quarryville. I felt like I had been transported into another world.

Everyone's shoes were left in a pile at the end of the path. I wasn't taking the chance of losing my new sandals, so I held onto them. I didn't know if I was able to keep them or not, I sure hope I get to keep them as a souvenir along with my matching dress. The grass felt amazingly soft, and silky smooth, I could lay down in it and take a nap, it felt so good. Some guests were doing just that in the distance. I kept walking around just enjoying the sensation on my feet.

In the distance I could faintly hear music. The sensation was enchanting, but I pressed on, following the music to the farthest end of the field. The more I walked the louder the music became until I was standing in front of a massive tent. A rock concert was being performed.

The crowd was so big that most people were outside on the grass dancing to the music. I couldn't even get close enough to see the band playing. *How peculiar to have a rock concert inside a circus*. This place truly was amazing, but you definitely needed to spend the entire day just to take everything in. I could spend hours just observing my surroundings.

Though intrigued, I remembered my priority was finding the side show and Eve. It was almost 1pm and surely, she was going to be there looking for me. I returned to the cobble path and put my sandals back on. I headed back the way I came breathing in the fresh lavender and mint.

Passing by the weeping willow tree I saw the twins still there. I didn't acknowledge them, but I heard one of them yell in my direction. "I told you!" Then they giggled more. Smiling, I shook my head. *Silly girls*, I thought to myself.

I dug into my pocket, searching for directions on the ticket. But instead, I found a cryptic message: "Welcome Home Nicole" I halted, my eyes fixed on the words as I reread them, wondering if I was hallucinating. Blinking my eyes and reading it again. Sideshow 1pm Little Black Tent. I flipped it over, but it was blank. I let out a frustrated sigh, scanning the sea of black and white tents again searching for any sign of the elusive little black one. But it was nowhere to be found. I felt a growing sense of unease, as if I was losing my grip on reality.

I turned right at the weeping willow tree and followed a picturesque pathway of wildflowers. The enticing aroma of cinnamon and sugar wafting from the elephant stand ahead drew me in. I couldn't resist the temptation of the deep-fried dough and approached the stand.

An older lady with short white hair had her back to me. "Excuse me, one elephant ear please." The lady took a moment before she turned around and when she did her face lit up with a warm smile that seemed almost familiar. It was as if she knew me, and I felt confused but smiled back.

The lady's smile lingered until I requested an elephant ear again. "Well now dear, you can't eat this right now, you will be late for your show, run along dear," her words leaving me in total shock "How did you know?" I asked bewildered. She shooed me away with her hand saying, "Don't worry dear, I'll bring you one a little later, now run along."

The lady watched as I stumbled away backwards, confused. I turned to continue down the path but then thought better of it and turned back around to ask for directions. But to my astonishment, she was gone. Not only had she vanished, but the entire stand had disappeared along with her.

I was growing increasingly uneasy with all the magic surrounding me. The disappearing elephant ear stand and the mysterious lady on the Cyr wheel had left me feeling perplexed.

I was no longer in the mood for the sideshow. This place was starting to feel like a surreal nightmare.

I glanced at my watch and saw that it was precisely 1 pm. Frustration boiled over, and I shouted aloud, "Where are you?" Irritated, I turned back around to continue down the path, but my feet froze in place when I saw the little black tent standing right in front of me.

CHAPTER
THREE

I couldn't believe my eyes; the black tent wasn't there just a moment ago! I rubbed my eyes, wondering if the magic of the circus was playing tricks on me. *Am I going crazy?* This was the only tent that was solid black, and while it was smaller than the other tents, I wouldn't call it little.

Unlike the other tents, which were bustling with people entering and leaving, this one seemed eerily quiet. There were no lines of excited spectators waiting to get in, no performers emerging from its entrance, and no music or laughter spilling out from within. It was as if the black tent was waiting for something, or someone, and I felt an inexplicable pull to approach it.

I walked around the black tent, searching for an opening. Finally, I found a small entrance and slid my way inside. For a few seconds, my eyes struggled to adjust to the complete darkness, and I stood still, waiting for my vision to clear.

Checking my watch, the glowing hands confirmed it was indeed 1 pm. *Surely, I was in the right spot.* I took a deep breath and looked around, realizing I was the only one there. The silence was eerie, and I could feel the weight of my solitude.

In the very middle of the tent, a spotlight shone down on a small area of the tent's floor, creating a circle of brightness in the darkness. I walked towards the light. I stood in the spotlight for a moment, before turning to leave.

Suddenly, I heard a man's deep, resonant voice say, "Hello, Mrs. Darlington." I stopped in my tracks, my heart skipping a beat, and turned back to the light to correct whoever it was that they had the wrong person. I opened my mouth to say, "I'm not Mrs. Darlington," but before I could utter a word, I realized that nobody was there.

I spun back around, thinking maybe it was a recording or some kind of trick, but as I stepped away, the voice called out again, this time closer to me. "I've missed you dearly," the words sending a chill down my body. His accent, I could not place.

But then, I felt his presence directly behind me, and all the hair on my arms rose as if electrified. Slowly, I turned around, my heart racing with anticipation and fear, wondering who or what I would face.

Even in the darkness, the deep crimson of the tailcoat adorning his foreboding frame was visible, like a splash of blood in the night. *He must be the Ringmaster,* I thought, my heart racing with fear. I was quite nervous as he stood there towering over me, his presence commanding and intimidating. I could tell he had dark hair, but it was too dark to see anything else, and his face was shrouded in mystery.

I began to tell him that he had the wrong person, but he took my hand gently, his grip firm but not unkind, and led me back into the light. I felt like a puppet on strings, powerless to resist. *Was this an act? Was this part of the circus?* "Excuse me,

I'm sorry, but you have me confused with someone else," I protested, trying to pull my hand free, but he held fast.

The strange man walked us into the light, and he turned to face me, his eyes gleaming with a knowing intensity. "I've been waiting a very long time for you, Mrs. Darlington," he said, his voice low and husky, sending shivers down my spine. He smiled at me as if he knew me intimately, and it was then that I curiously peered deep into his charming blue eyes, searching for answers. They looked like waves in the ocean, and I felt myself getting lost in their depths, like a sailor at sea.

Within seconds I was locked into a trance unable to look away. Instant pain engulfed my head, like a thousand knives stabbing at my brain. A scream came from my mouth, but I could only hear a deafening tone, like the sound of a thousand bells clanging in my ears.

My entire life was being replayed before my eyes, but it wasn't just this lifetime that was flashing through my mind. It was all my lifetimes! Memories long buried, forgotten and suppressed, came flooding back. I remembered every detail, every joy, every sorrow, every love.

And then, it hit me, the realization that I am Mrs. Darlington, and the sexy, tall ringmaster standing in front of me was thee, Bellamy Darlington, magical mastermind, and creator of Darlington Circus, but most importantly, he was my husband. My soulmate. My eternal love. The memories of our past lives together came rushing back, and I felt the weight of our centuries-long love story bearing down on me.

Flashes of my past lives with Bellamy, my many lives with the circus, and all the immortals who worked here bombarded my mind, like a tidal wave crashing against the shore. I remembered my life with Eve, who was way more to me than a roommate. She was my confidante, my partner in crime, my sister in every way that counted.

My memories were flooding my mind in the most intense and irrepressible way, like a dam had burst, releasing a torrent of emotions and experiences that I thought I had long forgotten. The sheer volume of thoughts was so overwhelming that my head began to pound, like a jackhammer drilling into my skull.

It was so painful, like a brain freeze that didn't end, until I was out of breath and my vision began to blur. I squeezed my head with both hands, trying to stem the flow of memories, but they kept coming, relentless and unyielding. My body began to shake from the pain, like a leaf in a hurricane, and I felt myself falling, falling, falling, until Bellamy caught me just before I hit the floor. And then, everything went black.

As I came to, Bellamy's embrace enveloped me, and my eyes adjusted to the blinding house lights that were now turned on inside the tent's interior. 'Oh, Daddy, I'm back! I'm back!' Tears streamed down my face as I clung to him, overwhelmed with joy and relief. The familiar scent of the salty sea filled my nose, and the warmth of his hug was soothing to my soul.

I held on tight, unable to stem the flow of tears, as Bellamy cradled me like a child. He pressed a small glass into my hand, and I obeyed his unspoken instruction to drink, my mind reeling from the sudden onslaught of memories. It always took time for my brain to adjust to the resurgence of my past, but in this moment, all that mattered was that I was back with my immortal family.

After drinking Bellamy's concoction, I sat up straighter, still cradled in his lap. A place I had deeply missed. Bellamy's gentleness was apprehensible, as if he feared I might shatter at any moment. I enveloped him in a tight embrace, and he reciprocated with equal tenderness. Tears flowed freely, as I was overcome with emotion.

Bellamy's soothing kisses on the top of my head and his gentle reassurances, "Let it out, cry it out." only seemed to release more tears. I was once again struck by the weight of my rebirth, the realization that I had been reincarnated yet again. The enormity of it all left me breathless and tearful, but with Bellamy's loving embrace, I felt a sense of safety and comfort wash over me.

As I took slow, deep breaths in through my nose and out through my mouth, Bellamy's supporting hand helped me rise to my feet. Though still dazed, my eagerness to reunite with loved ones propelled me forward. With Bellamy by my side, we stepped out of the tent, and I was met with a heartwarming sight of a line of familiar faces, all beaming with warm smiles.

As my eyes adjusted to the radiant sunlight, I beheld the bright, shining faces of my immortal family. The gentle rustle of their murmured greetings and the soft shuffle of their feet as they shifted in anticipation created a sense of comfort and belonging.

As I took in the vibrant sights and sounds of the magical circus, my earlier disorientation seemed foolish. This was my haven, my community, and my eternal family had finally found me again. Nineteen years had passed since our last reunion, and the warmth of their embraces and familiar faces soothed my soul.

Bellamy remained steadfast by my side, offering reassurance as the performers and crew members approached me with open arms and heartfelt gifts. "Take your time, my dear," he whispered, his British accent still present after all these years. "We can pause whenever you need." But I was too enthralled, too eager to reconnect with my loved ones and rediscover the memories we had shared. One by one, they came forward, showering me with affection and tokens of remembrance. Tokens that stirred long- forgotten joys and reminded me of the lives I had lived before.

Eve was among the first to embrace me, her warm smile and infectious laughter instantly putting me at ease. We shared a playful chuckle about her role as my roommate. A clever ruse to keep me safe until the circus could reunite us, likely orchestrated by Bellamy himself. Eve was more than just a friend; she was a sister, a confidante, and a kindred spirit.

The blonde Bally sisters, Pixie and Poppy, affectionately known as the "giggle mug twins" approached me with their signature giggles, their eyes sparkling with mischief. These talented aerialists, known for their breathtaking Spanish web act, enveloped me in warm hugs and presented me with a box of Linzer tarts. A sweet treat that held a special place in my heart, and one I hadn't yet experienced in this lifetime.

The twins, always playful and quick to tease, were still chuckling about our earlier encounter, which Bellamy had gently interrupted, sending them on their way. Their lighthearted banter and joyful energy reminded me of my brother Lucca from my current lifetime.

Velar, the handsome vampire who had earlier manned the ticket gate, bypassed the forming line, and strode confidently to the front. His earlier grin had blossomed into a wide, fang-baring smile, highlighting his razor-sharp teeth. I had only ever known Velar as an immortal, turned in the late seventeenth century, long before I joined the circus.

Despite being over four hundred years old, he appeared as a fit and attractive fifty years old, with salt-and-pepper hair, piercing emerald eyes, and a powerful physique that seemed chiseled from marble. As the strongman of our circus, his muscular build was imposing, yet his warm demeanor put everyone at ease. Though he could not tolerate true sunlight, Bellamy's enchanted circus allowed him to thrive in the daylight, his skin radiant with a subtle, otherworldly glow.

Velar swept me up in a bold embrace, spinning me around before setting me down, his deep, masculine voice filled with emotion as he declared, "I've missed you so much." His smile faltered for a moment as he caught Bellamy's watchful gaze, but he quickly recovered, his expression morphing into a sly smirk.

Bellamy, his best friend, and brother-like confidant, didn't react, but I knew he wasn't pleased. Despite this, Velar's warmth and enthusiasm were infectious, and I could not help but feel a deep connection to him.

The Blackwoods, one of the many families of witches from Jubilee, approached me with warm smiles. Mesidor, stood alongside his wife Ambrette and their son Clove, who had brought along an incredibly special companion - Orlow. He was a majestic African elephant with a single ivory tusk. When I saw him earlier, he had two tusks, deceived by Bellamy's magic.

As Orlow made his way towards me, the crowd could not resist showering him with affection, patting his wrinkled gray skin and offering gentle praise. Orlow was more than just a beloved animal, he was my cherished friend, I rescued from a cruel circus many years ago. Clove kindly takes care of him, and I was overjoyed to be reunited with my gentle giant.

I embraced Orlow, and he wrapped his trunk around me, lifting me up in his special greeting. I reveled in the warmth of his touch, feeling a deep connection to this magnificent creature.

As he sat me down, Ambrette approached me with a gentle smile, offering a fragrant bunch of rosemary and a selection of herbs. This was a tradition she had upheld for years, providing me with these special herbs to aid in recalling my past lives. My memories were always hazy in the early weeks, but with time, they would slowly resurface.

Ambrette's thoughtful gesture was a reminder of the love and support that surrounded me. I felt grateful for this family, who had stood by me through countless lifetimes, and for the memories we had shared. As I accepted her gift, I knew that with their help, my memories would soon return, and I would once again be whole.

During the welcome line I looked around the circus, my circus and smiled knowing that I was home again. The Rossi Family who does the Risley Act in the circus greeted me with homemade pasta. This entire family juggles everything and anything including their own bodies. It is quite amazing to see in person.

"Nee-cole!" Giuseppe yelled in his thick Italian accent. "Thank you so much." I said as he gave me a hug. "Come for dinner sometime, I make you spook-eti and meat ball." I loved and missed his big personality.

Behind Giuseppe were the clowns. "Joey!" I yelled at all of them. With all the makeup I couldn't tell who was who and that's what we called the clowns anyway at the circus.

As I continued down the line, I spotted Miss Poppet, her warm smile radiant as she approached me with a freshly baked elephant ear. "I told you I'd bring you one, my dear," she said, her eyes twinkling with kindness. I squeezed her in a tight hug, grateful for the motherly love she had always shown me.

Her specialty, baking sand tarts during the Christmas season, was a beloved tradition that brought joy to everyone in the circus. Bellamy would even close the circus to give her the time and space to create her magical baked goods, which people would eagerly line up for at her cozy bakeshop in our hidden town.

Miss Poppet was more than just a talented baker. She has always been a mother figure for me. So wise and compassionate, always ready with intelligent advice and a listening ear. She was the circus's collective grandmother, nurturing and guiding us all with her warmth and wisdom. As I took a bite of the still-warm elephant ear, I declared with a mouthful, "This is the most delicious thing I've tasted in this lifetime!" She smiled knowingly, her eyes sparkling with pleasure at seeing me enjoy her creation.

The sweetness of the treat was matched only by the warmth of Miss Poppet's presence, and I felt grateful for her constant support and love. She was a true treasure of the circus, and I felt lucky to have her in my life.

It's a peculiar sensation, realizing how deeply I have missed everyone, despite only recalling them today. My soul, it seems, has been longing for them all along. It's as if I had an unexplained ache in my heart, a void I could not quite pinpoint, until now.

Today, with memories flooding back, that ache has finally been soothed. I'm overwhelmed with a sense of reunion, of reconnecting with pieces of my past that I thought were lost forever. It's truly a unique experience, one that transcends words, and I'm grateful to be back with my circus family.

Years of shared experiences and memories had forged an unbreakable bond between us, a deep and abiding love that only grew stronger with time. This vibrant community, my circus family, was my true home, and I was finally back where I belonged.

As I gazed out at the sea of familiar faces, I noticed that the celebration seemed even more exuberant than in years past. *Did they miss me even more this time?* The thought filled my heart with warmth. I scanned the crowd, taking in the beaming smiles of the performers and crew, and felt a sense of pure joy wash over me. I was back.

Once the crowd dispersed, I found myself surrounded by my closest friends and the circus's leadership - Bellamy, Velar, and Eve. With my memories restored, I finally had the chance to ask Bellamy a question that had been weighing on my mind. "Daddy, why did it take you so long to find me this time? I am nineteen, and usually, you find me sooner."

Bellamy's expression turned uncertain, and he hesitated before responding, "I am sorry, baby girl. I have you now, and that's all that matters." His response only sparked more curiosity, and I delved deeper into my mind, searching for answers. But to my surprise, I could not recall my last life or the circumstances of my death. It was as if those memories were shrouded in a thick fog, refusing to surface. I found this peculiar and continued to probe my mind, but the memories remained elusive, leaving me with more questions than answers.

Bellamy was speaking with Velar when I uncaringly interrupted. "Why can't I remember how I died?" I muttered, shaking my head in despair, trying once more to recall the lost memories. But my mind remained a blank slate, and panic began to set in. I turned to Bellamy, seeking answers, but he exchanged a fleeting glance with Velar before responding, "Why don't you give yourself some time, let your mind rest for a bit? This is all very overwhelming for you."

His words full of wisdom, and I knew he was right. I needed to calm down and trust that my memories would resurface in time. I nodded in agreement, but before I could say anything more, Velar abruptly turned and walked away, leaving me feeling concerned and confused.

I decided to let the matter rest, trusting that my memories would return in time. Rejoining the circus was always a whirlwind experience, and today was no exception. Remembering who I was and my place within the circus was a lot to process, and the day's events had left me emotionally drained.

Despite the exhaustion, I was in awe of the circus's seamless operation, knowing the immense effort that went into keeping it running even with the help of Bellamy's magic. Magic! Oh magic! Bellamy's magic was a crucial part of that, and I was thrilled to have it back in my life. I had forgotten the wonder of magic until today, and now that I have it back, I am filled with joy and gratitude.

Darlington's Circus has a rich history that dates back to the late seventeen hundreds, founded by Bellamy himself. Initially, he followed a friend to London to help launch a circus venture, and soon he became a performer himself. However, Bellamy's secrets went far beyond his circus roots. He possessed magic and immortality long before the circus's inception. In fact, he is the oldest person I have ever known. But the circus's fate took a dramatic turn when a witch cast a curse, making everyone associated with Darlington's Circus immortal - everyone, that is, except for me.

If my memory serves me right, the witch's curse was a vindictive move aimed at Bellamy himself. She sought to punish him by forcing him to witness my mortal existence, watching me grow old and eventually perish, while he remained forever young and immortal. This ancient grudge was cast centuries ago, and the details have grown hazy with time, but the pain and longing remain.

Bellamy's appearance remains timeless, tall, handsome, and captivating, with dark hair and charming sea blue eyes that draw me in. Despite his youthful appearance, which suggests a man in his thirties, he has lived an astonishing four hundred plus years.

One of the most remarkable aspects of Bellamy is his extraordinary intelligence, honed by centuries of experience and learning. His vast knowledge and insight are a testament to the wisdom that comes with immortality.

More witches from the circus community warmly welcomed me with an array of delicious food and thoughtful, handmade gifts. These witches, though powerful, practice a benevolent craft, and their kindness is a blessing. They have performed the ancient ritual of Samsara, ensuring my reincarnation with each passing life.

Soon, we will gather again to continue this cycle, bound by a sacred promise. Life after life, I am reborn, and though I would not trade this precious connection for anything, a part of me longs for the gift of immortality, a privilege that has eluded me thus far.

Since Bellamy and Eve still had some tasks to attend to with the circus, I offered to wait by the majestic weeping willow tree. This magical tree holds a secret, it is the sole entrance to Jubilee, a hidden land created by Ambrette and Bellamy in the late seventeen hundreds.

Jubilee is a sanctuary for the immortals of Darlington Circus, a place where we can live safely, hidden from the rest of the world. It is a necessity, really, given the challenges of coexisting with humans and the difficulties of trust.

Especially the witches, I do not blame them, throughout history we have seen what society has done to witches. They have every reason to be cautious, given the dark history of persecution and fear that has haunted their kind for centuries.

As I sat on the bench, lost in thought, memories of my past lives at the circus flooded my mind. I recalled the first time I met Bellamy, when I was a young tightrope walker seeking refuge from a horrible situation. He took me under his wing, offering me a job and a sense of belonging. I was just sixteen years old then, and our connection was instantaneous.

We fell deeply in love, our bond growing stronger with each passing day. Our relationship has always been unconventional, perhaps that's what has sustained our love across countless lifetimes. As immortals, they don't adhere to the same rules as humans when it comes to love and relationships. Our love has been a constant, a beacon of hope and devotion that transcends time and circumstance.

My connection with Bellamy remains constant across every reincarnation. We are bound by marriage, a union we have renewed numerous times. More profoundly, he is my Dominant, and I am his submissive.

In our world, it is a natural dynamic, one we embrace with ease. I affectionately call him 'Daddy,' and he lovingly refers to me as "baby girl.'" Bellamy's inherent dominant alpha nature makes him the only man I trust implicitly, the only one I can surrender myself too completely.

Bellamy is my unwavering rock, my biggest supporter, and my guiding light. No matter how wild my dreams or desires may be, he is always there to encourage me, offering a safe and non-judgmental space to share my thoughts and feelings. He's my fierce protector, and I pity anyone who dares to cross his baby girl. With a wealth of knowledge and experience, he's also my trusted teacher, mentor, and advisor, always ready to share his wisdom and insights. His vast understanding of the world, gained through centuries of life, makes him an invaluable resource in navigating life's challenges.

While he's my rock, my anchor, and my safe haven, he's also my loving disciplinarian, though he's grown softer with time, preferring to spoil me rather than punish me. Still, I must admit that I occasionally crave a firm but loving spanking, which may explain why I sometimes playfully test boundaries and act out, seeking that thrilling spark of discipline.

Submitting to Bellamy comes naturally to me. I have absolute faith in him and always speak my truth, knowing he'll listen with kindness and understanding. I show him the utmost respect and devotion, never faltering in my commitment to our bond. I delight in pleasing him, and he knows I'll always strive to make him proud. Our dynamic works so effortlessly because Bellamy cherishes me deeply, and I bask in the warmth of his adoration. While many immortals choose different paths, this lifestyle is our haven, our sanctuary, and our love story.

As I waited for Bellamy, I strolled through my circus, discovering delightful added details at every turn. The sweet aroma of sugar from the floss vendors masterfully crafting enormous balloons of fluffy cotton candy for the guests.

Nearby, the majestic unicorns, paraded down the pleasant cobblestone path, accompanied by their dedicated equestrian director, Elmer. He came up to greet me earlier in the line and gave me the most thoughtful gift. It was a handmade scrapbook filled with cherished memories from the years I was away. He was a considerate and caring man, always thinking of others.

He spent many years training the animals at the circus. He was supposed to retire when the circus was cursed, but his love for the animals kept him devoted to his work. Now, he splits his time between the circus and the peaceful haven of Jubilee, where he can often be found in the gardens.

I peeked into one of the Big Top tents and was captivated by Lucy's death-defying Iron Jaw Act. The packed house held its collective breath as she gripped a black leather strap between her teeth and was lifted high into the air by a rope. I winced in sympathetic discomfort, my teeth aching in solidarity! But my discomfort was quickly replaced by delight as I watched the audience's faces mirror my own earlier wonder.

Lucy's performance reached its climax as she spun rapidly by her teeth, her body a blur, before vanishing into thin air, a classic disappearing trick elevated by Bellamy's magic. The crowd erupted into a standing ovation, and I couldn't help but beam with pride. My smile radiated joy, not just for the performers, but for the entire circus family and our beloved home. I was back, and it felt amazing!

As I watched the guests depart, I remembered that Bellamy would want us to jump tonight. That means the circus would vanish into the night, reappearing in a new location by dawn. I couldn't leave just yet.

In this life, I had a little brother and parents who loved me, and I needed to say goodbye. It hasn't always been that way in the past. Especially when they found me right away, I lived with Miss Poppet or if I'm older I have lived with Eve. But this time was different, I was an adult and I love my mortal family.

I sought out Bellamy, determined to plead my case. I knew he had his rules, but I couldn't bear the thought of leaving without saying goodbye to my family, especially my little brother Lucca. I found him in the backyard of the circus, amidst the bustle of performers packing up and cleaning up after the day's shows. As soon as he saw me, Bellamy's focus shifted, and he strode towards me with purpose, his eyes locked on mine. The performers nearby paused, sensing the weight of our impending conversation.

When Bellamy reached me, he cradled my face in his hands, his thumbs tracing the curves of my cheeks. Then, he leaned in, his lips meeting mine in a gentle, yet electrifying kiss. His love for me ignited a spark of magic, and I felt his lips tingle against mine, leaving me breathless. It was a kiss that always felt like a whispered promise of forever.

My eyes fluttered closed, and it took a few seconds for me to reopen them, still reeling from the intensity of the moment. It was a first for this lifetime, and I felt my heart skip a beat.

I gazed up at Bellamy, and his warm smile greeted me. "Daddy?" I asked, my voice hesitant. "Yes, baby girl?" he replied, his eyes sparkling with curiosity. I took a deep breath before continuing, "Can we stay one more day?" Bellamy's expression shifted, his eyebrows furrowing in surprise. "What's this about, love? You know the rules," he said, his tone gentle but firm.

I pressed on, my emotions rising to the surface. "I can't leave my family without a proper goodbye. I have a little brother, Lucca, and they love me, and I love them."

My voice trembled, and tears began to well up in my eyes. The thought of leaving them abruptly, without a chance to say goodbye, made my heart ache. Bellamy's expression softened, his eyes filled with understanding and compassion.

He wrapped me in a warm embrace. "Of course, baby girl," he whispered, his voice filled with understanding. "We can stay one more night, but that's all, okay? It's not safe for us to linger longer." I nodded eagerly, and he gently tilted my chin upwards, his lips meeting mine once more.

This time, his kiss was more passionate, he pushed harder, parting my lips seductively with his tongue. I was lost in the intensity of his embrace when he swept me up, cradling me effortlessly in his strong arms.

As I nestled in his arms, I felt the depth of our love, a bond forged over lifetimes. With our extra day granted, I was overjoyed and showered Bellamy's face with playful kisses. The performers nearby, still packing up, couldn't help but tease, their whistles and catcalls filling the air, "About time, Bellamy!" or "Get some, Bellamy!" But he ignored their good-natured jabs, his eyes locked on mine, his gaze piercing. "I've searched far and wide for you, baby girl, for what feels like an eternity. Are you ready to come home?" I smiled, "Yes."

After the last guest departed, the performers and crew headed home to Jubilee. Bellamy cradled me in his arms, carrying me to the willow tree, its branches swaying gently in the breeze. Velar joined us with a smile on his face.

As we reached the tree, I gazed upon the intricate carvings left by the workers of Darlington. And there, in the center, was a weathered but still proud declaration: B + N. Our initials, carved by Bellamy's own hand when we were married, the first time. Not only was it a symbol of our eternal bond, but also a poignant reminder of the time that had passed, but never felt like enough.

Bellamy gently set me down. I put my hand out to touch the trunk. After a few moments, the wood shimmered and transformed, revealing a wooden staircase that spiraled downward. I descended the stairs, Bellamy and Velar following closely behind. I suspected Eve was already waiting for us. As I reached the last step, I gazed out into the magical land of Jubilee. My home.

CHAPTER
FOUR

Jubilee was just how I remembered it to be, a breathtakingly beautiful magical town. Where the performers and crew of Darlington Circus could live in harmony and security, surrounded by their loved ones. Our supernatural community was thriving, with around four hundred residents who called this special place home.

As I gazed out upon the dazzling landscape, I noticed subtle yet wonderful changes since my last visit. Bellamy had added more homes, and the gardens had grown even more resplendent, with every flower and tree in vibrant bloom. But what truly caught my attention was the lush, soft grass beneath my feet, its gentle caress reminding me of its remarkable healing properties.

I immediately took off my black sandals. I stepped onto the lush grass, feeling its softness envelop my bare feet. It was like a wave of relief washed over me, and I realized just how much pain I had been carrying until it was all gone, replaced by a sense of rejuvenation. This enchanted grass was a blessing for our performers, who could come here at the end of each grueling day to heal their wounds and soothe their sore muscles. Even the animals loved to lay and roll in its embrace, basking in its restorative power.

Jubilee was a charming small town with magic soaring around like wind. Its homes and town square boasted stunning Gothic Victorian-inspired architecture, complete with intricately carved stonework and delicate spires.

Manicured lawns and vibrant gardens bursting with fresh produce. Crisp vegetables and juicy fruit trees surrounded the town, regardless of the season. The weather was always perfect, with gentle rains nourishing the earth when needed and warm sunshine illuminating our days. Bellamy's mastery of magic ensured that our every want and need was met, crafting a utopian haven where we could thrive in harmony.

One of the most wondrous aspects of Jubilee was its absence of currency. Everything was freely available or borrowed from a neighbor, fostering a sense of community and mutual support. We lived abundantly and untethered from the burdens of the outside world.

The profits from our circus endeavors were distributed among the performers and crew, allowing them to thrive in the mortal realm. If anyone had a need, they would simply inform Bellamy, myself (now that I had returned), Velar, or Eve, who collectively managed Jubilee along with the circus.

As the memories came flooding back, my excitement surged! I had missed being an integral part of the circus, working alongside Bellamy, Velar, and Eve to bring joy and wonder to our audiences. When the four of us come together, our creative synergy is unstoppable, yielding innovative ideas for performances and shows that leave our viewers in awe. Our passion for our craft shines through in every magnificent show we produce, and I couldn't wait to dive back in and be a part of it all once again.

I was admiring Jubilee when I saw Miss Poppet standing outside her adorable bakeshop in the town square. Her cozy home above the shop was a testament to her love of baking and her desire to be close to the heart of the community. When she spotted me, she beckoned me over with a wave of her hand, and I could not resist the invitation.

Without hesitation, I dashed across the street to her, eager to reconnect with my dear friend. We shared a heartfelt hug, and then she led me inside, where the heavenly aroma of freshly baked goods instantly made me hungry. She presented me with a little box tied with twine, filled with warm, flaky croissants straight from the oven. I did not wait and dove right in. "Mmm..." I moaned as the warm treat hit my tastebuds.

Miss Poppet's passion for baking was evident in every delicious treat she created, and her secret ingredient was the love she infused into each and every one. But what truly made her special was her kindness and generosity, she never let anyone leave her shop empty-handed.

We sat in a cozy nook at a small, circular wrought iron table by the shop's expansive bay window, bathed in warm, golden light. Miss Poppet's curious gaze encouraged me to share stories of my life since we last met. I told her about my family, art school, her eyes sparkled with delight, thrilled that I was pursuing the same passion that I had in a previous life.

I knew, however, that my time in school had come to an end, but I was happy to return to the circus. After a quick, but lovely visit, I made my way back to Bellamy and Velar.

When I returned to the other side of the street, I noticed Bellamy and Velar engaged in a serious and intense discussion, but they promptly stopped as I approached. I didn't pry into their conversation, instead, I turned to Bellamy with an enormous grin and exclaimed, "I'm ready to see Casmira!"

Bellamy's face lit up with a warm smile as he replied, "As you wish." With that, I took off running, feeling like a carefree little girl again, overflowing with excitement and joy at being back in this enthralling place.

I sprinted away from the town, down a narrow path lined with trees. The residential homes, with their charming facades, were mostly clustered to the right of the town square. Velar, and the other vampires, and the witches lay north of the square, nestled in the bewitching Emberlynn Forest. This magical woodland, full of lush vegetation and rolling hills. It was there, among the whispering trees that the witches honed their craft.

The forest was home to a diverse array of creatures such as Griffins, Centaurs, Beringian wolves, Tasmanian tigers, and Dodo birds. Not to mention bears, deer, and foxes. Even the occasional unicorn would roam through the underbrush, their horns shimmering in the dappled light. This bounty of wildlife provided an ample food source for Velar, although his true preference remained the rich, ruby red liquid of human blood. Meanwhile, my own sanctuary, shared with Bellamy, lay hidden to the far left, shielded from view by a vibrant forest.

South of Jubilee lay a stunning white sand beach, marking the entrance to the incredible Opal Sea. This shimmering body of water surrounds the town, forming a picturesque island. The enchanted water emits light through the teal water creating an adularescence glow. This mystical phenomenon was renowned for its healing and cleansing properties, capable of lifting even the darkest of moods. If anyone were struggling with a bad day, a mere dip in the ocean would instantly revitalize their spirit.

Bellamy held this place dear, beginning each morning with a refreshing swim. The sweet scent of the beach lingered on him throughout the day, a constant reminder of the sea's allure. When it came to Casmira's placement, Bellamy desired a spot by the water's edge, but we reached a compromise. Casmira now sits in a lush field, blanketed with healing grasses, nestled between the Emberlynn Forest and the Opal Sea. This serene location allows us to bask in the gentle, soothing energies of both the woods and the waves.

A winding path, carpeted with soft pine straw, led me through the woods, guiding me home. The gentle rustle beneath my feet was a familiar comfort, and I reveled in the softness I had forgotten until now. As I emerged from the woods, my heart swelled with joy. There she stood, just as I remembered her. Casmira, my enchanting Victorian home, beckoned me with her Gothic charm. I paused at the sturdy iron gate, adorned with intricate scrollwork, which swung open to reveal the slate-covered manor. With a sense of belonging, I called out, "Casmira, I'm home!"

As the wrought iron gate swung open, I followed the path to the steps, my heart racing with excitement. I had always been enamored with Victorian homes, and Casmira, a gift from Bellamy, is the grandest of them all. My house boasted four floors, a steeply pitched gabled roof, and four round towers, all encircled by a wrap- around porch. One of my favorite features was the stunning conservatory attached to the back of the house. With bouncy anticipation, I ascended the front steps to the massive teak front door, which swung open just as I reached it, inviting me into the warm embrace of my beloved home.

As I stepped inside, the warm aroma of cinnamon and spice filled my nose, immediately making me feel at ease. Casmira, my beloved home, always exuded a sense of warmth and coziness, and I was thrilled to be back within her comforting walls. The marble plated fireplace was crackling and burning in the main room. I had finally returned to my haven, my sanctuary, and I was exactly where I was meant to be.

As I entered the kitchen, I set the basket of freshly baked goods down on the dark, gothic wood countertop. The rich aroma of sweet treats mingling with the savory scents wafting from the stovetop. A delicious meal was simmering away, and a wave of relief wash over me, knowing I could finally leave waitressing behind. I did not have to cook or clean anymore! No more scrambling for tips that barely covered my rent! I was walking on air, my heart soaring with joy. Just hours before, I was a poor girl trying to make it through art school with no plans for my future and now look where I am!

One of the greatest joys of returning to the Circus was leaving behind the struggles of my past lives. I had never been born into wealth and privilege and had even spent time in an orphanage before Bellamy found me again.

As I reflected on my previous lives, I couldn't help but contrast it with my current circumstances. The difference was like night and day. I had gone from scraping by to living a life that was truly a dream come true for most people.

As I wandered through the downstairs rooms, I felt a deep sense of gratitude wash over me. My loving husband had thoughtfully preserved Casmira exactly as I had left it, a constant haven in an ever-changing world. His consideration and devotion touched my heart, and I felt grateful to have such a loving partner. With growing excitement, I ran up to the third floor, eager to see my bedroom once again.

As I approached the elegant French doors leading to our master bedroom, I hesitated, savoring the anticipation. This was no ordinary bedroom, it was our inner sanctum; a place that our souls intertwine with passion, and we become one.

Before me lay the majestic, oversized bed, meticulously made to perfection every day. The house, Casmira, was a marvel of efficiency and grace, never messy, dusty, or out of order. She cooked, cleaned, and assisted with tasks, making our lives effortless. I adored Casmira, I spoke to her as if she were an actual being.

As I entered my closet, I was surrounded by a stunning array of dresses, each one a masterpiece. I recognized some of my favorites, but others were new, still bearing tags for my size in this lifetime. Bellamy's love for dressing me was a delight, and his magic made it all possible. With just a snap of his fingers, he could bring any dress I desired to life.

As I pulled out an elegant, pleated back pencil dress, memories came flooding back from my life in the nineteen-forties. What a tumultuous time that was - World War II, the Holocaust, atomic bombs, and the beginnings of the civil war. Yet, despite the chaos, we had Jubilee to keep us safe, although it didn't keep Velar from fighting in the wars.

As I delved deeper into my closet, a stunning evening gown from nineteen-twelve caught my eye, transporting me back to a bygone era. Memories of Bellamy and I sharing a romantic dinner in England the night before I boarded the ill-fated Titanic came flooding back. As the painful recollection of my tragic demise on that fateful voyage began to resurface. I shook my head, trying to dispel the haunting memory, and quickly exited the closet, seeking to escape the bittersweet nostalgia that threatened to overwhelm me.

As I entered the bathroom, the sound of water filling the oversized bathtub greeted me. "Thank you, Casmira, but I'm not quite ready for a bath just yet," I called out, my voice echoing off the walls. The water ceased flowing instantly. I couldn't help but smile, knowing that my beloved home had missed me just as much as I had missed her.

Before heading back downstairs, I made a detour to the third floor's final door. I peeked into the red room, our intimate play space, where Bellamy and I would reconnect later that evening. I felt a mix of excitement and nerves, knowing it had been years since our last intimate encounter. The room, though potentially intimidating at first glance, held countless cherished memories with Daddy.

As I approached the king-size wooden canopy bed, I could not help but fantasize. The four posts were adorned with straps, a reminder of the times Bellamy would lovingly restrain me. I circled the room, taking in the various toys and sexy lingerie lining the closet. My face flushed as I recognized a black lace piece from a special night. I smiled at the provocative memory and closed the door, eagerly anticipating our upcoming encounter.

As I meandered back downstairs, Bellamy and Velar should be here by now. Approaching the front door, I glanced through the bay window and was surprised by the scene outside. Velar's arms were raised, his face red with anger, fangs showing, while Bellamy's eyes blazed with fury. I stepped out onto the porch just as Velar stormed out of the front gate. "What's going on?" I asked Bellamy, my concern growing by the second.

Bellamy's silence was unnerving, his eyes piercing as he gazed at me. I took a step closer, my concern growing. "What's wrong?" I asked again, hoping for a response this time. Without a word, Bellamy took my hand, leading us inside Casmira. We walked to the main room; his grip gentle but firm.

Only when we reached the fireplace did he release my hand, his eyes still intense. "Please, sit," he said finally, his voice low and serious. I quickly obeyed, settling into my favorite leather couch, my heart racing with anticipation. Bellamy's unusual silence only added to my unease, he was never at a loss for words, and I knew something significant was amiss.

The silence was unbearable, Bellamy's pacing a stark contrast to his usual calm demeanor. "Daddy!" I exclaimed; frustration etched on my face. He finally sat beside me; his eyes locked on mine. "Velar found the witch who cast the immortality spell on the circus." He revealed. My confusion deepened.

"Why? Were you looking for her?" I asked, but Bellamy's pause spoke volumes. "No, but Velar has been searching for her... for thirty years," he admitted. I sensed a hidden purpose behind his words. "Velar wants to find her so she can break the curse on you," he continued.

My confusion deepened, and I pressed on, "Why would she help us if she's the one who cursed us in the first place?" Bellamy's silence returned, and my patience began to wear thin. I asked again, my voice laced with a hint of desperation, "Daddy, what are you not telling me? Are you hiding something from me?" Bellamy's response was swift and firm, his eyes flashing with a warning. "I'm telling you what you need to know"' he stated, his tone brooking no further discussion.

The sudden intensity in his voice and the stern set of his jaw only fueled my growing unease, leaving me feeling like there was much more to the story than he was letting on.

I shot up from my seat, my eyes blazing with indignation as I repeated, my voice raised in protest, "What I need to know?"

Bellamy's expression shifted, his eyes widening in surprise, as he realized the depth of my upset. I never spoke to him with such defiance, and he knew it. Typically, such boldness would earn me a stern reprimand, usually a spanking. But in that moment, my anger and frustration at being dismissed and kept in the dark overrode any fear of consequences. I stood my ground, my glare challenging him to reveal the truth he was so determined to keep from me.

"Baby girl, I need you to trust me, I'm doing everything to protect you," Bellamy pleaded, his voice calm and reassuring. But I was having none of it. "By keeping secrets?" I shot back, my voice rising in anger. 'We tell each other everything!' I yelled, my frustration boiling over. "I know it's been nineteen years, but we're a team, we're married, we have had many lives together..."

My words tumbling out in a passionate torrent, when Bellamy cut me off, his voice like a bombshell. "It hasn't been nineteen years; it's been fifty years!"

My jaw dropped, and I felt like I had been punched in the gut, all the air sucked out of me. I could not process what I was hearing.

"What do you mean fifty years?" I stammered, my mind reeling. "I am nineteen... I reincarnate immediately every time I die." I repeated, as if trying to convince myself of the truth. But Bellamy's words loomed in my mind, a stark contradiction to everything I thought I knew about my reincarnation.

Bellamy grabbed my hands, his grasp warm and comforting. "It was different this time," he explained. "We've been searching for you for fifty years, scouring the earth for any sign of your rebirth. I had almost given up hope, thinking you might never return."

His voice cracked with emotion. "But then Eve found your birth certificate just a year ago, and we were faced with a difficult decision. We debated whether to let you live your life without knowing us, without remembering us. Maybe it would be better that way, we thought." His words were a mix of sadness and longing that tugged at my heart. I felt like I was being pulled into a world I did not understand.

My heart ached at the thought of Bellamy giving up on me, of him considering a life without me. His eyes welled up with tears, his voice cracking with emotion. "I thought I had lost you forever, that you'd never come back to me. That is when Velar tracked down the witch, and just today, he told me he found her."

Bellamy's gaze bore into mine, his eyes pleading for understanding. "But we don't need her now, I have you back, and I won't risk losing you again. Going to her would be playing with fire; What if she takes the curse off of everyone, are we ready to be mortal again, ready to die? How can I make that call for everyone?" His voice was a mix of fear, love, and uncertainty that tore at my heart.

I sank back into the cool leather couch, my mind reeling from the revelation. Thoughts swirled in a jumbled mix, as I struggled to process the truth. I tried to recall my past life, but my memories remained shrouded in fog. Bellamy stood over me, his eyes fixed on mine, He watched as I wrestled with the weight of my newfound knowledge.

I gazed up at Bellamy, my eyes searching for answers. "Why can't I remember how I died last time?" I asked, my voice laced with desperation. Bellamy's eyes widened. "I can recall all my past deaths, up to a certain point," I continued, my voice cracking. "I remember the circus curse, the Titanic, the yellow fever... and you, always by my side. But the last time... it's a complete blank." Tears began to fall, streaming down my cheeks as I accused, "You're keeping something from me, aren't you?"

The way Bellamy stood there, tears welling up in his cold eyes, told me he knew the truth. But he remained silent, his gaze fixed on mine, his expression a mix of pain and reluctance. A stinging sense of betrayal wash over me, knowing he was withholding something from me, and the weight of his secrets lingered in the air.

I could not bear the sight of my husband's paralyzed state any longer. With a surge of determination, I pushed myself up from the couch and stormed out of Casmira, the door slamming shut behind me matching my emotions. I paused for a moment, waiting for the reverberations to fade, then made my way down the stairs and back through the wooded path to the town square.

CHAPTER
FIVE

It was nighttime now in Jubilee. The crescent moon was so close I could almost touch it and the stars were shining so bright, the only time I could tell the sky was enchanted. My mind swirled with thoughts of Bellamy and the secrets he kept from me. Never before had he kept something from me, and it hurt deeply. I was torn between feelings of frustration and sadness, unsure which pain to confront first, the secret he was hiding, the delay in my reincarnation, or the fact that they had considered letting me live a mortal life, free from our eternal bond?

I found myself lost in thought, my feet carrying me through the quiet streets of Jubilee. I wandered back to the town square, where the only sound was the soft murmur of families settling in for the night. I longed for the comforting presence of Miss Poppet, but the bakeshop was dark and closed.

I continued my aimless stroll, passing by the shuttered shops and their sleeping owners. The cobblestone path matched the one in the circus and I followed it to the crossroads, the only one in our town.

I settled onto a bench at the intersection, my gaze drifting into the darkness of the Emberlynn Forest as my thoughts swirled in a jumble of emotions. The silence was broken by the sound of footsteps behind me. I turned expecting to see Bellamy's. But instead, Velar's imposing figure loomed before me, his emerald eyes gleaming in the faint moonlight.

"Velar," I said, my voice breaking the silence and startling him. He was surprised, clearly not expecting to see me sitting there. I assumed he was out on a hunt. "Nicole, what are you doing out here?" he asked, his brow furrowed in concern.

I raised an eyebrow, intrigued by his worry, Jubilee was the epitome of safety, after all. I waited for him to sit beside me on the bench before responding. "Bellamy and I had a fight," I admitted, my voice low. "I can't remember how I died in my previous life, and he won't tell me." I turned to Velar, "Do you know?"

Velar shifted uncomfortably, his body language screaming guilt. He knew the truth but was reluctant to share it. I pressed him, my voice laced with desperation. "What happened? Please, you are my oldest friend, can't you tell me?" He hesitated, his eyes avoiding mine. "I want to tell you, Nic, but I'm not the one who can."

My frustration grew, and I asked, "Is this what you and Bellamy were fighting about earlier?" Velar's expression turned solemn, as he leaned in closer. My heart raced, and I wondered if his vampire senses could detect my anger. He asked, his voice tinged with hope, "Do you remember anything from your past life? Anything at all?' I shook my head, disappointment washing over me. "No," I replied.

Velar put his arm around me, and we sat together in silence. My mind wandered back to the first time we met, when I started working at the circus. When everyone was still mortal. It was a simpler era, in the late seventeen hundreds. I remembered the thrill of learning, the rush of adrenaline as I soared through the air. Memories flooded back, bittersweet and a reminder of the life I once knew before the curse.

The first day I met him, he emerged from the backyard of the circus with an impressive array of rigging equipment in tow. His towering frame effortlessly shouldered the massive weight, his stride confident and unhurried, I admired his chiseled features. He introduced himself as Velar Hansen with a firm handshake.

I remember him showing me his fangs for the first time and explaining to me that he was a vampire. He was the first vampire I had ever met, and I remember how dumbfounded I was, to say the least. His nonchalant explanation had initially startled me, but my fear quickly gave way to trust. I knew instinctively that he would never harm me. Our friendship blossomed, built on a foundation of laughter and playful teasing.

But now, I felt a pang of hurt and betrayal, knowing he was keeping secrets from me, just like Bellamy. My thoughts crowded my mind as I sat there, leaning against Velar's firm body.

Time seemed to stand still, he looked identical to the first time we met, his rugged charm and striking appearance unchanged. The only hint of evolution was the ever-expanding canvas of tattoos decorating his pale skin.

As I leaned against Velar, his cold skin was a welcome respite from the warm night air in Jubilee. His whisper was barely audible, "I wish you could remember." I shared his longing, and asked hopefully, "Can you tell me anything about it?"

Velar shook his head no while looking down to the ground. "I thought I was never going to see you again…" He paused, collecting himself, before continuing, "That's why I sought out the witch, I had to find you. I never want to lose you again." I listened intently.

I was surprised by Velar's words, his tone revealing a depth of emotion I had never suspected. Our friendship had always been light-hearted and playful, but now, he spoke with a passion and intensity that made my heart race. I felt a flutter in my stomach as I sat up, repositioning myself to break the intimate contact.

I turned to face him, my voice filled with apology, "I'm so sorry, I had no idea this has affected you all so deeply." *What was going on? Why was Velar holding back?* Velar's response was cut short, his sentence hanging in mid-air as he hesitated, his eyes focused on the approaching Bellamy. I followed his stare, my confusion growing.

"There you are, Babygirl," Bellamy said, his voice dripping with affection. As he approached, his eyes locked onto us, a warm smile spreading across his face. But Velar's expression darkened, his eyes narrowing as he snapped, "I was out hunting, and Nic was sitting here alone."

The tone was accusatory, as if he were tattling on me. Bellamy's response was swift and laced with sarcasm, "I was giving her some space to cool off, but I guess she's found you for that!"

I sprang to my feet, positioning myself between them, my voice rising in protest. "Bellamy!" I shouted, pushing the two men apart. The tension between them was almost visible, as their words echoed in the night. I had never witnessed them speak to each other with such venom before, and it both shocked and frightened me.

The argument between Bellamy and Velar escalated, their voices growing louder and more heated by the second. Velar insisted that we needed the witch's help, but Bellamy's response was fierce and accusatory. "This is all your fault, Velar! And do not ever speak to my wife again!" I felt like a pawn between them, and I'd had enough. I stood tall and shouted, "I'm going home!" But Bellamy's response was dismissive, "Yes, go home. We'll handle this." I shot him a fiery glance, my anger and frustration boiling over. "No! I mean I'm going back to the real world!" I turned to leave, but my arm was seized in a firm grip, halting my escape. I tried to shake off the hand, but it held fast, leaving me trapped and furious.

Bellamy's grip on my arm tightened, and the two men's argument ceased abruptly, their attention fixed on me. Bellamy grasped my other hand, his voice laced with a gentle urgency.

"Babygirl, you can't leave Jubilee." I wrenched my hand free. "You're both keeping secrets from me!" I shouted, my eyes darting between them. "We've known each other for so long, but now it's like you don't want me here. You won't tell me what's going on, you won't share anything about my past life... I cannot remember anything!"

My voice cracked as I backed away. "I'd rather go back to my life and pretend I never knew either of you existed!" In my haste, I failed to notice the tree root behind me, and my feet tangled. Velar's quick vamp reflexes saved me from a harsh fall before I reached the dirt.

Instant silence filled the night. I looked at Bellamy, his eyes fixed on me with a mixture of concern and guilt. Velar's grip on my arms remained firm, yet gentle, as I stood up and composed myself. My anger and determination ignited, I turned to face the two men, my eyes blazing with a fierce intensity. In a calm, but measured tone, I issued a warning, "I am going to need some answers, or I'm out of here. For good!"

Bellamy and Velar exchanged a weighted glance, before nodding in unison. They agreed to reveal the secrets they had kept hidden, and we silently consented to discuss the matter further in private. We walked back to Casmira in total silence. Upon entering the house, I directed them to sit at the wooden kitchen table. I stood firm. As if anticipating my needs, Casmira had prepared a glass of wine, waiting for me like a comforting embrace.

I savored the wine, its rich flavor a brief respite from the tension, before sitting at the head of the table. I peered at Bellamy and Velar, urging them to begin. Bellamy's voice was laced with hesitation, "Baby girl, this is extremely hard to talk about... I did not think it would matter to you so much, not to remember." I listened, my patience running thin.

Then Velar spoke up and his words cut through me like a knife. "The reason you don't remember your past life is because I erased your memory." My jaw dropped, shock and betrayal etched on my face, as I turned to Velar with disdain. "How could you? Who gave you the right to do that?" Velar's gaze faltered, his eyes fixed on the table, as if unable to meet mine. Bellamy continued for him, his response was a quiet admission, "I did."

My eyes cut into Bellamy, my voice rising. "How could you do that to me?" I demanded, my words echoing off the walls. I was a maelstrom of conflicting emotions, anger, rage, sadness, and hurt all swirling together in a toxic mix. I tried to form words, but they caught in my throat. "Why did you...?" I trailed off, unable to finish the question. Velar's hand reached out from across the table, a gesture of comfort, but Bellamy swiftly intervened in anger. "I think it's best if you leave, Velar." I shook my head vehemently, my eyes locked on Bellamy. "No one leaves until I know the truth!"

I downed my glass of wine in one swift motion, only to have it instantly refilled by the attentive house. The two men had resumed their argument, their voices escalating once again. I reached for my glass, ready to take another hasty sip, but Bellamy's keen eye caught mine. "Alright, alright, I'll tell you." He said, his tone laced with a hint of surrender. I hesitated, my hand hovering over the glass, before finally setting it back on the table with a soft clink.

Bellamy's voice was laced with trepidation as he began again, "You're not going to like what I'm about to tell you." I sank back into my wooden chair, bracing myself for the words to come. "The reason you don't remember your past is because I didn't want you to. I was angry and hurt, and I made a grave mistake by forcing Velar to erase your memories. I am consumed by shame and regret, and I can only hope that someday you will find it in your heart to forgive me." Bellamy's eyes drooped, heavy with remorse, as he added, "I was so consumed by my own emotions, I wasn't thinking of the consequences."

I remained silent, allowing him to continue. He looked between me and Velar. "In your past life, I saw you... I saw you with Velar, and the two of you were together." Bellamy's voice cracked as he paused, his eyes darting to Velar, who turned to face me. His voice was laced with a deep longing as he spoke directly to me, "I loved you in your past life, with every fiber of my being." Bellamy's discomfort was visible, he looked downward, avoiding mine. I turned my attention to Velar, my voice confused, "So... we were together?"

Velar's solemn nod confirmed my suspicions, and my jaw dropped once more. I turned to Bellamy, whose eyes had finally met mine, filled with deep remorse. His voice was laced with anguish as he continued, "When I saw the two of you together, my world came crashing down around me. My magic consumed me like a raging storm, and I lashed out without control, striking with the ferocity of lightning."

He paused, collecting his thoughts before adding, "I never meant to hurt you, I swear it." His confession struck me, and I felt like I'd been punched in the gut. Finally, I asked the question that was stirring in my mind, "You killed me?"

Bellamy's face contorted in anguish, tears streaming down his cheeks as he begged for forgiveness. "Baby girl, please, I'm so sorry. I was consumed by grief and my magic took control. I didn't mean to hurt you, I swear it." But his words fell on deaf ears as I rose from my seat, my voice numb and detached.

"I don't know what I feel right now, but I need space. I don't want to see either of you." I stood frozen, my eyes fixed on the two men who I had known for so long, yet in this moment, they felt like strangers.

Bellamy's words trailed off as I raised my hand, a clear signal to stop. My voice was a fragile balance of calm and tremble as I addressed my husband, "I need you both to leave. Now." Bellamy opened his mouth to protest, but I cut him off, my tone firm but shaking. "It's been a long day, and I need some time to think."

Velar stood up, his eyes never leaving mine, and placed a gentle hand on Bellamy's shoulder. "Indeed, it has been a long day," he said, his voice low and agreeing, as he guided Bellamy towards the door. I knew he was encouraging him to leave, to give me the space I so desperately needed.

As the door closed behind them, I mechanically walked to the stove, ladled a bowl of stew, and sat down at the table, my mind reeling with questions.

How could I have been with Velar? How could I have betrayed Bellamy like that? What was going through Bellamy's mind when he saw me with his friend? How could he have taken my life? And did the entire town of Darlington know about this dark secret?

I took a few listless bites of the stew, my appetite gone, as my thoughts swirled in a mix of emotions. The silence of the room was punctuated only by the soft deafening clinking of my spoon against the bowl. I was lost in a sea of confusion, unsure of what to feel or think, or how to process the revelations of the day.

As the minutes ticked by, my mind remained a jumble of thoughts, each one colliding with the next in a chaotic dance. I must have sat at the table for an hour, lost in my reverie, sipping wine, and staring into the abyss of my own thoughts. The sound of running water upstairs broke the spell, and I felt the gentle nudge of the house urging me to take a bath. It was as if Casmira, the house itself, knew I had reached my limit.

I stood up, placed my bowl and empty wine glass in the sink, forgetting this chore was no longer necessary. I whispered a soft "Thank you, Casmira" in gratitude for its gentle prompting. Then, I trudged upstairs to the bathroom, seeking solace in the warm embrace of the bathwater.

As I sank into the warm waters of my oversized clawfoot bathtub, my thoughts inevitably drifted back to Bellamy, and the ache of missing him swelled in my chest. Regret and guilt washed over me, weighed down by the knowledge of my past betrayal. But even that couldn't justify his brutal actions.

The pain still lingered, a raw wound that refused to heal. I longed for someone to confide in, someone who might understand the tangled web of emotions in which I was trapped. Eve flashed in my mind, was she awake? Did she know the secrets of my past life?

I instinctively reached for my phone, only to remember that it was useless in Jubilee. So, I turned to the house, my voice echoing through the rooms, "Casmira, please call Eve for me."

The invisible speakers crackled to life, and I heard the brief ring of the phone before Eve's concerned voice filled the air. "Nicole, is that you? Why didn't you call me sooner? What is going on over there? I have been waiting for hours!" She finally paused, her words tumbling out in a rush, allowing me to respond to her urgent questions.

I hesitated a bit embarrassed, "Eve, do you know what I did to Bellamy?" The silence that followed felt like an eternity, and I could feel the weight of my shame bearing down on me.

But instead of answering my question, Eve asked, "Is Bellamy there with you now?" I was confused by the sudden change in direction. "No," I replied, my voice cracking, "I told him to leave. He killed me, Eve. I cheated on him with his best friend, and I don't even remember any of it!" The words spilled out, and with them, a torrent of tears. The wine I had consumed earlier likely contributed to the emotional release, but the pain and regret were all too real.

I was left with only silence on the other end of the line, and I was about to ask Casmira to reconnect me with Eve when I heard the unmistakable sound of the front door opening and closing, followed by footsteps ascending the stairs.

My heart sank, realizing Bellamy had returned. I was not prepared to face him yet. The footsteps grew louder, heavier, and soon they stopped right outside the bathroom door. In a drunken slur, I yelled, "Go away, Daddy!" But the door creaked open anyway, and I braced myself for the confrontation that was to come.

Eve's face appeared around the bathroom door, her raised eyebrows and warm smile a welcome sight. "Hey, lady, let's get you out of the tub and into bed, shall we?" She gently helped me out of the water, and we rummaged through my once-tidy closet, now a mess of clothes filled the carpet. I could not help but smile, knowing that the mess would be tidied up tomorrow by Casmira. As Eve slipped my satin nightgown over my head, I started chuckling.

I could not help but laugh at the irony. Just yesterday, I would have been mortified to be seen naked by Eve, but now, I was grateful for our open friendship. In an instant, we fell back into our easy, sisterly dynamic, and I realized how much she must have hidden herself during those months we lived together. Yet, she had always been there for me, a constant presence in my life. As she tucked me into bed, I reminisced about our friendship, feeling a deep appreciation for her unwavering support and love.

I still recall the day Eve first showed up at the circus, about a year after I had joined. She walked in with a confident stride, introducing herself with a radiant smile. "My name is Evangeline Milton, and I'm here to be an acrobat," she declared, her voice ringing with confidence.

This was before the curse that granted her immortality. I vividly remember watching her audition, mesmerized by her graceful movements, and daring aerial stunts. The entire circus was instantly enamored with our new acrobat, and I was no exception. Immature compared to her performance nowadays.

Eve handed me a mug, filled with a peculiar tonic concocted by the house. I protested, "I don't want to be sober," but she just smiled and firmly said, "Drink." I hesitated, then took a sip. The flavor was delightful, warm, and sweet. Tasted like warm milk infused with honey and cinnamon. Comforting. It was as if Casmira knew my preferences better than I knew myself.

After a few sips of the tonic, my sobriety returned, and with it, a crushing sense of self-reproach. Eve sat beside me on the bed, her empathetic look encouraging me to confront the secrets of my past. "Tell me about my past life, Eve." I asked, not sure if I really wanted to know. She replied with compassion, "Nothing was your fault, Nicole. You've lived multiple lifetimes, and in each one, you've loved and been devoted to the same man." She paused, choosing her words carefully before continuing, "Velar was just a fleeting temptation, something new and exciting. No one blames you for that, not even Bellamy."

Eve's words didn't bring me the comfort she intended. In fact, they only stirred up more turmoil within me. I couldn't bear the thought of myself with Velar, and yet... a nagging voice in my mind whispered, "That's why Velar wanted me to remember." I sat in silence, lost in the labyrinth of my own thoughts, trying to make sense of the shambles of my past life and the desires that had driven me.

Eve's words cut through the silence, gentle but direct. "I know you might not want to hear this, Nicole, but you once confided in me that Velar made you feel alive." She allowed the weight of that admission to settle before continuing, her voice laced with compassion. "Bellamy was a mess after...what he did to you. He was consumed by grief, unable to forgive himself for his actions." Eve's words were delicate as she carefully illuminated the dark corners of my past. I listened cautiously.

"After we feared, you were lost to us forever, Bellamy was overcome with despair. We had to appoint Briar as the new Showman, as Bellamy sank into a profound depression, unable to leave Jubilee. Velar, too, departed the circus and Jubilee, only returning when we rediscovered you. The rift between Bellamy and Velar grew insurmountable after Velar erased your memories."

Eve's eyes welled up with tears as she recounted the anguish, they all endured. I realized that Bellamy and Velar's silence wasn't about secrets, but about shielding me from the truth. As Eve finished speaking, tears streamed down her olive-toned cheeks, and I embraced my dear friend, feeling a sense of resilience wash over me.

Despite everything I was grateful to be back home in Jubilee. This was where my soul felt most at home, and I knew in my heart that Bellamy and I would weather any storm together. We were more than just lovers or friends, we were bonded.

As the night wore on, Eve filled me in on all the moments I had missed. She shared the news of a new couple in Jubilee, immortals who had found their way to our community and were now an integral part of our circus family. "Henry and Anise got married!" Eve exclaimed, her eyes sparkling with excitement. I couldn't help but feel a pang of regret at having missed such a joyful occasion. Eve was quick to offer a comforting perspective: "You get a whole new life to start over and make it what you want. How exciting!"

Eve saw my soul's reincarnation as a fresh start, a second chance at life. But for me, it wasn't quite that simple. With all my memories from past lifetimes still intact, it felt more like a continuation than a new beginning. I tried to explain to Eve that my soul wasn't starting from scratch. Instead, it was building upon the experiences and lessons of my previous lives. I was carrying the wisdom and scars of my past into this new life, aiming to do better, to grow and learn more. It was an evolution, not a reset.

Eve had a gift for lifting my spirits, and our bond was forged through lifetimes of sisterly bickering and unwavering friendship. I marveled at the transformation she had undergone since I first met her, and I couldn't help but wonder if I had changed as much. Eve's carefree, badass, and thick-skinned exterior was vastly different from the worried and vulnerable mortal she once was. I remembered how she used to cry over heartbreak, how her palms would sweat with nervousness before each act.

As I watch Eve now, I see her in a new light, knowing she has endured the agony of love and loss countless times. Yet, she has transformed her pain into a soaring strength, literally and figuratively. She dazzles as one of the world's premier aerialist performers, her grace and skill mesmerizing audiences.

Alongside Bellamy, she expertly manages the circus, her leadership and wisdom guiding the troupe with grace. And when I die and reincarnate, she tirelessly tracks me down, watching over me with a fierce devotion until I am safely back among my immortal family. At this moment, I am struck by the profound way my friend has grown.

CHAPTER

SIX

The next morning, the smell of freshly brewed coffee wafted into my consciousness, and I opened my eyes to find Bellamy standing beside me, a warm smile on his face as he offered me a steaming mug. My heart swelled with a deep longing for comfort and reassurance, rather than anger or resentment. I craved the solace of his embrace, the gentle promise that everything would be all right.

Without a word, I took a sip of the hot coffee, just the way I liked it, and set the mug down on my nightstand. Then, I reached up and wrapped my arms around Bellamy, seeking the shelter of his love.

He openly accepted my invitation. I nestled my head under his chin, feeling the gentle pressure of his embrace. It was then that I noticed he had not slept in our bed the night before, his side remained untouched. Yet, at that moment, neither of us needed words. His love and devotion flowed through his hold, filling me in a sense of security and care. I realized how deeply

I had needed this embrace, this reassurance that we were unbreakable. Our bond was unshakeable, a fortress of love that nothing could ever dismantle.

As I sat up to speak, my words were silenced by the gentle press of his lips on mine. The soft, sweet kiss deepened, and I slipped my tongue in his mouth, and we were instantly compelled to one another. I could feel the force of magic encircling us and it made my body tingle. The world around us melted away, leaving only the two of us, lost in the depths of our passion.

Bellamy mounted me. Oh, how I missed the smell of wild algae and sea fennel that lingered on his skin. I wanted him so badly, but he teased me with his mouth. While he kissed me deep his other hand reached for my throat and gave me a gentle but tight squeeze making all air leave my body for an instant. It turned me on to feel my life literally in his hands knowing I could trust him, knowing I was owned by him. Then his hand left my neck and went down to my chest and rested, caressing my hard nipples. He moved lower to my tummy, owning every part of me. Grabbing me as he moved his hand further, then holding himself there for my pleasure to grind on.

I could feel him hard against me. I wanted to feel him inside me. I eagerly moaned "Daddy." A second later his two fingers slid inside me pleasuring me yet teasing me. I arched my back when his finger met my clit. Then looking down at himself to adjust he thrust himself inside me. My mouth opened with a moan. Pleasure and pain became one in an instant. It always took me time to adjust to Bellamy.

An hour later, we lay entwined in bed, Bellamy's grin radiating warmth as he whispered, "Hello, my beautiful girl." I finally shook off the weight of yesterday's news, grateful to be back. With a newfound courage, I voiced the apology I had been holding back before our loving reunion. "Daddy, I'm so sorry for being with Velar I can't even imagine being with him." I honestly couldn't imagine it. Bellamy's response was laced with deep remorse. "My love, I hope you'll find it in your heart to forgive me someday for taking your memories and, most of all, for ending your life."

I spoke with a solemn intensity, "I forgive you, but please, never erase my memories again, and never take my life again."

Bellamy's hands cradled my face, his eyes locking onto mine as he vowed, "I will always find you, no matter where you are, or who you're with. I promise to give you the choice, always." His words pierced my heart, but I understood the depth of his commitment. I reassured him, my voice filled with conviction, "You are the one I always want to be with. You are my every-thing." Bellamy embraced me, his lips brushing against my fore-head in a gentle kiss, sealing our promise.

As the morning wore on, I grew eager to visit my parents' house, and I headed to the closet to select a dress for Bellamy's approval. After he made his choice, I slipped out of my satin nightgown, and his eyes followed me with intensity. Bellamy never missed an opportunity to admire me undressing, and I must admit, I savored his stare just as much as he did.

I teasingly pulled up my thong panties slowly as Bellamy watched. I loved teasing him, but it usually ended with his dick in my mouth. I saw him through the mirror starting to stroke himself. I was beginning to blush, knowing he was getting aroused again. But we did not have the time to play again this morning. I knew I had to hurry, or we would never leave the bedroom.

I swiftly slipped into a short black dress with long sleeves, its fabric hugging my curves. As I reached for my still-steaming coffee on the nightstand, I sensed Bellamy watching my every move, his desire growing with each step I took. I knew if I made eye contact, I would see his wanting eyes and I would be forced to oblige in whatever he wanted me to do. So, I quickly made my escape, dashing downstairs before he could get his hands on me.

As I entered the kitchen, the smell of freshly baked chocolate croissants was present, and I spotted the flaky pastries on the counter. "Thank you, Casmira!" I called out gratefully. I could not resist the temptation and took a bite, the soft, buttery croissant instantly melting in my mouth. In a moment of indulgence, I stuffed an entire pastry into my mouth just as Bellamy entered the kitchen. I turned my head, attempting to conceal my embarrassment, but Bellamy simply stood in the doorway, his arms crossed and a playful grin spreading across his face. "Don't hide it," he chuckled, his eyes twinkling with amusement.

I continued to hide my bulging cheeks, but Bellamy's words only encouraged me to laugh along with him, almost causing me to choke on my pastry. "I know you haven't had Casmira's cooking in nineteen years, so enjoy it!" he said, his laughter echoing through the kitchen.

Once I finally savored the last morsel of croissant, I could face him again. He flashed a smile and said, "Shall we, Mrs. Darlington? Are you ready to reunite with your...ahem... "fake" family?"

I shot him a stern look, my eyes widening in emphasis.

"Daddy, these are my real parents and my little brother in this lifetime, so please, for my sake, be on your best behavior."

Bellamy's grin only grew wider at my reprimand. I knew it irked him to have yet another family for him to meet and take me away from.

As I waited for Bellamy on the front porch, I admired the familiar yet strange surroundings, feeling a sense of surreal wonder. Being back in this enchanting world filled me with joy, and I reveled in the magic that surrounded me.

Suddenly, Bellamy's voice broke my daze, "Baby girl?" he called out, and I let out a startled "Ahh!" as I jumped, my heart skipping a beat. Bellamy's laughter erupted, contagious and infectious, and I could not help but join in, our laughter entwining like a joyful embrace. When we finally managed to compose ourselves, Bellamy brushed off his suit. A sly grin still playing on his lips. "I have a surprise for you before we head out," he said, his eyes sparkling with excitement.

My curiosity piqued, I turned to head back into the house, but Bellamy's gentle grasp on my hand guided me down the porch steps instead. "This way, baby," he said. I followed him willingly, my feet moving swiftly beside his as we made our way to the side of the house and into the backyard.

The forest loomed before us, its trees towering above, and Bellamy led me towards its edge, his grip on my hand never wavering. "Daddy, I'm not exactly dressed for a hike," I pointed out, my bare feet sinking into the lush grass as I gazed up at the dense foliage, unsure where this adventure would lead.

Without breaking stride, Bellamy extended his hand once more, and with a subtle gesture, my bare feet were now magically wearing sneakers. "Thanks, I suppose," I said, my tone hinting at my reluctance to embark on this impromptu hike. As if sensing my thoughts, Bellamy reassured me, "We're almost there."

The forest floor beneath our feet soon gave way to a winding trail, and the path ahead was decorated with a delicate carpet of pink and white flower petals, carefully laid out like a gentle welcome mat. The Southern Crabapple trees stood sentinel along the walkway, their beauty and fragrance were soothing as we strolled along the serene trail.

As I wandered along the petal-lined path, I felt as though I had stumbled into a whimsical fairy tale. The gentle rustle of the flowers beneath my feet and the soft chirping of birds overhead only added to the enchantment.

Before long, the soothing sound of flowing water filled the air, and I caught a glimpse of flowing water peeking through the foliage. And then, with a graceful sweep of his arm, Bellamy lifted a massive tree branch, revealing a breathtaking teal waterfall hidden behind it. The sunlight danced across the water's surface, and I could not help but gasp in wonder at the scene before me.

"I created this for you." Bellamy called out over the gentle roar of the waterfall, still holding the branch aloft like a curtain reveal. I stepped past him, my eyes fixed on the breathtaking sight before me, and stood at the edge of the magnificent cascade.

The water tumbled down, a mesmerizing sixty feet of shimmering teal, its hue identical to the Opal Sea's teal radiant color. "It's... it's beautiful," I stammered, my words faltering in the face of such wonder. My own waterfall nestled in my backyard was nothing short of a fantasy.

Bellamy stepped up behind me, his arms encircling my waist in a warm embrace, his face nuzzling into the curve of my neck as he breathed me in deeply.

"Thank you," my voice barely audible over the waterfall's gentle thunder, but he sensed my gratitude. He held me for a long moment, and after the tumult of the previous night, I felt a deep comfort in his arms. Yesterday, I had doubted my decision to return, but in this instant, surrounded by the serene beauty of the waterfall and the warmth of Bellamy's embrace, I knew with certainty that I was exactly where I was meant to be.

As we ascended to the circus grounds, the performers and crew were already in high gear, busily preparing for the day's opening. I overheard some of the crew members mention "lot lice," a term that indicated a throng of eager guests were already queuing up at the entrance, awaiting admission.

It was clear that the circus was poised to be just as bustling as it was the previous day, if not even more so. Before we could head across town to visit my family, Bellamy had some pressing matters to attend to. While I made our way through the backstage area, I spotted Velar in the backyard, diligently hauling aerial ropes.

As I stood there, undecided about whether to approach him, Velar suddenly noticed me and promptly dropped what he was doing, striding towards me with a purposeful gait. I was caught, and there was no escaping now. "Hey," he said, his face lighting up with a warm smile as he drew near. I returned his smile, taking a deep breath before continuing, "I wanted to let you know that I forgive you for taking my memories. I don't want to dwell on the past." Velar's expression hinted that he was expecting more, his eyes lingering on mine as if awaiting further revelation.

Uncomfortable by the awkward silence, I hastily sought to fill the gap, blurting out "I am sorry for what happened between us, in my past life." Velar's smile abruptly faltered, replaced by a visible scowl. He scanned our surroundings, perhaps searching for potential witnesses, his gaze lingering on the possibility of Bellamy's presence.

As he stepped closer, the scent of pine and leather wafted from him, and I had to tilt my head back to meet his eyes. He leaned in, his emerald eyes narrowing as he delivered a blunt rebuke "Well, I'm not." With that, he straightened up, turned on his heel, and walked away, leaving me feeling foolish for my naivety. Of course, he wouldn't apologize, he still had feelings for me!

What was I thinking? How could I be such a moron!

I walked away, berating myself with a smack to the forehead, before seeking out Bellamy. Hand in hand, we strolled towards the entrance gate, where the crew and performers greeted us with warm waves and smiles. No matter how many lifetimes I live I will never get used to being the center of attention.

When we stepped outside of Darlington Circus, the chill of the outside air surrounded us, a stark contrast to the warmth of the circus. The rain had subsided, leaving behind a dismal, gray sky. A car awaited us, its engine purring softly. I pushed aside thoughts of Velar, unwilling to dwell on the awkward encounter. And certainly, I had no intention of broaching the subject with Daddy.

Instead, I focused on the excitement of introducing Bellamy to my family. I knew they would never comprehend the truth about me, Bellamy, the circus, my reincarnation, magic, and so our secrets would remain hidden from them.

As we arrived at my parents' townhouse, I softly reminded Bellamy to be on his best behavior. While he was always courteous to everyone, I knew he sometimes found mortals a tad...trying. Unintentionally, he could come across as somewhat condescending, treating them like simpletons. Except, of course, when it came to me. I was the exception to his rule. We followed the winding path to the front door, where Bellamy paused, gazing down at the embroidered floor mat. "The Bonetti Family?" he queried, raising an eyebrow. I simply shrugged, and he flashed me a charming smile.

My parents warmly welcomed us, ushering us into the cozy home. "Mr. and Mrs. Bonetti, it's an absolute pleasure to meet you," Bellamy said, his eyes scanning the surroundings where I grew up. I observed him taking in the memories that lined the walls, his gaze lingering on the photos that told the story of my present life.

He seemed particularly drawn to the one from my high school graduation, a hint of regret flickering across his face. I knew he could not help but think he should have found me sooner, but I had cherished my childhood in this life. Just as we were settling in, my rambunctious little brother Lucca burst out of his bedroom, his energetic presence filling the hallway. "He keeps my parents young," I laughingly exclaimed to Bellamy.

My mother had prepared a delicious brunch of bruschetta and a creamy mushroom risotto. As we sat down to eat, I began to explain to my parents that Bellamy was from Darlington Circus. But before I could continue, my mother's enthusiasm got the better of her. "Darlington Circus!" she yelled, almost spilling her glass. My father maintained a stoic expression, but I knew he was secretly amused by her antics. Bellamy, however, was thrilled to encounter someone who shared his passion for the circus. He beamed with pride, flashing me a cocky smile that made me roll my eyes in good- natured teasing.

Bellamy warmly shared his proposal with my parents, explaining that he wanted to recruit me as an aerial performer for the traveling circus. My mother's face lit up again with excitement, and she eagerly began showcasing my gymnastic awards and trophies. She proudly revealed that I had even earned a grant through my gymnastics talents, beaming with maternal pride. Bellamy listened intently, his eyes shining with interest.

As my parents proudly displayed my gymnastics awards to Bellamy, I couldn't help but think about the secrets I kept from them. They had no idea about my true identity, the countless lives I'd lived, my immortal family, and the magic. I knew I could never reveal the truth, no matter how much I wanted to share it with them. The safety of the entire circus depended on it. A hint of melancholy washed over me as I thought about leaving this life behind, but it was quickly overshadowed by the thrill of my life with Bellamy.

Bellamy was discreet, wisely keeping the truth hidden from my parents. He didn't reveal that my exceptional gymnastic skills were honed over countless lifetimes, my soul instinctively recalling the familiar rhythms of aerial performances. Instead, he shared a knowing smile with me, a silent understanding that only we two shared.

Bellamy was delighted to meet Lucca, who bombarded him with a thousand questions. Bellamy responded with excitement, his eyes sparkling with a childlike wonder that only fueled Lucca's excitement. As he filled Lucca with tales of the circus, his passion was infectious, and listening to Bellamy's animated stories, I couldn't help but smile with pride, knowing that this magical world was mine as well.

My father brought up the topic of art school, expressing his desire for me to stay and complete my education. But when

I explained that I could continue my studies online, he acquiesced. *Another lie.*

As my father shook Bellamy's hand, a sense of relief washed over me. It was important to me that my father accepted the man he believed to be my new employer. Not that Bellamy needed anyone's approval, but he understood the significance of this moment for me. He knew that having my father's blessing brought me comfort and peace of mind.

Bellamy extended an impromptu invitation to my parents and Lucca, offering them a special experience at the circus for the day. He produced tickets from his showman jacket, explaining that we would be departing tomorrow, making this their only chance to use them. My parents were overjoyed, and my mother hurriedly retreated to her bedroom to change attire.

As the Showman, Bellamy had responsibilities to attend to, so we said goodbye to my parents and Lucca, departing ahead of them. As I left my childhood home, I felt a sense of relief, knowing that my parents had embraced Bellamy.

While our romantic relationship remained a secret, their approval somehow eased my conscience, making it simpler for me to leave them behind and continue my journey with the circus. It was not that Bellamy needed their validation, but having their blessing made my transition smoother for me.

Upon our return to the circus, I was struck by the sheer size of the crowd, which had swelled to twice its morning numbers. It was clear we would need to depart tonight; excessive attention was a liability for the circus and its immortal inhabitants.

Bellamy's plan was to relieve Briar, who had been filling in for him, but our arrival was met with an unexpected complication. Velar, his expression grave, hastened towards us, urgency in his voice. "Bell, we need to bolster security. A group of teenagers breached one of the fences and gained entry. I managed to escort them out, but the gate requires your repair."

Bellamy nodded, his eyes locking onto mine. 'I'll return shortly, after I address this issue.' I reassured him there was no hurry, as I intended to give my family a tour of the circus. With a nod, he set off to tend to the damaged gate, his magic the only means to restore it.

My parents and Lucca finally arrived, and I couldn't wait to share my circus world with them. Even if they couldn't know everything. As they entered, I reveled in their wonderstruck expressions, mirroring those of the other guests. My mother's face radiated pure delight, her smile so wide it seemed to transport her back to childhood.

My father, ever the logical thinker, scrutinized the surroundings, attempting to decipher the secrets behind the spectacle. His analytical mind struggled to comprehend the magic that defied explanation. I savored the reactions of all the guests, but children's wonder was always the most enchanting. Lucca's eyes shone like saucers, brimming with unrelenting joy. I basked in the moment, allowing my family to absorb the enchantment before I finally greeted them.

As soon as they spotted me, my mother exclaimed, "I knew this place was magical!" Her words were met with my warm smile. My father, meanwhile, remained speechless, his eyes scanning the circus with a mix of confusion and amazement. Lucca, bursting with excitement, bounced up and down, eager to explore every nook and cranny. I delighted in taking them on a comprehensive tour of the circus, ensuring we visited each and every tent.

We marveled at the death-defying tightrope performers in the Big Top, admired Orlow the elephant and Clove in another tent, and indulged in all the delicious treats. My parents savored whimsical alcoholic drinks, the hint of magic in the drinks had them feeling like they were floating. Lucca relished his favorite treat, a rich chocolate peanut butter milkshake. They had funnel cakes, French fries, deep-fried Oreos, and sizzling sausages. The magic soaring around the circus left the guests feeling like they were never full so there was always room for more.

My parents claimed their seats in the front row, eagerly awaiting Eve's mesmerizing performance in the Big Top. As she took her final bow, she gracefully glided over to greet them. She had met them when I moved in with her months earlier. After her short exchange with my parents, we settled in to watch Bellamy's grand finale, the pièce de résistance that would bring the evening's spectacle to a close.

Following his performance, the sky erupted in a shimmering spectacle, a dazzling firework display illuminating the darkness for miles around. Throughout the day, Lucca repeated queries about joining the circus or accompanying me on my journey tinged with an infectious excitement. I overheard my father's reassuring response, "One day you can join with Nicole." I gave Lucca a half smile knowing that he could never know the truth about the circus.

We shared a joyous day together, and I cherished every moment, knowing that our time together would soon be scarce. I reassured them that I would return to visit whenever possible, but the impending goodbye weighed heavy on my heart. I said goodbye to my loving parents and Lucca. I gave him the biggest hug of all. I was going to miss my little brother even if he did get on my nerves sometimes.

As I escorted my family to the entrance gate, I bid them a final farewell, my heart ached. I assumed Bellamy was busy overseeing cleanup and was preparing for our imminent departure tonight. With sadness I began my solitary walk back to the willow tree, lost in thought. Suddenly, Velar appeared beside me. "Nic, I'm sorry I was a jerk earlier." Startled, I halted my stride, turning to face the strongman, his unexpected apology catching me off guard.

I too regretted how our encounter earlier had ended, and I sought to clear the air. "I don't want things to be awkward between us, and I hope we can still be friends," I said, my voice sincere. Velar's response was unexpectedly a hearty chuckle that left me wondering. "What's funny?" I asked. Velar's smirk lingered as he paused, his eyes scanning our surroundings as if ensuring we were alone. "Oh, I've just heard this before, and I understand completely..." His trailing words only added to my confusion, and I pressed him for clarity. "And what?" I asked, my eyes locked on his, seeking answers. Velar's eyes darted around once more, as if he feared being overheard, before responding.

Velar took my arm firmly as he swiftly guided me between two tents, seeking seclusion. He didn't release his hold, instead, his hands encircled both of my arms, his eyes locking onto mine with an intensity that made my heart race. "Nic, I know you don't remember what we had in your past life, and I know that you love Bell, and I'm not here to disrupt that, Bell is like my brother." His voice was low and measured. He paused, his gaze piercing, as if choosing his words with care. Then, with a gentle sincerity, he continued, "I love you, Nic, and I will always love you." His words hung in the air like a promise, and I held my breath, my mind reeling with the weight of his confession.

My mouth dropped as he continued. "I know you may not want to hear it, but I need to be honest with you, and with Bellamy," Velar said, his voice filled with conviction. "I will leave if that's what you desire, but it won't change the way I feel. I will continue to love you, no matter what." His words were firm, and I released the breath I had been holding, my mind racing. I struggled to find the right words, and after a moment's pause, I replied, "Velar, I am sorry. I truly am. I do not recall our past, and right now, being back with Bellamy brings me happiness. Please, do not leave us because of this."

Velar nodded in understanding, his expression softening. "I promise, my feelings won't compromise our friendship," he said, his voice sounding sincere. As we strolled back towards the willow tree, the circus seemed eerily quiet, as if we were the only two left behind. The entrance gate was closed, and the performers had all retired to Jubilee, leaving us alone amidst the silent tents.

Eve and Bellamy awaited our return at the willow tree. We discussed the urgency of departing immediately, as the impending crowd the next day would pose a significant risk to everyone's safety. With a sense of relief, we descended the stairs into Jubilee. I was exhausted, my thoughts drifting to the comforts of Casmira, where a soothing bath in my spacious tub beckoned.

Bellamy's arm encircled my waist as we entered our town, his touch a gentle reminder of his presence. Just as we prepared to cross the street, a deafening crack of thunder and a blazing flash of lightning illuminated the sky above, sending the four of us tumbling to the ground.

The sky above us suddenly turned a deep, foreboding black, and the houses around us plunged into darkness. Bellamy sprang to his feet, his voice laced with panic. "No, no, this cannot be happening! No!" He frantically examined his hands, arms, and entire body, as if searching for something that was no longer there. "My magic... it's gone!" he exclaimed. As I struggled to my feet, I could barely make out the silhouettes of our neighbors emerging from their homes, their faces tilted upwards, gazing at the empty, dark sky in collective disbelief.

Were it not for the soft glow of the oil lanterns scattered throughout the town, total darkness would have engulfed us. I turned to face Bellamy, whose eyes were still wide with shock, but now fixed on something behind me. Eve and Velar were similarly transfixed, their eyes directed towards the entrance of Jubilee. I followed their line of sight, and my heart skipped a beat as I spotted Lucca standing there.

CHAPTER
SEVEN

Lucca was scared. He stood frozen in his tracks. The thunderous crack had left him looking small and vulnerable staring at a world he couldn't comprehend. The stairs behind him closed and immediately transformed into a real tree sealing our only exit out of Jubilee.

Velar turned to the showman; his voice laced with urgency. "Bell, what's happening?" Bellamy remained fixed on Lucca as he murmured, "A mortal entered Jubilee, and my magic is gone!" Eve's expression mirrored her confusion. "What do you mean?" she asked, shaking her head. Bellamy's eyes met mine. He mumbled under his breath, "No mortal may enter, lest the magic that dwells within its walls flees in terror, abandoning its owner..."

As I stood there in shock for a moment, two figures emerged from the darkness, their cautious footsteps echoing through the silence. Mesidor and Ambrette, the wise witches who dwelled in the hills of the Emberlynn Forest. They quickly approached Bellamy and Velar; their voices hushed as they discussed our predicament.

Meanwhile, Lucca ran over to me, and I wrapped my arms around my little brother. "What are you doing here? Why didn't you go home with mom and dad?" I asked. Lucca did not answer my questions, he remained fixed on the mystical surroundings, his voice full of awe. "Where are we? What is this place?" I didn't know how to answer those questions, but I didn't have to because we were now surrounded by everyone in Jubilee.

Bellamy waited for the townspeople to gather, his eyes scanning the crowd as he prepared to address them. We stood facing the sea of worried faces, our presence a symbol of unity amid chaos. Bellamy called out, his voice was calm and authoritative. "Please, everyone, remain calm. I have temporarily lost my magic." Eve and I exchanged a concerned glance (*lost our magic?*) "But I will recover it," Bellamy continued, his confidence unwavering. "I'll be working closely with my council." He gestured to the three of us beside him. "And together, we'll find a solution in no time."

The crowd before us looked far from reassured, their faces etched with worry and fear. Bellamy instructed them to return to their homes and await further instructions, but the sense of unease lingered. Without magic, we were trapped in a place that didn't exist, stuck in a void beyond the boundaries of the universe. My mind raced with the implications, my head pounding as I struggled to comprehend our predicament. One thought dominated all my concerns, I had to get Lucca back to my parents or they will kill me!

As we navigated the darkness, our footsteps led us back to Casmira, my beloved home. The sight that greeted us was nothing short of devastating. No longer a magical house filled with life, rather she just looked old and haunted.

The entrance creaked as we stepped inside, and the air that welcomed us was stale and void of the warm cinnamon scent that once filled the room. Bellamy wrapped his arms around me, holding me tight as if trying to shield me from the pain. I felt his sorrow seep into my bones. Casmira was more than just a home; she was a part of the family, and she was gone.

Together, we fumbled through the darkness, our hands groping for anything that could bring light to our despair. We opened drawers, rummaged through cupboards, and stumbled upon a few scattered lighters and candles. As Bellamy lit the first candle, the flickering flame cast a warm glow on his face, and I saw a glimmer of sadness in his eyes. "She fills the void when you aren't here," he said, his voice soft.

I felt a pang of guilt and realization, I had never stopped to think about how my absence affected those around me. I had always assumed they simply moved on with their lives, never considering the impact my reincarnation had on everyone. Bellamy's eyes seemed to well up with tears, but the dancing candlelight hid the truth. He stood still, lost in thought, mourning the loss of our beloved home.

Bellamy and I joined Velar and Eve in the kitchen, our faces illuminated only by the faint glow of the candles we lit. Eve disappeared upstairs, her footsteps echoing through the silence as she searched for more oil lanterns. Bellamy and Velar worked in tandem, their faces set with determination, as they coaxed a fire to life in the main room. Their hands moved with a practiced ease, yet a hint of uncertainty dawdled in my mind, wondering if they could build a fire without magic. The air was heavy with the scent of smoke, and the flickering sparks seemed to dance in rhythm with my doubts.

The crackling flames started to ease my concern. The glowing light was a small comfort in the midst of our despair. We all worked in silence, each lost in our own thoughts, our minds racing with the question, how do we get the magic back? As the light grew, Lucca's curiosity got the better of him, and he began to examine the pictures that decorated the walls of my dark home. His small face scrunched in concentration.

His eyes widened in confusion, and a hint of fear crept into his expression. I walked over and wrapped my arm around him, offering a reassuring squeeze. "I know this is a lot to take in right now, Lucca. But I'll explain everything, okay?" He looked up at me, searching for answers. I held my breath, anticipating his next question.

Then, he pointed to an old picture on the wall, a faded photo of Bellamy and I from our Appalachian trail adventure years ago. "Is that you?" he questioned. When I nodded a grin spread across his face. "Cool!" His fear was forgotten. I let out a sigh of relief, grateful for his response.

As I observed my little brother exploring the main floor, I couldn't help but think about the challenges ahead. Eve was still upstairs, and the men were still building the fire without. I chuckled to myself, wondering if they even remembered how to do it the old- fashioned way. Meanwhile, Lucca's curiosity led him down the hall, and I heard the creak of a door opening across from the dining room. He had discovered the library.

The library was pitch black, but I was prepared. I pulled out my lighter and candles, setting one down on a nearby table. The flickering flame illuminated the room. Lucca started to explore more. "Wow! Look at all the books!" he exclaimed. He began to read the titles aloud, his fingers tracing the spines of the books that lined the floor-to-ceiling shelves. "I didn't know you could read!" I teased, playfully giving him a hard time. But Lucca was too captivated to respond with his usual wit, his attention fully absorbed by the treasure trove of books surrounding us.

The shelves, stretching from floor to ceiling, filled the entire walls of the library, leaving only one wall with a window that framed a serene view of the gardens. This sanctuary was a treasure trove, housing some of the rarest and most coveted books in the world.

Bellamy's passion project had evolved into a remarkable collection after so many years. Among my many cherished volumes was a true gem, a four-hundred-year-old edition of Harry Houdini's "Natural Magick", its yellowed pages whispering secrets of the past.

As I gazed out the window, the blackness of the sky stared back at me, reflecting only the flickering candlelight and my own image. Meanwhile, Lucca's interest drew him to the coffee table, where he began to examine the scattered picture frames. These were snapshots of my past lives, frozen moments with loved ones now gone, and cherished memories of my circus family.

Lucca's fingers lingered on an old black and white picture, one that showed Bellamy, Eve, Velar, and me standing proudly in front of the circus entrance. Though I appeared older in the photo, my features remained unmistakable. Lucca's eyes narrowed; confusion etched on his face. "Is...is this you?" He asked, sounding unsure.

I hesitated, unsure of how to explain, but decided to tell him the truth. "Yes, that's me, but it was a long time ago." I began, but Lucca cut in. "How can this be you? You look old in this picture!" I walked over to him and sat down on the blue suede couch, facing him directly.

How could I simplify this complex concept for a ten-year-old? I thought to myself before asking, "Lucca, do you know what reincarnation is?" My little brother shook his head, his eyes still puzzled. "I didn't think so."

I took a deep breath, "Reincarnation is when your soul is reborn after you die," I explained. "Most people don't remember their past life, but I do."

I paused, studying Lucca's expression to see if he was following along. He rubbed his head, looking puzzled, and exclaimed, "So you remember your past life?!"

I nodded enthusiastically, hoping to convey the significance without revealing too much. "Yes, I do." Lucca's curiosity did not let up, and he asked, "Does Mom and Dad know?" I hesitated, knowing I had to tread carefully. "No, and they can't know, for my protection and the circus." I knew it was a lot to ask a ten-year-old to keep secrets, but I pushed that worry aside for now. It was the least of our concerns, considering the bigger picture.

Lucca remained engrossed in the photographs, but my attention was diverted by a sudden, loud knock at the front door. "I'll explain it all to you one day, but right now, we're in a dire situation, and we need to focus on restoring Bellamy's magic, or we'll be trapped in Jubilee forever," I said, my urgency evident in my tone. Lucca's eyes widened, and he quickly set aside the pictures, his curiosity momentarily replaced by concern. He followed me closely as we went to see who was at the door.

Eve opened the door to find Miss Poppet standing in the darkness, her flashlight casting eerie shadows. "Come in," I called out from down the hall. Miss Poppet stepped inside and switched off her flashlight, her eyes adjusting to the dim light within. "Good evening," she said with a warm smile. "I was wondering if Lucca would like to come to my house for a fresh funnel cake. I made it just before the lights went out, and I would hate for it to go to waste."

Her wise eyes met mine, and I knew she understood the importance of distracting Lucca from our terrible situation. Lucca's face lit up at the mention of the treat, and he remembered meeting Miss Poppet earlier at the circus. I handed him a flashlight, and with a grateful nod, the two of them set off into the darkness, bound for the bake shop. I watched from the front porch as they disappeared into the night, the faint glow of their flashlights fading into the trees.

The four of us huddled around the fire in the main room, its warmth a meager respite from the biting cold that had seeped into the circus. Without magic, the air felt hollow, and the silence was oppressive. Velar tended to the fire, adding logs to keep it burning strong, while Eve paced back and forth. Each of us lost in our thoughts, searching for a solution that refused to come.

As the night wore on, I decided to brew some coffee, the familiar ritual a comforting distraction from our predicament. It was clear we would not be getting any sleep anytime soon, not until we found a way to restore the magic that had vanished.

Eve trailed behind me into the kitchen, holding up a candle to light the space as I rummaged through the cupboards for coffee. I held the can up to the flickering candle to see the directions and began to read. Eliciting a chuckle from Eve. "I can't believe you have to read the directions!" She teased, her eyes sparkling with amusement.

I shot back, "Hey, I'm sorry, but I'm used to having a magical house that does everything for me!" Her grin grew wider as she retorted, "Spoiled bitch." I playfully stuck out my tongue, and for a moment, we forgot about the pressing issues at hand.

After the coffee was brewed, we returned to the main room, where Velar and Bellamy still sat in silence. The flickering fire was now raging. I handed each of them a steaming mug, and they accepted without a word, their eyes lost in the flames. I settled onto the hearth, feeling the warmth of the fire radiate through my back, a comforting sensation amidst the chill of the night. As I sipped my coffee, I watched each of my friends, their faces etched with worry and concern, the silence between us heavy with unspoken thoughts.

This was typically a time filled with laughter and excitement, as we prepared for the Samsara ritual, a celebration of life and renewal. But now, instead of joy and anticipation, we sat in stunned silence, our minds racing with thoughts of survival. Velar seemed to hold a thousand thoughts; his lips pressed together as if struggling to contain his words.

Bellamy slumped beside me, his face buried in his hands, his shoulders sagging under the weight of our circumstances. I remained silent, consumed by guilt and regret. If only I had been more cautious. If only I had not persuaded us to stay another day. The weight of my responsibility troubled me. Then, Velar cleared his throat, his voice ready to break the silence. *I knew he couldn't hold it in.*

Velar sprang from the oversized chair, his movements sudden and urgent. "Bell," he called, his voice firm but careful, waiting for Bellamy to acknowledge him. Bellamy straightened, his eyes locking onto Velar's intense face. Velar's words tumbled out in a rush, "I know you don't want to hear it, but we need to go see her." Bellamy's headshake was immediate, his face set in determination. "There has to be another way," he protested.

Velar was swift and forceful, "What are you going to do without magic? How is the circus going to jump? And how are we going to escape Jubilee?" The room fell silent, Velar's words hanging in the air like a challenge. I held my breath when Velar paused. Bellamy's face had been reddening with each passing moment, his anger and frustration growing.

Bellamy rose from the fireplace, his eyes locking onto Velar, the two alpha men standing toe-to-toe, their faces inches apart. The air was electric with tension, their body language screaming aggression. "I don't want to ever see that witch again!" Bellamy growled, his voice low and menacing, "and I'd appreciate it if you stopped bringing her up!" Eve swiftly intervened, her voice sounding annoyed. She put herself between the two dominant men. "Bell, what choice do we have?" she asked, her eyes pleading for reason.

Bellamy's shoulders relaxed slightly, his gaze shifting to me, as if I held the answer to their predicament. Velar and Eve waited patiently, their eyes fixed on me, expecting my opinion. Their stares bore into me, and my heart sank. I hated being caught in the middle, especially when it came to Bellamy.

It took me a moment to summon the courage, but I finally nodded in agreement, my eyes fixed on the floor. "I think this is our only option," I said. I hesitated, then I looked at Bellamy, my heart racing with anticipation. I was terrified of facing the witch, whose power was so formidable she had cursed an entire circus and everyone in it, everyone except me.

Something inside me shifted, a spark of trust igniting. I realized that Velar wouldn't suggest this course of action unless he was certain it was the right decision. My gut told me to trust him, to have faith in his judgment. Bellamy eventually relented, but his expression betrayed his discontent. He was not pleased that I had gone against him, but I knew he understood.

Eve nodded, her expression resolute. "Okay, great, we will go see the evil witch, but how are we even going to get there? We still don't have a way out of Jubilee." Her words were a stark reminder of our predicament. Then, Velar quickly said. "What about the witches? Maybe they can help us?"

Bellamy's expression lightened, and he nodded. "They'll help us. The Blackwoods offered their assistance as soon as I lost my magic." He paused, collecting his thoughts. "They have a coven, a community for all the witches living here." Mesidor and Ambrette Blackwood are the leaders, and their son Clove resides with them in a quaint cottage deep within the Emberlynn Forest. That is where all the witches and vampires live.

Eve and I gathered a few oil lanterns, and the four of us departed from Casmira, heading towards the hills. The darkness surrounded us like a shroud, casting an eerie gloom over our journey. It felt as though Jubilee was trapped in a box, and someone had slammed the lid shut. Without the flickering oil lanterns, total darkness would have consumed us. As we passed through the town, I noticed that several lanterns had already burned out, their extinguished flames an ominous sign. The gravel path wound its way up the hills, leading us into the forest, where the usual twinkling fairy lights had been replaced by an unsettling, creepy darkness.

As we trudged through the darkness, I couldn't help but feel a deep sense of sympathy for the people of Jubilee. Their reliance on Bellamy's magic was noticeable, and it was clear that we were woefully unprepared for a crisis of this magnitude. I made a mental note to myself, *once we escaped this predicament, we needed to develop a contingency plan, a backup strategy to prevent such vulnerability in the future.*

My thoughts were interrupted by the burning sensation in my legs, protesting the steep incline of the hills. I lagged behind my friends, my mortal limitations starkly contrasting with their immortal vitality. While they walked with effortless grace, I struggled to keep up, my humanity a stark reminder of our differing realities.

At last, the cabin came into view, a welcoming haven in the darkness. "Almost there!" I called out, urging myself forward. I paused to catch my breath, my lungs burning from the exertion. The others had already reached the cabin, their figures waiting patiently in the flickering lantern light.

They waited for me to catch up before knocking on the wooden door, its rustic surface weathered to a warm brown. Clove answered, his hazel eyes surprised as he took in the sight of Bellamy standing on his front porch.

"Hello, Mr. Darlington," he said, his voice tinged with shock. In the flickering light of the lantern, Clove appeared as a youthful teenager, his features smooth and unlined. But, like the others in the circus, he had long since ceased to age, his immortality a gift - or curse - that had frozen his physical appearance at a mere fraction of his true age, which was closer to two hundred years.

As we stepped inside the cozy cottage, Clove welcomed us and called out to his parents, his voice echoing through the rustic interior. Ambrette and Mesidor emerged from the shadows, their faces aglow with candlelight. They greeted us with a gentle nod, their mannerisms and attire a testament to their preference for a simpler time.

Unlike their son, they eschewed modern trappings, living off the land and shunning technology. Their clothing, too, was a throwback to the late eighteen hundreds, a style they seemed to cherish. Clove, on the other hand, had chosen a different path. His attire was more modern, reflecting his love of travel and exploration. Whenever the circus was on hiatus, he would venture out into the world beyond Jubilee, returning with tales of adventure and wonder.

Ambrette offered us a steaming pot of tea, which we gratefully accepted, and we gathered around the cozy table in the small dining room. Mesidor asked, "How can we be of service to you?" Bellamy hesitated, glancing at Velar, who nodded almost imperceptibly.

Bellamy continued, "We're seeking a way to leave Jubilee." He paused, his voice trailing off, before adding, "We believe we can find a powerful witch who can help me regain my magic." His tone apprehensive, as if he was reluctant to reveal the full truth. Mesidor's gaze met his wife's, and Ambrette's eyes narrowed, her voice laced with a hint of knowing, "You don't mean Sage, do you?"

Velar responded, "I know Sage is the one who cursed us, but we can't remain in Jubilee indefinitely. We've exhausted our options, and her assistance is our only hope for regaining our magic." Mesidor leaned in, whispering something to his wife, his eyes locked on hers. Ambrette's expression turned contemplative, her eyes distant, no doubt remembering her estranged sister, Sage, whom she hadn't seen in centuries.

She voiced her concerns, "But what if she refuses to help us? She was banished for her treachery, after all." Bellamy understood Ambrette's trepidation, and he shared her doubts about trusting Sage. Yet, he persisted, "I believe we must try."

Mesidor sought his wife's approval once more. Ambrette nodded, her consent given, and Mesidor declared, "You may use our cheval glass."

The four of us followed Mesidor up the creaky stairs to the cottage attic, the air thick with the scent of old wood and secrets. The space was sparse, with only a few dusty trunks and forgotten relics scattered about.

However, our attention was drawn to a majestic cheval glass, its ornate frame draped with a sheet. Mesidor ceremoniously unveiled the mirror, revealing its intricate carvings and the soft glow of aged glass.

"This cheval glass dates back to the Renaissance period," he said, his voice filled with reverence. Ambrette joined us, carrying a smoldering bundle of sage, which she waved around the four of us and the mirror, enveloping us in a fragrant, purifying haze. The smoke swirled, dancing in the flickering candlelight.

Mesidor's voice boomed through the attic, commanding our attention. "Listen well, travelers! This cheval glass is a powerful portal, but it can be dangerous if not used wisely. You must have a clear destination in mind before stepping through, or risk becoming lost in the vast expanse of the unknown."

Bellamy turned to Velar, his eyes inquiring, "Where do we need to go?" Velar's response was swift and decisive.

"Amsterdam." Mesidor's finger shot up, his brow furrowed in caution. "Be more specific, my friend." Velar's smirk hinted at a secret, and he elaborated, "The Paradiso in Amsterdam."

Mesidor's nod was curt, his approval granted. Bellamy's skepticism was visible as he shook his head at Velar, questioning, "Amsterdam, really?" Velar's fang glinted in the candlelight, his smirk growing wider, leaving no doubt that our destination was indeed the vibrant city of Amsterdam.

Eve's eyes rolled heavenward, exasperated by the men's banter, and she turned to Mesidor, seeking clarity. "How does this work?" she asked, her voice practical. Mesidor's response was straightforward. "Simply state your destination, take a step through the glass, and you'll arrive, just as you would walking through a door." *Easy enough.* Velar's brow furrowed, his mind racing with the implications. "And the return journey?" he queried. Ambrette's expression turned solemn, her voice gentle but firm.

"Once you step through, there's no coming back through the glass. Your only options are to re-enchant Jubilee or return to the circus's location."

Mesidor glanced at the old-fashioned watch strapped to his arm, his eyes widening in alarm. You better wait a few hours; I do believe it's still daylight in the Netherlands." Velar's eyes lit up with gratitude. "Thank you! I wouldn't have thought of that, I could have been fried by the sunlight!" Bellamy nodded in agreement. "Good thinking, Mesidor. We need to prepare anyway. This mission requires careful planning, and a few hours' delay won't hurt us."

As we waited for the sun to set in Amsterdam, Bellamy and Velar embarked on a mission to inform the townspeople of our plan, while Eve and I distributed candles throughout Jubilee. At Eve's house, I couldn't help but notice the transformations since my last visit, which, if my calculations were correct, had been approximately seventy years prior.

"Wow, I just love the bloody walls," I remarked, my candle casting flickering shadows on the bold, deep-red hue. Eve's smile hinted at her knowledge of my true opinion. I had never been fond of that particular shade. "Yeah, I was feeling bored one day," she admitted, and we shared a laugh. I wondered, though, if seventy years felt as fleeting to her as it did to me. To me, it seemed like only nineteen years had passed.

On our way back to the cottage, we made a stop at the bake shop to check in on Lucca and brief Miss Poppet on our plan. Lucca was fast asleep on the couch, and I didn't want to disturb him, nor did I want to see the sadness in his eyes when he learned I was leaving.

I knew he would be in capable hands with Miss Poppet, who would care for him as if he were her own. She gave me a warm hug, and we bid each other farewell. As we were leaving, Miss Poppet called out, her voice gentle but wise. "Remember, dear, time has a way of changing people. I am sure Sage is no exception." I nodded, taking her words to heart, as we departed the bakery.

Upon our return to the Blackwoods' cottage, Ambrette welcomed us with a savory stew, simmering over an open flame outside. As we gathered around the fire, enjoying the flavors and warmth, we delved deeper into our plan. Bellamy elaborated, "If we fail to re-enter Jubilee, I will need your help, Mesidor and Ambrette. In two weeks', time, please escort the townspeople through the cheval glass to this address." He handed Mesidor a small piece of paper, creased with precision. "It is a safe house, located in the real

world. A place where they will be protected and free from Jubilee."

Our safe house! I had completely forgotten about it. Despite being a part of our contingency plan, I had never actually seen it or knew its location. Velar and Eve were also aware of its existence, but I was certain they had never visited it either. This was the first time Bellamy had shared its location with anyone, and it struck me how grave the situation truly was. The weight of our predicament settled in, and I realized we were taking a significant risk.

After dinner, we ascended the stairs to the attic. *My first time through a cheval glass, how fun!* I was being positive. We formed a line, ready to enter the glass, and Mesidor offered a crucial warning, "Remember, don't hold hands. You never know if one person might be pulled in a different direction - you would not want to lose a hand!" His brief chuckle was followed by a serious tone, and he waved his hand dismissively. Then he continued, "Everyone, repeat after me: The Paradiso, Amsterdam." Our voices echoed in unison, "The Paradiso, Amsterdam." As I stepped through the shimmering portal, Ambrette's soft voice trailed behind us. "So, Mote it be."

CHAPTER

EIGHT

In a single step, I found myself in the alluring capital of the Netherlands. Even at night, the city's charm was undeniable. Edison bulbs cast a warm glow on the narrow streets, and the light danced across the long canals, creating a romantic ambiance. The street we stood on was lined with an astonishing number of bicycles. I had never seen so many bikes in my life!

We stood directly across from the Paradiso, a historic venue with a façade of faded brick and a clock tower that seemed to whisper stories of the past. The four of us paused, taking in the sights and sounds of our new surroundings. The grandeur of the building was a stark contrast to the chill in the air. A chilly wind swept through, and I instinctively wrapped my arms around myself, rubbing my hands to warm up. We had been so caught up in the excitement of our journey that we had not even thought to dress for the weather, and now the chill was starting to set in.

I turned to glance behind me, hoping to catch a glimpse of the portal that led back to Jubilee. But there was nothing, just the charming streets of Amsterdam stretching out in every direction. "Bellamy!" I called out. He hurried over to me, his face etched with worry. "Why haven't we ever used that before?" I asked, still trying to wrap my head around the sudden shift. Eve laughed and chimed in, "No kidding!" Bellamy shot us a disapproving look and said, "C'mon, girls. Let's move." He gestured for us to follow Velar, who was already on the move.

We hurried behind Velar, struggling to keep up with his rapid pace. Unaware of his own speed, he moved with vampire speed, forcing us to jog to stay behind him. I could not help but wonder how he knew the way, navigating the unfamiliar streets with ease. The cold wind whipped against my face as we raced past the tall, slender buildings, their ornate exteriors blurring together in a whirlwind of color and texture.

We trailed Velar across a bridge, then doubled back to ensure we did not lose him as he ducked into a narrow alley. The alley he chose was unexpectedly thronged with tourists, and we had to push through the crowd to keep up. As we finally broke through the mass, I saw what had drawn the tourists' attention. Neon lights illuminated the windows, and women in sexy lingerie beckoned from within, their provocative poses and flirtatious smiles captivating the onlookers.

We had entered the infamous red-light district, and the vibrant atmosphere was unmistakable. Ahead, Velar sauntered along, pausing to appreciate the women on display, while Bellamy maintained a steadfast gaze, his focus fixed on the path ahead. He was driven by a singular purpose. Eve and I lingered, taking in the sights and sounds of the debauchery, but we couldn't stop for long, we were losing the men.

As we picked up pace, the chill of the night air began to dissipate, replaced by a warmth that spread through my body. But my mind raced with questions. *Where were we going? What drove Velar's urgency to reach this mysterious witch?* I conjured up countless scenarios, each one more plausible than the last, yet none provided a satisfying answer. All I could do was hold onto hope – hope that she could help us.

As we finally came to a halt outside an old canal house, I doubled over, gasping for air. Velar's relentless pace had left me winded. I straightened up, eyeing the slim, weathered building with a mix of curiosity and fear. The darkness within seemed absolute, as if the house had been abandoned for years. Yet, Velar's confident knock suggested otherwise. He stepped back, his eyes fixed on the door, his expression expectant.

We stood in silence, our breathing suspended, as the door creaked open. The darkness within seemed to spill out, like a physical presence. I held my breath, my heart racing with anticipation, and Bellamy's hand found mine, as if sensing my fear. We all startled when a woman's voice pierced the night air, her tone a mix of irritation and wariness. "What do you want at this ungodly hour?" she demanded. Her face aglow in the faint moonlight.

Her gaze swept over each of us, before locking onto Velar, and her demeanor transformed in an instant. "Velar! You old vampire bastard, where the hell have you been?" She exclaimed, a sinister smile spreading across her face, as if she had stumbled upon a long- lost friend. And perhaps she had.

She tossed her hood back, revealing a cascade of fiery red hair that tumbled down her back like a wild inferno. Her beauty was breathtaking, leaving me wondering how such a radiant being could possibly be an evil witch. Velar and the witch embraced, and Bellamy's eyes widened in astonishment, mirroring my own surprise, as well as Eve's. It seemed Velar had been harboring a secret, one that had brought us to this mysterious doorstep.

After embracing Velar, her gaze shifted to Bellamy, her eyes lingering on him as she drew out his name, "Well, hello, Bellamy..." The way she prolonged the syllables made me feel uneasy. Bellamy, however, remained composed, his voice even as he replied, "Good to see you again, Sage." The witch's eyes sparkled with a

mischievous light, and she burst out laughing, "HA! Is it?" Her lips curled into a wicked grin, revealing a hint of malevolence beneath her charming exterior.

I took a step forward, intending to introduce myself, but she preempted me with a knowing smile. "Well, well, well, Nicole, right?" Her gaze flicked to Velar, and she nodded, as if confirming a secret only she was privy to. "You must be on... what?... your fourth or fifth life now, am I right?" She seemed fascinated by my reincarnation. Velar intervened, his voice low and urgent. "We actually need your help, Sage." The witch's attention snapped back to him, her eyes narrowing slightly as she scanned us all once more. "Of course you do. Come inside."

We followed behind Sage as she led us into the canal house, whose interior was a pleasant surprise after its unassuming exterior. The cozy kitchen was warm and inviting, with a beautifully restored old wooden table at its center. Sage gestured for us to take our seats around it. I settled in beside Bellamy, feeling a sense of comfort with him by my side.

A sleek black cat emerged from an adjacent room; its eyes fixed on us with a discerning look. As it took in our presence at the table, it let out a low hiss, its tail twitching with agitation.

"Play nice, Lilith," Sage scolded, her attention focused on the cauldron before her, rather than her pet.

The cat, seemingly unimpressed by our company, turned its back on us and padded over to Sage, its movement was graceful. With a deft flick of her wrist, Sage ignited a flame beneath the cauldron, the fire crackling to life with a mesmerizing intensity.

I watched, transfixed, as she worked her magic with a speed and precision that surpassed even Bellamy's skills. Her mastery was awe-inspiring, and I could not help but wonder how many years of experience lay behind her effortless technique. *Was she significantly older than Bellamy, or was her prowess simply a result of dedicated practice?*

Sage inhaled deeply through her nose, her chest rising with the breath, and then lifted her head towards the ceiling. She exhaled slowly, her gaze gradually lowering to fix on Bellamy, a malevolent grin spreading across her face. "So, where did all your magic go, Bellamy?"

She asked, her voice dripping with amusement, as if savoring our discomfort. Bellamy remained silent, but I could sense his thoughts mirroring mine. *How did she know?* Sage didn't wait for a response, her eyes glinting with knowledge. "I can't smell any magic around you," she continued, her tone dripping with intrigue. "For this is why you have come to me?" The question floating in the air.

I began to explain the circumstances surrounding my little brother's involvement with Jubilee, but Sage interrupted me with a knowing smile. "Oh yes, Jubilee," she said, her voice laced with annoyance. "I know my sister helped Bellamy create that world as a hiding place. How is she?" She asked with disdain.

Does she really want to know? Bellamy filled her in on the crucial role Ambrette and Mesidor had played in our journey, allowing us to reach her doorstep. Sage's face lit up with pleasure at the mention of her sister's involvement, but she didn't pursue the topic further, leaving me wondering about the dynamics between the two siblings.

Velar's words were laced with desperation as he pleaded with Sage, "We need the magic back, or we'll never be able to rescue our friends from Jubilee, and we can't return without it." The witch's gaze shifted to her black cat, just as it emitted a strange, cackling meow. It was as if they shared a secret understanding, their eyes locked in a silent conversation. Sage's attention snapped back to the four of us seated around her table, her eyes boring into Bellamy with an unyielding intensity. "Why should I help you?" she asked, her voice low and even, her gaze never wavering from his face.

Bellamy shot Velar a sideways glance, his expression Screaming, I told you this was a bad idea. But Eve, ever the optimist, chimed in, "Sage, why don't you come with us after we get the magic back? You can live with us, travel around, we could always use more witches at the circus."

Sage's response was a withering look, her eyes conveying that the circus was far beneath her refined tastes. "No, I've lived my circus days," Her tone thick with irritation, "and I have no itchy feet to come back to that place."

The witch then shifted to Velar, her eyes sparkling with mischief. "We did have our fun, though," she said, a sly wink accompanying her words. Velar's smirk was unmistakable, despite his evident discomfort. I couldn't help but roll my eyes at the unspoken history between them.

Bellamy shifted the conversation, his voice laced with a newfound vulnerability. "Sage, I'm not here to ask you to lift the curse on us. We're still living, and Nicole... well, she's still dying, just as you intended. But please, our entire family is trapped in Jubilee, and yours is too. Ambrette worked tirelessly to help build our town, our home."

Bellamy's gaze swept over us, before returning to Sage. "Please," he implored, "Will you help us?" In that moment, I witnessed a side of Bellamy I had never seen before, a raw, unguarded vulnerability that pierced my heart.

The witch seemed to revel in our uncertainty, her eyes gleaming with a mischievous light as she paced back and forth in front of her bubbling cauldron. Lilith rubbed against her feet, as if sensing her pleasure. The room was heavy with silence, each of us holding our breath as we awaited Sage's decision.

I couldn't help but feel a sense of desperation creeping in, if she refused to help us, would I ever see Lucca again? My anxiety must have been obvious because she halted her pacing. "Better you have your magic back than someone else," she declared with malice.

I exhaled a sigh of relief as the tension in the room dissipated. Bellamy's expression mirrored mine, while Velar's face lit up with gratitude. "Oh, thank you, Sage," he said, his voice filled with sincerity. Sage didn't acknowledge his thanks, too focused on rummaging through her shelves and cabinets in search of something.

Lilith jumped up onto the table, joining us as we watched Sage work her magic. With a flourish, she poured a dark liquid into a goblet, what looked like blood. She took a sip, then handed it to Velar, who accepted it without hesitation. "Thanks," he said, before gulping down the contents in one swift motion. That's when it hit me, it was indeed blood.

The dark blood glimmered like molasses in the candlelight as Sage poured the remaining liquid into the cauldron. She added a pinch of rosemary, a sprinkle of bay leaves, and a dash of Mug wort, the aroma of the herbs mingling with the metallic scent of blood. Eve whispered, "You forgot the salt!" with a playful grin. Sage's response was swift and wicked, "Salt is for good witches." Eve and I exchanged a stifled giggle, our eyes locking in a moment of shared amusement.

As we sat and waited, I felt the air thick with anticipation, heavy with the weight of our collective hopes and doubts. Sage busied herself prepping her cauldron with meticulous care. Minutes ticked by, each one feeling like an eternity, as we waited for the mysterious concoction to begin its magic. I wondered if it would work, *if she could really help us, or was she tricking us?*

The silence was intense, punctuated only by the soft clinking of ingredients and the gentle bubbling of the cauldron's contents, which seemed to be whispering secrets to each other. We waited and waited as Sage worked her magic. Her focus was both captivating and unnerving, her intense dark eyes made me afraid.

The four of us sat transfixed, watching as Sage stirred the bubbling concoction with a wooden spoon. Her humming began as a gentle murmur, gradually growing into a haunting melody that filled the room.

> "Magic lost and wandering free,
> Find your home, come to me.
> By my call, I summon thee,
> Come to me, so mote it be."

As the witch stirred the cauldron, she turned to face us. "This may take a while, since I'm calling the magic, and it could be anywhere in the world at this point." She walked towards Velar, her movements were graceful, and she pulled a soft blanket from a nearby chest. "The sun will be up soon, why don't you go lie down in the basement?" she suggested, her voice low and soothing.

Velar's white skin was paler than usual, almost translucent in the flickering candlelight. He didn't hesitate, his exhaustion evident in his swift nod. "Thanks," he murmured, before disappearing down the dark stairs, the basement door creaking shut behind him. Bellamy's raised eyebrows met mine, and I wondered if he was thinking the same thing, how did Velar know where the basement was?

Bellamy offered his help, but Sage was firm. "I just need you all to stay in my house. If you leave, I'll have to start over, and I'm not going to do that." She emphasized her point with a stern expression. Then, she turned to Eve and me, her tone softening slightly. "If you'd like, you can sleep on my couch through there."

She gestured towards a dark doorway, from which the cat had appeared earlier. Bellamy nodded in agreement, his eyes encouraging us to rest. "You two go get some rest on the couch, I'll stay up." The witch's expression turned annoyed, clearly disapproving of Bellamy's decision to stay awake. Bellamy leaned in to kiss me goodnight, and Eve pulled my arm, leading me into the dark room. The air was thick with the scent of old books and mystery, and I couldn't help but wonder what secrets the room held.

As we stepped into the darkness, I felt a sudden rush of fur against my legs, and I let out a startled gasp. "It's just Lilith,"

Eve said with a chuckle, amused by my reaction. But her laughter was short-lived, as candles around the room began to flicker to life on their own, casting eerie shadows on the walls.

Eve's smile faltered, and she froze, her eyes fixed on the dancing flames. The sudden, unexplained phenomenon seemed to fill the air with an unsettling energy, and I could feel all the hair stand up on my arms.

As the candlelight flickered, I scanned the room, taking in the eclectic array of knick-knacks that filled every nook and cranny. It was clear that Sage had lived here for a very long time. The shelves were overflowing with books, and the ones that couldn't fit were stacked haphazardly on the floor, creating a maze of paper and leather. Broomsticks of all shapes and sizes leaned against the walls, their bristles worn and wispy. And from the ceiling, dried flowers and herbs hung like a fragrant canopy.

As we settled into the couch, I leaned in close to Eve and whispered, "Do you really think Sage will help us?" Eve's smirk hinted at a secret, and she whispered back, "I think she'd help Velar." We exchanged a knowing smile, but I couldn't shake off the feeling of curiosity - and maybe even a hint of jealousy - about Sage and Velar's mysterious connection.

Eve seemed to sense my thoughts and whispered, "I believe this is where Velar was when he left the circus." The pieces clicked into place, and I nodded, understanding why Velar was so determined to come here. "Well, that all makes sense now," I said, feeling a sense of clarity. That's why he need an invitation when we arrived.

While we laid on the couch together our conversation flowed easily, touching on our past lives and shared experiences. And then, Eve finally spilled the beans about her new admirer -

Draven Graf. Her eyes sparkled with excitement, and I listened intently, happy to be her confidante. I chuckled at the mention of his name, Draven. He was the newest member of the Undying Council, which Bellamy and Eve were part of.

Eve was glowing as she described him, "He's from Switzerland, with blonde hair and silver eyes that seem to see right through you." She added with a sly grin, "And he's easy on the eyes." I teased, "Oh, Eve, you're smitten!" She blushed, but her smile remained, "We only met once, but there's something about him..." Her voice trailed off, and we both drifted off to sleep.

The next morning, I was abruptly woken up by Lilith jumping onto my stomach, her paws digging into my skin. I was so startled that I sprang up, my heart racing, and it took me a moment to regain my bearings and remember where I was. I rubbed the sleep from my eyes, and as my vision cleared, I could hear the murmur of Bellamy and Eve's conversation at the kitchen table in the next room. I stood up, stretching my arms overhead to shake off the slumber, and strolled out of the room to join them, Lilith trotting alongside me.

"Good morning," Bellamy said with a warm smile as I entered the kitchen. I returned the greeting. Sage handed me a steaming mug, and I took a sip, expecting the rich flavor of coffee.

Instantly my eyes widened in surprise as a bitter, earthy taste assaulted my tongue. As soon as Sage turned back to the cauldron, I discreetly spat the liquid back into the mug. "Not a tea person?" Sage asked, her voice tinged with amusement, somehow aware of my reaction. I apologized hastily, "I'm so sorry, I didn't know what it was." Sage just chuckled, her back still to me, as she continued stirring the bubbling spell.

Bellamy stood up, his eyes shining with anticipation, and asked Sage, "How's everything coming along?" He turned to me; his face filled with hope. "Sage told us earlier that she could start feeling the magic coming to her." I couldn't help but feel a surge of uncertainty at this news.

I stood up and leaned in, whispering into Bellamy's ear, "Shouldn't you be feeling it though, Daddy? You're the one who's supposed to be getting the magic, right?" My voice was barely audible, a look of puzzlement crossed his face.

Sage rolled her eyes and clarified, "I'm the one calling it, Bellamy. And when I receive it, I can transfer it to its rightful owner." I felt a flush rise to my cheeks as I realized Sage had overheard my question. After her explanation, we all exhaled a collective sigh of relief. Eve asked, "So, how much longer until the magic arrives?" Sage walked over to her bubbling cauldron, stirred its contents with a wooden spoon, and replied, "A Day or two, at most.

"A day or two!" I exclaimed; my voice laced with disbelief. Bellamy offered a reassuring smile, "Hey, it's all going to be okay baby girl. Just try to pretend like we're on vacation." I rolled my eyes, under normal circumstances that would have earned me spanking if we were home.

But this wasn't home, and the gravity of our situation hit me like a ton of bricks. I thought of my poor brother Lucca, stuck in a supernatural place, and my parents, who must be worried sick about both of us.

As the day wore on, Sage became increasingly devoted to her cauldron, rarely leaving its side for more than a few fleeting moments. Her stirring grew more rhythmic, her chants more insistent, as she coaxed the magic to come forth.

"Lost magic without a home, come to me, I call you here, come to me, so mote it be," she intoned, her voice weaving a hypnotic spell.

The air around us seemed to vibrate with anticipation, as if the very fabric of reality was responding to Sage's incantation. The cauldron's contents bubbled and churned, releasing wisps of steam that curled up towards the ceiling like ethereal tendrils, as if beckoning the magic to manifest.

With no TV to occupy us, Eve and I lounged on the couch, feeling a bit restless. To pass the time, we chatted about the circus, and Eve dished out all the juicy gossip about the performers and crew. She regaled me with stories of romantic trysts, rivalries, and secret talents, keeping me entertained. But inevitably, the conversation circled back to Draven. Eve's face lit up with a radiant glow, as she spoke about him. It was clear she was in love, and I couldn't help but wonder what this man was like.

I listened to Eve gush about Draven, and I realized that I had never seen her so thoroughly enamored before. Of all the years, she had many suitors, and men would often pursue her, but she had never been truly in love.

It was as if she had finally found her match. I felt a pang of sadness for my friend, knowing that she had been waiting for this kind of connection for so long. I wanted her to be happy, and if Draven was the one to bring her joy, then I was all for it. I smiled and listened intently as she continued to rave about him.

Just as the sun dipped below the horizon, Velar emerged from the basement, his voice booming through the room. "How's the spell

cooking, Sage?" he asked, his tone laced with hunger. Sage seemed to sense his craving, promptly handing him a goblet filled with a rich, crimson liquid. "It's fresh," she assured him, her eyes gleaming. Velar's face lit up with satisfaction as he took the goblet, his eyes fixed on the blood within.

I saw Velar down the entire goblet in one swift motion, his eyes closed in rapture as he savored the liquid. He savored the taste, his tongue darting out to lick his lips, which were now stained with a faint trace of crimson. His fangs gleamed momentarily, until his tongue washed away the remaining droplets.

Eve's curiosity got the better of her, and she asked, "Is it human blood or animal blood?" Sage's response was unsettling, her smile twisting into an eerie grin as she replied in a flat, monotone voice, "It's neither animal nor human." Eve's face paled slightly, her eyes widening in unease, but she wisely chose not to press the matter further.

Velar sauntered over to me, as Sage returned to stirring the cauldron. He leaned in close, his warm breath whispering in my ear, "Whatever was in that glass, I think it had magic in it."

His voice was low and conspiratorial. He straightened up and shrugged nonchalantly, as if sharing a secret. A cunning smile spread across his face, making me wonder what he knew that I didn't. With a fluid motion, he turned and strode back to Sage, leaving me with more questions than answers.

Perhaps Velar was craving more of the mysterious elixir, as he engaged in a hushed conversation with Sage, their words inaudible to me. My mind began to wander, pondering what secrets we had in my past life between us. *How did we end up together?*

While I found him handsome and cherished our friendship, the notion of a physical connection between us seemed unfathomable. Yet, a glimmer of possibility flickered in my mind... until Eve's sudden interruption shattered my reverie.

Eve's eyebrows shot up, and she flashed me a smirk, as if she had uncanny insight into my thoughts. Given our long history, it was entirely possible she could sense my inner musings. I felt a fleeting flush of embarrassment before swiftly redirecting my attention to Bellamy, who was slumped at the table, looking like he was on the verge of dozing off.

To break the momentary awkwardness, I announced, "Eve filled me in about Draven last night – Draven Graf, right, Eve?" I turned to Eve with a playful grin, trying to deflect any further scrutiny.

Eve's jaw dropped, her eyes wide with surprise, as if she'd been caught off guard. Velar and Bellamy swiveled their attention to us. Bellamy snorted, "Oh Eve, surely you can do better than Draven Graf?" Eve's face flushed, and she shot back, "Hey!" Velar chimed in with intrigue, "No way, isn't he a werewolf?"

I turned to Eve, my voice rising in excitement, "You totally left that part out!" Eve's gaze darted between us, her expression a mix of defensiveness and amusement. "You guys are unbelievable," she snapped. "So, what, he's immortal! I just didn't specify what kind of immortal!"

Velar cautioned, "Well, you have to watch out for werewolves." Eve retorted, "Oh yeah, just like they say to watch out for vampires?" She raised an eyebrow, her point clear. Velar's grin broadened, and he replied, his tone matter of fact, "Exactly."

The room erupted into laughter, and we all shared a moment of merriment. But our amusement was short-lived, as Sage, still focused on her cauldron, suddenly spoke up in a wicked, low tone, "What you really need to watch out for is witches." Her words left us feeling uneasy.

We all stared at Sage, and she seemed to sense our collective stare, slowly turning to face us with a hint of annoyance. "I'm not saying me," she clarified, her tone a touch defensive.

Velar quickly intervened, "Of course not, Sage. We're grateful for your help." Sage flashed him a half-hearted smile before she turned back to her cauldron. The tension dissipated, and the four of us exchanged a look of ease, our faces relaxing into more comfortable expressions. I felt a sense of relief wash over me.

As the night wore on, the silence in the canal house grew thicker, and boredom began to settle over us like a shroud. I couldn't shake the nagging thought that the magic might never return. *What then?*

The uncertainty gnawed at me, but I forced myself to push the doubts aside. I had to have faith in Sage's abilities; after all, she had been tirelessly stirring her cauldron for hours, her focus unwavering. Yet, despite her efforts, she hadn't left its side since yesterday, and the air was heavy with anticipation.

My mind began to wander, and doubts crept in like shadows. *How could I trust Sage, the very person who had cast the curse that ravaged our circus? The same curse that left me mortal while my friends remained frozen in immortality.*

The question burning within me refused to be silenced, and I blurted it out, "Sage, why did you curse the circus?"

The room fell still, as if time itself had paused. Bellamy, Velar, and Eve froze, their eyes wide with shock, Eve's mouth agape. I held my breath, realizing my question may have crossed a line, and Sage's expression might turn from helpful to hostile. The air was heavy with tension as I awaited her response, fearing I may have jeopardized our chance of getting Bellamy's magic back.

Sage's stirring ceased abruptly, and she turned to face me, her eyes flashing with irritation. "I did you all a favor," she snapped, her words full of venom.

I wisely remained silent, not wanting to provoke her further. But Eve, her voice trembling, pressed on, "But, why didn't you turn Nicole, Sage?"

Bellamy's sharp reprimand cut through the air, "Eve!" The single word was a warning, a subtle rebuke that made me feel like Eve's question had crossed a boundary. Yet, I couldn't help but share Eve's curiosity. The question still lingered in my mind, seeking an answer.

We recoiled in our seats as Sage approached us. "After I left the circus, my devoted sister chose to stay behind with that free-mason, Mesidor Blackwood." Sage's eyes rolled heavenward, her expression conveying a mix of disgust and annoyance at the mere mention of his name.

"I, on the other hand, traveled the world, honing my magical abilities, exploring all forms of magic, including the darker arts." Her gaze seemed to cloud over, as if the memories of her past still lingered, waiting to pounce.

Our eyes fixed on Sage as she resumed stirring the cauldron with a slow motion. Though her back was to us, her voice remained clear and steady. "As I grew older, the weight of mortality bore down upon me. The thought of leaving this world behind, of fading into nothingness, became unbearable. I became obsessed with cheating death, with defying the natural order."

Her stirring grew more rhythmic, as if the motion itself fueled her words. "I delved deeper into the dark arts, pouring all my knowledge and power into a single, forbidden spell. And finally, I succeeded in making myself immortal."

Sage's voice paused, her spoon hovering above the cauldron as if suspended in time. "But when I shared my secret with Ambrette, she refused to join me. She chose to remain mortal, to live a life bound by the constraints of time.

Sage's stirring slowed, and she fell silent, the only sound the gentle lapping of the potion against the cauldron's sides. Then, her voice cut through the stillness, stark and unflinching. "I was selfish, consumed by my own desires. And in a fit of rage and hurt, I cursed the circus, condemning all of you to eternal life."

She turned to Bellamy, her gaze piercing. "And I kept Nicole human, a constant reminder of mortality, to teach you all a lesson. Perhaps, one day, you would come to appreciate the preciousness of life, the beauty of its fleeting nature." With that, Sage's attention returned to the cauldron, her stirring resuming with a newfound intensity, as if she sought to lose herself in the swirling potion.

I turned to Bellamy, and my heart sank at the sight of his downcast face, his eyes fixed on the table as if unable to meet mine. Eve's voice trembled with emotion, her words spilling out in a rush. "But you knew she would die? You knew Nicole would eventually pass away?"

Sage's expression darkened, her eyes flashing with irritation. The hanging lights above started flickering as her voice rose in a sharp retort. "I'm no fool, I knew exactly what I was doing! And I know my sister, better than anyone. I knew she would find a way to keep you alive." The air seemed to vibrate with tension as Sage's words hung in the air, her gaze daring us to challenge her further.

Sage strode over to us, pointing a wooden spoon directly at me. "You're here now, aren't you?" she declared. I swallowed hard. The room fell silent, as if no one dared to breathe, let alone speak. Sage's glare swept across each of us, lingering on Velar for a moment before returning to her cauldron. She began stirring once more as if the tense confrontation had never occurred.

As the tension dissipated, Bellamy turned to Sage with a curious expression. "Sage, do you have any idea why Nicole's reincarnation took so long this time around?" he asked, his voice laced with intrigue.

Sage turned to him, their eyes locking in an intense gaze. "You're lucky she came back at all. I didn't think she would have," Sage said, her tone blunt. My eyes widened, and everyone looked at the witch, eager to understand more. "You think you can take a life and not pay a price?" Sage paused, collecting their thoughts. "I don't know if you're out of the woods yet, Bellamy, but if I were you, I'd be grateful for a second chance."

Bellamy's eyes found mine, and I saw the deep sorrow in them. He mouthed "I love you" to me, and I smiled knowingly, my heart filled with empathy.

As the hours dragged on, the darkness outside seemed to press in on us, and the silence grew thicker. Bellamy rummaged through Sage's pantry, munching on whatever he could find - spices and chocolates, an odd combination, but he seemed to savor each bite.

Eve and I sat at the table, our hands entwined in the soft fur of the black cat, our fingers gentle as we stroked its sleek coat. I was just about to stand up, to stretch my legs and shake off the numbness, when the room suddenly plummeted into an icy chill. Within seconds, our breath was visible in the air. The temperature drop was so rapid, so extreme, that it felt like a physical blow, leaving us all gasping in bewilderment.

As I turned to face the cauldron, a sight met my eyes that made my heart race. The potion was boiling over, a thick, fog-like steam billowing out of the top, obscuring the room in a misty haze. The fire beneath the cauldron died out in an instant, plunging us into an eerie silence.

Bellamy and Velar rushed to join Eve and me, their faces aglow with shock. We stood there, transfixed, as the cauldron continued to churn and bubble, its contents spilling over the edges like a miniature volcanic eruption. "It worked!" Sage exclaimed, her voice ringing out in triumph, her eyes shining with triumph.

We clustered around the cauldron, our faces bent over its rim, our eyes fixed on the churning potion within. The bubbles continued to overflow onto the floor, but Sage seemed unfazed, her attention solely focused on the cauldron's contents.

She ceased stirring, and we all held our collective breath, our gazes riveted on the swirling liquid as we waited with bated anticipation for the bubbles to subside. The room was silent, the only sound the gentle lapping of the potion against the cauldron's sides, until finally, the bubbles slowed and stopped, leaving the surface smooth and still.

As the steam dissipated, the cauldron's contents came into view, and we all gasped in unison. The liquid within was a mesmerizing swirl of colors, like a kaleidoscope come to life. "Wow!" was all I could manage to utter. Eve's curiosity got the better of her, and she asked with wonder, "What is that?" Sage's smile was boastful as she replied, "That's Bellamy's magic." Velar's chuckle was low and husky, "How colorful, Bell," he teased. Pride radiated from Bellamy's shining eyes.

He remained transfixed on the cauldron, his face inches from the swirling colors as he examined his magic with fascination. Sage's voice broke the silence, "I see seven colors of magic here, a truly rare occurrence." She turned to face us, noticing our bewildered expressions, and continued to explain. Her words were infused with ancient wisdom.

"Each color represents a distinct aspect of reality that can be manipulated. Red signifies energy, blue represents information, yellow is tied to the soul, orange governs matter, violet wields power over space and time, and white... white is the most crucial, for it embodies pure, organic magic." Sage's gaze shifted to Bellamy, her eyes locking onto his as she revealed the secrets of his extraordinary abilities.

Eve's voice was laced with confusion, "That's only six?" she pointed out, her brow furrowed in concern. Sage's expression turned grave, her voice dropping to a low, serious tone.

"Notice the thin, black thread swirling among the colors?" We all nodded in unison, still fixed on the cauldron's contents. "That is dark magic." *Rubbish.* Eve's protest was immediate, "But Bell doesn't practice dark magic!" Sage's gaze never wavered from Bellamy's face as she replied, her words laced with a hint of warning, "Just because you don't use it doesn't mean you don't have the ability."

We were all stunned to discover that Bellamy, of all people, harbored dark magic within him. I couldn't help but wonder if Sage's magic was predominantly dark, given her mysterious nature. As I watched, she pointed a bony finger at Bellamy and asked in a wicked voice, "Are you ready?" Bellamy's response was confident, "Yes."

Sage instructed him to disrobe, and he did so without hesitation, handing his clothes to me with a cocky grin. I couldn't help but stare, my mind wandering to the playroom and the illicit thoughts I had harbored there. Bellamy's physique was strong and chiseled, every inch of him exuding masculine charm. Even Eve seemed captivated, though she tried to hide it, rolling her eyes in feigned nonchalance when I nudged her with my elbow.

Bellamy approached the cauldron with a sense of purpose, his eyes locked on Sage, who stood waiting with an air of anticipation. She guided his hand into the pot, immersing it in the swirling colors of magic. We watched anxiously as Sage closed her eyes, her hands hovering above the cauldron like a conductor poised to orchestrate a symphony.

The room fell silent, the only sound the soft lapping of the potion against the cauldron's sides. We waited with collective anticipation, as we wondered what transformation was about to unfold.

Without warning, a fierce gust of wind burst into the room, sending us all grasping for the wooden table to anchor ourselves. The tempestuous blast howled and whipped around us, threatening to lift us off the ground. Sage's papers and lightweight items were swept up in the maelstrom, swirling around the room like confetti in a tornado.

The squall was so intense that I had to squint to keep my eyes open, my hair streaming behind me like a banner. As I clung to the table, I watched in awe as the liquid from the cauldron coalesced into a shimmering vortex above us, then encircled Bellamy's body.

The moment the magic touched him, it transmogrified into a vibrant colorful smoke that was absorbed into his being. As suddenly as it had begun, the wind died down, leaving an eerie stillness in its wake.

Bellamy's voice rang out, exuberant and unrestrained, "I'm back, I'm back!" He was so overcome with joy and relief that he swept Sage into a tight embrace, oblivious to his nudity. Sage's eyes widened in surprise, and with a swift flick of her wrist, she unleashed a jolt of magic that sent Bellamy stumbling backward.

The sudden shock only seemed to amplify his euphoria, and he burst into laughter, his eyes sparkling with mirth. He reached for his clothes, which I was still holding, and I playfully tugged them out of his grasp, teasing him. I couldn't resist the opportunity to keep him naked a little longer, savoring the sight of his lean, muscular form.

Our collective relief and gratitude were palpable as Bellamy's magic was restored, and we all breathed a sigh of joy. Bellamy hastily donned his clothes, his face still aglow with happiness, and thanked Sage profusely, his words tumbling out in a torrent of appreciation. Velar echoed his sentiments, their gratitude echoing through the room.

As the first hints of dawn crept into the sky, Bellamy turned to Sage with a request, "Could we stay one more night, since the sun is about to rise?" Sage, nodding in understanding, gestured with a graceful wave of her hand, "Follow me,"

We followed behind Sage as she descended a winding flight of stairs into the basement, the air growing thick with anticipation. "Velar, assist me," she commanded, and the two of them vanished into a shadowy recess, leaving us in a dimly lit room.

Moments later, they reemerged, carrying between them a magnificent silver cheval glass. My jaw dropped in awe as I beheld the stunning mirror, its surface glinting like moonlight. "This will be the quickest way back to Jubilee," Sage announced. I couldn't contain my excitement. I couldn't wait to get back home.

With the urgency of sunrise looming, we formed a line, each of us eager to pass through the silver cheval glass and return to Jubilee. "Remember, say 'Darlington Circus' as you step through," Bellamy reminded us, his voice filled with a sense of urgency. We all knew that Jubilee, a place of magic and wonder, was hidden from the universe, and direct passage was impossible.

As we prepared to leave, Bellamy turned to Sage with genuine gratitude, "Thank you again, Sage. Your help has been invaluable." Sage dismissed his thanks with a casual wave of her hand, "It was nothing, really." Bellamy flashed her a warm smile before stepping through the shimmering glass portal. I watched as Velar and Eve followed, their forms blurring as they disappeared into the mirror's silvery depths.

As the last one remaining, I stood before the cheval glass, its silver surface beckoning me to step through. I took a deep breath, ready to reunite with my loved ones in Jubilee. "Darlington Circus," I whispered, preparing to leave. But just as I was about to step forward, Sage's hand closed around my arm, her grip firm and unexpected. I turned to her, startled, and met her piercing dark gray eyes. "I believe I have something for you," she said, her voice low and mysterious.

Sage's grip on my arm guided me back upstairs, our footsteps echoing. We returned to her mystical cauldron. I followed her gaze as she peered into the cast-iron pot, its contents now a clear liquid with an ethereal white smoke swirling through it, like a whisper of secrets. I wondered what mysterious gift she had in store for me.

As I leaned over the cauldron, my eyes met Sage's, and I sensed her impatience. I stood there, perplexed, before asking, "Well, what is it?" Sage's posture straightened, and she declared, "Well, clearly, Bellamy wasn't the only one who lost something!" My memories! The realization hit me like a whisper from the shadows.

Sage beamed with pride, her eyes sparkling with a hint of mischief. "I must have called both at the same time - brilliant, utter brilliance!" She applauded once, the sound echoing through the room, and then glanced down at Lilith, who was sitting by her feet, the cat's eyes gleaming with an otherworldly intelligence. Lilith let out a low, menacing cackle, as if in agreement with Sage's triumphant declaration.

I stood transfixed, peering into the cauldron's depths. My mind was racing with doubt and fear. The liquid memories seemed to swirl, taunting me with secrets and unknown truths. At that moment, I hesitated, unsure if I genuinely wanted to reclaim my past.

What if my memories altered everything with Bellamy? What if there was a valid reason for my forgotten life?

Sage moved closer, her hand reaching into the cauldron, scooping up the liquid as she had done for Bellamy. But before she could apply it to my skin, I took a step back, my voice firm, "No."

CHAPTER
NINE

"Get out of here!" Velar's screaming voice gave me goosebumps as two teenagers fled in terror, sprinting out of the entrance gate. I was inside the circus, my eyes widening in disbelief at the scene before me. The tents and vendor stands were now in shambles, the result of a brutal invasion by intruders from my own hometown.

The destruction was heartbreaking, tents torn and shredded like ravaged fabric, vendor stands overturned and looted, and graffiti scrawled across every surface. I felt a lump form in my throat as I took in the devastation.

The sight was sad, a stark reminder of the cruelty and disregard that lurked in the world.

Eve sprinted towards me; her face twisted in a fury that looked like it could ignite a fire. "What took you so long to get back here?" she demanded. I hesitated, unsure of how much to reveal. "I was just thanking Sage for her help," I said, trying to sound convincing.

Eve's anger boiled over, and she kicked a graffitied sign that lay on the ground, sending it flying. "This is going to take Bellamy forever to fix! Fucking mortals!" She spat in anger. Realizing her words, she quickly added, "Not you, of course." I nodded, knowing she was just upset. "I know." I said, trying to sound understanding. But the truth was, I couldn't argue with her assessment. The destruction was senseless, and it was hard to fathom why anyone would do such a thing.

Bellamy spotted my return and sprinted towards Eve and me. "You two, head to Jubilee and alert everyone that we're back." He instructed with authority. "Velar and I will stay behind to ensure the premises are clear, so we can jump as soon as possible and avoid drawing more unwanted attention."

Bellamy led us to the once-majestic weeping willow tree, now a mere shadow of its former self. With a gentle touch, he placed his hand on the trunk, and his magic stirred. The tree's branches seemed to whisper in response as the entrance to Jubilee shimmered into existence.

Velar stood watch, his eyes scanning the surroundings with a fierce intensity, making sure no one else was in the circus. The passageway appeared revealing the stairs down to Jubilee. The two men began a thorough sweep of the devastated circus, leaving Eve and me to make our way home to spread the word.

A voice pierced the darkness, shouting, "They're back!" Eve and I stood still, peering into the darkness. The townspeople emerged slowly, their lit candles casting flickering shadows on the ground. I felt a pang of sorrow, knowing their ordeal had been far from easy. The darkness seemed to have deepened since our departure and the oil lanterns that once illuminated the town now extinguished. Then, a small figure pushed through the crowd, and I saw Lucca's eager face.

He flung himself into my arms, squeezing me tightly. "I never thought you were coming back!" he exclaimed, his voice trembling. Though the darkness obscured his features, I sensed tears in his eyes, and my own eyes welled up in response.

As the crowd gathered around us, Eve took a deep breath and shared the news about the circus's destruction. Her words were swiftly followed by a beacon of hope, "Bellamy and Velar will arrive soon to re-enchant Jubilee!" The announcement sparked a wave of celebration, and the townspeople erupted into cheers and applause. Faces lit up with joy, and people jumped up and down with excitement.

As I held Lucca close, a sudden pang of worry struck me, my parents must be frantic with concern. I turned to Eve, my mind racing. "Keep everyone here, Eve. As soon as Bellamy arrives, we'll jump. but I need to get my brother back home." I spoke hastily, my urgency clear. Eve nodded understandingly. "Be quick, though!" she called out as I turned to leave, Lucca's hand grasped tightly in mine. Together, we sprinted up the stairs, bound for the circus.

As we reached the circus, I shouted out, 'Bellamy!' But my call was met with silence. The devastated landscape stretched out before us, devoid of any sign of Bellamy or Velar. Lucca's eyes widened in disbelief as he took in the ruins of the circus. Just yesterday, he had seen the splendor of Darlington's Circus, full of life and magic. Now, the stark contrast was jarring.

I grasped Lucca's arm, urgency propelling him forward. We had to find Bellamy without delay. Lucca resisted, his feet dragging as he protested, 'I don't want to leave!' But I knew every minute counted. My parents must be frantic, and I feared they might have already alerted the authorities. The thought of police arriving and complicating our situation further spurred me on.

Lucca and I raced around the circus, desperate to find Bellamy, but instead, we stumbled upon Velar. 'What brings you two up here?' he asked, his eyes narrowing with concern. I explained our situation, "I need to find Bellamy, we have to get Lucca home!" Velar's expression turned grave, and he nodded swiftly. He understood the gravity of the situation and without a word, Velar joined our search, his urgency matching our own.

Velar began explaining Bellamy's whereabouts, but his words were interrupted by a sudden flash of memory from my past life. I recalled a moment of joy, laughing with Velar, feeling his arms around me, and our lips meeting in a tender kiss. The recollection was so vivid that I felt like I was reliving it. "Nicole!" Velar's sharp tone broke the spell, and I blinked, shaking off the nostalgia. "Where is he?" I repeated, refocusing on the present. Velar's eyes narrowed, "Nic, I told you, Bell is securing the front gate, boarding it up so we can jump out of here."

As we approached the front gate, I heard a familiar voice calling out in the distance "Nicole! Lucca!" My heart stopped as I recognized my mother's voice on the other side of the fence. Lucca sprinted towards her, and I followed close behind, my feet pounding the ground. Just then, Bellamy appeared from one of the torn tents near the entrance gate, his eyes locking onto us with a sense of urgency. He must have heard my mother's voice too, and knew we had to act fast.

Bellamy expertly opened the gate, and with a swift motion, he ushered my parents through the throng of onlookers, safely guiding them into the circus. I gazed out at the sea of faces beyond the gate, a mob of curious spectators eager to get inside the circus. The sun was rising, casting a golden glow over the scene. Bellamy swiftly sealed the gate behind them, his magic subtle yet effective, unnoticed by the crowd.

As the gate creaked shut, my mother enveloped Lucca and I in a tight embrace. 'Where were you? What happened?' she asked, her voice trembling with worry. My father's eyes scanned the devastated circus, his expression a mix of shock and relief. I braced myself for their anger, but instead, they held us close, their fear and gratitude overwhelming. They were too shaken to scold, too relieved to have us back unharmed.

Bellamy quickly concocted a story, explaining to my parents that a tornado had struck the day before, forcing us to take shelter in a nearby storm cellar. He continued, 'While we were away, trespassers sneaked in and vandalized the abandoned circus.' My parents exchanged confused and shocked glances, clearly perplexed by the news. They hadn't heard anything about a tornado.

My mother's hands flew to her mouth as she took in the devastation surrounding her. The sheer extent of the damage was convincing enough; they didn't question Bellamy's fabricated story for a moment. The ravaged circus stood as stark evidence, silencing any doubts they might have had.

My parents, still shaken but relieved, grateful that we were all safe. As they prepared to leave, I shared a bittersweet goodbye hug with Lucca, who didn't want to leave. Though he had asked to stay multiple times, it wasn't until he was about to depart that I felt a strong desire for him to stay.

As Bellamy approached the gate, my eyes began to well up with tears. In a spontaneous plea, I asked, "Can Lucca join the circus?" I knew I should have asked Bellamy first, but I couldn't help myself. I continued to persuade my parents, "He's eager to learn and we could really use his help. Just look around - we could use all the hands we can get." I gestured to the devastated circus, hoping my parents would see the sense in letting Lucca stay.

I glanced over at Bellamy, hoping he'd support my plea, but he remained stubbornly silent. Lucca, however, continued to beg, his persistence starting to make me regret bringing it up in the first place. Yet, to my surprise, my parents began to waver, their expressions softening. Despite my initial doubts, Lucca's enthusiasm was winning them over, and I could see the hint of a smile on my mother's face.

Just as Lucca's persistence was starting to wear thin, Velar intervened, his deep voice a welcome addition to the conversation. 'I could use a young man like him to help me with the horses,' he said without letting his fangs show. Lucca's face lit up, and he redoubled his efforts, pleading with renewed enthusiasm. My parents exchanged a whispered conversation, their faces thoughtful.

They seemed to appreciate the idea that my video game- obsessed little brother would rather engage in physical labor at the circus. My dad, in particular, looked relieved. After a moment, they relented, and Lucca let out a triumphant whoop, his joy so infectious that even Bellamy winced, covering his ears. We shared warm goodbye hugs with our parents and Lucca beamed with happiness. I couldn't help but feel a sense of excitement and relief myself.

After Bellamy escorted my parents through the crowded gate, Lucca took off towards Jubilee, and I followed suit, but Bellamy's firm grip on my arm halted me. 'Babygirl, you didn't even ask me,' he said, his tone laced with disappointment. I knew I was in for a scolding.

With a childlike whine, I pleaded, 'He's my brother, Daddy!' I gazed up at him with a pitiful pout, my eyes locking onto his captivating blues until he relented. A warm smile spread across his face. "As you wish," he conceded, his voice softening. I knew he couldn't stay mad at me; he adored me too much. I planted a grateful kiss on his cheek, 'Thank you, Daddy.' With a playful swat on my behind, he sent me off to catch up with Lucca, and I skipped ahead, feeling carefree and loved.

Before we could return to Jubilee, Bellamy needed to impart some of his magic to Lucca, just as he had done with me. This would allow Lucca to enter our enchanted town without disrupting the magic. With a gentle gesture, Bellamy placed his hand on Lucca's shoulder. Lucca's eyes widened with delight as he exclaimed, 'That tingles!' His infectious laughter filled the air, and I couldn't help but smile at my brother's wonder.

Upon our return to Jubilee, Mesidor and Ambrette welcomed us at the entrance, inquiring about Sage's whereabouts. We expressed our gratitude once more for their generosity in lending us the cheval glass and shared the news that Sage had played a crucial role in restoring the magic. Bellamy added with a sly grin, "Apparently, she has a soft spot for Velar."

Velar retorted with a chuckle, "Jealous, Bell?" The two immortals exchanged playful banter before turning serious. Bellamy was ready to begin the process of re-enchanting Jubilee, infusing the town with magic once more.

Without delay, Bellamy raised his arms to the dark sky, his eyes closed in concentration. I couldn't help but be captivated by the intensity of his magic, his strength and handsome features illuminated by the faint light. Colors began to emanate from him, reminiscent of the vibrant hues we had seen in Sage's cauldron.

The colors swirled around him, mesmerizing the onlookers as the sky transformed, filling with brilliant sunlight. The homes of Jubilee flickered to life, electric lights dancing across the town. In mere seconds, the magic had been restored.

Lucca's eyes remained wide open, frozen in wonder. 'I thought they were lying to me!' he exclaimed, his voice full of disbelief. The crowd around us erupted into gentle laughter at his bewilderment. At that moment, I knew I had made the right choice in bringing him here.

There was something about this place that felt meant for him, though I couldn't quite put my finger on it. I smiled at Lucca and asked, 'Are you ready to meet Casmira?"

As we strolled back home, Lucca revealed that the Bally girls had taken it upon themselves to enlighten him about Jubilee's enchantments. Miss Poppet had regaled him with tales of my numerous lifetimes, and Lucca was utterly captivated. I worried that the complexities of our world might overwhelm him, but he proved eager to learn, bombarding us with a flurry of questions. His curiosity was insatiable, and I couldn't help but smile at his enthusiasm.

As we approached the front gate, it swung open, welcoming us inside. "Oh, Casmira, I'm overjoyed to see you're back to yourself!" I exclaimed, stepping into the warm interior. Lucca's eyes widened in wonder as I gave him a tour of the magical house.

Just then, Bellamy entered, noticing Lucca's amazement, "When we move on to the next town, I'll build a room especially for you," he said. Lucca's face lit up with excitement as he quickly asked, "Does this mean I can stay?" Bellamy paused, then smiled, "For as long as you like." His gaze met mine, and I knew it was time to jump.

Bellamy stepped out onto the porch, and Lucca's curiosity followed as he watched through the front doorway. Bellamy's magic swirled around him once more, and this time, the entire town of Jubilee began to vibrate.

The sensation lasted mere seconds before Bellamy's arms dropped to his sides, he turned to Luccas and flashed a smug smile. "We have arrived," he announced. "Wicked." He spoke. He was in awe, struggling to understand the sheer scale of Bellamy's power. And just like that, Darlington Circus had vanished from Quarryville, Pennsylvania, leaving behind no trace of its existence.

CHAPTER

TEN

After several days of tireless effort and late nights, Darlington Circus was finally restored to its former glory. Bellamy's magic had played a significant role in the reconstruction, but the entire community had pitched in to ensure he didn't exhaust himself.

As a special touch, Bellamy had even built Lucca his own room on the second floor of Casmira, tailored to his love for Star Wars. The room was designed to resemble the interior of the Millennium Falcon, complete with intricate details and a winding tunnel slide that led to the outside, exiting behind the house. Lucca was over the moon with joy, he embraced Bellamy with the biggest hug, his face beaming with delight.

Bellamy revealed that the special room was a gesture of appreciation for Lucca's dedication to helping the circus get back on its feet. And indeed, Lucca had been pitching in tirelessly since being welcomed to stay. I suspected, however, that his motivation was also driven by his innocent crush on the charming

Bally twins. It was heartwarming to see him form friendships so effortlessly, and his eagerness to impress them was quite endearing.

I kept my parents informed about our adventures every few days, and Lucca eagerly snatched the phone to excitedly share stories about the circus and his new bedroom. During one of our calls, Bellamy had arranged for a homeschool teacher from Jubilee to join the conversation, introducing her to my mother. This way, they could discuss Lucca's educational needs and ensure his continued learning.

Lucca begins each day with a morning meeting with Ada, his homeschool teacher, before heading to his duties at the circus. This was my mother's one condition for allowing Lucca to join us on the road: education comes first. After speaking with Ada, my mother was relieved to know that Lucca was in good hands.

Ada, a master gardener in Jubilee, and her husband Briar, a circus performer, have become like family to Lucca. Ada has taken a shine to him, and he thrives under her guidance. When Bellamy presented her with a check from his showman coat, Ada graciously accepted her new role as Lucca's teacher.

Since our return from Amsterdam, fragments of my past life had begun to resurface, haunting me with memories I'd rather keep buried. Shame and guilt lingered, stemming from my past affair with Velar. Moreover, the fear of recalling the traumatic event where Bellamy's magic struck me, kept me from confronting these memories. I continued to suppress the recollections, hoping to keep them locked deep within my mind.

I kept the memories concealed, even from myself, and especially from Bellamy. In moments of introspection, I regret not standing firm and refusing Sage's offer. Her persistent nature wouldn't accept no, and now I'm left grappling with the consequences.

The memory of her sinister smile lingers, as if she knew the turmoil she was unleashing by restoring my memories. Maybe she was evil after all. I push the thought aside, wondering if I'm being unfair in questioning her intentions. Regardless, I have more pressing concerns. Tonight was Samsara, and I must prepare myself.

The ritual typically takes place a few days after my return to the circus, but due to our recent loss of magic, it was postponed. However, as soon as the circus was restored, Bellamy emphasized the urgency of performing the ritual without delay. "It's not safe to wait any longer, we must do it immediately!" he stressed before leaving from Casmira this morning. His concern was justified, and I knew he was right.

Samsara was a sacred ritual we performed every time I returned, ensuring my reincarnation upon each subsequent death. This ancient cycle of mortality and rebirth had been my fate for so many lifetimes. Ambrette, with her vast knowledge, discovered the ritual's secrets after Sage's curse befell the circus. Bellamy had sought the witches' assistance to grant me immortality, but they refused to wield dark magic, and Bellamy respected their boundaries. Instead, Ambrette led the tradition, ensuring my continued existence. I am forever grateful for her gift.

This evening, the townspeople of Jubilee will gather to witness Bellamy and I take part in a magical union through tantric sex, also known as sex magic. This ancient practice aims to connect us on a profound spiritual level through slow, sensual, and intentional lovemaking, without seeking climax. While not all residents of Jubilee partake in this ritual, many join in the celebrations, which have been described as a giant sex orgy.

I wanted to keep Lucca shielded from the ritual, so I asked Miss Poppet to kindly watch over him and host him for the night above her charming bakeshop. The ritual would take place in the serene Emberlynn Forest. Miss Poppet gladly agreed, as she delighted in Lucca's company. Indeed, the entire town of Jubilee had taken a liking to him, and I think it was a welcome change for everyone to have a fresh face in town.

Later that morning I headed up to the circus. As I practiced aerial ropes with Eve in the backyard, Velar appeared, and I couldn't help but greet him with a smile. My memories of him, though still suppressed, stirred something within me. I appreciated his dedication to training Lucca and admired his rugged physique, evident even in the torn sleeves of his shirt. Revealing his muscular arms as he approached.

I couldn't help but gawk, his form commanding attention. "Hey, mind if I put Lucca on a horse?" he asked. I hesitated, "Um, I think that'll be okay..." My uncertainty was met with a reassuring nod, and I knew Velar would keep Lucca safe. "Thank you," I said as Velar walked over to where Lucca waited.

Eve caught me staring as Velar walked away. A knowing grin spread across her face. "Girl, get it together!" she teased, her laughter echoing through the air. I feigned innocence, playing dumb, but she wasn't having it. "Let's face it, every time you interact with Velar lately, you've been...awkward, to say the least," she said with a chuckle. I tried to brush it off, but my cheeks betrayed me, blushing like a beet.

"Velar has been helping Lucca, and I just appreciate that," I said, trying to sound casual despite the memories of our past lingering in my mind. I still hadn't shared with anyone, not even Eve, that Sage had restored my memories. It was a secret I kept hidden, even from my closest friend.

Eve's question caught me off guard, "Do you think Velar will be at the ritual tonight?" I hesitated, unsure. He had always been present in the past, but this time felt different. "I don't think he will," I replied, trying to sound convincing. Eve raised an eyebrow, a sly grin spreading across her face. 'Oh, I think he will,' she said, her tone hinting at a knowing secret.

After my encounter with Velar, I felt emotionally exhausted and bid Eve farewell, declaring I was done for the day. I decided to head home and prepare for the upcoming ritual. 'See you later!' Eve called out as I made my way back to the tree, taking a leisurely stroll through the circus. I waved to the crew and performers, observing the wonder on the guests' faces, and soaking up the playful, whimsical atmosphere that Darlington Circus was known for.

Upon returning to Jubilee, I noticed the town square was relatively quiet, with most residents busy working at the circus. I followed the familiar path home to Casmira, looking forward to some solitude and preparation for the evening's events.

As I entered Casmira, the soothing aroma of brewing tea filled the air, and I poured myself a steaming cup. The silence of my home was a balm to my soul, and I felt a sense of peace wash over me. I wandered through the rooms, my gaze lingering on the treasures and trinkets collected over countless lifetimes. Each object held a story, a memory, a piece of my history.

I traced the intricate patterns on an ancient vase, ran my fingers over the worn leather of a beloved book, and paused before a faded photograph, its subjects long gone but still dear to my heart. In this quiet, peaceful space, I was surrounded by the accumulated memories of a lifetime – many lifetimes – and I felt the weight of my experiences, the depth of my existence.

The manor was a treasure trove of antiques and trinkets, each one telling a story of its own. My favorite painter's work covered the walls throughout the house. Among them, 'The Singing Butler' held a special place in my heart, it was my most treasured painting.

As I gazed deeper into the painting, I couldn't help but see Bellamy and myself twirling across the canvas, our movements graceful and carefree. And if I looked closely enough, I could even imagine Velar and Eve joining in the image holding the black umbrellas. The playroom, on the other hand, was a more intimate space, filled with the painter's more sensual and erotic works.

As I soaked in the warm bath, I was startled by the sound of my front door opening and closing. I assumed it was Lucca returning home, and I didn't think much of it. But as I appeared from the bathroom, wrapped in my black silky robe, I was taken by surprise to find Velar standing before me. His sudden presence was unexpected, and I felt a flutter in my chest as our eyes met. The soft glow of the candles cast a warm light on his chiseled features, and for a moment, we just stood there.

I tightened the robe around me, feeling a flutter of surprise. "I thought you were Lucca," I admitted, my voice slightly nervous. Velar's grin was warm and teasing. "No kidding," he chuckled, his eyes sparkling with amusement. I asked again, trying to hide my curiosity, "Why are you here?"

But instead of answering, Velar took his time, his emerald eyes roaming over me with a slow, deliberate intensity. I felt a flush rise to my cheeks as he finally spoke, his deep. "How are you adjusting to being back here?" I hesitated, unsure of how to respond. My eyebrows furrowed in confusion, and Velar noticed my uncertainty. "Lucca's a natural with horses." he added, his tone casual, but his eyes still probing mine.

I was relieved when Velar shifted the conversation, and my gratitude poured out. "Lucca is thriving here, thank you so much for training him!" Velar's face lit up with a warm smile. "Not a problem at all. That kid cracks me up; he's got a special spark." As Velar continued sharing stories about Lucca's progress, my mind began to wander, and a memory suddenly resurfaced. It was as if the conversation had unlocked a door in my mind, and the past came flooding back..."

Velar was teaching me how to drive a car for the first time, and what a car it was ... *a sleek beige nineteen-thirty Bugatti Royale with a black roof, fit for a king.* The memory was fond, but I quickly pushed it away, not ready to confront the emotions it stirred.

I nodded, pretending to have been fully engaged in our conversation. "Yes, I think Lucca would love that. Thank you, Velar." My mind was still lingering on the memory I had pushed away. Velar stared at me as if he was examining my body, and he continued to stand in the doorway, seemingly unaware of the turmoil in my thoughts that I possessed.

I forced a bright tone, trying to shake off the thoughts. "Velar, I really must get ready for Samsara tonight!" I adjusted my robe, using the motion to break the spell. "Actually, that's why I came here. Do you want me there?"

I hesitated, unsure of how to respond, but eventually found the courage to say, "No, you don't have to be there," To my surprise, he didn't appear offended; instead, a grin spread across his face showing his fangs that made me quiver inside. "Would it be uncomfortable for you?" he asked, his voice low and probing. He leaned into the doorway, his eyes fixed intently on mine,

awaiting my response. The air between us grew thick with tension, and I felt my heart race as I searched for an answer. Finally, I managed to stammer out a reply...

"I suppose it would be uncomfortable for you, since I don't have any memories of us." *Liar*. His response was surprisingly detached, "I understand." He delivered the words with a mat-ter-of- fact tone, before turning to walk down the hall. I stood frozen, watching the imposing figure disappear from view, feeling a pang in my heart. The ache was a mix of regret, longing, and unresolved emotions, leaving me with a sense of emptiness as I stood there.

I knew how he felt about me, I felt it ever since I got my memories back. His love and affection were obvious, but I was too consumed by shame and uncertainty to confront my own emotions. The tension between us was suffocating, and my face still burned from our earlier exchange.

My mind raced with questions, *was he toying with me? Did he know that Sage had restored my memories?* Just as I was about to retreat to my bedroom, the front door opened and closed once more. I held my breath, my heart skipping in anticipation, as I turned to face him once again.

Lucca burst into the room, his face beaming with excite-ment. I exhaled a sigh of relief, grateful for the distraction. He eagerly shared his adventures horseback riding, his eyes spar-kling with joy as he declared his dreams of becoming a perform-er. I couldn't help but smile at his infectious enthusiasm, my heart warming with happiness for him.

After he finished recounting his exploits, I informed him that he would be spending the night at Miss Poppet's place.

"Alright!" he exclaimed; his voice filled with glee. "She lets me eat whatever I want!" he added, already racing down the stairs to his room, his excitement echoing through the hallway.

Later that evening, Eve arrived to assist me in preparing for Samsara. As part of the tradition, I was required to remain in Casmira until the ceremony began, separated from Bellamy until the ritual. I assumed he would be preparing for the occasion at Velar's place. As she helped me get ready, I mentioned that I hadn't seen Bellamy since he had departed early that morning to open the circus.

As we entered my room, I spotted an elegant white box sitting on my bed, courtesy of Bellamy, I'm sure. I couldn't wait to discover what he had selected for me to wear tonight.

Eve's enthusiasm was infectious, and she urged me to "Open it, open it!" with excitement. I carefully untied the bold red bow securing the box, and as I lifted the lid. As I peered into the box, I was surprised to see he chose the color white when he usually picked me something in black.

Eve detected my discontent right away. "Hmm, well, try it on." She suggested. I acquiesced and took out the delicate white spaghetti strap lingerie. The satin fabric shimmered in the light, and the see-through design was paired with matching white stockings.

Eve then presented me with a dazzling white mask adorned with sparkling accents, which complemented the outfit perfectly. While the overall effect was undeniably beautiful, I couldn't shake the feeling that something was off. This wasn't the type of attire Bellamy typically chose for me, and the disconnect left me feeling odd.

Casmira had thoughtfully poured us each a glass of champagne that appeared on the nightstand. After a sip I slipped into the satin lingerie, striking a pose for Eve's approval. She declared it. "Absolutely adorable!" We both giggled, sipping our bubbly, and lost in conversation. Eve regaled me with stories of her adventures during our time apart, and I was captivated by her tales.

It was a rare and lovely moment, just the two of us reconnecting after so long. But our tranquility was short-lived, as the distant rumble of drums echoed through the air. A knot of tension formed in my stomach, and I met Eve's gaze, sensing a shared unease. She nodded solemnly, her eyes locking onto mine, and said, "It's time."

As I stepped outside, a mix of excitement and nervousness swirled within me. I always felt a sense of trepidation, eager to get this over with. I stood on the porch, and I paused to appreciate the magical night sky. The moon cast its silvery glow, and the stars twinkled like diamonds against the dark canvas of the Jubilee sky.

In the distance, a colossal fire blazed, its fiery tendrils illuminating the darkness as I gazed through the woods from the front porch of Casmira. I adjusted my matching white masquerade mask, ensuring it was securely in place, when Eve's voice broke the silence from behind me. "Are you ready?" she asked, her words laced with anticipation. I turned to face her; my response filled with anxiety "As ready as I ever am."

With a graceful nod, Eve acknowledged my unease, then gently took my hand, and wrapped it around her arm, guiding me towards the rhythmic beat. The drums grew louder and more insistent as we approached the Emberlynn Forest, their pulsing rhythm drawing us deeper into the woods.

We walked at a measured pace, the trees parting like a curtain to reveal a clearing. I heard cheers and chanting my name.

The mob's passion grew more frenzied as I appeared from the shadows.

The crowd was a sea of masked faces, a tradition dating back centuries, allowing individuals to conceal their identities and indulge in promiscuous and dissolute activities. Some residents had already shed their inhibitions, wearing risqué lingerie or nothing at all, signaling their willingness to participate in the ritual.

Others, clad in more modest attire, had come to bear witness, and offer their support, though they would likely depart before the night's festivities reached the end. As we approached the roaring fire, the masked crowd erupted into cheers and whistles.

Eve escorted me to a raised platform, where Bellamy and Ambrette awaited our arrival. Ambrette greeted me with a graceful nod, her long white gown shimmering in the flickering light. I returned the gesture, captivated by the intricate multi-feathered mask on her face.

Bellamy stood proudly naked, his muscular physique illuminated by the dancing flames. His piercing blue eyes sparkled with mischief behind the ornate horned Venetian carnival mask, adding an air of enigmatic mystery to his already commanding presence.

As I ascended the stairs to join my spouse on the stage, he extended his hand, and I took it, feeling a surge of anticipation. The drums fell silent, and the ceremony commenced. Ambrette's voice rose in a haunting Latin chant, her words weaving a spell of enchantment.

Meanwhile, men began to feed the fire with more wood, the flames erupting into a blazing inferno that cast a golden glow on the stage. The heat was palpable, and I could feel it radiating onto my skin, my forehead growing warm as the fire crackled.

As we stood on the stage, exposed to the gaze of the crowd, Bellamy slowly removed my robe, his movements deliberate and controlled. Ambrette's subtle nod had signaled his cue to begin. His eyes narrowed and were fixed on what lay beneath my robe.

Quickly I followed his gaze down at myself to see what he was concerned about. My nipples were visible through the sheer fabric. *Was he staring at them?*

Now it was my turn. Bellamy stood facing the crowd and I was on my knees in front of him. When I found a comfortable position, I reached for my husband's hardness and stroked him in my hand before parting my lips. I guided him gently and licked him. I felt his body shiver from my teases. Then I put him inside my wet mouth, sucking slowly and deep.

Ambrette chanted and Bellamy grew. My mouth watered as I took him down my throat. His hands on the back of my head, greedily forcing me to swallow all of him. My eyes opened and I pulled myself away gagging. Something pulled my gaze into the crowd and there was Velar staring at me.

I stopped, I felt embarrassed for some reason. Bellamy looked down at me to see why I suddenly stopped. Unsure of what to do I quickly resumed my role. *How could he be here?* That was all I was focusing on now.

My hands held onto the back of Bellamy's thighs as he thrusted, his body covered in sweat from the burning fire ignited a spark inside me making me take him deeper. Wanting to show off to the crowd or maybe show off to Velar. When Bellamy moaned the crowd erupted into a raucous, debauched cheer, their voices echoing through the night like a chorus of unbridled hedonism.

Just as Bellamy was going to orgasm Ambrette motioned for me to stop. He was not pleased, but he knew this was how the ritual went. It was now time for him to fuck me. Bellamy gently helped me off of my knees. He took my hand and escorted me to an altar.

I looked out to the crowd briefly but didn't see Velar. *Was I imagining him before?* The altar was covered in beautiful linen and white candles burned all around us. He hoisted me off my feet and laid me down on the well-crafted table. He reached up and swiftly removed my white lace panties that he held up to the crowd.

Cheering ensued as he threw them into the fire. Then he mounted me. I laid under him, surrendering myself to him fully. Sweat fell from his glistening body onto mine. I could feel my heart racing with anticipation. He lowered his head slowly towards mine. "Good girl." Bellamy purred.

His tongue licked my mouth in an upwards motion making my lips part for him to enter. Teasing me with his tongue as his sweat fell from his face and body onto mine, making me melt into the earth. He kissed me slow and deep, taking his time sucking on my tongue and biting my bottom lip. The bonfire burned hot, and I was over stimulated. I wanted him now.

Bellamy made his way down to my neck kissing and sucking on me, making me arch my back wanting him to fill me. He knowingly continued to tease me, making me moan. Finally, he pushed himself back and I laid anxiously waiting for his next move.

He slapped my thighs to make them open wider. I spread my legs for him to fit between them. Without taking his eyes off of mine he slid inside me. It hurt so bad I closed my eyes tight managing the pain and then I arched my back opening my eyes to the crowd. From my vantage I saw everyone upside down.

This time he didn't move. Velar stood in the crowd of debauchery watching me as Bellamy slowly fucked me. I tilted my head back, his emerald eyes locked into mine as Bellamy pushed himself in and out of me. I was aroused and even more so that he was watching me. Velar didn't turn his attention away from me. I wondered if he was as turned on as I was.

I scanned the crowd and could see many participating in the sex ritual. Men and woman kissing and fucking. When Bellamy was about to cum Ambrette told him to stop and the drums stopped causing the crowd to go silent. I looked up at Bellamy who kept thrusting. I tried pulling myself away, but he grabbed my thighs and kept fucking me while holding me down. "Stop," I yelled. But he couldn't hear me, like he was in a daze. He had become a ravenous animal that couldn't control himself.

The more I pushed away from him the more he held me down and thrusted himself filling me in pain. "Stop!" I pleaded. In a flash Velar was on the stage. In one swoop he had pulled Bellamy off of me. At once I sat up and covered my body in front of Velar. "Are you ok?" He asked. I nodded my head yes in a bit of shock. We both turned our direction to the ground where Bellamy was.

Velar's sudden intervention had sent Bellamy tumbling off the stage and landing with his back on the ground. He was stunned and disoriented. As I remained seated on the altar, still trying to process the chaos, Bellamy picked himself up and returned to the stage, his eyes locking onto me with concern.

He immediately approached me, apologizing for his loss of control. Then he turned to Velar, gratitude etched on his face. "Thanks for stopping me," he said, attempting to diffuse the tension with a joke, "I guess I just couldn't help myself; she feels too amazing!" The crowd laughed, but my attention was fixed on Velar, who now stood beside us, his presence radiating an air of protection.

Ambrette's voice rang out, her declaration echoing through the night air: "So mote it be!" The drums pulsed with renewed fervor, marking the ritual's triumphant conclusion. The crowd erupted into jubilant cheers. I knew that when my time on this earth finally came to an end, I would be reborn once more to come home to my immortal family.

As the festivities continued, some revelers bid each other farewell and departed, while others remained, indulging in the intoxicating revelry by the bonfire, with wine flowing like a river.

Bellamy draped himself in a robe, his expression one of gratitude as he thanked Ambrette and Mesidor for their role in the ritual. Meanwhile, Velar approached me, holding out my robe with a bit of mystery in his eye. I swiftly took it avoiding his gaze. But then, his breath caressed my ear as he leaned in, his whispered words sending a shiver down my spine. "I prefer you in white."

I froze, my mind racing with the realization that it was Velar who had given me the lingerie to wear tonight. The same words he had whispered in my ear, "I prefer you in white," were the exact words he had spoken in my past life, a memory that had lain dormant until now. It wasn't until he repeated them, that the recollection came flooding back, and I remembered his preference clear as glass.

Just as Velar disappeared off into the night, Bellamy scooped me up from behind. His strong arms cradled me as we departed the stage. I waved a farewell to the crowd, masking my inner turmoil with a smile, as we made our way off into the woods.

Bellamy carried me all the way back to Casmira, his silence a stark contrast to the tumultuous thoughts racing through my mind. Once inside, he directed me to the playroom, a place I knew all too well, where my punishment awaited with anticipation.

Bellamy removed his mask, revealing a face etched with frustration and silence. He had been edged twice, a rare occurrence, as he was usually the one in control. His eyes flashed with eagerness as he laid me down on the bed, swiftly binding my legs and wrists to the black straps hanging from the bedposts. He didn't seem to notice or care that the straps were too tight, cutting off circulation to my wrists.

Before I knew it Bellamy was licking me and then fingering me so fast and hard, taking his frustration out on me. He pulled an oversized dildo from a drawer near the bedside. It's been a while since I've used that, but he didn't seem to care. Instead, he squirted lube on it and plunged it inside me. Bellamy appeared ravenous. I was no longer thinking about Velar.

I thoroughly enjoyed Bellamy having his way with me. I love being his submissive. He moved on top of me. "Open your mouth." He demanded. I obeyed and my mouth was full of his hardness. When I started sucking, he moaned again, "Good girl." I sucked him deeper. Just how he liked it. Then he started fucking my mouth as I laid there only using my tongue to pleasure him.

I was squirming unable to breathe as he continued to fuck my mouth. Finally letting up so I could breathe. "Yes, baby girl," he moaned as he stroked my hair.

"Ready?" he asked as I opened my mouth for more. He stuffed himself inside my mouth again, deeper each time. When he had enough, he let me breathe. Then he made his way down to my dildo. He pushed it in and out over and over.

The feeling made me squirt and he played in my wetness. He turned me onto my stomach, and he pushed himself inside me. I was in full pleasure. Being owned by him made me feel so good. After a short while he exploded inside me.

We lay there for a while, entwined in each other's embrace, as Bellamy tenderly played with my hair and showered me with gentle kisses. At that moment, I could feel how much he loved me, and I felt the same way. I didn't want to be anywhere else. Bellamy asked, "Why didn't you wear the lingerie I picked out for you? Don't get me wrong, I did enjoy that beautiful white outfit on you."

I hesitated, deciding not to reveal the truth about Velar. "Oh, I just felt like wearing white tonight," I said, trying to sound convincing. He kissed my forehead, and we said goodnight. As he drifted off to sleep, snoring softly, I lay awake, my mind flooded with memories of Velar. I wished I had never regained my memories from Sage. After tossing and turning I asked Casmira for sleepy tea and within seconds a hot mug was on my nightstand. I sipped the soothing brew, and soon, my eyelids grew heavy, and I slipped into a peaceful slumber.

CHAPTER

ELEVEN

The day after every Samsara a grand feast is held in celebration of my rebirth. A joyous occasion akin to a birthday party, but far more significant. As I awoke, the clinking of dishes from the kitchen greeted me, a symphony of sounds that signaled Casmira's busy preparations. The entire manor was filled with the mouthwatering aromas of a traditional thanksgiving feast.

Our Samsara celebration featured an abundance of delectable dishes: tender turkey and ham, slow cooked to perfection; creamy mashed potatoes, infused with butter and love; sweet and sticky candied sweet potatoes, topped with fluffy marshmallows that melted in my mouth; savory stuffing, packed with herbs and spices; and an assortment of pies and other treats, each one a masterpiece of flavor and texture.

As I stepped out of the shower, my mind was still savoring the delights of the upcoming feast, and my mouth watered thinking about it. Just then, Bellamy stirred awake, his voice warm as he greeted me, "Good morning, baby girl."

He hoisted himself up, his muscles flexing as he leaned back against the wooden headboard, his naked form on full display. I couldn't help but gaze intently as he stretched his arms overhead, his biceps bulging, before placing them behind his head, his eyes fixed on me through the doorway. I felt a blush rise to my cheeks as I replied, "Morning Daddy," my voice soft, my smile bashful. I quickly made my way to my closet, searching for the perfect outfit to wear.

As the morning wore on, my stomach began to rumble in anticipation of the feast to come, knowing that everyone in Jubilee would be gathering at our manor by noon. I wandered over to my bedroom window, gazing out at the lush meadow beside the house, where two long tables sat side by side.

Just then, Bellamy appeared behind me, his strong arms wrapping around my waist, pulling me close as he breathed softly into my neck. I recognized the gentle pressure of his embrace, a subtle signal that he desired more of my attention. I inhaled deeply, savoring the familiar scent of the sea, feeling my heart race in response to his touch.

Finally, after what felt like an eternity, I was released from the playroom. I dashed down the hall, racing against time to shower and get ready before our guests arrived.

To my dismay, I now had to wash my hair as well, courtesy of Bellamy's careless indulgence deciding to deposit his seed in my tresses. He lingered behind, oblivious to my haste, typical of his laid-back nature. I couldn't help but think, "Mortal or immortal, men are all the same - always leaving their mark, literally!'

As I hastily scrubbed away in the shower, my mind wandered to the age-old dichotomy between men and women. How could they be so oblivious to the world around them, so cavalier about time and consequences?

I noticed a few lingering marks on my skin, souvenirs from Bellamy's passionate embrace. I hadn't even felt him biting me. I rushed through my routine, anxious to get downstairs before our guests arrived.

Meanwhile, Bellamy seemed utterly unconcerned about the impending celebration, his relaxed demeanor suggesting he was in dire need of a nap rather than a sense of urgency. His nonchalance was a stark contrast to my own frazzled state, a reminder that men and women often inhabit different worlds, even in the same household.

As guests began to emerge from the woods, Bellamy and I made our way out to welcome them. Eve was among the first to arrive, and she whispered to me with a sly grin, "So, how was last night?" I playfully nudged her with my elbow, and she burst out laughing.

I then took my seat at the head of the first table, with Bellamy sitting at the opposite end. Eve made her way to the head of the other table. Velar, who was noticeably absent, was supposed to sit at the other end across from Eve. I scanned the crowd of residents, searching for his face, but he was nowhere to be found.

Everyone began to settle in, finding their seats around the tables. I noticed Lucca already seated across from Pixie and Poppy. They were a few seats away from me, and I couldn't help but observe the playful banter between Lucca and the others. Teasing him good-naturedly about his endearing crush on the twins, Lucca laughed it off with a grin.

He clearly relished the sense of belonging that came with being part of our immortal family. It warmed my heart to see him so at ease, surrounded by people who accepted him with open arms. The way he interacted with my immortal loved ones was a joy and put a smile on my face.

In Jubilee, joking and teasing are a way of life. Velar often reminds us, "If you're easily offended, you won't survive here." Living among immortals, I sometimes forget how blunt and crass they can be.

After centuries of life, they've become desensitized to certain things. This numbness is just another aspect that sets immortals apart from mortals. It may sound harsh, but many immortals view mortals as naive and ignorant. Some, unfortunately, believe they are superior, a mindset that can lead to condescending attitudes and behaviors.

Miss Poppet approached me at the table, a warm smile on her face, and presented me with a basket of freshly baked sourdough bread. I rose to embrace her, then carried the basket up to the house to set aside for later. This treat was all mine, not to be shared!

As I ascended the steps of Casmira, I was shocked by the abundance of gifts that adorned my wraparound porch. It seemed everyone had brought a present! I couldn't wait to unwrap them, but I knew I'd have to contain my excitement until later. I must confess, I have a delightful weakness for receiving gifts.

When the time came to dine, we all gathered in wonder as the windows and doors of Casmira swung open in unison. I couldn't help but steal a glance at Lucca's reaction as he witnessed two white tablecloths effortlessly floating out of a side window. His jaw dropped in amazement as the fabric seemingly came to life, stretching and settling perfectly onto the two tables.

Lucca's eyes widened in awe as plates, cups, silverware, and napkins began to fly out of the windows, arranging themselves into precise place settings for each of us. The magic of Casmira was truly a sight to behold!

Next, an abundance of dishes emerged, spread across the tables in a lavish display, ensuring everyone had access to the bounty. "Is it Thanksgiving!" Lucca exclaimed, his enthusiasm infectious. The group erupted into warm chuckles, and I couldn't help but laugh at his joy. Though Bellamy was seated at the far end of the table, partially obscured from my view, I could sense his gaze upon me. He always seemed to be watching me, his attention a constant presence that I'd grown accustomed to.

Just as I was about to savor a bite of candied sweet potatoes, I sensed a presence behind me. I turned around to find Velar leaning into my ear as he whispered, "I love that dress on you." With a genuine smile, he straightened up and sauntered off to take his seat at the head of the adjacent table. My heart skipped a beat as I felt his gaze upon me, but I maintained a steady composure, keeping my eyes fixed forward.

As I took a bite of my food, I couldn't help but feel the weight of Bellamy's gaze upon me, his eyes boring into me like a gentle pressure. I couldn't bring myself to meet his gaze, nor Velar's, both alpha men waiting with bated breath for my next move.

Instead, my eyes drifted down to the soft blue dress I wore, and instantly, a memory came flooding back, *Velar presenting it to me as a gift, our eyes locking in a store window as we both fell in love with the fabric's gentle hue.*

I shook my head trying to banish the memory.

Overwhelmed, I hastily excused myself and rushed into my house, seeking solace in the sanctuary of my bedroom. I tore off the dress, letting it fall to the floor, and collapsed onto my bed in just my bra and panties.

Moments later, Bellamy appeared in the doorway, concern etched on his face. "Everything okay, baby girl?" he asked, sitting beside me on the bed. I scrambled for a plausible explanation, "I spilled gravy on my dress and needed to change." Bellamy's expression softened, and he nodded, accepting my excuse without question.

Bellamy selected a sleek black dress with long sleeves, his eyes shining with admiration as he helped me slip it over my head. "You are the most beautiful girl in the world," his voice filled with warmth, as he smoothed the fabric down my body. "Thank you, Daddy," I replied, feeling a sense of comfort and security in his presence.

Bellamy escorted me back to my seat at the feast, his protective presence commanding attention. I could feel Velar's gaze upon me, but I was determined to make a statement. As he leaned in to kiss my cheek, I grasped his hand, pulling him back to me. With a boldness I didn't know I possessed, I pressed my lips to his, wrapping my arms around his neck.

He responded with a fierce passion, our kiss burning with intensity. I knew Velar was watching. As I returned to my seat, a coy smile spread across my face, a declaration of my feelings for all to see.

As the last guest departed and the feast came to a close, I could finally unwind. Velar and Bellamy sat on the front porch, sipping scotch, and enjoying the enchanted evening air. Eve and

I retreated to the kitchen, giggling, and sharing stories about my brother's infatuation with the Bally girls.

We were having the time of our lives, maybe even a little too much fun, what we used to call 'Nanty Narking'. I hadn't laughed so hard since my return, and the wine only added to the merriment. But as the night wore on and our drinks flowed, our conversation took a more serious turn. In a moment of tipsy curiosity, I began questioning Eve about Velar, my words slurring slightly as I asked...

"Tell me more about Velar leaving the circus." Eve set her glass of wine down, her eyes narrowing slightly as she asked, "What exactly do you want to know?" She seemed hesitant, unsure of how much to reveal. I glanced towards the front door, nodding discreetly towards my ear, hinting that Velar might be listening in. Eve followed my gaze, then chuckled and whispered, "Don't worry, those two are too absorbed in their scotch to pay us any mind. Trust me, nobody's listening to us!"

I chuckled, knowing Eve was probably right. "Do you think I was happy with Velar?" I asked. Eve's eyes widened, and she replied, "Oh, I don't know, Nic, that was so many years ago... Why are you asking? Are you having feelings again?"

I quickly shook my head, trying to appear convincing. "No, not at all. I just... I don't know, I guess I was just trying to imagine it." The lie rolled off my tongue, but the guilt lingered. I couldn't even confide in Eve, my best friend, about regaining my memories.

The shame and embarrassment of my past with Velar felt too overwhelming. I wanted to keep those memories buried, hidden from the world and myself. I think Eve sensed something was troubling me, because she reached out and said, "You know you can tell me anything, right?" I nodded, knowing it was true. Eve had always been a trusted confidante.

Casmira, seemingly intuitive, refilled our goblets without asking, and we continued drinking and talking into the early hours of the morning. As the clock struck the witching hour, Eve slurred a goodnight and stumbled out of Casmira. Velar, ever the gentleman, offered to escort her home, and the two of them disappeared into the darkness, their footsteps rustling down the wooden path that led towards the town square, where Eve's residence lay.

That night, I surrendered to Bellamy's embrace with the passion of a first love. His salty sea scent transporting me to a place of pure passion. I had feared that our connection might have faded, but our love remained strong, perhaps even more intense.

Yet, my emotions were now tangled in a web of conflicting desires, as the memories of my past life with Velar resurfaced, colliding with my present feelings for Bellamy. The regret of yielding to Sage still lingered. As Bellamy slumbered beside me, I lay awake, my mind consumed by the ghosts of my past, re-living the moments I shared with Velar, unable to shake off the haunting memories.

I spent the night in restless torment, my mind a maelstrom of memories I had desperately tried to suppress. Visions of stolen kisses with Velar in a circus tent, of shared laughter and stolen glances, flooded my consciousness. The weight of my guilt was crushing. When my alarm sounded, I couldn't muster the strength to rise. And when Bellamy attempted to rouse me, I dimly recall mumbling a weak excuse, pleading exhaustion, and begging him to leave me be.

When I slowly came to, my hair was being gently stroked, and found Bellamy's concerned gaze upon me. "Hey baby girl, are you feeling rested?" he asked, his voice with worry. I turned to face the clock, and my eyes widened in surprise, it was evening, and I had slept the entire day away. The sun would soon dip below the horizon. I reassured him with a faint smile, "I just needed to catch up on sleep." It wasn't entirely a lie; the truth was, I had been tormented by unthinkable thoughts throughout the night, and exhaustion had finally claimed me.

Bellamy invited me to join him in bidding farewell to Velar, a reminder that the time of year had arrived when Velar embarked on his annual trip to Alaska. For thirty days, he immerses himself in the vampire festival, reveling in the darkness that envelops the land for an entire month. Bellamy's question hung in the air, and I finally responded, "Sure, I will go with you."

Velar's departure brought me a sense of relief, a feeling I couldn't quite explain. Perhaps his absence would be a blessing in disguise, allowing me to finally shake off the lingering thoughts that had plagued me.

The old adage echoed in my mind, out of sight, out of mind. Maybe, just maybe, I would finally find some peace and get some much-needed rest.

I dressed in the long black and white vertical striped dress Bellamy had chosen for me, pairing it with shoes and a black fascinator that perfectly complemented the outfit. Bellamy carefully placed it on my head, and with a final adjustment, we set off for the circus, ready to bid Velar farewell.

Upon arriving at the circus, Bellamy headed to the front to assist with securing the gate, as the circus had officially closed for the day.

Meanwhile, Lucca beckoned me over to the backyard, his voice ringing out with excitement. "Watch this!" he shouted, his eyes sparkling with pride. I held my breath as I watched him sprint towards one of the galloping horses, his feet pounding the ground in rhythm with the horse's hooves. In a daring display of agility, Lucca launched himself into the air, landing gracefully on the horse's back as it continued to gallop unfalteringly. "Bravo!" I exclaimed, my hands erupting into applause as I cheered him on.

From behind me, I sensed a presence, and a low, smooth voice spoke, "He's doing great, isn't he?" I recognized the voice as Velar's, but I didn't turn around, my eyes remaining fixed on Lucca's impressive display. "He is amazing!" I exclaimed, trying to sound casual despite the nervousness creeping up my spine. "Thank you for training him," I added, attempting to sound grateful. Velar stepped up beside me, his eyes never leaving mine. "He's such a good kid," he said, his voice filled with warmth. Then, he turned to face me, his gaze locking onto mine, his smile hinting at something more. "You did the right thing by bringing him here, you know," he said.

That was the first time anyone had ever spoken to me about Lucca with such kindness, and I felt a surge of pride as a protective older sister. I opened up to Velar with sincerity, "I felt an inexplicable sense that he belongs here." Velar's smile broadened as he extended a small white box towards me. "What's this for?" I asked, hesitant to accept the gift. "I can't take this," I protested, but Velar insisted.

I reluctantly opened the box, revealing a stunning gold locket that sparked a flood of memories. It was the same locket Velar had given me in my past life. "Velar, I can't accept this," I stammered, but he cut me off. "Nic, this is yours. I'm merely returning it to its rightful owner." Little did he know, I had regained my memories, and this locket was from our past. I took the locket, a mix of emotions swirling within me. "Oh, well, in that case, thank you very much," I said, trying to sound casual despite the chaos inside.

Just as Lucca bounded over to us, I swiftly hid the locket in my pocket, concealing it from view. We made our way to the front gate, where Bellamy awaited. The circus had officially closed its doors, and Velar was preparing to embark on his journey. Bellamy offered to jump to Barrow, but Velar declined, cautioning that it wouldn't be wise to reveal our existence to the vampires, particularly Jubilee.

Velar embraced Bellamy in a warm, brotherly hug, then turned to Lucca and Eve, sharing a similar farewell gesture. With a playful grin, he joked to Eve, "Don't run off to marry Draven while I'm gone, Ok? Wouldn't want to miss that wedding!" Eve responded with an eyeroll and a witty retort, "Don't party too hard at your lame festival." Velar chuckled and teased, "Don't be a vampire hater now that you're a werewolf lover!" Velar teased. The lighthearted banter filled the air as they shared a moment of camaraderie before his departure.

I embraced Velar, and for a moment, he held me close, his cold chest rising and falling as he breathed me in. But the tender moment was short-lived, as Bellamy's low growl pierced the air, prompting Velar to release me and flashed a cocky smile in Bellamy's direction. I shook my head, exasperated by the two men's antics. We stood there, watching as Velar vanished into the night.

CHAPTER
TWELVE

Two weeks had passed since Velar's departure. Bellamy surprised everyone when he jumped us away to the Caribbean Islands. Darlington Circus flourished on One Happy Island. After a successful run the Circus went into hiding. Bellamy placed us in the lush Gourie Forest in Jamaica.

The performers scattered, seeking sun-kissed adventures and relaxation. Many indulged in beachside luxuries, while Eve, Arabella, and Anise, fellow performers escaped to a singles resort, eager to mingle and make memories.

Lucca and the bally girls splashed into fun at the water parks daily, while I reveled in precious family time. I flew my parents out for a week-long vacation, and Bellamy treated them to an all- inclusive resort experience. My dad indulged in golf and buffet delights, while my mom rejuvenated at the spa every day.

We shared laughter and memories, and I cherished this rare opportunity to connect with my parents. As we strolled to lunch, my mom turned to me with a warm smile and said,

"Some life you're living now!" Her words filled me with gratitude and joy.

In this fleeting moment, I felt like I had it all. The warmth of the sun, the love of my family, and the thrill of our adventures together. And yet, a wistful thought crept into my mind, to be immortal, to never have to say goodbye, to never have to restart anew.

To be able to stay with my immortal family forever, to spare them the search for me, of wondering if I was reborn. It was a tantalizing dream, one that promised eternal joy, but also eternal longing. For in immortality, would I not also be cursed to watch as loved ones grew old and frail, while I remained forever young?

As we savored the final bites of our lunch, my parents prepared to bid farewell and return to PA. But Lucca was determined to make the most of our time together, regaling them with video after video of his impressive horseback riding skills. His tricks and talents left my parents beaming with pride, their faces glowing with pride and joy. It was a heartwarming moment, one that filled me with gratitude for this special time together and the opportunity to see my brother shine.

In a moment that will forever be etched in my memory, Bellamy dropped a bombshell that left us all stunned. With a beaming smile, he announced that Lucca was officially joining the Darlington Circus family!

My mother's eyes welled up with tears of pride, her heart overflowing with joy for her little boy's achievement. My father, the stoic, held back until he saw the impressive paycheck that came with Lucca's new role. Then, he couldn't help but shed a tear of his own. Lucca, overwhelmed with excitement, flung his arms around Bellamy, gratitude and happiness radiating from every fiber of his being. It was a moment of pure elation, one that we'll treasure forever.

After we got back from dropping my parents off at the airport we checked into another resort where we would be staying for another week. As we settled into our new oceanside room, Bellamy's eyes gleamed with desire, his hands eager to reclaim my body.

He swiftly lifted my dress over my head, and in the same motion, a soft clinking sound filled the air. We both froze, our gazes following the sound to the floor, where the delicate necklace Velar had given me just before his departure lay gleaming, its chain broken. The sudden appearance of the token, a symbol of Velar's affection, a reminder of the complex web of relationships that bound us together.

Bellamy leaned down and picked up the necklace, his eyes studying it with a knowing glint. "Where did you get this?" he asked, his tone measured. I sensed a hint of accusation, but his calm demeanor put me at ease. I snatched the necklace back, my defensiveness rising. "It's mine, isn't it?" I asserted, my voice firm.

Bellamy's expression remained serene, his voice even. "Actually, it was a gift from Velar... from your past life." The statement hovered between us, a precarious balance of truth and emotion. I felt a flush rise to my cheeks as I gazed at the locket, my mind scrambling for an explanation. But Bellamy, ever the peacemaker, swiftly intervened. "It's fine, really. It's not a big deal."

As I attempted to compose myself, a dam burst within me, and memories of Velar came flooding back. The ache of longing for his embrace, the warmth of his love, and the bitter taste of shame for my dual desires all swirled together. Overwhelmed,

I hastily excused myself, seeking the refuge of the restroom, where I could temporarily escape the turmoil brewing inside me.

I paced back and forth in the hotel bathroom, the white tiles blurring together as I struggled to contain the emotional storm brewing inside me. The sound of Bellamy's concerned voice calling out from the other side of the door, "Is everything okay?", only made me feel more trapped. I forced a lie through my tight throat. "Yes," but his hesitation told me he saw right through it. The door remained fixed, as if he was waiting for me to crack open the truth. My agitation grew with each passing moment, my emotions building towards a volcanic eruption.

The floodgates of my mind burst open, and memories I had long suppressed came rushing back. Velar's piercing gaze, Bellamy's gentle touch - both men, both loves, both intertwined in my thoughts. I recalled the tender moments, the whispers of affection, the vulnerable confessions. Memories of passion and intimacy with each of them, separately, yet equally intense. The memories swirled together, a bittersweet reminder of my divided heart, my love for two men who had claimed equal parts of my soul.

A wave of nausea washed over me as I leaned against the door, desperate to remain silent. Bellamy's shadow loomed on the floor, a constant reminder of his presence, his patience. I struggled to calm my racing breath, my mind racing with memories. And then, like a bolt of lightning, it hit me!

The memory I had long suppressed, the day I died. It came back to me with crystal clarity, no longer a fuzzy recollection. Every detail was vivid, every moment accounted for. The floodgates of my memory had finally opened, and the truth came rushing out.

The world around me melted away, and I found a strange sense of serenity. Bellamy's knocks on the door grew fainter, his voice a distant hum, as I delved deeper into the recollection. The memory unfolded like a forgotten tapestry, its threads weaving together to form a vivid picture. I became lost in its depths, the present moment fading into insignificance. Only the past existed, and I was trapped in its grasp, reliving the moments that had shaped me.

Velar and I had just finished a routine in the Big top and we had left the stage. It was our last act of the day. I was so happy it went flawless, and I remember I leaped in his arms, and he kissed me. It wasn't our first kiss, but it was still new and exciting.

The Circus had been going on and everyone including Bellamy was working in the circus. Velar and I decided to sneak back to Jubilee. I felt like a little girl sneaking around with him. He made me feel so naughty. I was always such a good girl for Bellamy. With Velar I had no rules. I had freedom and boy; did he love when I explored my freedom.

We went to Velar's house in the Emberlynn Forest, and I honestly just wanted some time with him because over the past few weeks we only saw each other briefly. We kept it a secret. Nobody knew and selfishly I didn't seem to care that I was doing this behind Bellamy's back. He had become increasingly consumed by his responsibilities with the circus, leaving little time for me. Not that I blamed him for this.

Bellamy knocked again, losing my concentration. I focused my mind and tuned him out once more. Where was I? The memory was clear now. The day I died.

We were in his house, in his bed. He was rubbing my arm as he held me. I remember having a deep conversation about life, we talked about running away together and leaving the circus. I brought up becoming a vampire, but Velar said it wasn't the lifestyle he wanted for me. Especially because I love the sunlight so much.

We had just made love and I laid naked in his arms, gazing into his emerald eyes. "I knew you couldn't keep your fangs away from her!" Bellamy shouted in anger. Within seconds Velar was standing in front of me blocking me from Bellamy. Bellamy was enraged and lifted his hands towards Velar. Velar lost all control of his body and was lifted off the ground and pushed into a corner where Bellamy's magic encircled him, keeping him imprisoned.

I sat scared on the bed. "Bellamy," I started to explain. He walked over to me. His magic swirling around his body as he grabbed my naked legs pulling them to him. "You want to be a little slut now?" He said. I turned my head around to face him and he immediately slapped my ass with his hand. "Turn around" He demanded, the sound of his pants hitting the floor echoed through the room.

I had never been treated this way by him before. I know I had hurt him, but he was violently hurting me. "I own you." He said as he thrusted inside me. Harder each time, in and out, over and over again. Not waiting for me to adjust. No doubt I was being punished.

He grabbed my hair and pulled my head back whispering in an irate voice "I own you!" I started crying, not only because I felt so guilty and ashamed for what I had done, but also because of the pain I was now feeling.

"Daddy, you're hurting me." I pleaded. Bellamy didn't stop. He fucked me harder and harder; I looked down at the sheets that were starting to fill with blood. My arms had bruises and *my hips felt like they were going to break the harder he held them. I cried out, "Stop." But he only fucked me harder. Punishing me. Then his hand wrapped around my neck, squeezing tightly.*

Velar fought against Bellamy's magic, but I knew there was no use. Bellamy's magic was stronger than whatever vampire powers he had. I waited for his anger to subside, but it only intensified, until suddenly, a sharp snap pierced the air. Velar's scream followed, a raw and anguished cry, "No!" In that instant, I realized that I was the one who had shattered, my neck snapping like a brittle twig. My life force ebbed away, leaving nothing but irreparable damage in its wake.

That was my last memory of my previous life.

As the memory faded, my eyes fluttered open, and tears streamed down my face. The knocking on the door persisted. "Baby girl," Bellamy cooed, his words a stark contrast to the brutality he had unleashed upon me.

My mind reeled with the realization that he had lied about my demise. It wasn't magic, it was his dark magic, the same magic that almost ruined Samsara.

I flung open the bathroom door, and Bellamy recoiled, taken aback by my tears and accusation. Our eyes locked in a fierce stare. "You lied to me!" I spat, my voice trembling with rage. "You wanted me dead because you couldn't bear the thought of me with someone else!"

Bellamy's eyes darted wildly, his mouth stumbling over words. "Nicole, I was heartbroken... I own you..." I cut him off, my voice rising. "You killed me!" His face crumpled as he realized I had regained my memories. He swallowed hard, but I didn't give him a chance to speak. I turned on my heel and fled the room, unsure of my destination, but driven by a desperate need to escape the truth and the man who had shattered my life.

I fled the hotel, desperate to escape the suffocating weight of Bellamy's lies. A cab whisked me away to the forest, where I was hiking through the dense underbrush, my feet pounding out a rhythm of anger and betrayal. I didn't glance back; didn't dare to confront the emotions I was trying to outrun.

The circus grounds finally came into view, and I sprinted towards the willow tree, its branches like open arms welcoming me to Jubilee. Once in Jubilee I ran all the way to Casmira. I got inside only to realize I didn't want to be there either.

Exhausted and parched, Casmira refilled every sip of cool water in my cup. But even the soothing liquid couldn't quench the despair that had taken hold of me. The thought of facing Bellamy soon was unbearable. I couldn't stay there, couldn't face myself.

I fled my magical house and found myself running towards the forest hills, my feet carrying me swiftly. I knocked on a cabin door, my tears streaming unabashedly. "May I use your cheval glass?" I asked, my voice cracking.

Clove's kind eyes and nodding head were all the comfort I needed. He ushered me in, and I collapsed into the safety of his presence, finally allowing myself to surrender to the anguish that had been building inside me.

I trailed behind Clove, my feet creaking on the wooden stairs as we ascended to the attic. The air was thick with anticipation. He carefully unveiled the cheval glass, its surface glinting in the dim light. I offered a silent thanks, my heart pounding in my chest. With a resolute breath, I stepped forward, the glass's silvery veil immersing me.

"Barrow, Alaska," I whispered, the words barely audible. The world around me began to blur, and I felt the familiar sensation of being pulled through the portal's mystical embrace.

The attic, Clove, and the circus faded into the distance, replaced by the vast, snowy expanse of Alaska's wilderness.

CHAPTER
THIRTEEN

The icy wind slapped me like a thousand frozen needles, its bitter chill piercing through my clothes. I shivered, my teeth chattering, as the harsh reality of my impulsive decision hit me like a blizzard. I had forgotten that Barrow, Alaska lay far north of the Arctic Circle, where the unforgiving wilderness and subzero temperatures could swiftly claim a life.

My numb hands frantically rubbed my arms, a futile attempt to kindle warmth. The urgency to find shelter screamed in my mind, for I knew that if I did not escape the biting cold soon, it would consume me whole, leaving me a frozen statue in this desolate landscape.

The sky above was a deep, foreboding shade, almost black as coal. Snow swirled around me, casting an eerie silence over the deserted town. I stood frozen, gazing up at a sign that I could not pronounce 'Utqiagvik'. The name felt strange on my lips, a harsh whisper in the wind. As I scanned my surroundings, the darkness revealed a few skeletal buildings in the distance, their windows like empty eyes staring back. The biting cold and desolation suffocated me. *Why would Velar come here?*

Panic set in as the cold overwhelmed me, my teeth chattering uncontrollably. I sprinted towards the buildings, my feet pounding the snow-covered ground.

Every second felt like an eternity, my body screaming for warmth. I was ludicrously unprepared, having left the Caribbean's balmy embrace only to plunge into this Arctic nightmare without so much as a coat or scarf. My mind raced with self-reproach: *Idiot! What was I thinking?* The buildings loomed ahead, a potential sanctuary from the biting wind and snow.

Door after door, I was met with rejection. Noone was home and the doors were locked. The cold and darkness closing in around me like a vise. The streets were eerily silent, devoid of life. Panic's icy grip began to tighten, my breath coming in short gasps.

Just when I thought I was truly alone, I spotted a cluster of shadowy figures in the distance. I waved my arms wildly, a desperate beacon of hope. As I drew closer, the figures solidified into four men, their faces weathered and rugged. They eyed me warily, their expressions unreadable. I approached them with a mix of trepidation and gratitude, my teeth chattering uncontrollably.

I was still a distance away when, in the blink of an eye, one of the men materialized beside me. My heart skipped a beat as I let out a startled yelp. The vampire's sudden appearance had me trembling even harder. "Hi there, I was hoping you could help me," I stammered, my voice barely audible over the wind. He flashed a disarming smile, his eyes glinting with mischief. "Sure thing, little lady. Come with me."

Despite my reservations, I followed behind him, my body shivering uncontrollably. His attire seemed ludicrously inadequate for the harsh climate. A thin t-shirt and jeans that offered little protection against the biting cold.

Yet, he seemed utterly unfazed. As we approached the others, his grin grew wider, making me regret my decision to come here. I pushed on, driven by the desperate need for warmth and shelter, but my gut screamed warnings I dared not heed.

As we reached the group, they swung open the massive door of a warehouse-like structure, revealing a dimly lit interior. I hastened inside, relief washing over me as I escaped the merciless wind and snow.

Though the air inside was still chilly, it was a reprieve from the biting cold outside. As I looked around at the four men, my skin crawled with fear realizing they were vampires. They were all grinning at me with their fangs showing, their eyes gleaming with an unnerving intensity. I felt like fresh meat, trapped in their midst. The air seemed to vibrate with an unspoken tension, and I sensed that I was in a precarious situation, at the mercy of these mysterious and unsettling strangers.

The bald vampire's piercing gaze bore into me as he asked, "Where did you come from?" My mind raced, hesitant to reveal my true origin. The Caribbean was too far-fetched. "I'm from... um, Juno," I stammered, grasping for the first Alaskan town that came to mind. The vampires exchanged skeptical glances, their grins faltering for a moment.

I knew I had to think fast, to come up with a more convincing reason for my presence in this Arctic tundra. "I'm here for the vampire festival," I blurted out, hoping to deflect their suspicion. The bald vampire raised an eyebrow, his smile returning, wider and more unsettling than before.

The vampires exchanged perplexed glances, their eyes returning to me with a heightened intensity. The one who had escorted me in asked, his voice laced with curiosity, "How do you know about the festival?" But before I could respond, another interrupted, his tone tinged with suspicion, "How do you know about vampires? Are you working at the feeding booths?"

I stood frozen, my mind reeling from the cold, the shock, and the unsettling gaze of these creatures. My silence only seemed to heighten their interest, their eyes devouring me like prey. I sensed their hunger, their thirst, and felt like a vulnerable morsel, trapped. The air was heavy with tension, and I knew I had to speak, to deflect their attention, or risk becoming their next meal.

I cast a desperate glance towards the door, my mind racing with escape plans. "Well, I got separated from my friend," I said, attempting to sound nonchalant, "I better go look for him." I turned to make a swift exit, but the vampire was too quick.

He stepped into my path, his eyes glinting with a sinister light, his fangs bared in a cold smile. "You'll freeze out there, little lady," he sneered. I forced a brave tone, despite my heart racing like a wild animal, "Oh, I'll be okay." But my words were hollow, and I knew they could hear the fear pounding in my chest.

Before I could make another move, a voice from behind me echoed, "I think we'll keep you here for now." The words sent a chill down my body, and I knew I was trapped, at the mercy of these bloodthirsty vampires.

Something inside me snapped. Every instinct screamed at me to flee. I made a desperate lunge for the door, but it was too late. The bald vampire's hand slammed against the metal, blocking my escape.

The others closed in; their movements eerily synchronized. They formed a tightening circle around me, their eyes fixed on me like predators. I felt like prey, trapped and helpless. As they began to pace around me, their footsteps echoing off the walls, I knew I was doomed.

My heart raced, my breath came in short gasps, and my mind raced with the certainty of my impending death. I was surrounded and outnumbered. The silence was oppressive, heavy with anticipation, and I knew I was running out of time. I was going to die.

I clung to the thought that I would reincarnate again, that Bellamy would find me again, that the ritual would protect me. But as the vampires closed in, their fangs bared and their eyes gleaming with hunger, my courage faltered. I crumpled to the floor, my legs tucked into my chest, my eyes screwed shut against the horror.

Tears burst forth, hot and uncontrollable, as I succumbed to despair. The vampires' menacing growls and the sound of their footsteps encircling me faded into the background as I retreated into a world of despair, my mind screaming silently for Bellamy, for safety, for escape.

The doors exploded open with a deafening crash, and in the same instant, I was swept up into a strong embrace. I kept my eyes clenched shut, paralyzed by fear. The sound of yelling pierced the air, but it wasn't until I finally opened my eyes that I realized it was Velar's voice thundering through the room.

His voice was with fury as he yelled at the other vampires, his arms holding me tight against his chest. I felt a surge of relief wash over me, mixed with a dash of confusion. *How did he find me?* The question swirled in my mind as I gazed up at Velar's fierce expression, my heart still racing from the ordeal.

Velar's words were lost on me, uttered in a language I could not understand, later I came to find out it was Iñupiaq. However, the other vampires comprehended all too well, their faces pale and fearful as they cowered before him.

I, on the other hand, felt a wave of relief wash over me, gratitude flooding my heart. Velar's strong arms cradled me protectively as he strode out of the building, the cold air hitting us like a slap.

Only when we were safely outside did he address me, his voice firm but laced with concern. "What are you doing here?" he asked, his voice panicked. His eyes scanned me as if searching for signs of harm. I felt a sudden chill, but this time, it wasn't just from the cold.

My lips were frozen, my voice unable to escape the icy grip of the wind. I simply shook my head, my eyes fixed on Velar's concerned face. He nodded understandingly, his gaze never leaving mine. "We'll be inside soon," he promised, his voice a warm whisper in the frozen landscape. Velar sprinted with his vampire speed, the snowdrifts swallowing his feet as he trudged through the blizzard carrying me.

Finally, Velar stopped in front of a small, weathered house. He produced a key from his pocket and unlocked the door, ushering me inside with a gentle hand. I stumbled in, grateful to be inside. Velar followed close behind, shutting out the cold and the darkness.

The chill in the air was visible, the house's interior almost as cold as the exterior. Velar swiftly wrapped me in a blanket, his movements efficient and gentle. I sat on the hearth, my eyes fixed on him as he worked to kindle a fire, his hands moving with a quiet urgency. I blew on my frozen fingers, trying to coax some warmth into them, and rocked my body back and forth, seeking comfort in the motion.

The cold had seeped into my very marrow, my bones aching with a dull, relentless pain. I felt like I'd never be warm again, like the chill had taken up permanent residence in my soul. Velar's presence was a beacon of hope, his calm and capable demeanor a reminder that safety and warmth were within reach.

Velar made tea as I warmed by the fire. I thawed out slowly, my frozen limbs regaining feeling, my voice returning from its hiding place. Finally, I could speak, and my questions tumbled out in a rush. "How did you find me? How did you know I was here?" I asked, my eyes fixed on his face, searching for answers.

Velar paused in his task, his gaze meeting mine, and his words were like a gentle revelation. "I can still feel you," he said, his voice low and husky. "I think it's from consuming your blood from your last lifetime. It never went away." The fire crackled, but I barely heard it, my mind reeling with the implications of Velar's words. The connection between us was still alive, a thread of fate that bound us together across time and space.

I stared at Velar, "I thought that ended when I died," I said. His eyes held a deep intensity, his gaze piercing through the flames. "So did I," he admitted, his voice low. "Until I felt you again. I knew you were alive before Eve found you. That's why I came back to the circus. For you."

I lifted my tea to my lips, the warmth a comforting distraction from the tumultuous emotions within. The silence that followed as we sat there, lost in our own thoughts, the only sound the crackling of the fire.

As the warmth seeped back into my bones, I ventured a lighthearted question, hoping to dispel the somber mood. "So, where's this vampire festival? Looks like a ghost town around here." Velar's quick wit sparked a smile, "Well, vampires are dead, after all." I chuckled, feeling a pang of nostalgia for our banter. His humor was calming, and I reveled in the familiarity of our exchange.

I hesitated to share the details of my argument with Bellamy, unsure of how Velar would react. As the fire crackled and spat, Velar handed me another steaming mug of tea, his eyes crinkling at the corners as he smiled. Not as good as Casmira's tea, but it would suffice. I took a sip, feeling the warmth spread through my chilled body, and savored the comforting silence between us.

I sank into a state of numbness, my mind reeling with the events of the past few hours. The tea in my mug was a distant warmth, a comforting blur as my thoughts raced back to the vampires, to the memory of Bellamy fucking me to death, to our fierce argument and my hasty departure.

The memories swirled in my head refusing to settle. Guilt pricked at my conscience as I thought of Bellamy, likely frantic with worry, but I couldn't bring myself to face him.

The hurt and anger still lingered, a raw wound that I couldn't yet bear to confront. So, I sat, lost in the silence, my tea growing cold in my hands as the fire crackled on, a steady heartbeat in the stillness.

Velar's gentle prodding broke the silence, his voice a soft prompt. "Why are you here, again?" I set my mug down on the hearth, the ceramic clicking against the stone.

"Bellamy and I had a fight," I admitted. Velar's nod was a subtle encouragement, his eyes never leaving mine. "I went through the cheval glass." His eyebrows arched, a silent question, but he remained silent, waiting for me to continue. I hesitated, then asked, "May I have more tea, please?" Velar's movements were fluid as he rose and walked to the small kitchen, the teapot on the stove emitting a soft whistle. He poured the steaming liquid into my mug, his expression a mask of calm understanding.

Velar returned to my side, handing me the refilled mug. I took a sip, my gaze wandering around the small, unassuming house. The living area was sparse, with a worn sofa and a faded armchair, the walls bare of any decorations. It was a space that screamed 'bachelor pad', devoid of any feminine touch.

My curiosity got the better of me, and I asked, "Whose place is this?" Velar's response was nonchalant, "It's mine." My eyes widened in surprise, "Really?" I exclaimed. "I had no idea you had a home outside of Jubilee," I admitted.

Velar settled into his worn armchair, the creaking of the old leather echoing through the silence. He gazed into the flames; his eyes lost in thought. "It's not much, but it's a place to stay during the festival, and when I need to escape," he said, his voice low and contemplative.

The pause that followed was heavy with unspoken words, and I sensed a depth of emotion beneath his calm exterior. I summoned the courage to ask the question that had been lingering in my mind, "Is this where you were when you left the circus?" Velar's gaze remained fixed on the fire, "Mostly." The single word spoke volumes, hinting at secrets and stories left untold.

I swiftly shifted the conversation, eager to avoid the topic of Amsterdam and Sage. "So, where is this festival, exactly?" I asked, my curiosity piqued. Velar's eyes lit up with excitement, and he leaned forward, his voice taking on a conspiratorial tone.

"Why? Do you want to go?" he asked, his gaze sparkling with amusement. I hesitated, feeling caught in a snare of fear and curiosity. "I just don't want to run into those other vampires," I admitted.

Velar's chuckle was warm and reassuring, and he paused, his smile still playing on his lips. "Don't worry," he said, his voice filled with conviction. "I'll protect you." My heart swelled with gratitude, and I smiled, knowing that Velar's promise was unshakeable.

Velar had quickly left his place leaving me waiting patiently for his return. As I wandered through Velar's humble abode, I began to notice the subtle details that revealed the nuances of his character. The simplicity of his home, both here in Alaska and in Jubilee, spoke to his unassuming nature. Every surface was clean and uncluttered, a testament to his minimalist approach to life. He did not crave extravagance or excess; his needs were few, and his desires even fewer.

The silence of Velar's home enfolded around me, the only sound the crackling of the fire as I waited for his return. The warmth and comfort of his chair lulled me into a gentle doze, my tea forgotten on the hearth. The creak of the front door broke the stillness, and I stirred, my eyes fluttering open as Velar stepped inside, a bag slung over his shoulder. With a casual toss, he sent the bag my way, and I caught it.

My eyes widened in surprise as I pulled out the contents, black leather pants, a silver sequined top, and a black leather jacket. The outfit was a far cry from my usual attire, and I could not help but feel a thrill of excitement at the prospect of donning such a daring ensemble. Velar's knowing smile hinted that he had anticipated my reaction, and I could not help but wonder what other surprises the night had in store.

Velar's eyes seemed to gleam with amusement, as if he had divined my thoughts. "It's just to wear to the festival so you can fit in better and not look so obviously human. The only mortals here are in the feeding booths." His grin grew wider, his fangs glinting in the firelight.

"And I know you don't want to be one of them." He stated. The way he said it, with a bit of mischief and a dash of protectiveness, made my heart race.

As I emerged from the bathroom, the leather outfit on me, and I felt a newfound confidence coursing through my veins. "I'm ready to go!" I declared, striking a pose for Velar's benefit. His eyes narrowed slightly as he took in my appearance, and I couldn't resist a playful flourish. "Do you approve?" I asked flirtatiously. But his response was characteristically serious, his tone a gentle rebuke. "I'm not Bellamy, Nic. I don't need to approve." The reminder was subtle, yet poignant.

Velar's words, though not intended to wound, pierced my heart like a dagger. I felt a mix of sadness and longing, as I struggled to contain the truth. Oh, how I yearned to confide in him, to reveal that my memories had returned, and with them, my feelings. But the weight of my loyalty to Bellamy remained, a burden I couldn't shake. The painful truth was that my love for Bellamy had never wavered, a constant ache that lingered deep within me. I stood there, silenced by my emotions, as Velar's gaze searched mine, unaware of the turmoil brewing beneath my surface.

Velar's rugged truck rumbled to life, and we set off into the night, the darkness of Barrow's streets swallowing us whole. As we drove, Velar revealed that he had this truck for many years and this house even longer. I realized how little I truly knew about my mysterious friend.

The streets began to fill with people or vampires rather, and I sensed the electric energy of the crowd. Though smaller than the throngs that flocked to Darlington Circus, the gathering was sizable, and the air was alive with anticipation. Vamp Fest banners and posters plastered every available surface, their vibrant colors and bold graphics beckoning us towards the heart of the celebration.

As we entered the festival grounds, I was surrounded by a sea of bodies, the air thick with music and laughter. Velar's hand closed around mine, his grip strong and reassuring, as he navigated us through the mass of people outside. I felt a surge of comfort and security in his embrace, his towering height and broad shoulders making me feel tiny and delicate in comparison.

The sense of vulnerability was unexpectedly exhilarating, and I felt a thrill of submission wash over me as I surrendered to his guidance. With Velar by my side, I felt sheltered from the world, his presence a bulwark against the unknown dangers that lurked in the shadows.

As we entered the festival grounds, a gauntlet of booths lined the entrance, mortals offering their lifeblood to satiate the thirst of eager vampires. The air was heavy with anticipation, the queue of vampires waiting their turn to taste the forbidden pleasure.

Once we stepped inside the vast venue, the warmth encircled us by a massive bonfire crackling at its center. The flames cast a golden glow on the assembled crowd, revealing a surprising mix of species. Not all who attended this gathering were vampires, and I spotted other creatures mingling freely with excitement.

As we ventured deeper into the venue, the thumping rhythms and electric energy of the rock band on stage drew us in. The crowd was entranced, their bodies swaying in time to the music. Velar leaned in, his voice raised above the din, explaining that a new band would take the stage every few hours, the music flowing uninterrupted for the entire four-week duration of the festival.

He handed me a cup, the aroma of spiced cider wafting up from the vendor's special brew. I took a sip, the warmth spreading through my chilled bones as I surrendered to the infectious beat and let the music wash over me.

The mysterious drink in the beer bottle-like container was a puzzle I could not decipher, the label's strange symbols and letters defying my attempts at pronunciation. I took a bold swig, the flavors exploding on my taste buds. "Not bad," I said, nodding in approval.

Velar's eyes narrowed. "Go easy on that, Nic. It's far stronger than any alcohol you've ever had." I playfully rolled my eyes, dismissing his caution, and took another sip. Velar's brows shot up in exasperation, his head shaking in a silent reprimand, as if I was recklessly courting danger.

As we stood amidst the sea of revelers, the pulsating rhythms and deafening guitars rendered conversation all but impossible. But then, a sudden shift in the crowd's dynamics caught my attention. A path cleared, and three figures emerged from the throng, their eyes fixed on us. Velar's tap on my shoulder was accompanied by a shouted introduction, his voice carrying above the music. "These are my buddies!" His gesture drew my gaze to the approaching trio.

As Velar's friends approached, their imposing figures drawing nearer, he introduced me with a nod. "This is Killian, Roderick, and Nate." I offered a hesitant greeting; my voice barely audible over the music. Oh, how I wished for Eve to be by my side, to witness the awe-inspiring sight before me.

My gaze lingered on Killian, his massive frame and chiseled features leaving me spellbound. He stood tall, exuding a warrior's confidence, his oval face a map of sharp angles and rugged beauty. I couldn't help but stare, my eyes drinking in the sight of these three formidable men, their presence both captivating and intimidating.

Killian's majestic appearance left me breathless, his long blonde hair cascading down his back like a river of gold. His piercing silver-blue eyes seemed to gleam with an otherworldly intensity, as if he were a deity descended from the realm of the gods.

The Fae heritage was unmistakable, their slender ears tapering to delicate points, their skin a radiant canvas of pale perfection. I was surprised, realizing that Velar's associations extended far beyond the circus boundaries. These beautiful beings, with their ethereal grace and mystical aura, were a far cry from the rough-and- tumble world of Darlington Circus.

As the night wore on and the drinks took hold, my inhibitions melted away, and I succumbed to the irresistible sound. I weaved through the crowd, drawn to the stage's magnetic energy, as the music reached a frenetic pace.

The vampire girls, their black leather outfits gleaming like dark armor, descended upon me, their movements fluid and sensual. We spun and twirled together, our laughter and joy infectious, our bodies lost in the music's thrall. But in a moment of carelessness, I released one of their hands, and my momentum sent me stumbling into the solid wall of a stranger's back.

As I spun around to apologize, my eyes widened in horror as the glass bottle slipped from the stranger's hand, shattering on the floor with a loud crash. The liquid contents splashed upwards, drenching his black pants and boots. My gaze shot up, locking onto the stranger's piercing eyes, and realizing he was a vampire.

My heart raced as I took in the sharp jawline and the pale skin that seemed to glow in the dim light. "I'm so sorry!" I exclaimed; my voice laced with genuine regret. "Let me get you a new one, please!" I offered, my hand instinctively reaching out to make amends, as if seeking to repair the damage I had caused.

For a fleeting instant, I braced myself for the worst, my mind racing to summon Velar's protective presence. But to my surprise, the vampire merely shrugged, his expression softening into a carefree smile. "Nah, don't worry about it. Enjoy the festival," he said, his voice low and smooth, as he turned back to his friends and resumed dancing. I exhaled a sigh of relief, my tension melting away like mist in the sun.

The vampire's nonchalance was infectious, and I threw myself back into the music, lost in the whirlwind of color and sound. The girls and I twirled and laughed together; our joy unbridled. It was as if the very air was alive with magic, and I realized that these vampires, the ones within the festival's embrace, were a far cry from the menacing vampires I had first encountered in Barrow.

As the night wore on, Juliet and Philomena, my new vampire friends, showered me with drinks and laughter. I was having the time of my life, my senses heightened by the music and the infectious energy of the festival. Reaching for another bottle, courtesy of Juliet's generosity, I felt a sudden presence behind me. A hand swooped in, eclipsing mine, and claimed the bottle before I could grasp it. I turned to face the interloper; my vision slightly blurred by the alcohol.

"That's enough," Velar's deep voice insisted. My speech slurring slightly as I protested, "Excuse me?" But before he could respond, I noticed Juliet and Philomena had swiftly disappeared into the crowd, abandoning me to Velar's mercy. Not eager to surrender to sobriety just yet, I stumbled away from him, weaving through the mob of revelers, and made a beeline for another bar on the opposite side of the stage, the music and laughter swallowing me whole once more.

The female vampire bartender wearing her midriff-baring top, raised an eyebrow in expectation of my order. Before I could even form the words, I was swooped up and slung over a broad shoulder, my legs dangling helplessly in mid-air. Velar's shoulder, to be precise.

His iron grip held me fast, my face pressed against the supple leather of his jacket, the scent of which filled my nostrils. I struggled and squirmed, but it was a futile effort, Velar's strength was unyielding, his hold unbreakable. I was at his mercy, a captive of his unrelenting grasp.

Velar finally set me down on the passenger seat of his truck and drove us back to his house. When he parked, I almost fell out of the truck door, but he was there before I hit the ground. He gently grasped my elbow, steadying me until I regained my balance. Once inside his home, he tended to the fireplace, adding kindling to the smoldering embers.

I collapsed onto the plush couch, my exhaustion and alcohol- fueled haze threatening to consume me. I gestured lazily, patting the seat beside me, inviting Velar to join me. He obliged, his tall frame settling into the cushion, his proximity both comforting and intimidating. The crackling flames cast a warm glow, illuminating the space between us, as we sat in silence, the only sound the gentle popping of the fire.

I inched closer, my body gravitating towards him, our legs touching, sparks flying. My desire for him was undeniable. I traced my fingers along his thigh, my touch tender, exploratory.

Velar's voice was laced with amusement, his words a gentle rebuke. "I told you not to drink so much." I remained silent, my actions speaking louder than words. The soft whoosh of my jacket slipping off my arms filled the silence. Then, with deliberate slowness, I peeled off my silver top, my bare skin exposed to his gaze.

"Nic, you're drunk," Velar stated, his voice laced with a mix of amusement and arousal. I responded with a defiant "So?" I straddled him, my legs wrapping around his waist, and leaned in, my lips seeking his in a drunken kiss. But Velar caught my face in his hands, his fingers gentle but firm, holding me at bay.

"You're drunk, and this is a bad idea," he whispered, his eyes locked on mine. I was beyond reason. I wanted him, needed him, and I couldn't deny it any longer. I leaned forward again, my lips brushing against his, the kiss soft and tender. As I pulled back, my eyes locked on his, I whispered, "I miss you."

I AWAKENED TO A THROBBING MIGRAINE, MY HEAD POUNDing in rhythmic agony. Groggily, I sat up in Velar's bed, disoriented and confused. The bed was empty, and the room was dimly lit, with no sign of Velar anywhere.

I rubbed my temples, trying to alleviate the pain. I was still wearing my leather pants, and I hastily threw on my shirt, my mind foggy. As I looked around, I realized it was still dark outside, and my confusion deepened. *Where was Velar? And why was it still dark outside?* The events of the previous evening came flooding back, and I winced, my head protesting the memories.

I struggled to recall the events of the previous night, but my memories were hazy and fragmented. The only clear recollection was the vibrant festival, the music and laughter still echoing in my mind. I called out for Velar, my voice loud in the silence, but there was no response.

I swung my legs over the side of the bed and stood up, my head spinning. I stumbled out of the bedroom, my feet carrying me towards the warmth of the fire. The flames danced and crackled. The heat was inviting, and I sank down onto the couch, letting the warmth seep into my bones. *Where was Velar?*

Just as I was starting to feel like I was alone in the house, Velar walked through the front door, his expression stern and unyielding. "Hey," I said, my voice laced with a mix of pain and regret, still rubbing my temples in a vain attempt to soothe the throbbing ache.

Without a word, Velar handed me a couple of pills and a glass of water, his silence deafening. I swallowed the pills gratefully, feeling a twinge of shame wash over me. "I'm sorry about last night," I said embarrassed. "I don't remember much after we left the festival." Velar's gaze narrowed, his eyes piercing mine. "Nic, when did you get your memories back?" he asked, his voice calm, but laced with an undercurrent of tension.

I shook my head, feeling a wave of embarrassment wash over me. "I was so drunk, I don't remember anything," I admitted shamefully. Velar's expression darkened, his eyes flashing with anger.

I knew he was upset that I had kept my memories hidden from him, just like I had with Bellamy. "It doesn't matter," I said, trying to brush it off. "I just have them back, okay?" I added my tone a little sharper than I intended, hoping to deflect the conversation and avoid the inevitable confrontation.

Velar's anger boiled over, and he spun around to face me, his voice thundering through the room. "It does matter, Nic! I can't believe you kept this from me! Why did you come here? What do you expect me to do?"

The questions came rapid-fire, his frustration and hurt evident in every word. But then, seeming to remember my fragile state, he reined in his emotions, his voice dropping to a softer, more controlled tone. "When did you get your memories back?" he asked, his eyes still flashing with intensity, but his words gentle enough not to exacerbate my throbbing headache.

I avoided his gaze. "From Sage." Velar's expression darkened. "You knew all this time?" He shook his head, his jaw clenched in frustration. I knew I had made a mistake coming here. "I shouldn't have come," I admitted, feeling a pang of regret. But before I could say more, Velar spoke up, his voice firm. "Bellamy is on his way." The words felt like a threat. Then, without another glance, he turned and walked out the front door, leaving me feeling uneasy.

I slumped by the fire, the crackling flames mesmerizing as I succumbed to self-reproach. *What had I done? What was wrong with me?* The weight of my mistakes bore down on me like a physical force.

Bellamy was en route, summoned by Velar's displeasure. The two men I loved, both angry with me. The thought was suffocating. I felt like a burden, a nuisance they'd rather be rid of. All I wanted was to escape, to flee to the safety of Casmira. But I knew I couldn't run from my problems forever. The fire's warmth couldn't penetrate the chill of my regret, and I shivered, lost in my misery.

I gazed out the window, my eyes scanning the horizon for the familiar sight of Darlington Circus's black and white tents. My heart raced with anticipation and anxiety, knowing that my reckless decision to come here had put the entire circus at risk. As soon as the tents came into view, I planned to make a swift exit.

My mind raced with questions, *where had Velar gone? What had Velar revealed to Bellamy about my mistakes? And what words would Bellamy have in store for me?* I felt like a chastened child, consumed by regret and self-doubt. The weight of my mistakes bore down on me as I waited for the Circus.

Time dragged on, and the silence felt oppressive, as if Velar had walked out hours ago. I grew increasingly restless, wondering what was taking Bellamy so long. Doubts crept in, taunting me with the possibility that he might not come for me at all. Maybe he assumed I was with Velar last night, and his absence was a stark reminder of my mistakes.

My mind raced with endless worries, each one compounding my guilt. I knew Bellamy had to ensure the safe return of the entire circus to Jubilee before he could even think about coming for me. The weight of my actions hit me like a ton of bricks, I had put everyone in a difficult position, not just myself.

The waiting game was excruciating, with only my regrets to keep me company. I felt like a burden, a liability they'd rather be rid of. The fire crackled, a stark contrast to the cold dread that had taken up residence in my heart.

Just as I was wallowing in self-pity, the Circus materialized from nothing in a second. Velar burst through the front door, his movements swift and urgent, as if he'd been waiting for the circus's arrival with bated breath. A hint of panic flickered in his eyes, and his usual calm demeanor was replaced by a sense of haste. He moved with a purpose, his long vampire strides eating up the distance as he hastened towards the circus. The sudden flurry of activity jolted me out of my misery, and I rose from my seat, my heart racing with a mix of anticipation and trepidation.

Velar swooped in, grabbing a bag and mine. I realized with a start that he was coming with us, his expression grave with urgency. "We need to move quickly," he instructed, his voice

pressing. "We can't risk anyone discovering the circus so as soon as we're inside and down in Jubilee, Bellamy will need to jump us out of here immediately." His words were laced with a sense of danger.

We burst out of the house, Velar slamming the door shut behind us and locking it. I sprinted ahead, my feet pounding the ground, but Velar quickly caught up, effortlessly keeping pace with mine. Without breaking stride, he swept me up into his arms, carrying me with ease as we raced towards the circus.

The gates loomed ahead, and Eve, alert and watchful, flung them open just in time for us to dash through. We hurtled into the circus, the black and white tents were a blur as we sped towards the heart of the encampment, Velar's powerful legs devouring the distance with grace and precision.

We tore through the circus, our footsteps echoing off the tents as we dashed towards the willow tree. Down the stairs we plunged into our hidden world. Eve's voice rang out, urgent and clear, "I didn't see anyone else out there!" Velar's response was immediate, his words tumbling out in a rush "It won't take them long to find us. We have to leave now!"

He sprinted out of sight, leaving Eve and me to follow at a close pace. Before we even reached the wooded path, the familiar vibration hummed to life beneath my feet, and I knew we were already gone, whisked away to a new and unknown destination.

As soon as we were alone, Eve's curiosity got the better of her. "So, what were you doing in Barrow?" she asked, her eyebrows raised with intrigue. I collapsed onto the soft, healing grass, feeling its gentle energy coursing through my veins to alleviate the lingering hangover.

Looking up at Eve, who towered over me with an expectant gaze, I relented. "I got my memories back," I revealed. Eve's arms shot up in excitement, her eyes wide with disbelief. "No way! When did that happen?" she exclaimed, her voice full of wonder and excitement, as if she couldn't wait to hear the entire story.

I turned my head away, my cheeks flushing with embarrassment. The soft grass beneath me seemed a safer focal point than Eve's inquiring gaze. "It happened in Amsterdam," I admitted. Eve's eyes narrowed in confusion. "Why didn't you tell me?" she asked, disappointed.

I sighed, knowing I had let her down too. "I didn't tell anyone, Eve. That's why Velar and Bellamy are upset with me." I explained, my words dripping with regret. Eve's expression softened, understanding slowly dawning on her face. She offered me a gentle smile and pulled me to my feet, our hands entwined. Together, we strolled towards Casmira.

The gate opened as we approached. Part of me was so happy to be home from Alaska. The other half was dreading what was going to happen inside. Eve wanted to head home, but I dragged her inside because I was too much of a coward to face them alone.

As we entered, Bellamy sprang to his feet, his face set in a stern expression. He strode towards us with purpose, his voice firm. "Nicole, go upstairs and wait for me." I didn't dare look at Velar or Eve, instead I stomped up the two flights of stairs. Below, I heard Eve ask Velar, "How was Vamp fest?" but Velar's response was lost in the distance, drowned out by my own footsteps and the turmoil in my mind.

I sulked in the playroom, my heart heavy with anticipation. I knew I was in trouble. Bellamy's worry and frustration were obvious, and I braced myself for the consequences of my actions. Running away, putting myself in danger... and who knew what else Velar had told him? My mind raced with the possibilities, each one ending in a stern lecture and punishment. I swallowed hard, my pout deepening as I waited for the inevitable.

I heard the footsteps approaching, and my heart raced in anticipation. I knelt on the floor, my head bowed in submission. As the door opened, I tilted my face downwards, my eyes fixed on the floor.

Bellamy's boots came into view, and I felt his presence behind me. He grasped my hair, his fingers weaving a gentle braid. The soft tug on my scalp was a surprise, a tender gesture instead of the reprimand I'd expected. Then, his hand settled on my forehead, his magic coursing through my body, soothing me. The tension in my mind eased, my thoughts quieting as the tingling sensation spread.

Bellamy opened the drawer, his eyes fixed on me. "Get undressed." I compiled without hesitation, shedding my clothes before returning to my kneeling position, submissively awaiting his next command. "Stand up and come to me."

I rose, my heart pounding, and approached him by the bed. My gaze fell on the belt lying on the bed. "Do you know why you're being punished?" he asked, his voice firm. I nodded, knowing I'd pushed boundaries. "Bend over onto the bed." I obeyed, my body tensing in anticipation.

I waited with anticipation. His black belt was laying on the bed and I watched as it was slowly pulled out from my vantage. Crack! "Ow" I cried as I arched my back from the pain. Bellamy calmly cooed "Be still." Then crack. Again, and again. Tears fell from my eyes. I felt Bellamy's hand on my ass. Rubbing and soothing the red marks that he left.

Bellamy pulled me into his embrace, holding me securely. "You belong to me," he whispered, his voice filled with a mix of authority and tenderness. I nodded, still sniffling. "Don't ever run away from me again," he demanded, his eyes boring into mine. We sat together in silence for a moment, the tension easing.

Then, Bellamy spoke up, "Velar told me you were upset when you arrived at his place yesterday. He suggested giving you some time to calm down." I wondered what else Velar had shared with Bellamy, and why he would intervene on my behalf. Bellamy continued, "I'm just glad he took care of you, but please, don't ever run away from me again. Okay?" I shook my head agreeing. "Good girl," he said, his voice calm.

I indulged in a long, hot shower, seeking solace in the warm water. I wasn't ready to face Velar or Eve just yet, so I hid in my room, getting dressed in the closet. As I stood in front of the mirror, Bellamy appeared behind me, his reflection surprising me.

He lifted my dress, his eyes examining the tender skin he'd punished earlier. His fingers traced the soreness, his touch gentle. He smiled at me through the mirror. I smiled back, feeling a flutter in my chest. The tension between us dissipated, replaced by a sense of connection and understanding.

Bellamy's lips brushed against my hair as he kissed my head, his gentle gesture a contrast to the firm tone that followed. "Eve has gone home, and Lucca is having dinner with the twins in the town square," he informed me, his voice clear and authoritative.

Then, his dominant voice took on a slightly stern quality, "You, me, and Velar will be having dinner together tonight. We have matters to discuss." He didn't wait for my response or acknowledgement, simply turning and exiting the room, leaving me to follow his instructions.

CHAPTER
FOURTEEN

I indulged in a leisurely getting-ready process, scouring my closet for the perfect outfit. Clothes scattered across the floor as I tried on dress after dress, finally settling on a stunning long red velvet number with a daring high slit. I let my hair cascade down my back, adding subtle curls and a touch of makeup to complete the look. Bellamy's patience wore thin as I took my time, his voice booming from downstairs, "Dinner is ready!" The prompt jolted me out of my reverie, and I made my way downstairs, the velvet dress flowing behind me like a crimson river.

As I descended the stairs, Bellamy awaited me with a captivating smile. "You are absolutely stunning, Mrs. Darlington," he said, his sea blue eyes gleaming with admiration. He offered his hand, and I placed mine in it, feeling a spark of electricity as he escorted me towards the back of the house.

We glided past the kitchen, the aroma of dinner wafting through the air, and entered the dining room. Velar rose from his seat, his eyes locking onto mine with a warm smile. "You look beautiful," he said, his voice filled with sincerity. Bellamy pulled out a chair for me, and I sat down, feeling a blush rise to my cheeks as I murmured my gratitude.

I peeked around Velar's broad frame, my eyes scanning the area behind him. Behind him was the 'Singing Butler' painting, its subjects frozen in mid-dance, their faces a blur of joy and mystery. I felt a strange sense of connection. A fleeting moment of happiness suspended in time. As I gazed at the painting briefly, I sensed a deeper meaning hidden beneath its graceful lines.

My hand trembled slightly as I reached for the glass in front of me, taking a sip to stall. Bellamy and Velar seated themselves across from me, their eyes fixed on mine. I darted a glance at Velar, relieved to see his expression had softened since our last encounter. Bellamy, too, seemed in good spirits, his smile reassuring. Emboldened, I finally asked, "What's going on?" I held my breath, awaiting their response.

Bellamy's gaze flicked to Velar, a silent understanding passing between them before he turned back to me. His eyes filled with compassion, he said, "We know you're struggling now that your memories have returned. Velar and I have discussed it, and we want you to know that we're here for you, no matter what."

His words were a reminder that I wasn't alone in this journey. Velar's nod of agreement and the warmth in his eyes reinforced Bellamy's promise, and I felt a small sense of comfort.

Bellamy's words added to my confusion, and I looked at him, then Velar, seeking clarification. Velar said, his excitement restrained, "We don't want to pressure you into making a choice between us. We just want you to let go of your doubts and see what happens naturally." Bellamy shot him a sideways glance, his expression a mix of annoyance and warning. Then, his eyes returned to mine.

Bellamy's hands held mine, his grip warm and reassuring. His eyes locked onto mine, filled with a deep intensity. "You will always be mine," he whispered, his voice trembling with emotion. "I will always be your Daddy, baby girl."

Then, with a visible swallow, he continued, "But if being with Velar is what you truly desire, I will let you go." The sacrifice in his eyes was almost too much to bear, and my heart swelled with love and desire for him.

For a second, I was taken aback, unsure what to make of Bellamy's words. Was he really giving me permission to explore a relationship with Velar? Bellamy's expression remained serious as he said, "We don't want you to feel torn between us, to the point where you feel like running away again." Velar leaned in; his emerald eyes sparkling. He said, "Your life, your happiness, is precious to us. Figuring out what you want, what truly fulfills you, is crucial. And as immortals, we have the luxury of time, unlike mortals, we don't have to force a choice."

As I settled back in my chair, I was struck by the unusual display of vulnerability from these two men, especially seeing them exhibit it together. It dawned on me that they might be fearful of losing me, but I pushed the thought aside. Bellamy's voice brought me back to the moment, "So, what we're saying is that this is your decision. Whatever you desire, we want it too. However, we should establish some rules." Velar's eyes rolled heavenward.

Bellamy loved rules. "What rules?" I asked, intrigued.

Bellamy's eyes gleamed with a hint of excitement, "Well, you must have my permission before... indulging in any activities with Velar. And I must always know your whereabouts...

Oh, and one more thing. No running away." He spoke with a smooth, velvety tone, his British accent sending a thrill through my veins. "So, really, it's nothing you're not already accustomed to, my dear."

I savored a sip of wine, feeling a sense of relief wash over me as I processed their words. I nodded, grateful for their understanding. "Thank you, I feel much better about things."

Bellamy beamed with satisfaction, "Good!" Velar's smile revealed his fangs, and I returned it, feeling a sense of ease with these two men. Just then, Bellamy excused himself, only to return promptly with a pair of plates and a goblet of blood for Velar. The domestic scene was almost surreal, but I enjoyed it.

My stomach growled with anticipation as I gazed at my plate, loaded with a succulent T-bone steak, a generous serving of mashed potatoes, a flaky biscuit, and a side of lima beans. I took a bite of the steak, and it literally melted in my mouth.

The flavors exploded on my taste buds, and I couldn't help but take another bite, eager to experience it again. I had realized I hadn't eaten anything since I ran away to Alaska.

Before swallowing, I added even more to my mouth, and Velar caught my gaze, an amused smile spreading across his face. "Remember to chew," he teased, chuckling. I laughed, my mouth still full, and nodded enthusiastically, the delicious food rendering me speechless.

Bellamy's smile grew wider as he wielded his magic to slice my steak into bite-sized pieces. Velar chimed in, his tone playful, "Come on, Bell, don't spoon-feed her! She needs to learn how to eat like a civilized being."

Bellamy's eyes twinkled with mirth, "Life is a delicate balance of magic and good food." Velar interjected, his voice dripping with arrogance, "And good sex!" Bellamy's smile never wavered, "Agreed." I couldn't help but laugh at their banter.

As we finished our main course, the pièce de résistance arrived, my all-time favorite chocolate crème pie, adorned with a generous dollop of whipped cream. I took a bite, and my eyes closed in rapture as the rich flavors danced on my taste buds.

I was so entranced by the dessert's deliciousness that I didn't even notice the pair of eyes watching me, a smile playing on Velar's lips. It wasn't until I paused, my fork hovering mid-air, that I caught his gaze, and my own smile faltered for a moment before I returned to savoring my treat while I danced in my chair.

The two men wore matching smirks, their eyes sparkling with amusement. I followed their gaze to their plates, and my cheeks flushed as I realized they hadn't even taken a bite yet, while I was already close to finishing mine.

"How is it, baby girl?" Bellamy asked, his smile growing wider. I couldn't help but grin, "It's the most delicious treat I've had in a long time." Velar and Bellamy exchanged a knowing look, their smirks still in place, before they finally began to indulge in their own desserts.

As I savored the last bite of my pie, Velar and Bellamy engrossed themselves in a conversation about an upcoming circus performance. Bellamy noticed my empty plate and gestured, "Baby girl, time to get ready for me, okay?"

But I was reluctant to leave the cozy ambiance and the entrancing companionship that had so thoroughly captivated me. I crossed my arms, pouting like a child, "But, Daddy, I don't wanna go yet!" My voice was laced with a playful whine, hoping to persuade him to let me stay a little longer.

Bellamy's gaze locked onto mine, his eyes serious and unwavering. "Go on darling," he said, his tone firm but gentle. I knew better than to test him, so I reluctantly bid Velar goodnight and began my ascent up the stairs, dragging my feet in a playful show of resistance.

"Good girl," Bellamy called out behind me, his approval sending a warm flutter through my chest. I smiled to myself, feeling a sense of contentment as I reached my bedroom, the soft glow of the lamp casting a cozy ambiance.

On the bed lay a black silky lingerie set, a signal Daddy wanted to see me in the playroom. I felt a thrill of excitement as I changed into the outfit, adjusting it slightly to fit my curves.

After a few jumps I was able to squeeze into the sexy lace outfit. The corset top was a bit snug, revealing my weight gain since returning to the circus. My breasts spilled out of the silk top as I made my way to the playroom, wondering if tonight's session would involve punishment or play.

As Bellamy entered, I cast my eyes down, a sign of respect. He moved behind me, his skilled fingers weaving my hair into a braid. His gentle touch sent shivers down my back, and I felt a deep longing for him. I was eager to please him, to make him proud.

"You'll be a good girl for me tonight, won't you?" he whispered.

"Yes Sir." I replied, my voice barely audible. "Good," he said, his voice low and soothing.

Then he took a blindfold and pulled it over my eyes. Everything is instantly black. Not a shadow, just eerie darkness. I still closed my eyes under the mask listening to Daddy's voice. I heard him undressing and his belt hit the floor. "Open." I opened wide anticipating feeling him on my tongue, but instead it was a blob of spit.

I kept my mouth open, and he slid inside. Gagging me deeper and deeper. I was gagging and gasping for air when finally, he stopped. "Daddy" I whimper. "Good girl," he moaned. It turned me on, hearing him in such pleasure. "Are you ready to be Daddy's slut tonight?" Not a real question, but rather his expectations of me. "Yes," I said anxiously.

I was still wearing the blindfold when he gently escorted me to the bed. He instructed me to lay down with my head hanging off the bed. I obeyed. He slowly started rubbing and lightly fingering me.

Almost teasing me. He was making me incredibly wet by the way he touched me. Bellamy was at my mouth again pushing my lips apart to get inside. I sucked on him nice and slow as he instructed.

I felt a sensation down at my inner thigh and at the same time I felt his hands on my tits tugging on my nipples. He was playing me like an instrument. My mouth was too full, and I tried to move my mouth free. "Relax." He soothed. I instantly relaxed. "Daddy" I moaned, as he fell out of my mouth.

As Bellamy swept the blindfold from my eyes, I was met with a shocking sight. Velar was poised above me, his eyes burning with intensity. I gasped, my gaze darting up to Bellamy, who stood over us, his intense eyes full of arousal. The sudden reveal left me reeling, my mind racing to process the unexpected turn of events.

"Good girl, now spread your legs." I obeyed like a good little wife, eager to please him. I spread myself wide open in front of Velar. His eyes were fixed on me with an unblinking intensity, like a predator sizing up its prey. His expression was primal, his features sharpened by a hunger that seemed to simmer just beneath the surface, leaving me feeling like a tantalizing morsel he was eager to devour.

I felt his fingers glide inside me, and I held my breath. He rested his large self against me and slowly rubbed himself against me, parting his way. Bellamy began slowly kissing me, distracting me from what's happening with Velar. When I felt Bellamy's tongue in my mouth Velar pushed himself deep and slow inside me. My mouth opened in ecstasy.

I had to adjust to his massive size and soon I was enjoying the pleasure. Bellamy stood at my head that was hanging off the bed. He told me to open my mouth again. I obeyed. He pushed his hardness into my mouth, and I sucked him deep. Both men moaned and breathed heavily. Hearing their animalistic groans made me wetter and more aroused.

Moments later the men switched positions and Bellamy was now fucking me and Velar was trying to get inside my mouth. When I didn't open right away, Bellamy commanded, "Open up, baby girl." I obeyed and Velar slid in. Both men were using me, groping me and owning me. Velar held my face and fucked it making me drool and gag all over him. At the same time, Bellamy was fucking me hard and rough.

The two men took their time, enjoying themselves. I orgasmed over and over again until I was about worthless. I was so worn out that I couldn't wait for them to finish. I was sucking Velar on my knees when I felt him grow harder in my mouth. Then I felt a sudden release, a burst of intensity that left him breathless and trembling. I swallowed all of his saltiness. Velar kissed my cheek afterwards in bliss before departing the play-room.

When Velar left the room Bellamy instructed me to stay put. He quickly returned holding a belt. "I'm going to punish you now." I gave him a smile and said, "Yes Daddy." I leaned over the bed and waited. I held my breath as the suspense grew. CRACK! Pain ignited across my bare ass. I arched my back, but Bellamy quickly mounted me and fucked me like a wild animal until he came inside me.

He wrapped his arms around me, his gentle kisses soothing my skin. "I love you, baby girl," he whispered. We cuddled together, basking in the warmth of our embrace. Bellamy reassured me, "Remember, what happened with Velar was ok and it's your choice, and we'll only explore that path again if you so desire it." I nodded, still processing my emotions. While the experience had been pleasurable, I was still uncertain about my feelings. Bellamy's love and adoration filled me, helping me feel safe and cherished.

When it was time to get up, Bellamy walked into the shower with me. Kissing me and holding me. I watched as he stepped out of the shower, wrapping a towel around his waist. He gazed at me with affection, and I expressed my gratitude. "Thank you, Daddy," I said, feeling a deep connection with him. Bellamy's eyes warmed with love, and he replied, "I love you, baby girl, in every way." With a gentle smile, he turned and walked out, leaving me to shower in peace.

CHAPTER
FIFTEEN

It's been a while since our salacious night together, and no one, including me has yet to mention it. Instead, we've been focusing on our shared passion for the circus, with me thriving in my role as an aerialist and Bellamy supporting me every step of the way. Our connection has only grown stronger, built on mutual respect, trust, and a deepening friendship.

Just a few days after my brief trip to Barrow, the four of us, Bellamy, Velar, and our Eve and I, decided to add an extra show to our schedule. I was initially hesitant, knowing how hard everyone already worked each day, but to my surprise, the performers and crew were eager to take on the challenge. The excitement was vibrant as we brainstormed ideas for the new show.

Darlington Circus was renowned for its exceptional talent, and our performers, the best in the world, relished the opportunity to push the boundaries of their craft and maintain our top-notch reputation.

Velar and I started each morning with an invigorating work-out together, followed by aerial training sessions that pushed me to new heights. Once he was satisfied with my progress, he'd hand me over to Bellamy for further training.

I was learning so much and loving every minute of it. With each passing day, I felt more at home in the circus, surrounded by people who had become my family.

Lucca's horse-riding act has been a crowd favorite, but I'm fiercely protective of him and limit his performances to just one or two shows a day. The circus is thriving, and we jump town to town, sometimes staying longer if the audience is particularly enthusiastic.

Bellamy expertly determines our schedule, ensuring we strike the perfect balance between work and rest. Meanwhile, Lucca has formed a special bond with the bally girls, often spending his evenings with them in Jubilees town square.

One evening, Bellamy was preparing for a late-night performance with Eve, so Velar and I decided to have dinner at his place. Of course, I asked for Bellamy's permission first. As we sat in his cozy home, I couldn't help but compare it to his house in Alaska.

After admiring the warm decor of the dining room, I turned my attention to Velar, who was gazing at me with an intensity that made my heart skip a beat. His piercing eyes seemed to see right through me.

Velar's unassuming nature belied a depth that I couldn't quite grasp. Despite his rugged appearance, he carried himself with a quiet confidence that made me feel like a vulnerable young girl in his presence. Sometimes, his piercing gaze and authoritative demeanor left me feeling intimidated, but also with a thrill of excitement. His brand of dominance was distinct from Bellamy's, not necessarily more powerful, but it was as if he possessed a quiet ownership of me, a claim that resonated deep within my soul.

I blurted out the question, catching Velar off guard. "So, what did you think of our threesome?" His gaze locked onto mine, and for a moment, he was frozen in time. Then, a sly grin spread across his face, revealing his fangs. "It was rather lovely," he said, his tone dripping with pleasure.

I pressed on, my curiosity getting the better of me. "Whose idea, was it?" I already knew the answer, but I wanted to hear him say it. "Bells," he replied, his eyes glinting with amusement. Of course it was. Horny scoundrel. "And why did you agree to it?" I asked, as his gaze raked over me. "Do you think I could say no?" Velar's eyes seemed to bore into my soul, as if daring me to challenge him further.

Velar's eyes narrowed, his gaze piercing mine. "I almost took you in Alaska," he revealed, his voice low and smooth, like honey. My eyes widened in shock, my mind reeling with the implications. "Really?" I asked, excitedly. Velar's nod was almost imperceptible.

"I just had to ask Bell first," he said, his eyes locked onto mine with an unspoken message. The air was thick with tension as he seemed to be conveying a secret. His gaze burned with an intensity that left me breathless.

Velar's voice dropped to a whisper; his words laced with a hint of vulnerability. "When you died last time, Bellamy and I... we clashed. My grief and anger consumed me, and I directed it all at him. I was consumed by a fierce desire to see him suffer, to make him pay for the pain he had caused me. If only he could feel the sting of mortality, I thought, he wouldn't be standing here today."

His gaze fell, his eyes fixed on his hands as if they held a secret. I leaned in, my heart pounding in anticipation. "I promised him I'd never let that happen again," he continued, his emerald eyes snapping back to mine, piercing my very soul. "Do you understand?" The weight of his words hung in the air, and I nodded, my throat too dry to speak.

Bellamy and Velar's relationship was a longstanding one, predating my connection with either of them. They were more than just business partners, running the circus together like two sides of the same coin. Their bond was fraternal, built on a foundation of trust and respect that only comes from weathering life's storms together.

Both alpha males, they'd had their share of fiery disagreements, but their mutual respect always prevailed. It was clear that they were intertwined in a way that made it impossible for one to exist without the other for too long.

After dinner, Velar accompanied me home, his goodnight kiss leaving a lingering sense of warmth. It felt like a natural culmination of our evening together. I stayed up, awaiting Bellamy's return, and when he finally arrived, he looked more fatigued than usual. 'How was your night?' he asked, his eyes searching mine. I shared the details of my dinner with Velar, and Bellamy's face softened into a gentle smile. "I'm happy you're happy," he said, his voice filled with sincerity. And in that moment, I truly was.

As I descended from the aerial rig, exhausted but exhilarated from the show, I made my way back to Jubilee. Suddenly, a guest approached me. He was an older man with dark hair, dressed in jeans and a blue shirt. Initially, he seemed kind, his eyes fixated on me as he complimented my black sequin costume. I smiled, thanked him, and tried to continue on my way, but his grip on my arm stopped me short. His grasp was firm, his fingers digging into my skin.

Every hair on my arm stood on end as his grip tightened. Fear coursed through my veins like ice water. I tried to shake him off, but his grasp only hardened. I turned to face him, my heart racing, and he demanded, "Where is the traveling trailer?"

His eyes seemed to bore into mine, as if searching for a secret. I knew I had to tread carefully; Darlington's magic was not something to be shared with outsiders. I forced a calm tone, hoping to deflect his suspicion, "Oh, we park them in a secure area, away from the circus grounds." My voice barely hid the tremble within.

"Show me," he growled, his voice sending shivers down my spine. My instincts screamed at me to flee, but I forced a calm smile and said, "Unfortunately, I can't do that. Enjoy the rest of your time here at the circus." I turned to leave, but my heart sank as I felt his eyes on me, following me. I quickened my pace, my senses on high alert. I dared not lead him to the willow tree. I had to lose him in the crowd, but his footsteps echoed mine.

I slipped under the roped fence, entering the restricted backyard area, and made my way to Clown Alley. The silence was a stark contrast to the lively atmosphere out front. I settled onto a trunk overflowing with colorful costumes, taking a moment to catch my breath. The mirrors lining the walls reflected my exhausted expression. Just as I began to relax, the tent flap behind me burst open with a sudden jolt. I spun around to face the intruder, and my heart sank. The strange man in the blue shirt stood in the entrance, his eyes fixed intently on me, his presence seeming to fill the entire space.

I sprang to my feet, my heart racing like a drum. "Excuse me, but this area is restricted to circus members only," I declared, trying to sound braver than I felt. But the stranger didn't seem to hear me, his eyes fixed on me with an unblinking gaze. "There you are, pretty lady," he drawled, his voice dripping creepy. He advanced towards me with a slow and deliberate pace. I felt like a trapped animal, my breath caught in my throat as he closed in on me.

"Sir, you need to leave," I tried to sound firm, but my voice trembled with fear. My legs felt like lead, refusing to move. "How much for a night with you?" he sneered, his eyes roaming over me like a predator.

"What?" I asked, confusion and outrage wrestling for dominance. "You must be a prostitute; how much are you worth for the evening?" His words were like a slap in the face. My face flamed with anger. "No, I'm not!" I yelled; my fists clenched at my sides. I wanted to strike him, to erase the vile suggestion from his twisted mind.

The stranger's smile grew wider as he closed in on me. "You are free then," he sneered. Before I could react, he pounced, pinning me against the costume cage. I struggled to break free, but his grip was strong for a mortal man. In desperation, I reached for the nearby makeup box and hurled it at him.

The box burst open, sending colorful contents flying, but the stranger didn't flinch. He seized my arms, holding them captive. His body pressed against mine, making my skin crawl. He leaned in, his hot breath on my face, and I tried pushing away. "What do you say, pretty lady?" His lips inches from mine, ready to claim a kiss.

I squeezed my eyes shut, desperate to escape the stranger's clutches, and jerked my head away from his vile breath. The next instant, a blood-curdling scream filled the air. I opened my eyes to see the creepy man flying across the room, hurled by an unseen force.

Velar stood tall, his eyes blazing with fury, his magic crackling with energy. The stranger crashed to the ground, dazed and helpless. Before he could even attempt to rise, two burly guards appeared, pinning him down and dragging him away from Darlington Circus, banishing him forever.

Velar grasped my hand, pulling me up from the ground. I trembled, still reeling from the unexpected assault. "Are you okay?" he asked with concern. I nodded, trying to appear braver than I felt, but the truth was, I was far from okay. Velar escorted me back to Jubilee, where I remained trying to process the trauma.

I'm still unsure why that incident left such a lasting impact on me, but perhaps it was a stark reminder of my own mortality. As a human, I'm vulnerable to harm and death, and the recent news headlines only serve to drive that point home. It seems like every day, people are losing their lives over trivial matters, and that realization is both haunting and humbling. The fragility of life is a daunting truth to confront, and I can't help but wonder if I'll ever feel truly safe again.

Growing up in this life, the news was dominated by tragic stories of school shootings and senseless acts of violence, like road rage incidents ending in gunfire. It's heartbreaking to see the world descend into such chaos and brutality.

I recall a time when people showed empathy and kindness towards one another, but that seems like a distant memory, lost in the pre-technology era. Those simpler, more compassionate days are now a nostalgic relic of the past, and it's disconcerting to see how far we've strayed from that sense of community and humanity.

One morning, I woke up to find Bellamy pacing back and forth across our bedroom, his eyes fixed on something in the closet. As I sat up, he pulled out an old suitcase, its worn leather and faded labels showing our countless adventures past. "What's going on?" I asked, my voice still filled with sleep.

Bellamy's face lit up with a warm smile as he approached me. "Baby girl, you've been cooped up in Jubilee for three weeks now. Everyone's worried about you, and I think it's time we got away from it all. Just the two of us. A little escape, a little romance... what do you say?"

His eyes were hopeful, and I couldn't help but feel a thrill of anticipation at the prospect of a secret getaway with the man I loved. I hesitated, trying to sound more convincing than I felt, "Oh, thank you. This is just what I need." Truthfully, I'd been stuck in a rut. Bellamy's suggestion sparked a glimmer of hope. "But what about the Circus?" I asked, my mind racing with logistics like a ringmaster juggling too many balls. "Who'll keep the show going?"

Bellamy paused, his packing momentarily forgotten, and sat beside me on the bed. As he smiled, "My love, I've got it all under control. The Circus will be tucked away in a forest, and everyone will get a well-deserved break. You just focus on yourself for now. Let me handle the rest." He reassured me with a gentle touch on my hand, his fingers intertwining with mine like the threads of a tapestry.

As he resumed packing, I couldn't help but wonder, "Well, what about Lucca?' Bellamy's response was swift and effortless, like a skilled acrobat landing a tricky somersault. "Miss Poppet will keep a watchful eye on him, darling. She'll make sure he's safe and sound." My excitement began to build, and I playfully replied, "Ok, no more questions, Daddy." Bellamy chuckled, his eyes twinkling with amusement.

Later that afternoon, when the bustle of Jubilee had subsided, Bellamy grasped my hand, and with a mischievous glint in his eye, he jumped us into the heart of a dense forest somewhere I didn't know.

Mesidor, ever the gentleman, offered us the use of his cheval glass, but Bellamy just winked and said, "Not this time, my friend. We're taking to the skies!" I was perplexed, but my curiosity was piqued. "An airplane?" I questioned. Bellamy nodded, his smile growing wider. "Are you ready Mrs. Darlington?" I couldn't help but jump with excitement as I replied, "Yes, I'm ready!"

As we emerged from Jubilee, our suitcases in hand. We made our way through the empty circus and approached the front gate. Velar escorted us out, his eyes shining with a warm smile. He scooped me in a gentle hug, his lips brushing against my cheek in a soft kiss. "Don't worry, Bell," he whispered, "I'll keep everything under control."

Bellamy nodded in appreciation, his eyes locking onto Velar's in a silent understanding. "See you in two weeks," he said, his voice reassuring. With that, we stepped out into the forest as we embarked on our adventure.

As we wandered deeper into the forest, I found myself awestruck by the towering trees that surrounded us. Their trunks were as wide as houses, their canopies a vibrant green umbrella that filtered the sunlight. I craned my neck, my eyes glued to the sky, trying to take in the sheer scale of these natural wonders. "Redwoods," Bellamy whispered, his voice full of reverence, as he followed my gaze. "They are indeed magnificent."

His smile grew, his eyes full of delight, as he watched me drink in the beauty of these ancient giants. We bid farewell to a few fellow performers, also escaping the circus for a brief respite, their faces fading into the distance as we ventured further into the forest's embrace.

With Bellamy's arm wrapped around me and our suitcases securely in hand, I felt a thrill of excitement as he raised his magical staff to the sky. The air around us began to shimmer and glow, and before I knew it, we were lifting off the ground!

We didn't soar to dizzying heights, but just enough to clear the underbrush, and then we began to move at a breathtaking pace. The wind rushed past us, whipping my hair into a frenzy as the trees blurred together in a green and brown haze. For a moment, I closed my eyes, my heart racing with a mix of fear and exhilaration. As I opened them again, I saw the wonder in Bellamy's eyes, his face alight with a mischievous grin, and I knew I was safe in his care.

Before long, we reached a winding road, where a sleek black car awaited us, its driver standing at attention. We slipped into the soft interior, and the vehicle glided smoothly through the mountains, the scenery unfolding like a breathtaking canvas. I succumbed to the comfort and fell asleep, only to be gently roused when we arrived at the airport. As we pulled up to a luxurious private jet on the tarmac,

I remembered Bellamy's penchant for exclusivity. "Good morning," he said with a smile, as I sat up, rubbing the sleep from my eyes. "Do you want to know where we're headed?" "Yes, please!" I replied, my voice carrying over the hum of the engines. Bellamy's eyes twinkled and I knew that our destination was going to be somewhere truly extraordinary.

As we ascended the jet plane's stairs, Bellamy revealed our destination with grandeur, "The Irati Forest in Spain, my love. We'll be staying in a secluded cabin, deep in the woods." I was surprised to say the least. The Irati Forest was more than just a place, it was the fabled source of Bellamy's magic, the very place where he got his immortality and power. He had spoken of it a long time ago, calling it the "king of all forests."

I wondered if this was his first return to this sacred place since his transformation centuries ago. The prospect of exploring this enchanted realm alongside him was thrilling. With a sense of awe and curiosity, I followed closely behind my husband, eager to embark on this remarkable adventure.

As I stepped into the sleek jet, Bellamy greeted me with a champagne flute, its delicate bubbles sparkling in the light. "Thank you," I said, feeling like a queen. Bellamy knew me better than I knew myself, understanding the depths of my soul.

He had orchestrated this dream vacation with precision, tailoring every detail to my desires. The mountains, hiking, bonfires, and s'mores – all my favorite things, carefully woven into an unforgettable experience. I felt seen, loved, and pampered, surrounded by the opulence of the jet and the thoughtfulness of his gestures. As we soared into the skies, I knew this journey would be a treasured memory, crafted with love and care by the one who knew me best.

As we touched down in Donostia, we collected our sleek, sporty convertible, and Bellamy took the wheel. The wind whipped through my hair as we cruised through the picturesque countryside, the top down and the heat on, allowing me to bask in the breathtaking views.

Rolling hills, emerald forests, and charming villages unfolded like a masterpiece of nature and art. I felt carefree and exhilarated, my hair flying in the wind, as I gazed out at the stunning scenery. He smiled, clearly delighted to see me so happy. Leaving the circus behind, I felt a sense of liberation wash over me. The rush of the wind, the sun on my face, and Bellamy's joyful energy all combined to create an unforgettable experience.

After we parked the convertible, he retrieved his sleek, black staff, its shiny surface reflecting the dappled forest light. "We need to venture deep into the woods," he said. "Rather than hiking, we'll take to the skies once more." I nodded eagerly, my heart racing with anticipation. Bellamy surveyed our surroundings, his gaze darting back and forth, ensuring we were alone. Satisfied, he raised his staff to the sky, and its tip began to glow with a soft, ethereal light. We lifted off the ground, hovering momentarily before soaring through the trees, the wind rushing past us in a gentle whisper. The forest floor below grew distant, and the canopy above became a vibrant green blur as we flew deeper into the Irati Forest.

His face was shining with a carefree spark. He revels in the thrill of flight, but rarely gets to indulge in this pleasure. Even in Jubilee, it's a rare treat for him. I couldn't help but smile at his uncontained happiness, my heart soaring alongside his.

The crisp air invigorated my senses, and I embraced the rush of the wind on my face. As we flew over the forest floor, a herd of deer grazed peacefully below, their large eyes gazing up at us in wonder. Suddenly, they sprang into action, bounding away with graceful leaps as we soared directly above them, our shadow fleeting across the forest floor like a whisper.

As he gently guided us down to a secluded clearing, my tense body relaxed, grateful to be back on solid ground. "I think this is the perfect spot," he declared, his eyes twinkling with enthusiasm. I gazed around at the lush, vibrant forest, the trees stretching out as far as the eye could see. "This is where our cabin shall be," he announced. Then it dawned on me, Bellamy was going to conjure our cabin into existence with his magic!

I settled into a comfortable nook atop a gnarled tree root, feeling the subtle hum of the forest's energy beneath me. The vibrations soothed my senses, calming my mind and transporting me to a state of serenity. From this enchanted perch, I witnessed Bellamy's mastery of magic unfold. With graceful gestures and whispered incantations, he coaxed the trees and wood to conform to his vision.

The trees seemed to shift and rearrange themselves, their branches weaving together to form the framework of our cozy cabin. The cabin began to take shape, its walls and roof blending seamlessly into the surrounding foliage.

The camouflage was so convincing that even from mere feet away, the cabin seemed to disappear into the forest's embrace. When Bellamy's arms finally fell to his sides, signaling the completion of his handiwork, I couldn't contain my excitement. "It's amazing!" I Shouted.

I approached Bellamy, who was beaming with pride, though slightly winded from his magical exertions. I couldn't contain my eagerness to explore our new hideaway. With a nod, he granted me permission to venture inside.

I pushed open the sturdy, dark green door and stepped into a snug, welcoming space. The small room was furnished with a charming table and two chairs, perfect for intimate moments. To the right, a cozy kitchen beckoned, complete with a crackling fireplace that sprang to life as I entered, just like Casmira's magical flames. The cabin's rustic charm and my husband's thoughtful touches made me feel grateful for this enchanted retreat.

As the evening chill began to settle over the woods, I reveled in the cozy warmth of our cabin retreat. The soft glow of the fireplace and the gentle crackle of the flames created a soothing ambiance, a perfect respite from the crisp night air.

I wandered to the back of the cabin, discovering a plush king- size bed, invitingly adorned with soft linens and a fluffy duvet. A sleek half indoor half outdoor bathroom beckoned to the left, its modern amenities a delightful surprise in this rustic haven.

After exploring every nook and cranny, I made my way back to the kitchen, where Bellamy awaited me with a warm smile, his eyes sparkling with satisfaction. The scent of freshly brewed tea or coffee wafted through the air, enticing me to sit and stay a while, basking in the comfort and tranquility of our enchanted cabin.

I embraced Bellamy, my arms wrapping tightly around him. "It's beautiful," I whispered, my voice filled with emotion. "Will this do for a couple weeks, baby girl?" he asked, his eyes knowing. "It's perfect," I replied.

Bellamy's lips met mine in a long, slow kiss, his passion and love pouring into me. I knew what he desired, and I was eager to surrender to his embrace. With a gentle sweep of his arms, he lifted me up and carried me to the bed, laying me down with tender care. His fingers traced the curves of my body as he undressed me, his touch igniting a fire within me. The cabin's warmth and coziness melted away, leaving only the two of us, lost in our own little world of love and desires.

As I stood naked Bellamy eyed me up and down, examining his property. I watched as he took his clothes off slowly. His body, ever so masculine, sexy and firm. He mounted me and started kissing my lips. Then he moved to my neck and kissed all the way down to my breast. Then he sucked on my nipples, taking his time with each breast.

Just as he was about to claim me fully, a sudden noise outside the cabin caught our attention. We froze, our bodies tense, our eyes locked on the door. We held our breath, waiting for the sound to repeat itself, but the silence was deafening. He cautiously approached the window, his movements stealthy, and peered out into the darkness.

He scanned the surroundings, his eyes searching for any sign of movement, but there was nothing. "It's probably just an animal," he whispered, his voice reassuring. Yet, the momentary distraction had only heightened our passion. Bellamy returned to me, and we resumed our intimate embrace, our passion reignited.

About ninety minutes later, he and I lay entwined in the cabin bed, our naked bodies still basking in the warmth of our love. As I attempted to rise, his gentle grasp on my waist pulled me back, his soft command to stay. I snuggled deeper into his embrace, my body molding to his, and let out a contented sigh.

After a few blissful minutes, a tap on my arm signaled my release. I pressed a tender kiss to his cheek and rolled out of bed. A quick refreshing cleanse in the bathroom, and my growling stomach reminded me it was time to eat. The promise of a warm meal and a cozy evening by the fireplace beckoned me, and I couldn't wait to indulge.

As I opened the food storage suitcase, the aroma of dried herbs and spices wafted out, teasing my senses. I pulled out a packet of dehydrated stew, labeled for two servings, and a sturdy cast iron pot that had been cleverly stored alongside it. I hung the pot from a hook over the crackling fire.

As the water inside began to boil, I added the contents of the packet, the mixture of dried vegetables, meat, and seasonings swirling into the pot like a savory storm. A quick stir with a wooden spoon, and the stew was left to simmer, its tantalizing aroma filling the cabin, making my stomach growl with hunger.

Just as I was stirring the stew, Bellamy emerged from the cozy nook of our cabin, his eyes sparkling with hunger. I couldn't help but smile, knowing he must be famished after exerting his magical energies throughout the day.

As we sat down at the intimate table, I turned to him with a curious gaze. "Can you tell me again how you came to possess your magic. I recall it happening here, in these very woods, but the details have grown fuzzy in my mind." My eyes locked onto his, eager to hear the story once more, and perhaps uncover new secrets hidden within his enchanting past.

His gaze drifted, his eyes clouding like the forest mist that shrouded the trees outside. He toyed with his spoon, his fingers tracing the wooden grain as if searching for a hidden truth. The silence between us grew thick, before he finally laid the spoon to rest on the table with a soft clink. "It was a time of grandeur and darkness, the late sixteens hundreds, during the Medieval Era," he began, his voice low. "My brother Hugh and I, we were traversing the rugged terrain of Spain, trekking through this very forest, when fate struck. A poisonous snake sank its fangs into Hugh's flesh, and... everything changed."

Bellamy's gaze dropped, his eyes veiling the anguish that still lingered within. I had forgotten that he once had a brother, a mortal life, before his transformation. It was hard to fathom that the man before me, with his ageless beauty and timeless strength, was once vulnerable and human.

His centuries-long life had somehow preserved his youth, leaving him with an eternal appearance that belied his true age. My mind wandered to Velar, whose weathered face and graying hair spoke of a life well-lived, yet seemed to pale in comparison to Bellamy's enduring vitality. The contrast was striking, a constant reminder of the mysterious forces that had shaped their lives.

As Bellamy's voice pierced the silence, I snapped back to attention, my mind refocusing on the tale unfolding before me. His eyes clouded with deep sorrow, as he continued, "I tried to save Hugh, to suck out the venom, but it was too late. I screamed for help, but we were alone, surrounded by nothing but trees and desperation. Hugh's eyes grew heavy, his consciousness slipping away, and I knew we were doomed."

His voice cracked, but his eyes remained dry. "Then, like a miracle, or a curse, we were surrounded by strangers. Thirteen women, their faces aglow with an otherworldly light, appeared out of the darkness. I begged them to save my brother, and they brought us to their sacred place, a cave in Zugarramurdi."

I hung on to his every word, my heart aching in empathy. He spoke with a quiet intensity, as if the memories still haunted him. "The witches tried everything, their chants and incantations filling the cave, but it was too late.

Hugh's life slipped away, and I was left holding his cold, still body. I wept uncontrollably, consumed by grief, when one of the witches approached me. She spoke with a gentle sorrow, apologizing for their failure to save my brother. And then, in a gesture of guilt and compassion, the entire coven decided to bestow upon me a gift... a gift that would change the course of my existence forever."

I was transfixed on him. He hesitated, as if the memories still pained him, before continuing, 'I was bewildered, unsure what to make of their words, but before I could process, the witches encircled me, their chanting growing louder, more urgent. It was as if the very fabric of reality was shifting.

And then, in the blink of an eye, I felt it. The surge of magic coursing through my veins! The witches' instructions were hasty, yet stern: hide your power, beware its cost. Little did I know, that was only the beginning. Years passed before I discovered the truth - I was immortal. My body never aged since that day. Whether by design or accident, the witches' gift had forever altered my fate."

Bellamy's voice trailed off, and I couldn't help but wonder if he still desired the gift of immortality. I quickly pushed it aside. He resumed, his tone was of gratitude and incredulity, "Those witches, in their compassion, bestowed upon me a portion of their power. Why would they do such a thing? It seems almost absurd, even to this day." He shook his head, as if still grappling with the magnitude of their generosity. "And yet, their kindness didn't stop there. They aided me in retrieving Hugh's body, ensuring he received a proper farewell, a dignified burial, and a chance for our family to find closure."

I reached out, my hand bridging the gap between us, and Bellamy's fingers intertwined with mine, a gentle grasp that conveyed a deep understanding. His eyes full of memories of the past swirling in their depths, as he continued, "I never had the chance to thank them, and it wasn't until the Spanish witch trials in sixteen-ten that I realized the true extent of their sacrifice. Those innocent women, crucified for their gifts... It was a harsh reminder of the dangers of being different.

I hid my magic for many years, afraid of suffering the same fate." His head shook. I felt a pang of sorrow, my heart aching for the burdens he had carried for so long. And in that moment, I wondered if the weight of his immortality had become too much to bear, if the accumulation of centuries had left him weary of living.

The question lingered in my mind, unspoken, as I gazed at Bellamy, my heart heavy with the weight of possibility. *What if the reincarnation spell were to break, and fate were to tear us apart?*

I couldn't bear the idea of losing him, of never knowing him. The same fear extended to the others, Velar, and the rest, what if I never saw them again? The uncertainty gnawed at me, a constant reminder of the fragility of our connections and the transience of life.

After dinner, Bellamy's eyes gleamed with mischief as he announced, "I have a surprise for you!" My mind was still reeling from the emotional rollercoaster of the past few hours, so I couldn't quite muster the same level of enthusiasm. I raised an eyebrow and playfully rolled my eyes, "Oh boy, this should be good..." He just chuckled and waited patiently for me to close my eyes. As soon as I did, he swiftly tied a blindfold over my eyes, plunging me into darkness. My curiosity piqued; I wondered what he had in store for me now...

Before I could utter a word, a strange, tingling sensation washed over me, like a gentle, electric caress. It was as if my entire body was humming, every cell alive and vibrating. The sensation lingered for a few tantalizing seconds, leaving me tingling. And then, with a gentle tug, Bellamy removed the blindfold, revealing a sight that left me laughing out loud.

I stood there, wearing a tiny black thong bikini, utterly bewildered. "What in the world...?! It's freezing outside!" I protested, trying to cover myself with my hands. But he just burst out laughing, clearly enjoying the view. I pouted, trying to sound as indignant as possible,

"Daddy!" But he just chuckled, "Ah, baby girl, I thought our little adventure wouldn't be complete without a relaxing soak in the hot tub. He winked, looking mischievous, leaving me blushing and laughing despite myself.

I watched as Bellamy pulled open the curtains in the back of the cabin. Snow fell as I peered out through the window and saw a bubbling hot tub. "Oh my God!" I yelled and excitedly jumped up and down. Bellamy watched as my tits bounced and asked, "Can you do that again?" I jumped again for his pleasure and my excitement.

I sprinted out into the snowy night, my bare feet sinking into the cold powder, as Bellamy gave chase, laughing and hurling small snowballs in my direction. The icy crystals stung my skin, but I didn't let that deter me, I was too caught up in the joy of the moment. By the time we reached the hot tub, my feet were numb and protesting, but as soon as I immersed them in the warm water, they began to tingle and sting.

I yelped in surprise, but Bellamy quickly scooped up my feet in his hands. His fingers began to glow with a soft, golden light, and a strange, tingling sensation spread through my feet, as if they were being infused with magic. I couldn't help but laugh at the peculiar tickling feeling, and in mere seconds, my feet were healed, warm, and toasty once more. Bellamy's eyes twinkled with mischief as he smiled, "All better, my love?"

As we soaked in the hot tub, the gentle snowfall above us created a mesmerizing spectacle, each flake vanishing into the steaming water like a fleeting whisper. The snowfall gradually tapered off, leaving behind a peaceful stillness. I settled into Bellamy's embrace, sitting on his lap as he wrapped his arms around me, the warm water felt like a soothing embrace.

The tension in my body melted away, replaced by a deep sense of relaxation and contentment. "I could live here," I sighed as I nestled deeper into his embrace. The warmth, the tranquility, and the sense of being cocooned in this magical moment with Bellamy made me feel like I had found a little slice of heaven on earth.

As we lounged in the hot tub, sipping our wine and enjoying the peaceful night, we eventually found ourselves facing a dire situation. An empty wine bottle! Bellamy and I engaged in a playful standoff, each trying to convince the other to brave the freezing snow and dash back to the cabin for another bottle. But Bellamy, with a sly grin, refused to use his magic, instead reveling in the prospect of watching me make a mad dash through the snow.

I hesitated, knowing the cold would be biting, but the wine had loosened my inhibitions, and I couldn't resist the challenge. With a playful shriek, I leapt out of the hot tub and sprinted towards the cabin, the snow crunching beneath my feet. Bellamy's laughter echoed through the night, and I couldn't help but laugh too, feeling carefree and joyful in the midst of our silly game.

In a moment of drunken bravery, I declared, "I'll be right back!" and took off running into the snowy night, leaving a trail of steam behind me like a tipsy superhero. Bellamy's laughter and 'Hurry back!' echoed through the darkness as I stumbled into the warm cabin, only to realize I had completely forgotten my mission.

I wandered around, trying to shake off the fog, until my eyes landed on a tantalizing box of chocolates on the counter. My stomach growled in protest, and suddenly, it all came flooding back, I had come for food! Grabbing a handful of chocolates, I made a beeline for the hot tub, not wanting to spend another second in the cold. I emerged back into the night.

I hastily returned to the hot tub, chocolates in hand, and presented them to Bellamy with a flourish, as if to say, "Ta-da! Mission accomplished!" He received them with a charming smile, but as I quickly submerged myself in the warm water to thaw out, I noticed he was gazing at me expectantly.

When I resurfaced, he asked, his eyes sparkling with mischief, 'Where's the wine?' I laughed, realizing my drunken mistake, and replied, "Uh, I forgot it." Bellamy chuckled, and teased, "Well, I suppose you'll just have to go back for it... again!" I playfully rolled my eyes.

I burst into laughter, and Bellamy, caught off guard by my infectious giggles, joined in. We laughed together, our bellies shaking, tears streaming down our faces, for a full five minutes. It was as if our laughter had taken on a life of its own, filling the night air with pure joy.

And then, without even needing to ask, Bellamy waved his hand, and a bottle of wine magically appeared before us, floating through the air like a tiny, winged messenger. We laughed even harder at the absurdity of it all, and I raised the bottle in a toast, "To forgetfulness, and magic, and the joy of being with you!"

As the evening wore on, I settled into the warm water, straddling Bellamy's lap, our bodies swaying gently in the hot tub's embrace. I gazed deep into his piercing blue eyes, like shimmering sapphires reflecting the moonlight, and felt my heart flutter.

His lips met mine in a tender, loving kiss, our gazes locked in a sweet, intimate moment.

The world around us melted away, leaving only the two of us, lost in the depths of each other's eyes. I began to hum softly, a Robert Frost poem. I sang to my husband, my love, my soul-mate. The music seemed to dance on the steam rising from the water, weaving a spell of passion and devotion around us.

"Whose woods these are I think I know.
His house is in the village though.
He will not see me stopping here.
To watch his woods, fill up with snow."

"My little horse must think it queer.
To stop without a farmhouse near
Between the woods and frozen lake
The darkest evening of the year."

"He gives his harness bells a shake.
To ask if there is some mistake.
The only other sound's the sweep
Of easy wind and downy flake."

"The woods are lovely, dark and deep,
But I have promises to keep,
And miles to go before I sleep,
And miles to go before I sleep."

CHAPTER

SIXTEEN

The next morning, Bellamy and I embarked on a hike through the enchanting woods, breathing in the invigorating air. The snow from the previous day blanketed the forest floor creating a scene from a fairytale. The gray sky hinted at an impending snowfall. Before we set out, I laced up my boots and zipped my coat up on the cabin porch, preparing for our adventure.

The haze of my hangover lingered; Bellamy conjured up a mysterious elixir to soothe my throbbing head. He stepped out of the cabin, looking refreshed and revitalized, his eyes full of playfulness. I flashed him a radiant smile.

"Ready, Daddy?" I asked, my voice tinged with excitement. The great outdoors beckoned, and I was eager to immerse myself in its wonders. Bellamy, ever the enigmatic ringmaster, replied with a sly smile, "Oh yes, baby girl."

I playfully scooped up a handful of snow and began shaping it into a snowball. Bellamy, anticipating my mischievous intentions, quickly followed suit. "Are you sure you want to play?" he asked, amusement dancing in his eyes. I tossed the snowball at him, but he dodged it with ease, and it grazed his side instead.

Undeterred, Bellamy retaliated with a swift throw, catching me off guard. The snowball slammed into my backside, sending me tumbling forward into the soft, powdery snow. "Daddy!" I yelped, laughing. Bellamy chuckled, his grin mischievous, as he helped me up from the snow. "Okay, okay, I don't want to play anymore!" I pouted. His smile grew wider as he turned to lead the way, muttering under his breath, "I didn't think so."

After a couple of hours of hiking, we arrived at the river's edge, just as the snowflakes began to fall gently around us. Bellamy busied himself refilling our water bottles, while I took a moment to rest and soak in the breathtaking scenery of the forest.

The snow-covered trees sparkled like diamonds, transforming the landscape into a serene winter wonderland. The forest, now cloaked in white, resembled a masterpiece painting, its beauty so captivating that I couldn't help but pause and admire the tranquil scene.

A soft, mysterious hum suddenly resonated through the air, making me jump. I spun around, scanning my surroundings, but the sound seemed to be coming from within me.

Perplexed, I unzipped my coat and searched every nook and cranny, but the hum persisted. It wasn't until I slipped my hand into a hidden pocket of my jacket that I discovered the source. It was the necklace Velar had given me. I was taken aback, knowing I hadn't packed it. I quickly realized Velar must have secretly placed it in my coat during our farewell. *Sneaky Bastard*.

I stood frozen in shock, the necklace still clutched in my hand, as it emitted a soft hum, and the locket began to radiate a gentle glow. This was strange, the necklace had never made a sound or glowed before.

Without hesitation, I put it on, and as soon as the clasp clicked into place, a holographic projection of Velar materialized before me. I could see him clearly, yet simultaneously, I could see through him, as if he was a ghostly apparition.

"What is this?" I muttered. "You're in danger, now!" Velar's hologram exclaimed, his voice urgent and panicked. I instinctively glanced towards Bellamy, who was now approaching me with a concerned expression. Alarmed, I quickly removed the necklace, and Velar's projection vanished into thin air.

When Bellamy reached me, he immediately sensed something was amiss, his eyes narrowing at the pale terror etched on my face. "What's wrong?" he demanded, swiftly scanning our surroundings for potential threats. I struggled to articulate the words, my voice trembling as I held up the necklace. "Velar...he said we're in danger."

Bellamy's expression turned grim, and in a flash, he produced his staff, expanding it with a swift motion. He swept me into his arms, and we hurtled through the trees at a high speed, the ground below blurring into a black and white smear. I couldn't begin to explain the eerie apparition of Velar, but Bellamy's urgent actions spoke volumes - we were in grave peril, and every second counted.

I clung to Bellamy with a desperation I'd never felt before, my arms wrapped tightly around him as we hurtled through the forest. When we finally slowed to a stop, I scanned our surroundings, searching for any sign of the danger Velar had warned us about. The snowy forest seemed tranquil, devoid of any threat. I wondered what could possibly be amiss, we were alone, and no one knew our location. Yet, Bellamy's urgent manner suggested otherwise.

As we burst into the cabin, he quickly seated me in a chair and pressed a glass of water into my hands. "What did Velar say?" he demanded, his eyes piercing with concern. His usual calm demeanor had given way to worry, and I felt scared. I began to recount the message, but before I could finish, a sudden noise outside the cabin made us both freeze, our hearts pounding in unison.

We sat in silence, our ears strained, waiting for a response to Bellamy's authoritative call, "Who's there?" But the stillness was oppressive, punctuated only by the flickering of the lights, which danced like fireflies before suddenly extinguishing altogether. The darkness was absolute, except for the lone candle on the nightstand, its flame casting eerie shadows on the walls.

I gripped Bellamy's arm, my heart racing, as the room plummeted into an unsettling chill. The air was heavy with the acrid scent of sulfur, making my stomach roil. And then, the final candle's gentle flame was snuffed out, plunging us into total darkness. I couldn't contain my terror, and a scream tore from my throat, echoing through the blackness.

Bellamy rose to his feet, releasing my hand, and I felt a pang of fear. "No," I whispered, my voice barely audible, as I watched him approach the door with caution. He slowly turned the handle and pushed it open, revealing a scene that made my heart race. The sun was dipping below the horizon, casting a golden glow over the snow-covered landscape, which was now being blanketed by a thick, swirling storm.

Bellamy stepped out onto the porch, his eyes scanning the surroundings with an intensity that made me nervous. He was about to turn back when his body suddenly jerked, as if he'd seen something that made his blood run cold. He flung himself backward, hitting the cabin wall next to the door with a thud. I sat frozen for a moment, my mind racing, before I mustered the courage to follow him outside, my heart pounding in anticipation of what I might see.

A figure shrouded in a hooded cloak stood motionless on the porch, its face obscured by the shadows. Bellamy demanded, "Who are you?" The figure took a slow, deliberate step forward, its presence seeming to fill the space around us. Then, a voice like crackling ice spoke, sending a chill through my veins. "Can it be...Bellamy Darlington?" The words heavy with an unspoken menace, and I could sense Bellamy's tension as he awaited a response.

As we stood transfixed, a bony hand emerged from the cloak's darkness, its fingers grasping for the hood. With a slow, deliberate motion, the woman pulled it down, revealing a face that seemed chiseled from the very woods themselves.

Her long gray hair cascaded like a river of moonlight down her back. Her eyes, glinting with an otherworldly intensity, locked onto Bellamy as she repeated her query, "Bellamy Darlington?"

Bellamy's gaze flicked to me, then back to the woman, his expression a mask of caution. "Yes, I am," he replied, his voice firm. "And who are you?" But the woman didn't respond. Instead, she turned towards the darkness of the woods and let out a piercing cry, "Sisters, Sisters, come!" The words echoed through the forest, summoning some unknown force from the shadows.

The woman's gaze swiveled back to us, her lips curling into a malevolent grin. "I'm sorry to have frightened you," she said, her voice dripping with sarcasm. The wind began to howl, and the snow fell in thick, heavy flakes. Reducing visibility, but we could see them, twelve more cloaked figures emerging from the darkness, their footsteps slow.

They formed a straight line, their faces obscured by the hoods. The wind died down, but the snow continued to fall, shrouding them in a veil of white. And then, in unison, they pulled down their hoods, revealing thirteen women standing before us. Bellamy's whisper was barely audible over the pounding of my heart: "Witches."

"Sisters, behold Bellamy Darlington!" The witch cackled, her voice carrying across the clearing to the assembled witches. They gasped in unison, their faces lighting up with an unsettling excitement, as if Bellamy was a long-awaited messiah. Bellamy's eyes narrowed, his confusion evident. "Who are you?" he demanded, taking a step forward.

The witch's gaze gleamed with a knowing intensity as she glided back onto the porch, her movements eerily graceful. "My dear, fear not," she croaked, her voice like a rusty gate. 'I am Petri, and my ancestors placed a mark upon you many moons ago." Her bony finger extended, pointing at Bellamy with an accusing intensity. "We have awaited your arrival for far too long..." The words trailed off.

"What mark?" I asked, curiously. Petri's gaze snapped towards me, her eyes flashing with irritation, as if I'd disturbed a centuries- long slumber. Her nostrils flaring as she sniffed the air around me. "You are mortal," she declared, her tone dripping with disdain. I didn't bother responding, instead, I shot Bellamy a sideways glance, seeking answers. "What do you want from me?" Bellamy demanded, his voice firm, his eyes locked on Petri with a hint of warning.

Petri's lips curled into an evil grin as she addressed Bellamy. "We have awaited your arrival for centuries." Her gaze swept towards the assembled witches, and with a regal wave of her hand, they sprang into action, gathering firewood with an eerie efficiency. Petri's attention snapped back to us, her eyes glinting with a dark intensity.

"I am a descendant of the great Petri de Joangorena, who was martyred at the stake during the Spanish Inquisition. But before she and her sisters were silenced, they passed down a prophecy... a tale of you, Bellamy."

Bellamy's expression turned uneasy, his eyes darting towards me before returning to Petri. "They gave you magic and immortality?' she sneered; her voice laced with disdain. Bellamy nodded curtly; his jaw clenched. "Yes, that's right."

Her gaze seemed to bore into his soul, her voice taking on a sinister tone. "Well, my ancestors felt deeply remorseful for their inability to save your brother. And so, they made a vow. That if you ever returned to these woods, they would grant immortality to the one you hold dearest.

I remained silent, my eyes fixed on the witches as they worked in eerie unison, constructing a colossal bonfire that seemed to rise from the earth itself. The flames erupted with an otherworldly intensity, casting flickering shadows on the surrounding trees.

I couldn't read Bellamy's expression, but his gaze was fixed on Petri with a mixture of fascination and wariness. As for me, a sense of dread crept up my spine. My intuition was screaming that something was terribly amiss.

"How did you know Bellamy was here?" I demanded. Petri's expression turned petulant, her eyes flashing with irritation. "Oh, mortal," she sneered, "We share the same magic, and

I could feel his presence since yesterday. We simply chose not to reveal ourselves… until now."

Her apology was mocking, and her laughter made me feel terrified. The other twelve witches joined in, their cackles echoing through the clearing like a chilling chorus.

I leaned in close to Bellamy, my voice barely audible over the crackling flames. "This is what Velar was warning us about," I whispered urgently. "I think they want your magic." Bellamy didn't respond, his eyes locked on Petri with an unnerving intensity.

Instead, he spoke in a low, resolute tone, "I want her to be immortal." My eyes widened in shock, my mind racing with the implications of his request. Before I could protest, Petri's bony hand grasped my arm, pulling me towards the blazing bonfire with an unsettling strength.

"So, you wish to defy mortality?" Petri asked wickedly as she led me closer to the bonfire's golden glow. I cast a hesitant glance back at Bellamy, seeking reassurance, but his expression was eerily serene, despite the warning I had whispered moments before. His calm demeanor was a stark contrast to the turmoil brewing within me. Yet, when he nodded his head in encouragement, I trusted his judgment and followed Petri, my heart pounding in my chest.

The witches had conjured a blazing inferno in the snow, its flames towering at least ten feet high. The fire's fury was mesmerizing, its heat so intense that it melted the snow around us, leaving a circle of slushy earth. I felt the sweat trickling down my face as we drew closer, the warmth suffocating.

Petri's grip on my arm finally relaxed when we reached the fire's edge. The witches began to chant in unison, their voices rising and falling in a hypnotic cadence, but the words were lost on me, a mysterious incantation in Spanish that only they seemed to understand.

I spun around, frantically scanning the snowy landscape for Bellamy, but he was nowhere to be seen. My eyes darted back and forth, searching for a glimpse of him, but he had vanished into the darkness. A sense of panic set in. *Where had he gone?*

Petri's voice broke the spell, her words dripping with an unsettling sweetness. "Drink this, child," she cooed, thrusting a cup towards me. I recoiled, my instincts screaming warning. The liquid inside was a murky, noxious brew that reeked of rotten eggs.

I shook my head, refusing to touch it. Petri's expression turned cold, her eyes glinting with a sinister light. "Drink it," she hissed, her voice like a snake slithering through the snow.

The witches' chanting grew louder, and I was terrified, and my fear was plain to see. Where was he? Just as I thought I couldn't take it anymore, the chanting abruptly ceased, and an unsettling silence fell over the forest. I stood frozen, unsure of what would happen next. "Drink, drink it now," Petri urged, her voice low and menacing. I hesitated, the cup hovering near my lips. Petri's smile grew wider.

Just as I was about to give in, the cabin door creaked open, and Bellamy emerged, his staff at the ready. "Drink now, if you want to live forever," Petri taunted, her eyes locked on mine. I raised the cup, pretending to surrender, but with a swift motion, I flung it into the fire, shattering the silence.

The fire erupted in a blaze of dark green flames, as if the very essence of the witches' magic had been unleashed. The witches, including Petri, crumpled to the ground, their powers momentarily broken. Bellamy acted swiftly, sweeping me into his arms and conjuring his staff to life.

With a swift motion, we soared into the night sky, leaving the stunned witches in our wake. But they quickly regained their footing, their eyes blazing with fury as they mounted their broomsticks and gave chase. The air was soon filled with the sound of whooshing brooms and the witches' cackling cries, as they pursued us through the darkness.

I clung to Bellamy's chest, my arms wrapped tightly around him as he soared through the forest, his staff guiding us with precision. A blazing fireball hurtled towards us, but Bellamy expertly dodged it, his reflexes honed to perfection. The wind whipped through my hair as we flew at breakneck speed, the trees blurring together in a green blur.

Ahead, I spotted the road, a beacon of safety in the darkness. I dared a glance back, my heart racing, and saw the witches still hot on our heels, their broomsticks streaking through the night like spectral fingers.

Bellamy shouted, "I see the car! You'll have to drive; I'll handle the witches!" My heart sank, but there was no time to hesitate. We landed beside the rented sports car. Bellamy thrusted me towards the driver's side door. I scrambled in, my mind racing.

Before I could even buckle up, Bellamy sprinted to the passenger side, his eyes fixed on the witches closing in. With a swift gesture, he summoned the trees to do his bidding, their trunks crashing down to block our pursuers. But the witches were relentless, appearing through the clearing like specters.

Bellamy leaned out the window, his arm extended, and more branches fell, only to be dodged by the agile witches. I floored it, the sports car surging forward with a roar. The wind whipped through my hair as I pushed past the speed limit.

Just then I heard Velar's voice through the car's speaker, "Velar, we're in trouble! Thirteen witches are on our tail!" Bellamy blurted out. Velar's response was laced with concern, "Where are you?" Bellamy swiftly replied, "Spain!"

Before Velar could offer any assistance, the two began arguing about why Bellamy brought us here in the first place, their voices raised in urgency. Suddenly, a loud thud shook the car, and I swerved to avoid losing control.

Bellamy grabbed the wheel, his reflexes lightning-fast, and straightened us out just in time. He spun around to gaze out the back window, his eyes widening in alarm. "They're gaining on us!" he yelled. My knuckles turned white as I gripped the steering wheel, pushing the car to its limits on the treacherous winding roads.

Bellamy leaned out the passenger window, unleashing his magic to hinder the witches' pursuit, but they were unforgiving. Every time we thought we'd shaken them off, they reappeared mere moments later, their relentless cackles echoing through the air.

Velar's voice crackled through the car speaker, "Drive to Sage!" I didn't know where I was headed, but I kept my foot on the gas, desperate to shake off the witches. Bellamy rapidly programmed the GPS, and Velar rattled off the address. I sped on, my heart racing, as we zigzagged through the winding forest roads.

The witches had ceased their fireball attacks, but I knew they were still hot on our trail. "Once we clear the forest, they won't dare follow us on brooms without being seen," Bellamy called out, "Time to switch!" I nodded gladly, my eyes fixed on the road ahead, as Bellamy smoothly slid under me. Taking control of the pedals and then the wheel as I slid into the passenger seat, never once lifting my foot off the gas.

I was still trembling, my nerves frazzled from the intense drive. Grateful to be free from the wheel, I kept a vigilant eye on the rearview mirror, tracking the few witches who persisted in their pursuit. "They'll have to land soon," Bellamy said, his voice calm and reassuring. He noticed my anxiety and placed a comforting hand on my thigh. "They won't dare risk exposure to mortals."

Velar's voice crackled through the car speaker once more, "I'm alerting Sage to your arrival. In the meantime, stay vigilant!" The line went dead, and I turned back to scan the horizon. The witches had vanished from sight, and I felt a small sense of reprieve wash over me. But my relief was short-lived, as I knew our ordeal was far from over.

The GPS display glowed with an ominous forecast, twelve hours of driving lay ahead, with no break in sight. Bellamy simply removed his hands from the wheel, and a burst of light filled the car, imbuing it with a magical autopilot. The vehicle began to drive itself, gliding smoothly through the darkness. He flashed me a smug, self-satisfied grin, his eyes gleaming with pride in his handiwork. "Magic has its perks," he said.

The initial hours of the drive passed in a daze, our minds reeling from the chaos we'd left behind. We remained vigilant, scanning the horizon for any sign of the witches. "What just happened?" I finally asked, breaking the silence.

Bellamy's shoulders rose in a casual shrug. "Sage will fill us in when we arrive." Though we'd long since shaken off the witches, my gaze kept drifting to the side view mirror, haunted by the fear that they might reappear at any moment.

CHAPTER
SEVENTEEN

Bellamy roused me from my slumber as we arrived in Amsterdam, the city's vibrant lights and sounds a stark contrast to the tense silence of our drive. "We need to conceal the car," he whispered urgently, his eyes scanning our surroundings. I sat up straight, bleary-eyed, as he navigated the sports car down a narrow alley and into a parking garage.

We abandoned the vehicle with haste, hurrying down the alleyway with quickened steps. Bellamy pulled up his hood, and I followed suit, our faces hidden from prying eyes. He set a brisk pace, his long strides forcing me to almost run to keep up, my heart racing with anticipation and a hint of fear.

I sprinted to catch up with Bellamy, my breathing labored. "Are we near Sage's place?" I asked, feeling winded. Bellamy's response was laced with caution. "I parked a distance away, hoping to throw the witches off our trail. If we're lucky, they'll follow the car's magical scent before finding us."

My confusion deepened. "What do you mean? Why would they even find it?" I pressed, my anxiety spiking. Bellamy's expression turned grave. "They can detect the magic; they can smell it. That's how I think they tracked us in the forest. Our car reeks of it, and they'll follow that scent until they find us."

Bellamy ducked into the familiar alley, the same one we'd traversed with Velar and Eve before. As I caught up to him at Sage's front door, it swung open, and we hastily entered, seeking refuge.

I was still gasping for air when I spotted Velar, and my instincts took over. I rushed into his embrace, feeling a sense of security wash over me as he held me tight. "Thanks for your help," Bellamy said to Velar, but his expression was far from grateful. His face was red with anger, his emerald eyes blazing. "How could you be so foolish, so irresponsible, with her?" he thundered, his voice echoing off the walls.

Bellamy bristled; his irritation evident. "Like I was supposed to anticipate a witch ambush?" Velar's anger only intensified, his head shaking in disbelief. "You were being reckless, Bell! Why did you even go back there?" he yelled, his voice cracking with emotion.

I instinctively positioned myself between the two men, using my body to separate them as they squared off against each other. Velar's eyes blazed with fury; his fangs bared in a snarl as he continued to berate Bellamy.

Meanwhile, Bellamy's magic churned around him like a tempest, his eyes flashing with anger as he grew more enraged by the second. I felt like I was standing between two ticking time bombs, waiting for one of them to detonate. The air was electric with tension, and I could sense the violence simmering just below the surface, threatening to erupt at any moment.

"STOP!" I screamed at the top of my lungs, my voice echoing through the room. The two men froze, their faces twisted in anger, before turning their attention to me. My outburst seemed to snap them out of their fury, and they ceased their fighting. Their chests heaving with exertion.

Sage, who had been watching the exchange with a look of exasperation, chimed in, her voice dripping with sarcasm. "Are you boys finished yet?" Bellamy and Velar remained silent, their gazes fixed on Sage, who looked like she had better things to do than referee their squabble. Her expression was a perfect blend of annoyance and disinterest, as if she was tired of their petty bickering.

"My apologies, Sage," Bellamy said, his tone conciliatory. "Can you explain what the witches are after, exactly?" Before Sage could respond, Velar cut in. "Do they want your magic, Bellamy?" Bellamy turned to Sage, his eyes seeking answers. She, however, seemed lost in thought, her brow furrowed as she began pacing back and forth across the room. Her silence was palpable, and we waited patiently, our eyes fixed on her, as she gathered her thoughts.

"It seems you've crossed paths with elder witches," Sage explained, "and if she's a descendant, as she claims, then I believe that's what they're after. Your magic." Velar's eyes widened in shock as he grasped the implications. "If those elder witches get their hands on your magic, they could potentially dominate the entire world."

But Sage cut him off with a calm, yet annoyed tone, "Not quite true." She continued, her pacing steady and deliberate, "The elders must be desperate, as they don't possess all of their original magic. If they did, they wouldn't have waited for you to come to them; they wouldn't have needed to search for you."

We watched intently as Sage paced before her cauldron, her words dripping with ancient knowledge. Without turning to face us, she began to reveal the secrets of the elder witches. "Take a seat, and listen closely, for there are things you should know about these elder witches..." We settled in at the wooden table, our ears tuned to Sage's every word. "The elders are descendants of the witches who were persecuted during the Spanish witch trials. They are the leaders of their coven, wielding immense power and unwavering loyalty to their ancestors."

Bellamy and Velar were engrossed in Sage's words, but I was still struggling to understand. "So, what exactly do they want from Bellamy?" I asked, my confusion evident. Sage's response was straightforward and unsettling. "They want their magic back."

My eyes widened in alarm, and Bellamy instinctively wrapped his arm around me, offering comfort. Sage hastened to clarify, "Now, mind you, not all elders are evil, some are good witches like me." Velar's sudden snort of laughter was quickly disguised as a cough, but the hint of amusement lingered in his eyes.

Sage rolled her eyes, her expression a mix of exasperation and patience, and continued, "Anyway, during the Spanish Inquisition, in the sixteenth century, six powerful witches were crucified. It was a time of great fear and persecution, when countless men and women were condemned and burned at the stake, accused of witchcraft." Her words painted a vivid picture of a dark and turbulent era.

"As the trials unfolded, the accused witches seethed with anger, which gradually consumed them, transforming into a deep- seated hatred. The darkness of their magic eventually claimed their souls, except for one. Amidst the chaos and persecution, this lone witch chose a different path. Instead of succumbing to hatred, she prayed for those who condemned her, and her soul was spared. Her descendants continued to practice witchcraft in secret, unlike the elder witches who had surrendered to their hatred. This lone witch's legacy became a beacon of hope, a testament to the power of compassion and forgiveness in the face of darkness and despair."

We sat in stunned silence, digesting the weight of Sage's words. "Could a descendant of that one good witch help us?" I ventured, breaking the stillness. Sage pondered for a moment before responding, "I'm not sure... she's likely hiding from the elders as well and finding her would be a challenge."

We sat around the table, lost in thought, considering our next move, when suddenly Sage's head snapped towards the door and she exclaimed, "They've found you!" The room fell silent as we strained to listen to the outside world. "You need to use the cheval glass," Sage urged, her voice low and urgent, as she swiftly led us down to the basement.

As we gathered before the cheval glass, Sage whispered urgently, "Get back to the circus!" But before we could move, a knock at the front door froze us in place. Our eyes darted to each other, filled with fear and uncertainty.

A creepy voice on the other side of the door sent shivers down our spines, "Bellamy, I think you have something of mine..." The chanting from upstairs grew louder, and Sage gestured frantically for us to hurry. Bellamy grasped my hand, and together we stepped through the glass.

In a split-second Darlington Circus surrounded us. Bellamy and I waited anxiously for Velar to follow, and within moments, he and Sage tumbled onto the cobblestone floor. Sage sprang to her feet, brushing off her clothes with anger. "What in the world were you thinking, bringing me here?" She demanded, her voice rising in indignation.

Velar stood up, a hint of sheepishness on his face. "We are out of options, Sage. The witches were about to break down your door. I had no choice." We rushed to their side, eager to intervene. Sage's eyes rolled heavenward.

The circus was eerily deserted, its black and white tents standing silent sentinel. The performers and crew were still in Jubilee, leaving the usually vibrant space feeling abandoned and eerie. Yet, despite the emptiness, I could sense Bellamy's pent-up energy, his readiness to spring into action. We took off in a sprint, racing back towards Jubilee with Sage lagging reluctantly behind. As we burst out of the weeping willow entrance, Mesidor's sharp eyes instantly detected our return.

Bellamy's voice boomed through the invisible speakers, echoing across Jubilee. "Attention, all residents! We require immediate assembly. We have an emergency meeting scheduled in one hour, gathering outside Casmira." The announcement reverberated through the island.

Following Bellamy's announcement, the community sprang into action, mobilizing to gather those who had ventured into the outside world. I swiftly briefed Eve on the unfolding situation as she rushed to join us, her concern etched on her face.

Together, Bellamy, Velar, Eve, Sage, and I made our way to Casmira. The door opened and a soothing brew of hot tea simmered on the stove. As we stepped inside, Velar's urgent tone cut through the calm atmosphere, "We need a plan, and we need it now."

As we gathered around the dining table, Lucca burst through the door, and I gave him a warm embrace. Moments later, Miss Poppet followed, her expression relieved. "Bently and his family are en route to us as we speak," she informed Bellamy and me. "Thank you for watching over Lucca," I added gratefully, "Anytime dear." She said as she walked out of Casmira.

Bellamy sat in contemplative silence; his thoughts consumed by the weight of their situation. Eve, meanwhile, acknowledged Sage's presence with a warm greeting, "Hello, Sage." Sage's response was characteristically terse, "Oh, hi again." Eve pressed on, curious, "So, you returned with them?" Sage's eyes rolled in exasperation, "Not by choice."

Velar attempted to inject some levity into the tense atmosphere, "I couldn't leave my favorite wicked witch behind." Though his quip fell flat, Sage's smirk hinted at a glimmer of amusement.

As the silence stretched on, Lucca excused himself to his room, leaving the rest of us to our thoughts. I voiced the question that had been nagging at me, "With the witches searching for us, how can we ever leave Jubilee again?" Velar's reassuring gaze met mine, "We will figure it out."

Just as the room fell silent, Bellamy burst out, "Oh yeah, how exactly?" Velar's chair scraped against the floor as he sprang up, his eyes blazing with intensity. He leaned in, his face inches from Bellamy's, and hissed, "We wouldn't be in this mess if you hadn't recklessly returned to that place! What were you thinking, putting yourself and Nic in danger?" Bellamy shot to his feet, his voice raised in defiance, but before the argument could escalate further, Sage slammed her hands down on the table, the force of her gesture silencing the room.

Bellamy and Velar sank back into their chairs, which mysteriously slid forward, pinning them to the table. Their mouths opened and closed in comical silence, like fish gasping for air. Sage's eyebrows shot up in warning. "The next outburst that doesn't concern the elders, I'm walking out, and you'll be on your own!" The two men's shoulders slumped in defeat.

When Sage finally released them from her spell, they nodded in unison, agreeing to put aside their bickering and focus on the crisis at hand. Eve's voice rang out, urgent and worried. "We still need a plan, and we have to present it to the entire Jubilee community in just a few minutes, but we have nothing!"

"I have an idea!" All eyes turned to Lucca, who had been quietly observing from the stairs, Velar's face lit up with curiosity, and he strode over to Lucca, asking, "Oh yeah, little man, what'cha got?"

Lucca's response was characteristically straightforward, "If we don't have a plan, we just pretend everything is fine." Velar's chuckle filled the room, and Bellamy, rising from his chair, nodded thoughtfully. "You know, that might not be a bad idea, Lucca."

"Bellamy," I exclaimed, my voice mixed with surprise and disagreement. But Bellamy pressed on, his tone resolute. "Let's not alarm anyone just yet. The less they know, the better. We'll assure them everything's under control and we'll keep them safe." Velar attempted to interject, "Bell, I don't think we should deceive them..." but Bellamy cut him off. "It's not deception, Velar. We're preventing panic. If everyone flees, where will they hide? The vampires, the witches, they're all safe here in Jubilee." Velar shook his head, his disapproval clear.

Bellamy continued, undeterred. "We'll need to bolster security, jump quicker and farther, and hide more effectively." He turned to me, seeking my opinion. Though my instincts sided with Velar, I reluctantly agreed with Bellamy, seeing no alternative at that moment. Velar, about to protest, caught Sage's gaze and instead shook his head and exited the house.

Lucca's request to visit the Bally girls was met with a swift nod from me, and he eagerly darted out of the house. The remaining four of us, Sage, Bellamy, Eve, and I, gathered around the table. Sage broke the silence, her with unease. "I can sense the witches' presence in my home, and I fear I cannot return until this situation is resolved." Her words were a stark reminder of the danger that lurked beyond Jubilee's borders.

Bellamy extended a warm offer to Sage, "Make Jubilee your home, we welcome you with open arms." Sage's response was tinged with a sense of longing, "I would like to see my sister now." Bellamy nodded understandingly, "I'll take you to her." I trailed behind them, my mind torn between Bellamy's pragmatic approach and Velar's impassioned argument. My thoughts swirled with uncertainty, vacillating between the two perspectives like a pendulum.

As we walked to Mesidor and Ambrette's home, I spotted Velar heading up the hill towards his house. I longed to speak with him, but I knew Bellamy wouldn't approve. We soon arrived at the witches' residence, and Bellamy knocked on the door. Ambrette answered, her eyes widening in surprise as she took in Sage's presence. "Hello, Sister," Sage said, breaking the silence.

Ambrette's face lit up with a warm smile. "It's been over two hundred years since we last saw each other!" She exclaimed. Sage quipped, "Oh yes, much too soon." Ambrette embraced her sister, but Sage stood stiffly, her hands at her sides, clearly uncomfortable. "Alright, alright," she said, hinting for her sister to release her. Ambrette chuckled and invited us inside for a private conversation.

Upon entering, Mesidor and Clove joined us, and Mesidor's eyes widened in surprise. "Well, I'll be damned!" he exclaimed, taking in Sage's presence. Sage swiftly retorted, "I see my sister is feeding you well, Mesidor." He chuckled and approached his wife, Ambrette.

Meanwhile, Clove eagerly approached Sage, exclaiming, "So, you're my wicked Aunt Sage?" He paused looking her up and down before saying, "Wow, I'm thrilled to meet you!" Sage stood stiffly, scrutinizing her nephew before responding, "The pleasure is mine, Clove. You bear a striking resemblance to my father." Ambrette beamed with pride at the compliment her sister paid their family.

"What brings you here, Sage?" Mesidor inquired. Sage gestured to Bellamy, deferring to him for an explanation. Bellamy took the lead,

"We require your assistance once again, please." Mesidor's gaze swept over his wife and son before nodding resolutely. "We're here for you, Bell. What do you need?"

Bellamy elaborated, "We're being pursued by thirteen elder witches. As the most skilled witches in Jubilee, we hoped you might aid us." He emphasized the need for discretion, "For now, this must remain confidential until we devise a plan. Our priority is to keep everyone safe and avoid panic."

After Bellamy finished explaining the situation, Mesidor and Ambrette conferred in hushed tones. Sage, possibly overhearing their conversation, interjected, "Yes, that's why I'm here. I assisted Bellamy in his escape, and just before they breached my home, Velar pulled me through the cheval glass."

Bellamy continued, "We're currently awaiting the return of everyone to Jubilee, and then we must jump out of here."

Mesidor's eyes narrowed, "What do you need?" "We need to find a way to hide from the thirteen elders," Bellamy stated. Sage agreed to stay with the Blackwoods and work on a spell to conceal Darlington Circus.

I left to assist Eve, who was in charge of gathering everyone back in Jubilee. On my way to find her, I spotted Velar, and without hesitation, I approached him. He saw me coming and walked towards me, his expression stern.

As soon as he reached me, he said, "Why are you siding with Bell, knowing he's wrong to keep a secret this huge? I know you don't truly agree with him." I sensed his disappointment and anger. "I don't want to panic anyone," I replied, trying to reason with him.

I had no desire to quarrel with Velar, and I dreaded even the slightest hint of discord between us. Perhaps sensing my reluctance, he grabbed me in a warm embrace, his strong, tattooed arms wrapping around me like a shield.

I felt his love and affection pour over me, and I reveled in the safety of his muscular arms. Tilted my head up, our eyes met, and he leaned down, his lips meeting mine in a gentle, loving kiss. The world around us melted away.

In the distance, I spotted Bellamy heading back to Casmira, and I couldn't help but wonder if he had witnessed our intimate moment. "We need to go now," I urged, tugging Velar's hand.

After a brief hesitation, he followed me back to the house, our hands clasped together the entire way. As we entered Casmira, I released his hand, and we found Bellamy waiting for us by the front door. "Sage is going to be working with Mesidor and Ambrette," he informed us.

Just then, Eve burst through the door, her voice ringing out, "Everyone's back! We're ready to jump!"

CHAPTER
EIGHTEEN

As Bellamy stepped outside, the familiar vibrations of the jump enthralled us, transporting us to a new town across time and space. Eve headed to the kitchen in search of sustenance, while Bellamy returned inside, his expression etched with concern. I quickly approached him, sensing his unease. "Are you okay?" I asked, noticing the deep furrows on his brow.

Velar, overhearing our exchange, joined us, his eyes narrowing with interest. "What do you mean?" he pressed, seeking clarification. Bellamy's gaze met Velar's, and he stated gravely, "We'll need additional help to defeat the elders." His words were a stark reminder of the challenges ahead.

Eve emerged from the kitchen, a handful of cookies in her grasp, and a look of nonchalance on her face. She must have overheard Bellamy's concerns from the kitchen, as she casually suggested, "Why not ask the Undying Council?" While stuffing her face with a cookie, Bellamy nodded in agreement. "I was just thinking of that." Velar's expression turned concerned, "Will they help us?" he asked.

Although I wasn't well-versed in the inner workings of the Undying Council, Bellamy, as a council member himself, had previously described it to me as a governing body for immortal beings, akin to a supernatural government.

Just as Bellamy was briefing Velar on the Undying Council meeting, Lucca burst into the room, exclaiming, "Those girls drive me crazy!" His frustration with the Bally girls was half-joking, half- serious. I knew they loved teasing him, but I suspected he secretly enjoyed it too. I sent Lucca to his room, allowing us to focus on planning, and turned my attention back to Bellamy.

Interrupting him to ask about the timing of the next meeting or if one could be scheduled. I hoped they had a plan in place. Bellamy's response caught me off guard, "Baby girl, we are going to a ball."

"A ball?" I echoed; my annoyance evident. "How can we even think of attending a ball at a time like this?" I protested, incredulous. Eve rose to her feet, her calm demeanor a stark contrast to my frustration.

She explained that the Undying Council's annual ball was scheduled for that weekend, followed by a meeting of council members the next day. It seemed like the perfect opportunity to attend the ball and seek the council's aid.

Eve's excitement was evident as she expressed her confidence in Bellamy's ability to request assistance during the meeting. I felt a wave of relief wash over me as I grasped the plan, but Velar shook his head in disagreement, his skepticism evident.

"I don't think Nic should go, she should stay in Jubilee," Velar said, directing his comment to Bellamy. My anger flaring up instantly. "Excuse me? What do you mean? Keep me here? I want to help, and you can't keep me locked up in this town!" I protested, my voice rising.

Velar, noticing my ire, turned to me, his expression softening. "I'm sorry, Nic, I just don't want anything to happen to you." I turned to Bellamy, my arms crossed, my eyes fixed on him, waiting for his decision.

Bellamy's calm, reasonable voice cut through the tension, "I believe the four of us need to attend the ball together. We can network with various factions and garner support from council members. We require all the help we can muster.

Velar, your connections with the vampires will be invaluable. Eve, your relationships with the Fae and werewolves, particularly Draven, will be crucial. I'll focus on rallying the witches and other immortals. And, Nicole, your charm and humanity may prove to be a unique asset."

Bellamy's smile hinted at his confidence in me. Velar added, his voice laced with a hint of pride, "Nic will be the first human to ever set foot in the Undying Ball, a true historical moment."

I wasn't sure if being the first human to attend the Undying Ball was good or bad. I sought reassurance from Bellamy, who offered a comforting smile. "She will help persuade them," he said, his confidence in me evident.

I wasn't convinced I was up for the task, but I put on a brave face and asked, "When do we depart?" "In four days," Bellamy replied, his eyes gleaming with determination. The countdown has begun, and I could feel the weight of our mission settling upon me. I felt like I was going to vomit.

As a novice to the Undying Council, I felt apprehensive about attending the ball. Seeking guidance, I turned to Eve and asked, "What should I expect at the ball?" Velar nodded in agreement, his eyes also seeking answers. Eve gazed upwards, as if rummaging through her memories.

Finally, she focused on us once more and said, "The Undying Ball is like any other ball, just with immortals. It'll be a blast, I'm sure." I exchanged a skeptical glance with Velar. "Do you buy that?" I asked. He waited until Eve had departed before responding, "Not for a second." With that, he followed her out the door, leaving me to ponder the unknown.

As Bellamy believed the elders could sense the vibrations, we refrained from jumping for the next couple of days, saving our jump for when we departed for the Undying Ball. In the meantime, Sage collaborated with Ambrette and Mesidor to track down the descendant witch who remained in hiding. I accompanied Lucca to Miss Poppet's residence once more, and she graciously agreed to watch over him while we attended the ball.

Eve and I prepared for the grand event together at Casmira, adorning ourselves in exquisite ball gowns. My dress, a radiant light gold that shimmered like the sun, added a touch of luminosity to the room, while Eve's stunning red gown perfectly accentuated her curves, showcasing her beauty with effortless elegance. As we stood together, our dresses complemented each other harmoniously, creating a breathtaking spectacle.

As we completed our preparations, Bellamy summoned us downstairs, where he awaited us with a debonair smile, looking impeccably dashing in his black tuxedo with tails. With a charming compliment, he addressed me as Mrs. Darlington, causing a blush to rise to my cheeks. I stood on my tiptoes and leaned in to greet him with a kiss. Playfully, I inquired about his preference for my hair, already aware of his fondness for it when worn down. He confessed that it was lovely, but his true affection lay with my hair flowing freely. With a nod of consent, he ran his fingers through my locks, and in mere seconds, my long brown hair cascaded down in luscious, loose curls. Eve's jaw dropped in awe, exclaiming, "Stunning!" as she gazed at my transformed look.

"Look at you!" Velar's voice drew my attention, his gaze roving over me with appreciation. Clad in a tailored tuxedo that accentuated his muscular physique. I couldn't help but admire his transformed appearance.

"I don't recall seeing you ever dressed up," I said. "You wouldn't know, would you? I only dress this well for your funerals." Velar and I shared a laugh at his dark humor, while Bellamy tried to stifle our merriment, suggesting it was time to depart.

With my arm linked through Bellamy's, he escorted me out of the house. To maintain our stealth, Bellamy jumped us to another town before heading to the Blackwoods' residence. Upon arrival, we found Mesidor waiting for us, and he led us upstairs to the attic, where the cheval glass awaited. After a brief struggle with my dress, which nearly tripped me up I made it up the stairs.

Bellamy revealed the cheval glass, his expression solemn as he announced our destination, the iconic Empire State Building in New York City. My excitement surged as I exclaimed, "New York City!" With a gentle grasp of my hand, Bellamy positioned me at the forefront, followed by Eve, and then Velar. We stepped through the glass.

We arrived at the Empire State Building under the stars, our path illuminated by the bright glow of streetlights. As we navigated through the deserted streets, we encountered a handful of homeless individuals and revelers stumbling through the night.

Bellamy took my hand, his grasp warm and reassuring, and together we entered the iconic landmark.

A statuesque woman, resplendent in a flowing black gown, greeted us with a warm smile, addressing Bellamy as Mr. Darlington. He acknowledged her with a nod, and she led us to a bank of elevators, her slender fingers pressing the button with grace. As the doors slid shut, she bid us a silent farewell.

As the elevator plummeted downward, defying our expectations, we exchanged perplexed glances, our silence punctuated only by the soft hum of the machinery. The doors finally slid open, revealing a sight that left me utterly bewildered. Instead of finding ourselves on a floor of the Empire State Building, we stepped out into a mystical realm, as if we had traversed a portal akin to those that led to Jubilee.

Entranced, I remained frozen in place, drinking in the wonders of this enchanting world, while my immortal companions continued on their way, oblivious to my captivated state. The beauty and magic of this new world held me spellbound, my senses struggling to absorb the splendor that surrounded me.

Before us lay a breathtaking castle, its grandeur and beauty surpassing anything I had ever seen. Lush gardens stretched out as far as the eye could see, adorned with the largest, most vibrant red roses I had ever laid eyes on. The scene was so picturesque, it seemed plucked straight from the pages of a fairy tale.

Yet, it was even more stunning than any magazine spread could ever hope to capture. As we stood there, people began to emerge from unseen portals, just as we had, their appearances as sudden and mysterious as our own. The sheer scale of this enchanted place was staggering, rivaling that of a sprawling resort, with secrets and wonders waiting to be uncovered.

I was so captivated by the breathtaking scenery that Bella-my had to call out to Eve and Velar to wait for me, allowing me a moment to absorb the magic of my surroundings. Eventually, I snapped out of my trance-like state and hastened to catch up with my companions.

As we walked, Eve enthusiastically pointed out the extrav-agant attire of the arriving guests, their opulent gowns and suits rivaling those seen on the red carpet of a prestigious award show. The atmosphere was one of glamor and sophistication, with every attendee seemingly determined to outdo one anoth-er in their sartorial splendor.

As we trailed behind the crowd, we crossed a majestic draw-bridge leading to the castle's imposing entrance. Upon enter-ing, we found ourselves in a grand foyer, where Bellamy guided us to a reception desk in the lobby. A receptionist greeted us with a warm smile, inquiring, "How may I assist you?"

Bellamy replied with a charming smile, "We will be stay-ing the night." The young lady asked, "Name?" to which he responded, "Bellamy Darlington." Moments later, she handed him two room keys, and he promptly entrusted our luggage to her care, ensuring its delivery to our quarters.

I felt as though I had stepped into a fairy tale, the enchant-ment of the surroundings and the effortless luxury of our treat-ment leaving me utterly enchanted.

To our left, a procession of immortals flowed towards a magnificent ballroom, and we joined the crowd. As we walked, I found myself fascinated by the diverse assembly, attempting to discern the nature of each immortal we passed.

Vampires, Fae, witches, and werewolves in human guise mingled effortlessly, their ethereal beauty and grace on full dis-play. Eve, with her vast knowledge, pointed out a chimera and other creatures, her whispered explanations only adding to my wonder. I was utterly astonished by the surreal surroundings and the fantastical beings that inhabited this mystical world, my senses reeling from the sheer magic of it all.

Upon reaching an unoccupied high table, Bellamy turned to us with a solemn expression, his voice low and urgent. "Let us not forget our purpose here. We must make a favorable impression and secure their assistance in our quest to vanquish the elders."

He scanned the crowd, his gaze lingering on the sea of faces before returning to us. "In order to maximize our efforts, we must split up and mingle with the various factions. We will cover more ground and forge more alliances this way."

Velar, attempting to lighten the mood, slammed his hand on the table and exclaimed, "Divide and conquer!" However, Bellamy's stern expression remained unyielding, his focus fixed on the task at hand.

As we dispersed, I remained by Bellamy's side, while Eve drifted off into the crowd and Velar ventured in the opposite direction. Bellamy presented me to a succession of immortals, and I greeted them with a firm handshake, anxious that my human nature might be discovered. Yet, no one ever alluded to it, and I began to relax, observing that each immortal appeared remarkably mortal at first glance.

It wasn't until you engaged with them on a deeper level that their extraordinary qualities became apparent, subtle hints of their supernatural essence peeking through the façade of humanity.

The melodious strains of a piano wafted from an adjacent room, drawing me in with irresistible force. I excused myself from Bellamy's conversation with a charming couple and followed the enchanting music. I couldn't help but seek out the source of such beauty.

As I entered the room, I beheld a colossal figure seated at a grand piano, his massive frame seeming to overflow from the instrument. His eyes were closed, lost in the harmony he created, and I marveled at how he had managed to navigate the doorway without difficulty. The poor bench beneath him appeared to be on the verge of collapse, its legs buckling under the weight of this gentle giant, as if it might cry out in protest at any moment.

As the final notes faded away, I applauded spontaneously, my hands coming together in a soft clap. "That was beautiful," I exclaimed, genuinely moved by the performance. The room was empty except for the two of us, and my words seemed to startle the giant pianist, who quickly rose from his seat, his face flushing with embarrassment.

"I'm so sorry, I didn't mean to intrude," I apologized, feeling a pang of regret for interrupting his private moment. The bench, now freed from the weight of its massive occupant, seemed to breathe a sigh of relief, its legs no longer straining under the pressure.

As he approached me, his towering frame casting a long shadow, he remarked, "I've never seen you here before." His piercing gaze scrutinized me, making me feel even more diminutive. I stammered, "This is my first year," my nervousness evident in my trembling voice. The giant's eyes narrowed, his scrutiny intensifying. "Are you a new immortal?" He inquired, his tone hinting at a mixture of curiosity and suspicion.

I panicked, regretting my decision to wander off without Bellamy's protection. I frantically scanned the doorway, searching for a glimpse of my companion, but the giant's looming presence made me feel trapped. He took a step closer, his voice low and commanding, "Who are you?" I stuttered, my voice barely audible, "M-my name is Nicole."

The giant's gaze remained skeptical, his eyes boring into mine as he demanded, "What kind of immortal are you?" My mind raced, searching for a convincing response, but before I could fabricate a reply, Velar appeared out of nowhere, his timing impeccable.

"There you are, love," he said with a charming smile, and I grasped at the lifeline he offered, exclaiming, "I was looking for you!" Velar's eyes crinkled at the corners as he nodded, then gestured towards Atlas. "Well, I see you've met Atlas." But before Velar could finish the introduction, Atlas cut in, his deep voice laced with disapproval, "She's with you?" He didn't wait for a response, simply shaking his head and returning to the piano, his fingers beginning to dance across the keys once more.

Velar ushered me out of the room, but I quickly turned back to face Atlas, calling out, 'It was lovely meeting you!' as a polite farewell. Once we were back in the bustling ballroom, Velar grasped my shoulders, his eyes serious as he admonished, "Don't you know not to make friends with an Ogre?" I was taken aback, my mind racing with the revelation. "An Ogre?" I repeated, hardly able to believe I had just met a actual Ogre.

Velar noticed the attention we were drawing and swiftly swept me into a dance, his hands holding mine as we twirled across the floor, our movements graceful and fluid. The music and laughter swirled around us, masking the tension that lingered beneath the surface.

I followed Velar's lead, trying to mimic the steps of the unfamiliar dance. We glided across the empty dance floor, our movements fluid and graceful. As we twirled, I caught sight of Eve in the distance, engaged in conversation with a man.

"Look, there's Eve, talking to someone," I said, peeking over Velar's shoulder. He swiftly turned us to get a better view. "Ah, that's Draven Graf," he said, unimpressed. I eagerly requested, "Let me see!" Velar obligingly spun us around again, allowing me to catch a glimpse of the mysterious figure. With my heels giving me a boost, I could see him clearly over Velar's shoulder. "Wow, I can't believe she's talking to him! We should go say hello."

Velar swiftly spun us around again, his eyes locking onto mine with a firm "No". I searched his face for an explanation, and he pulled me close, whispering in my ear, "She can do better than a werewolf." I knew Velar had a long-standing aversion to werewolves, so I decided to shift the conversation. "Did you manage to speak with anyone we needed to?" I asked, attempting to steer the topic towards our mission.

Velar's gaze swept the surrounding area before returning to mine, his eyes locking onto mine with an intense spark. Without warning, he pressed his lips to mine, and I responded instinctively, our kiss deepening for a fleeting moment.

I broke away, my cheeks flushing, as I nervously glanced around, worried that Bellamy might have witnessed our intimate exchange. "The vampires aren't going to help," Velar finally replied to my earlier question, his voice nonchalant. "They prefer to mind their own business." I slowed our dance, frustration simmering beneath my surface. "Well, did you even try?" I pressed, but Velar remained silent.

With a sudden flourish, he spun me around, releasing my hand, and I stumbled right into Bellamy's broad chest, my heart racing from the unexpected turn of events.

"There you are, baby girl," Bellamy said, his deep voice warm and familiar, as he effortlessly swept me into his embrace, our hands entwining like a well-rehearsed waltz.

I glanced around, searching for Velar, but he had vanished into the crowd. Bellamy's smile was radiant, his eyes shining with optimism. "I think we'll have a productive meeting tomorrow." I hesitated, unsure how to break the news about the vampires' refusal to help, so I simply smiled and nodded, letting the music guide our movements. As the melody came to a gentle close, we slowed to a stop, our bodies swaying in harmony.

"She's here," Bellamy announced, rising from his bow and guiding my gaze towards a vision in white. Amidst the sea of guests, a stunning woman in a flowing ball gown and updo stood out, her pointed ears visible through her elegantly styled hair.

Bellamy led me towards her, and as we approached, a line began to form, but we bypassed it, and Bellamy introduced me with a gentle pride, "President Olivia, I want you to meet my wife, Nicole."

Turning to me, he added, "Olivia is the President of the Undying Council." The beautiful Fae woman smiled warmly, her voice like music, "It's delightful to finally meet you, Bellamy has shared so much about you. I'm thrilled you could join us at the Undying Ball." I thanked her, and as she turned her attention to Bellamy, I spotted Eve across the room, beaming with a radiant smile. Excusing myself, I wandered over to join her, and she introduced me to Draven Graf.

A handsome man with piercing silver eyes and chiseled features, his blonde hair swept back, revealing his chiseled jawline. He took my hand, his lips brushing against it in a gentle kiss, "I've heard wonderful things about you, Mrs. Darlington. It's an absolute pleasure to meet you." His accent danced across my name.

"Please, call me Nicole. It's lovely to meet you," I said, smiling at Draven. As we chatted, a server circulated, offering flutes of sparkling liquid that resembled champagne. We each accepted a glass, and I toasted,

"Cheers," our glasses clinking in unison. Draven's glass touched Eve's, and then mine, before I took a sip. The taste was sublime. Draven leaned in, his voice low and mysterious, "Be cautious with those," he whispered to Eve, who smiled knowingly and took another sip, her eyes sparkling with amusement.

As I stood there, I began to feel like an outsider, observing the effortless rapport between Draven and Eve. Deciding to explore further, I excused myself and wandered into the vibrant ballroom, intent on discovering more of its secrets.

However, as I traversed the room, I started to experience a strange, disorienting sensation. The space around me seemed to undulate in waves, and the colors from Bellamy's magic swirled before my eyes, leaving me disconcerted and uncertain.

Suddenly, it clicked, the drink! I recalled the mysterious liquid and wondered if it contained magic, and whether it was safe for humans to consume. Alarmed, I swiftly set my flute down on a nearby table, deciding to err on the side of caution. "Be cautious with those," he had told Eve.

Panic began to set in as I turned back around, only to find Eve and Draven had vanished from their previous spot. I frantically scanned the ballroom, desperate to locate Bellamy or Velar, but they were nowhere to be seen.

The swirling colors and distorted space around me were making my head spin, and I felt myself on the verge of collapse.

The room seemed to be closing in, and I struggled to maintain my balance, my vision blurring at the edges.

I stood there, dazed and disoriented, gazing out at the ballroom for what felt like an eternity.

The next thing I knew, Bellamy, Velar, and Eve were by my side, and we had somehow made our way back to the foyer. Bellamy pressed a glass of water into my hand, and I sipped it gratefully, trying to clear the cobwebs from my mind. Eve turned to Bellamy, her voice laced with apology, "I'm so sorry, Bell, I totally forgot the drinks had magic in them."

As I began to regain my bearings, I noticed the three of them staring at me with a mixture of concern and amusement. "What's going on?" I asked, still trying to shake off the haze. Velar chuckled, "Still can't handle your alcohol, it seems."

Bellamy's expression turned apologetic as he explained, "The drinks served here contain magic, and it's not suitable for mortals, Babygirl. I'm so sorry."

Once I felt steadier, I stood up, and Bellamy handed the key to Velar, instructing him, "I still have matters to attend to here, can you see them safely to our room?"

Before Velar could respond, Eve piped up, "I'm still catching up with Draven, I'll go find him." Bellamy nodded understandingly, and Eve skipped off, eager to rejoin the ball.

Meanwhile, I was relieved to be heading to the comfort and safety of our room, grateful to escape the enchanting but overwhelming atmosphere of the Undying Ball.

Bellamy's lips brushed against my cheek in a gentle farewell, and then Velar's hand enveloped mine, leading me away from the foyer. We strolled down an elegant hallway, ascending a grand staircase to the floor where our room was located. Velar produced a key and unlocked the French doors, which swung open to reveal a lavish suite.

Inside, a spacious living area beckoned, flanked by two bedrooms, one on either side of the suite, each door perfectly aligned across from the other. The suite exuded luxury and comfort, a serene oasis amidst the enchantment and wonder of the Undying Ball.

I collapsed onto the plush living room couch, my extravagant ball gown spreading out around me like a cloud. "Ready to shed that yet?" Velar asked with a chuckle, but I shook my head, too exhausted to even contemplate the effort required to remove the gown. "I'm never drinking again!" I declared, clutching my head in mock despair.

Velar's laughter filled the room as he handed me a steaming cup. "Don't worry, it's just tea," he said with a sly grin. I sipped the soothing brew, feeling my fatigue lift with each successive swallow. Before I knew it, the cup was empty, and my vitality was restored.

I mustered the energy to rise from the couch, excusing myself to change out of the cumbersome gown. Velar promptly stood up, his eyes sparkling with courtesy, and asked, "Do you need any assistance?" I was about to dismiss the offer with a playful eyeroll, but then I remembered the intricate corset back of my dress, and my pride surrendered to practicality. "Yes, please," I admitted with a gracious smile. Velar followed me into the bedroom.

Velar's fingers worked the laces, and once the gown was loose enough, I stepped out of it, revealing my bare torso, clad only in panties. I sensed Velar's gaze lingering on me, and I swiftly shifted the focus, inquiring, "What are your thoughts on tomorrow's meeting?" Velar's shoulders rose in a noncommittal shrug, and he replied, "I think Killian will address the vampire council, but I doubt they'll get involved." His casual tone irked me, and I pressed for more, "Why not?" Velar's expression turned deep, and he explained, "Vampires tend to keep to themselves, avoiding entanglements with other... creatures. We're nocturnal beings, without magic; it's hard to see how we can effectively aid in a conflict against witches with their formidable powers and spells."

I nodded, grasping his perspective as a vampire. I hadn't considered their unique viewpoint. As I finished dressing, I turned to Velar, who remained fixed on me, his gaze unwavering. "Don't you want to rejoin the party?" I asked, curious. Velar's lean frame relaxed against the doorframe, his arms crossing over his chest as he replied, his eyes never leaving mine, "This is where I want to be."

My heart skipped a beat. I felt an overwhelming pull towards him, and before I knew it, I had closed the distance between us, my lips meeting his in a gentle, yet deliberate kiss. This time, there was no interruption, no distraction, just the two of us, lost in the moment.

Velar's hands encircled my waist, pulling me into the hardness of his body. I melted into his embrace, savoring the sensation of his tongue dancing with mine. His fangs grazed my lips, and I sensed his hunger, a primal urge that stirred my own desires.

Memories of our past life flooded back, and I recalled the ecstasy of his bite. I yearned for him to taste me again, to feel his fangs pierce my skin.

With a deliberate motion, I exposed my neck, inviting him to take what I knew he desired. Velar's gaze locked onto mine, seeking reassurance, and then his teeth sank into my flesh. A fleeting pain gave way to a torrent of pleasure, intensifying my longing for him. I craved more, my body responding to the intoxicating mix of pain and delight.

Feeling him suck blood from my neck felt so intimate. Blood ran down my chest and dripped on the floor. Soon I was feeling lightheaded and that's when Velar finished. He licked my neck clean and slid his tongue to the blood that ran down my chest.

In one motion he removed my top and sucked on my nipples teasing me ever so gently. "I've been waiting to taste you again." He said smiling. I smiled back. I quickly realized Bellamy is going to see my bite marks. *What was I thinking?*

I bid Velar a goodnight, citing a need for a shower and some rest. Once alone in the bathroom, I confronted my reflection in the mirror. The woman staring back at me appeared older, worn by the experiences since my return to the circus. I knew I could conceal the bite marks from the others, but Bellamy would undoubtedly detect them. I wondered how he would react, what he would say or do. After my shower, I retreated to the bedroom I shared with Bellamy, seeking the solace of the bed.

Despite my exhaustion, sleep eluded me, and I finally gave up, slipping out of bed with a quiet sigh. The darkness of the night filled the room as I tiptoed out of the bedroom, careful not to disturb the silence.

I had expected Eve and Bellamy to return by now, but the stillness suggested otherwise. As I wrapped myself in a blanket found on the couch, a sudden chill swept through the living area, and I turned to face the source of the cold breeze coming from the balcony.

As I stepped out onto the balcony, the chill of the concrete beneath my bare feet was a stark contrast to the warmth of the living room. The moon cast its silvery glow over the lush garden below, and I stood transfixed, lost in the beauty of the night and my magical surroundings.

Velar's voice from behind startled me, "Couldn't sleep?" He wrapped his arms around me, holding me close. I didn't respond, simply surrendering to the comfort of his embrace. His breath tickled my ear as he asked, "How's your neck?" I tilted my head to meet his gaze and replied, "It's fine, nothing Bellamy can't heal."

His tone took on a hint of disapproval as he said, "Let me know if Bell punishes you too harshly, okay?" The implication in his words left me wondering how much he knew about what went on in the playroom.

The prospect of Bellamy's reprimand didn't concern me, and I offered Velar a reassuring smile, saying "Okay" to placate him. As I turned to face him, our bodies aligned, and I felt his hardness press against mine. Velar's gaze locked onto mine, his eyes burning with intensity, and I sensed a hunger in him that went beyond mere blood. The night air seemed to vibrate with tension as we stood there, our bodies entwined, the only sound the soft rustling of the garden below.

Velar's hand cradled my chin, guiding me towards his lips. Our kiss was a slow, sensual embrace, the passion between us clear. Without breaking the connection, he swept me into his arms, carrying me to his bedroom. The door closed behind us, plunging the space into darkness. He laid me on his bed, and I surrendered, helpless with anticipation. The only sound was our ragged breathing, the silence between us electric with expectation.

I lay there, my senses heightened as velar undressed. The sound of his pants hitting the floor making me moan in anticipation. He climbed onto the bed, and I tried to move but he gently restrained me, his hands holding me in place as he positioned himself above me. With a swift motion he removed my panties, and I remained still eager for what came next. His finger tranced the straps of my nightgown.

As he gently pulled down the straps, my anticipation grew, and I couldn't help but crave him at that moment. I reached up, seeking his face, and he leaned into my touch, his skin warm against my fingertips. My hand wandered to his mouth, and I traced the contours of his lips, grazing a fang with my thumb. His sudden shudder betrayed his own eagerness, and I knew in that instant that our desire was mutual.

I pulled the back of his head to mine and our mouths found each other in the darkness. I kissed him and he kissed me back. His hands were groping me, grabbing my tits and my hips. His hand made his way down and he started slowly rubbing me making me incredibly wet. I wanted him so badly. He continued to tease me. I was growing impatient and wrapped my legs around him pulling him towards me.

Velar's pace slowed, leaving me breathless and yearning. "We can't, Nic," he whispered, his voice husky with restraint. "Why?" I demanded, frustration edging my tone. "Did you ask Bell?"

He knew the answer, and I knew I hadn't. With a gentle shift, Velar moved from hovering over me to lying beside me. I reached for the lamp on the nightstand, flooding the room with light. I shielded my eyes, momentarily blinded. "Why didn't you ask Bellamy?" Velar pressed, his voice tinged with curiosity. "I didn't know if you wanted me again," I admitted, my words laced with a hint of deception. The truth was, I was certain he still desired me, and the thought sent my heart racing.

As I finally opened my eyes, Velar's naked form and radiant smile greeted me. "Yes, I do want you," he affirmed, his emerald eyes sparkling with warmth. But when his gaze began to wander, I hastily wrapped myself in a blanket.

Velar's laughter was gentle, but his expression soon turned serious. "I still love you, Nic, since your last life," he revealed, catching me off guard. I averted my gaze, my heart conflicted. I loved him, but my heart belonged to Bellamy.

As Velar dressed, I watched, my emotions in turmoil. He sat beside me once more, his lips claiming mine in a long, yearning kiss that only intensified my desire.

When I stood to leave, he stated, "I'm always here, Nic, whenever you want." I knew he was waiting for me to seek Bellamy's permission. "Rules are rules." he said as I closed the door behind me.

CHAPTER
NINETEEN

The next morning as I emerged from the bedroom I found a lively conversation between Bellamy, Velar, and Eve going on. They were reminiscing about the previous night's ball, their laughter and stories filling the air. Even Velar, typically reserved, was fully engaged, his eyes sparkling with amusement. Bellamy's gaze met mine, and he smiled, presenting me with a steaming cup of coffee. "Good morning, my beautiful girl," he said affectionately.

I raised an eyebrow, inquiring about his whereabouts the night before, but Eve intervened, "You went to bed so early, Nic!" I exchanged a glance with Velar, wondering if he had confided in Bellamy about our encounter, but I chose to keep silent. As I joined them, I noticed Velar basking in the artificial sunlight streaming through the floor-to-ceiling windows, his expression serene.

When Velar finally turned his attention to me, he asked with a hint of nonchalance, "How did you sleep?" I paused, considering my response before quipping, "Like the dead." With a sly smile, I turned back to Bellamy and Eve, who were still reveling in the merriment of the previous night. "When is the meeting?" I inquired; my curiosity piqued.

Bellamy's expression suddenly turned serious as he checked his watch, took a swift sip of tea, and announced, "Now!" His tone abrupt and authoritative, signaling the end of our leisurely morning and the start of a new, potentially crucial, gathering.

"Oh shit, I need to fix my hair!" Eve exclaimed, leaping up from her seat and hastening into the bathroom, the door closing behind her with a slight slam.

Bellamy, meanwhile, adjusted his attire in the hall mirror before turning to me with a reassuring smile. "The meeting will be just fine, don't worry your pretty little head," he said. His gaze then shifted to Velar, and he instructed, "I'd prefer it if you two remained here until our return. No wandering around."

Velar nodded in acquiescence. I, however, crossed my arms in protest, my voice laced with discontent. "What? Stay here the entire time?" I asked, my tone incredulous.

Bellamy's gaze swept over me, his eyes seeming to say, "Who do you think you're talking to?" He sauntered towards me, his intimidating stare never wavering. With a gentle yet commanding gesture, he reached out and tucked a stray lock of hair behind my ear. "It won't be long, I promise," he stated in his calm, firm tone, "and I've booked a massage for you at the house spa."

Eve emerged from the bathroom, overhearing our exchange, and chimed in, "Oh, how thoughtful!" Bellamy pressed a soft kiss to my forehead, his eyes narrowing as he whispered, "We'll discuss the bite marks on your neck when I return, naughty girl." I felt a thrill of arousal as I watched them exit the room, Bellamy's parting words lingering in the air like a promise.

I swiftly concealed my enthusiasm, aware of Velar's observant gaze. "Where's the spa?" I inquired, attempting to sound nonchalant. Velar's knowing smile hinted that he was aware of my fondness for massages.

I rummaged through the suitcase to see what other attire Bellamy had packed for me, but to my surprise, there was only one remaining outfit. A stunning royal blue summer dress. The simplicity and elegance of the dress caught my attention, and I couldn't help but wonder if Bellamy had intentionally chosen it for me.

Prior to my massage, I persuaded Velar to join me on an adventure through the opulent halls of the mansion. Though he was initially hesitant to defy Bellamy's instructions, I was determined to explore this enchanting castle, even if it meant facing consequences later. Having never been inside a castle before, my curiosity was piqued, and I begged Velar to indulge me. Eventually, he relented, and together we set out to uncover the secrets within the grand estate.

As we descended the stairs to the ballroom, I was struck by the stark contrast to the previous night's vibrant atmosphere. The grand space, once teeming with life and music, now lay empty and silent, like a forgotten whisper. I wandered through the room, searching for any hint of the revelry that had taken place mere hours before. A discarded decoration, a stray confetto, a lingering guest, but found nothing. The castle's impeccable tidiness was almost surreal. Velar, seeming to delight in my perplexity, offered a single explanation, "Magic."

Of course, it was magic! I chide myself for my momentary forgetfulness. Velar's knowing smile and the gentle pressure of his hand on mine were all the encouragement I needed. As we entered the magnificent library, I felt like a kid in a candy store.

Towering shelves lined the walls, packed tightly with books that seemed to stretch up to the ceiling. In the center of the room, a spiral stairwell beckoned, leading down into the depths of the library. Velar and I leaned over the railing, peering into the unknown. "More books," he said, his tone unconcerned. But I was enchanted. Without hesitation, I dashed down the stairs, eager to explore the treasures below, leaving Velar to follow behind.

I paused at the first landing, entranced by the cozy nook overflowing with books. I devoured the titles, running my fingers over the spines, before continuing my descent to the next floor, and the next. My excitement was palpable; I felt like a kid in a wonderland, eyes wide with awe. I had never seen such an extensive collection of books in one place. Before venturing further down, I gazed upward, searching for Velar. He was leaning over the railing, a gentle smile on his face as he watched me with an air of amusement. "Had enough yet?" he asked, his tone playful, as if he knew I was just getting started.

Disregarding Velar's teasing, I ventured down to the final level of the library, my curiosity driving me forward. But as I reached the last floor, I was met with an eerie atmosphere that made me regret my solo exploration.

The air was thick with dust, and the darkness seemed to press in around me. I suddenly felt a pang of longing for Velar's presence, his reassuring calmness. Just as I was about to retreat back up the stairs, a faint noise echoed from behind a nearby bookshelf. I froze, my heart pounding in terror, as I strained to listen.

The rustling persisted, but it seemed to be coming from something small. I tried to reassure myself that it was just a mouse scurrying through the shelves. However, my curiosity got the better of me, and I found myself cautiously approaching the source of the noise. As I peered behind the bookshelf, the rustling abruptly ceased, and I was met with an unexpected sight.

Lying on the ground, as if deliberately placed, was a book. I stepped closer, my confusion growing, and read the title: 'The Legend of Sleepy Hollow' by Washington Irving. The classic tale gave me a chill, and I wondered why it was left here, in this dusty, forgotten corner of the library.

As I reached for the book, it suddenly swung open, and I let out a blood-curdling scream, scrambling backward in terror. Velar appeared by my side in an instant, his eyes scanning me with concern as he helped me up. We both gazed in disbelief at the book, which seemed to be moving of its own accord.

A hand emerged from its pages, and Velar's grip on my arm tightened. We exchanged a stunned glance, our minds racing with questions. Then, a peculiar little figure climbed out of the book. He was a short, comical man dressed in a long suit and top hat, looking like a character from a whimsical tale. Velar and I stood frozen, struggling to comprehend the surreal scene unfolding before us.

As we watched, the little man tidied himself up, then carefully placed the book back on the shelf. "Ahhh!" he yelled, spinning around to face us. His eyes widened in surprise, and I could sense that he was not of this world. "I'm sorry, we didn't mean to scare you," I apologized. Velar whispered in my ear, "He's a goblin."

The goblin composed himself, his initial fright giving way to a stern expression. "That's enough fright for one day," he declared, wagging his finger at us. "What are you doing here?" he demanded, his eyes narrowing. I began to explain, but the goblin cut me off. "This floor is forbidden; you shouldn't be here!" Velar stepped forward, positioning himself protectively in front of me. "If it's forbidden, why are you here? " he challenged, his eyes locked on the goblin.

He quickly noticed Velar's fangs and suddenly became more courteous. "I'm Wren, President Olivia's researcher," he introduced himself, "and I travel through books."

My eyes widened in amazement, recalling the book he had just emerged from. "You mean you actually enter the stories?" I asked, stuttering in confusion. "Ah, yes, it's the best way to truly immerse oneself in the narrative, don't you think?" Wren replied, his eyes twinkling. Still bewildered, I asked, "So, you were just in Sleepy Hollow?"

Wren was already rummaging through other books, his attention easily diverted. "Oh, yes, I was visiting my book friend Ichabod Crane, but that dreadful headless horseman was terrorizing the town again, so I made a quick exit. He scares me to death."

My jaw dropped in awe. "Can you enter any book?" Velar asked, curiously. The goblin halted his rummaging and said sternly, "Absolutely not. Only this floor contains the enchanted books, and no, before you ask, no, you may not go inside a book."

He must have noticed my face fall because he added, "I'd get in trouble if you got lost, and I don't want President Olivia upset with me." "I understand," I said, trying to hide my disappointment. Velar gently took my arm, and we began our ascent up the flights of stairs, leaving the enchanted books and Wren behind.

That encounter with Wren left me in awe, and I couldn't help but feel a pang of envy towards the goblin's extraordinary ability. Velar and I enthusiastically discussed the possibility of entering other worlds through books we had read. "I wish I could live in Moby Dick," Velar said, his pirate past making his longing understandable. I, on the other hand, couldn't choose just one place to step into, I wanted to experience them all!

My mind daydreamed about visiting my favorite book world, the city of Starlight, and I lost myself in the fantasy. Velar gently nudged me, bringing me back to reality, which was already magical now that I was back with the circus and my immortal companions. We continued our exploration of the castle's towering spires and gazed down at the alligators swimming in the moat below.

As we ventured through the castle, I realized it was fortunate we'd left our room behind. The air was thick with unspoken desire, and I couldn't ignore the growing sexual tension between us. Every touch, no matter how brief, sent my heart racing.

When Velar helped me up from the library floor, I felt an intense surge of passion. He was always there to rescue me, and I couldn't help but be drawn to his chivalrous nature. His proximity was both thrilling and intimidating, leaving me breathless and eager for what might come next.

When the time came for my massage, I welcomed the respite from Velar's intense presence. I craved a moment of tranquility, free from the complexities surrounding me. Bellamy's thoughtfulness always made me feel pampered, and I adored him for it. Who wouldn't cherish being spoiled by the one they love? Upon arriving at the spa, a statuesque woman escorted me to a private room.

I disrobed and reclined on the massage table, awaiting her return. As the lights dimmed and soothing music filled the air, her skilled hands began working out the knots in my back, releasing tension I didn't even know I carried. Initially, it was uncomfortable, but soon, her expert touch melted away my stiffness, leaving me feeling relaxed and supple.

The massage was so divine that I drifted in and out of consciousness, completely losing track of time and my surroundings. My mind was serene, free from thoughts and worries. I was utterly at peace.

The moment I became aware of my tranquility, I was pulled back to reality. The skilled therapist had worked out all the knots in my back, expertly soothing the pain away. After she finished, she excused herself, leaving me to bask in the aftermath of the massage.

I remained on the bed, savoring the bliss. Then, I heard the door creak open. Initially, I thought it was the therapist returning to check on me, but as a masculine form settled on top of me, I knew it was Velar. His sudden presence sent a thrill through my relaxed body, and I felt my heart race with anticipation.

As I lay there, I felt a warm breath on my neck, causing my body to arch in response. I was so consumed by desire that I didn't even think to ask permission, and as I turned over, I was surprised to see Bellamy above me, his eyes burning with intensity. "Oh my, you startled me," I whispered, still trying to process the sudden turn of events.

Bellamy's smile was sly and knowing as he gazed into my eyes and asked, "Were you a good girl while I was away?" His eyes narrowed, and before I could even respond, he commanded, "Turn over." I knew exactly what he wanted, and my body, still slick with oil from the massage, was more than willing to comply. As I obeyed, Bellamy's hands caressed my oiled skin, and then he slid inside me, our bodies moving in perfect sync.

I moaned as he held himself inside me so I could adjust to his vastness. Then he slowly started to thrust in and out of me. I spread my legs open wider to help ease the pain, but he kept fucking me. Then he fucked me harder. He went deeper and deeper. Faster and faster. Enjoying me purely for his pleasure. I thought to myself, *Was this my punishment?*

He was pounding me now and I knew I was being punished for the bite marks on my body. When Bellamy was close to cumming he started to growl like a wild animal, and it set me off. "Daddy" I moaned as I came and hen he unleashed himself inside me.

When Bellamy caught his breath, he gently lay on top of me, careful not to crush me with his full weight. I whispered, "how did the meeting go?" "Oh, it went great!" His voice trailed off, and I could feel his body relaxing, almost drifting off to sleep.

Bellamy rolled off me, allowing my lungs to expand fully once more. "The werewolves, Fae, and witches are all on board to help us!" He exclaimed. I was overjoyed I sprang off the table, wrapping my naked body around Bellamy in a tight embrace. "And an Ogre is also helping as well!"

Bellamy began to recount the meeting, his eyes widening in surprise when I asked, "Atlas?" He let out a deep, rumbling laugh, his voice low and husky as he replied, "Ah, yes, you've met Atlas, I see." I smiled knowingly, "He seems like a kind ogre."

As Bellamy dressed, he chuckled, "Atlas took a liking to you, it seems. He initially thought you were with Velar, but once I clarified that you were my wife and the esteemed Mrs. Darlington of Thee Darlington Circus, he couldn't refuse our request." While he finished recounting the Undying council meeting, I slipped into my blue dress.

We then headed to our room to collect Eve and Velar, who were already prepared and waiting. Eve asked with a hint of envy, "How was your massage?" I returned her question with a sly smile, "How's Draven?" Her face lit up, and she blushed, clearly smitten. With our bags in hand, courtesy of Bellamy and Velar, we exited our room, ready to head home.

As we approached the front door in the foyer, a voice echoed from the grand staircase behind us. President Olivia stood at the top, her presence commanding attention. Bellamy bowed respectfully, and we followed suit. When she descended to the bottom of the stairs, she addressed Bellamy, "I think it's best if you travel through our cheval glass."

Her gaze swept across us all before focusing on Bellamy. "Stay hidden, and we'll be prepared when you need us." She instructed. Bellamy expressed his gratitude once more, and a servant escorted us to a room housing an enormous cheval glass. Its massive size allowed us to step into it together, which we did. Bellamy directed us, "Say Darlington Circus" and in unison, we repeated, "Darlington Circus."

CHAPTER
TWENTY

In an instant, we found ourselves back at the circus entrance. Upon our return, we decided to split up and reconvene later at Casmira. Bellamy headed off to confer with Mesidor and Ambrette, tasked with rallying the witches of Jubilee to join our cause. Eve dispersed among the townspeople, spreading the word.

I made my way to inform Lucca of my return. Before we parted ways, Bellamy urged us to hurry, sensing the circus had stayed in one place for too long. I lost sight of Velar, but assumed he'd retreated to his home to rest, exhausted from the night's events. Daylight had arrived, and though Velar could tolerate the artificial sunlight, I knew he needed rest. Fatigue had caught up with all of us, it seemed.

Lucca's attention was diverted to Pixie and Poppy outside Miss Poppet's bake shop, and he quickly pursued them, utterly uninterested in my return. I engaged in conversation with Miss

Poppet, sharing tales of the Undying Ball. Well, censored versions.

However, when I realized my visit had overstayed its welcome, I rose from my chair to bid her farewell. Just then, we both froze, our eyes locking in a mutual moment of awareness, as we sensed the familiar vibration. Bellamy had jumped us, transporting us to our next hidden destination.

Bellamy's voice resonated from the enchanted sky, followed by an announcement from the unseen speakers, "The Circus will open tomorrow, and all hands are required on deck." My jaw dropped in disbelief as I turned to Miss Poppet, wondering what Bellamy was thinking. I quickly bid her farewell and rushed back to Casmira, determined to find Bellamy and demand an explanation.

Lucca and I arrived at Casmira's gate simultaneously, nearly colliding. Inside, Bellamy waited by the crackling fireplace, his expression unreadable. My anger got the better of me, and I burst out, "We can't possibly open the circus tomorrow! It's far too risky!"

Lucca, sensing the tension, swiftly dodged upstairs to his bedroom, eager to avoid the impending confrontation. Just then, Velar burst through the front door, almost splintering it from its hinges. "Bell, we can't open the circus tomorrow!" he demanded, his voice echoing through the room.

Bellamy stood tall, his legs spread wide, his hands clasped behind his back, exuding an air of superiority. His gaze seemed to regard us as inferior, which, given his vast age of over 400 years, perhaps we were.

I felt a flutter in my chest as Bellamy stood before me, his confident stance and wise, aged eyes stirring a thrill within me.

My face grew warm, and I sensed myself becoming lightheaded as our gazes locked.

He seemed to sense my thoughts, his smile hinting at a knowing glint. Just as my knees began to weaken, Casmira opened the front door, breaking the spell. I suspected Bellamy's magic was at play, saving me from my own vulnerability.

Eve burst into the room, breathless, having evidently sprinted across Jubilee in response to Bellamy's declaration, just like the rest of us. She joined our gathering by the fireplace, her eyes fixed intently on Bellamy. "Hey Bell, what's going on?" she asked, her tone implying he'd lost his damn mind.

Bellamy ran his hand through his hair, a hint of exasperation showing. "I have a plan, so let's not jump to conclusions," he said, his calm demeanor a contrast to our collective anxiety. We all settled in on the couch, eager to hear his plan. "Well, what is it?" Velar asked, his arms crossed with skepticism.

Bellamy explained, "The witches can track the elders... or at least, they will be able to." My friends and I exchanged perplexed glances, clearly puzzled. Bellamy elaborated, "To track the elders, we need something of theirs, just like they use my magic to track me." Velar's eyes narrowed. "So, it's a trap?" Bellamy nodded in confirmation. "So, we are the bait?" Eve questioned. "Essentially." Bellamy's straightforward response left a knot in my stomach.

"The Cask of Amontillado!" Velar exclaimed, his eyes sparkling with excitement. Our confused expressions prompted him to elaborate, his smile faltering as he realized we weren't familiar with the reference.

He leaned in, his tone turning serious. "It's like Edgar Allan Poe's story, where a man seeks revenge by luring his enemy into a trap, burying him alive in a catacomb." Velar's smile returned, his fangs gleaming. Eve's sarcastic comment, "Can't wait to read that book," was met with Bellamy's thoughtful silence.

Then, to my surprise, Bellamy nodded in agreement with Velar, "I'd like to read that." I felt uneasy, sensing the danger in Bellamy's plan, but my trust in him won out. Without looking at Eve or Velar, I nodded in agreement, my heart racing with trepidation.

As Velar and Eve engaged in a hushed conversation, I trailed behind Bellamy into the kitchen, my anxiety escalating with each step. I observed in silence as he uncorked a bottle of wine and poured four generous glasses, his movements seemingly effortless.

My mind raced with apprehensions, yet Bellamy's nonchalant demeanor suggested he was unfazed, almost as if he was hiding something. He handed me a glass filled to the brim with wine, his smile unsettling. "Cheers," he said, his tone lighthearted, but my nerves remained on edge.

As night fell, the four of us gathered on Casmira's front porch, surrounded by the soft glow of twinkling lights. Eve and I snuggled together on the swing, while Velar sat cross-legged on the floor. Bellamy perched on the railing, his eyes gleaming with magic.

With a flick of his wrist, the sky transformed, ushering in a crisp, cool night. I nestled closer to Eve as the wind whispered through the trees, and suddenly, a soft blanket descended upon our laps, enveloping us in warmth. I smiled at Bellamy, my eyes locking onto his, knowing that his magic was behind this cozy gesture.

Our conversation about the circus was light and easy, until Velar suddenly shifted the topic. "Nic, I don't think you and

Lucca should go to the circus tomorrow." Before I could respond, Bellamy interjected, "She's not going to be."

My eyes widened in surprise and annoyance, fixing Bellamy with a stern look. "Baby girl, I can't risk losing you," he explained, his tone soft but firm. I turned to Eve, expecting her to disagree, but she nodded in agreement with Bellamy. Deep down, I knew they were right, my presence would only distract them and potentially put them in harm's way. With a quiet nod, I acquiesced.

The night wore on, and we shared a few more bottles of wine before Bellamy sent Eve and Velar home, citing the need for rest before the big day ahead. As they departed through the front gate, I headed upstairs to ensure Lucca was settling in for the night as well.

I slipped into Lucca's room, expecting to find him wide awake, but instead, he was fast asleep. The TV cast a faint glow, and I crept towards it, trying not to disturb him. As I turned it off, I heard a faint stir behind me and froze, holding my breath to avoid waking him. But when I turned back, he was still peacefully asleep.

A warm smile spread across my face, feeling grateful to have my little brother living with me. It was a reminder that I was still connected to the real world, a world beyond the magic and wonder that Bellamy brought into my life. Perhaps, I thought, Bellamy felt the same way about me when I returned to him, a connection to the mortal world, a reminder of the life he once knew.

I anticipated Bellamy's desire for me that night, and as I emerged from the shower, I found him waiting in bed, his arms open in invitation. I reached for a silk nightgown, but his voice whispered sweetly, "No, I prefer you naked." My gown fell to the floor, and I slipped into bed beside him, our skin meeting in a tender embrace. The world outside receded, and all that remained was the two of us, lost in the intimacy of the moment.

As I snuggled under the covers, I felt Bellamy's warmth envelop me, his chest a comforting haven. His embrace tightened, "Do you want me to share you, baby girl?"

My heart raced, memories of our previous threesome flooding my mind. I longed for Velar's presence, my desire for another night like the Undying Ball burning bright. Bellamy's eyes gleamed with knowledge, his teasing tone igniting a fire within me. His kiss was intense, his body pressing against mine with a hunger that left me breathless. I wondered if Velar had revealed our secret to Bellamy, but my thoughts were lost in the passion of the moment.

His sultry blue eyes locked onto mine, and he whispered, "I know you do," his voice dripping with seduction. I felt his hardness pressing against me, his body grinding into mine with a tantalizing rhythm. His lips claimed mine in a fierce kiss, leaving me breathless and yearning for more. My mind raced with thoughts of our previous encounter at the Undying Ball, wondering if Velar had shared our secret with Bellamy. The thrill of possibility only fueled my desire.

Bellamy's voice was firm and commanding, "I need you to earn it." I nodded, understanding the unspoken challenge. With a determined gaze, I nodded my head and made my way down under the covers. When my mouth reached him, I took him slowly into my wet mouth. "Good girl," he moaned. His moaning further turned me on, and it put me into an even deeper erotic trance where I began sucking even deeper.

I knew he wanted me to show him how naughty I could be, how slutty I had become. I made him moan like I had never heard him before. I sucked and stroked him until he exploded into my mouth. "Good girl," he groaned. I nestled my head against his thigh, feeling safe and protected. He gently pulled me close, wrapping his arms around me in a warm embrace. Together, we drifted off to sleep, surrounded by a sense of comfort and tranquility.

With a mix of nerves and determination, I woke up early, eager to contribute in some way. I knew I wasn't allowed to directly participate, but I was determined to help in any way I could.

My mind raced as I made my way to the kitchen, where a secret pantry lay hidden behind a floor-to-ceiling painting, "The Cigar Girl," I had shared the location with Casmira, and Bellamy's magic had made it possible. I listened carefully, ensuring I was alone, before pulling the painting open like a door and slipping inside.

As I fumbled through the dimly lit space, I stumbled upon the collection of herbs I had gathered during my many lifetimes. "Casmira, can you brighten things up here?" I asked aloud, and instantly, the room was filled with light. "Thanks," I said, scanning the shelves lined with glass jars labeled with familiar names. Lavender, Gingko, Evening Primrose oil, Echinacea, Turmeric.

The sight of the herbs transported me back to when I first began exploring the world of witchcraft, fascinated by Bellamy's magic and the witches of Jubilee. Although Bellamy's powers surpassed anything I could hope to achieve, I had developed a passion for the craft over the years. Just as I was about to give up and leave the hidden room, something long forgotten caught my eye...

My old witch's knot pendant. I picked it up, feeling a surge of nostalgia as my fingers traced the intricate design. The four interwoven points, representing earth, air, fire, and water, seemed to hum with a gentle power.

Bellamy had gifted me this symbol of protection and unity when we first exchanged our vows. I remembered him explaining the ancient significance of the knot, how it bound two lives together in marriage, and how it would shield me from harm. With a sense of purpose, I fastened the pendant around my neck, feeling its familiar weight settle into place. With the knot's protection and power coursing through me, I set to work with renewed determination.

As the silence was broken by the creaks and groans of footsteps above, I froze, my heart racing. I wanted to escape the hidden pantry before I was discovered. I swiftly gathered my supplies and slipped out from behind the painting, just as Bellamy entered the kitchen, his arms crossed and a hint of amusement playing on his lips. "What's got you so busy?" he asked, his eyes radiating curiosity.

I held up the three witch's knot bracelets I had crafted, and his expression turned from playful to impressed. He knew the significance of the knots and admired my handiwork as he stepped closer. "I wanted to contribute, even if I can't be there in person," I explained. "A protection bracelet, made with love." He extended his hand, and I tied the bracelet around his wrist, the knot symbolizing our bond and protection.

Just as I finished tying the bracelet, the front door opened, and Bellamy thanked me with a gentle kiss. Velar and Eve entered the kitchen, and I held up the matching witch's knots. "I made these for you," I said, offering them the bracelets. Eve's eyes lit up as she asked, "What's the meaning behind these?" "They're protection bracelets," I explained, helping her tie it around her wrist.

Velar's comment caught me off guard, "You shouldn't feel guilty about not being able to help us." I didn't respond, realizzing he had struck a chord. I focused on tying the bracelet around Velar's thicker wrist, glad I had made them large enough. Velar tried to reassure me, "Enjoy your day, relax, we'll be back before you know it." His words were comforting, but I couldn't shake off the feeling of helplessness.

As Lucca bounded down the stairs, his energy was infectious. He joined us in the kitchen, where something sweet was baking in the oven. I didn't catch what it was, too distracted by the impending departure of the trio. I followed them outside and stood on the front porch, watching until they vanished into the woods.

Returning inside, I found Lucca already indulging in a freshly baked Dutch baby pancake. The aroma was irresistible, so I grabbed a plate and joined him. We savored the treat in comfortable silence, our hunger momentarily taking priority over conversation. As I poured myself a steaming mug of freshly brewed coffee, Lucca's eyes widened in wonder, and I couldn't help but smile at his delight.

After breakfast, I knew I had to keep Lucca occupied, or perhaps it was myself who needed the distraction. "Are you scared?" Lucca asked, his eyes searching for reassurance. "No,

they're unstoppable, everything will be fine," I said, trying to sound convincing despite my own fears. The elders were formidable and terrifying, and the thought of them seeking to steal Bellamy's magic made my stomach twist with anxiety.

I attempted to divert Lucca's attention with games and puzzles, but he remained restless, his mind fixed on the impending attack on the circus. Together, we waited in tense anticipation, feeling helpless as our loved ones faced the threat of the elders' attack.

As I paced back and forth in the library, Lucca burst in, "Why haven't they attacked yet?" he asked, his eyes wide with worry. I hesitated, unsure of what to say. "It's only midday, they'll come," I replied, trying to sound convincing, but my words felt hollow. The truth was, I had no idea what was taking the elders so long. I didn't want to admit it, but the more I thought about Bellamy's plan, the more I doubted its success. The idea of using our loved ones as bait felt increasingly precarious, and my anxiety grew with each passing moment.

Panic set in, and my mind raced with worst-case scenarios. What if they'd already been attacked? *What if they needed my help?* I had to check. I turned to Lucca; my voice laced with desperation. "Lucca, I need you to stay here, okay? Do you understand me?" I demanded, my eyes pleading for his cooperation. He nodded slowly, "Yes."

With that I sprint towards the front door. I flung it open, but it slammed shut with a force that nearly knocked me off balance. I tried again, pulling with all my might, but the door refused to budge. It was as if some invisible force was determined to keep me trapped inside. I grasped the doorknob, my hand refusing to let go, and the door swung open once more. This time, I stumbled forward, my body crashing into the door as it slammed shut again.

I stood up, dusting myself off, and called out in frustration, "Casmira!" The front door creaked open, as if surrendering to my determination. I stepped out into the bright sunlight, making my way towards the weeping willow tree. My heart raced as I followed the worn-out path to the entrance. I took a deep breath, preparing myself for what I might find. Cautiously, I ascended the stairs and peeked out into the circus. Everything seemed calm and ordinary, so I continued towards the main gate entrance, my senses on high alert for any sign of trouble.

The sun shone brightly over Darlington Circus, casting a warm glow over the bustling crowds. The air was filled with the sweet scent of sugary treats and the sound of laughter and applause. I surveyed the scene, my eyes scanning the crowd of happy faces, performers and patrons alike. Everything seemed peaceful and joyful, just as it always was in this enchanted place. With a sense of relief, I continued down the cobblestone path.

I had only taken a few more steps when a deafening explosion shook the ground, sending me tumbling to the cobblestones. The blast wave reverberated through my body, leaving my ears ringing and my head spinning. As I struggled to my feet, I saw that I was not alone, many others lay nearby, dazed and disoriented.

The air was filled with the cacophony of screams and cries for help. Despite my instinct to rush towards the chaos and assist, I knew I had to prioritize my own safety. Bellamy's stern warnings echoed in my mind, and I knew he would be furious if I intervened. With a heavy heart, I turned back towards Jubilee, my senses reeling from the shock of the explosion.

I raced back to the weeping willow tree, my heart pounding in my chest, as another explosion rocked the circus. The ground trembled beneath my feet, and I watched in horror as the crowd erupted into more chaos. People scrambled in all directions, unsure of where to seek safety. I felt helpless, frozen in place, as the circus descended into pandemonium.

Soon, the circus workers rushed towards the tree, seeking refuge. I stepped aside, allowing them to hurry down the stairs to safety. Bellamy appeared, his magic swiftly creating a new exit for the fleeing guests. Without noticing me, he vanished into the chaos, leaving the crew members to guide the terrified crowd to freedom through the new side entrance he had created.

I remained steadfast by the weeping willow tree, guiding the stragglers to safety in Jubilee. The explosions continued to rock the circus, causing the tree to tremble and more people to flee down the stairs. As the chaos slowly subsided, the frequency of the blasts dwindled, and eventually ceased. The circus was finally empty, the guests and performers having escaped through the tree or the gate.

My anxiety grew as I waited for Bellamy, Velar, and Eve to appear. I scanned the front gate, my eyes fixed on the entrance, but my fear kept me rooted to the spot. "Where are they?" I whispered to myself. I couldn't bring myself to leave the tree, my sole comfort in this terrifying ordeal.

As the minutes ticked by, my anxiety gave way to despair, and tears streamed down my face. I felt powerless, unable to do anything but wait. Just as I thought I was alone, Miss Poppet emerged from the entrance of Jubilee. She approached me with a gentle smile and said, "Come on, dear." I hesitated, unwilling to leave the spot where I last saw Bellamy, Velar, and Eve. But Miss Poppet's warm hand on my arm encouraged me to follow her, and I reluctantly descended into the safety of Jubilee, my heart heavy with worry and fear.

Miss Poppet, offering a comforting embrace as we strolled towards the town square. My mind raced with unanswered questions, my thoughts consumed by the whereabouts of Bellamy, Velar, and Eve. *How could they just vanish?* The uncertainty was unbearable.

Despite their immortality, a nagging fear lingered, had they somehow died? Just as we entered the cozy confines of Miss Poppet's bake shop, a triumphant cry echoed through the square. "They're back!" My heart skipped a beat as I spun around, hope and relief washing over me like a wave.

I flung open the door and my heart leapt with joy at the sight of Velar and Eve approaching. But my excitement was short-lived, as my eyes scanned the area behind them, searching for Bellamy. My heart sank like a stone when I realized he wasn't there. A wave of nausea washed over me, and my legs buckled beneath me. I collapsed to the ground, struggling to catch my breath.

Velar was by my side in an instant, his concern etched on his face. "Nic, are you okay? What's wrong?" I managed to choke out the words, "Where's Bellamy?" Eve rushed up to us, her eyes wide with alarm. "Bell isn't back yet?"

She turned to Velar, seeking answers, but he remained silent. He gently lifted me up, and I frantically scanned the entrance once more, willing Bellamy to appear. "Where is he?" I sobbed, my desperation palpable. Eve wrapped a comforting arm around my waist, trying to reassure me. "He will be okay, Nic."

The three of us stood in anxious silence, waiting for any sign of Bellamy's return. A few concerned townsfolk approached us, offering their assistance, but we knew there was nothing anyone could do.

Eve firmly suggested we head back to Casmira, her eyes filled with worry. Velar, determined to uncover some answers, considered returning to the circus to assess the situation. I grasped his arm, holding him back. "No, Velar, stay here in Jubilee," I urged, my voice laced with concern. "The police will likely be investigating the explosions at the circus. It's not safe for you to go back there." Velar hesitated, then nodded in agreement, his eyes never leaving mine.

He finally convinced me to head back to Casmira, and we began our somber walk. I was reluctant to leave the entrance, still holding onto hope that Bellamy would appear at any moment.

Just as we turned our backs on the entrance and started towards home, I heard a faint shout in the distance. "I got it!" Bellamy's triumphant cry echoed through the air, and I spun around to see him waving something in the air, a broad grin spreading across his face. My heart soared with relief and joy, and I rushed back towards him, Velar and Eve close behind.

As I sprinted towards him, my heart overflowed with relief and joy. I leapt into his arms, wrapping my legs around his waist, and buried my face in his neck. The familiar scent of the sea and his sweat mingled together, a comforting aroma that soothes my frazzled nerves.

As he walked towards the cheering crowd, his arrogant smile returned, and he whispered in my ear, "Baby girl, I'm immortal, remember? A few elders can't bring me down." His confidence and charm were infectious, and I couldn't help but laugh, my worries melting away in his embrace.

Bellamy held aloft the elders' cloak, triumphant, as the crowd in Jubilee gathered around. "We have what we need to track the elders!" he declared, his voice ringing out across the square. Mesidor and Ambrette made their way through the crowd, their faces set with determination.

I watched as Bellamy handed the cloak over to them. They hastened back to their cottage, no doubt to begin their spell. Once the crowd had dispersed, Bellamy whisked us away to a hidden location, declaring that we would remain in hiding until we could devise a plan to evade the elders.

I had every confidence that with Sage's expertise, they would ensure our safety and locate the elders. For now, we would bide our time, waiting for the perfect moment to strike back. Sage has proven to be a valuable addition to our community in Jubilee. Initially hesitant to leave the Blackwoods' cottage, she has gradually become an integral part of our little family.

She's been lending a hand to Mesidor in the gardens, and even cultivated an entire garden of tulips, which she says reminds her of her homeland in the Netherlands. Ambrette has been raving about her culinary skills, claiming she's been whipping up delectable dinners every night.

It seems we may have misjudged Sage initially, perhaps she's not as evil as we thought. Her contributions and kindness have slowly won us over, and she's begun to feel like one of us.

CHAPTER
TWENTY-ONE

The entire community stayed in Jubilee to ensure our safety. The witches' progress was slower than anticipated, even with the elder's cloak in their possession. Days turned into weeks, and weeks dragged into months. Three long months of hiding. Restlessness settled over us all, including myself.

Sage and the Backwoods finally discovered the reason behind the elders' relentless pursuit, Bellamy's magic was traceable. They could sniff it out if they were within a hundred-mile radius. So, we devised a plan to lure them away, and just as they closed in, Bellamy would whisk us off to a new location, where we'd hide until they picked up the scent again.

It was a cat-and-mouse game, with the Blackwoods and Sage expertly tracking the elders' movements. Sometimes it took days, other times weeks, but we remained one step ahead, always on the move, never staying in one place for too long.

While our nomadic existence allowed us to escape the elders, it was clear that this lifestyle couldn't be sustained indefinitely. We couldn't forever, never truly living in the real world. Bellamy, in particular, was growing increasingly restless, his anger simmering just below the surface.

Every few weeks, he and a small group of men would venture out to gather supplies, jumping to a nearby town and then dispersing to collect essentials like food, dry goods, and newspapers to keep us informed of what was happening in the real world.

They'd also fetch whatever else we needed that couldn't be found in Jubilee's isolated community. These brief excursions into the real world were a reminder of what we were missing, and Bellamy's frustration was growing. He longed to break free from this hiding game and reclaim his life, but the danger posed by the elders kept us trapped in this endless cycle.

During these brief excursions, Lucca and I would sneak away to the circus, eager to seize the opportunity to contact our parents. We'd fabricate stories about our travels, exaggerating our performances and Lucca's skills, careful not to reveal the truth about our hiding place.

Our conversations were always hurried, as Bellamy refused to linger, anxious to return us to the safety of Jubilee. We'd steal a few precious minutes to reconnect with our loved ones, our words laced with deceit, but necessary to maintain the illusion of a normal life.

As we exited the playroom, exhausted from a grueling session, Bellamy's expression turned thoughtful. "Will you be alright tomorrow night, while I'm away?" he asked with concern. I offered a reassuring smile, trying to alleviate his worries. But he continued to scrutinize me, as if searching for any sign of doubt. Then, without warning, he posed an unexpected question, "Would you feel safer if Velar stayed with you?"

I felt a surge of flustered emotions, as if Bellamy had somehow infiltrated my thoughts. *How did he know I'd been thinking about Velar?* It was as if he had a direct line to my innermost musings. I gazed at him, perplexed, my words caught in my throat.

Bellamy's laughter broke the silence, his eyes sparkling with amusement at my bewildered expression. "It's okay, my love," he teased, his voice low and playful. "I know Velar would jump at the chance to spend a night with you. And I know you enjoyed his company last time... and his kiss." He paused; his eyes locked on mine. "I just want you to ask me, and to be honest with me. I promise I won't be upset. I trust you, and I trust Velar."

I finally summoned the courage to ask, my voice barely above a whisper. "Can Velar spend the night?" Bellamy's smile was immediate. "Yes, he may."

He turned and walked towards our bedroom, leaving me feeling perplexed and a little frustrated. I trailed after him, my confusion giving way to irritation. "What do you mean?" I demanded, feeling upset, but I didn't know why. *Was it because he wasn't jealous? Didn't he care that I wanted to spend time with Velar?*

The memory of our past conflicts, including the time he'd killed me over Velar, made his nonchalance all the more baffling. "What's going on, Bellamy?" I asked, feeling a pang of uncertainty. "Do you not love me anymore?"

As I stood there, my emotions simmering, Bellamy's calm and possessive tone soothed my nerves. "Baby girl, I love you. You will forever be mine. I own you." His words were a gentle reminder of our bond. "I know you love me, and I know you love Velar. That's okay." He paused, his sincerity evident. "I promised myself I'd never let jealousy come between us again. I lost you once because of it, and I won't risk it again."

I wrapped my arms around his neck, my love for him overflowing. "I love you more," I whispered. As I relaxed my hold, he smiled knowingly. "I know." He began dressing, his eyes locked on mine. "If you want to have a little fun while Daddy's away, I'll allow it." His eyebrows raised, his tone turning playful. "Only because you asked for permission, my Darling." He winked, his eyes sparkling with anticipation. "I can't wait to hear all about it."

That night, my mind raced with anticipation, making sleep elusive. I lay awake, staring at the ceiling, my thoughts consumed by the prospect of tomorrow night with Velar. My restlessness was contagious, and Bellamy's gentle stirrings beside me told me I was keeping him awake.

Feeling guilty for disturbing him on the eve of his big day, I tried to settle down. But my tossing and turning continued until Bellamy, with a soft snap of his fingers, conjured a cup into existence on my bedside table. Without a word, I reached for the potion and drank it down, feeling my eyelids grow heavy as sleep finally claimed me.

The next morning, I groggily emerged from bed to bid Bellamy farewell. Though it was only for a night, his absence would be felt. My nerves were also on edge, anticipating the evening ahead with Velar. After a tight embrace, I watched as Bellamy vanished into the willow tree alongside a handful of men, who nodded their heads in respect as they passed me. With a heavy heart, I turned and trudged back to our home, the silence echoing through the empty spaces.

As I strolled through the front gate, which swung open with a soft creak, I savored the crisp morning air of Jubilee. The sky above was a brilliant blue, and I couldn't help but feel a sense of tranquility wash over me. But my peaceful reverie was shattered when I turned to face the door and found Velar standing before me, his eyes locked on mine with an uncharacteristic nervous energy.

My heart stopped as I took in his tense posture, his usual confidence momentarily replaced by a vulnerable intensity. Without a word, he closed the distance between us, his movements swift and purposeful, leaving me little time to prepare for what was to come.

I stood rooted to the spot; my feet seemingly anchored to the ground as Velar's piercing gaze held mine. "Hey," he said, his deep voice low. I managed a calm reply, "Hey Velar," It was absurd to feel so nervous around someone I'd known for so long, yet my heart raced like a wild animal. I forced myself to move, reaching the door just as it swung open, and Velar followed closely behind.

As we entered the main room, the fireplace roared to life, casting a warm glow over the space. I began to speak, but Velar cut in, his words tumbling out in a rush. "I'm sorry, I couldn't wait until tonight. Bellamy came to see me this morning and told me... well, you know." My eyes narrowed, a knot forming in my stomach. Typical Bellamy, always meddling and pushing the boundaries.

My face flamed with embarrassment as I confirmed, "Yes, I did ask." His eyes blazed with intensity, and he closed the distance between us, pulling me into a fierce, passionate kiss. His hunger was visible, and I knew it went beyond mere thirst.

As our lips parted, they lingered, hovering close, our breaths mingling. "I think tonight you should sleep at my house," he whispered with desire. Before I could respond, he added, "That way, there won't be any distractions." My gaze faltered, dropping to the floor, but I nodded my head in agreement, my heart racing with anticipation and a hint of trepidation.

A wave of relief washed over me after Velar's words, grateful that the truth was finally out in the open without me having to muster the courage to reveal it myself. It dawned on me that Bellamy's meddling was likely intentional, sparing me the discomfort of confessing my desires. He always seemed to be one step ahead, anticipating and orchestrating events to his advantage. I marveled at his uncanny ability to read people and situations, leaving me in awe of his mastery over the intricacies of human relationships.

Velar settled into the chair in front of the fire, stretching his arms above his head in a languid motion. "So, what do you want to do today?" he asked, his eyes fixed on me. I pondered for a moment before suggesting, "Let's take a walk." Without waiting for his response, I headed towards the front door. Velar quickly fell into step behind me, his long strides easily keeping pace.

As we strolled along the wooded path, he reached out and took my hand, his fingers intertwined with mine. We walked in comfortable silence until we reached the town square, where I discreetly disentangled my hand from his, aware of the watchful eyes of the townspeople. Velar understood the unspoken gesture.

Our stroll through the town square led us to Miss Poppets' bakery, where the sweet aroma of freshly baked goods wafted out into the street. Velar's eyes lit up as he watched me devour three muffins in quick succession, leaving him laughing. Miss Poppets herself handed me a batch to go, and we continued our leisurely walk.

Our shopping excursion took us to The Jubilee Boutique, where Velar surprised me by purchasing a stunning dress that matched the black and white pattern of the circus tents. I couldn't resist trying it on, and Velar's admiring gaze as I emerged from the dressing room made my heart skip a beat. The dress was a showstopper, its flowing design and daring backless cut leaving me feeling like a true performer. "I'm going to have to take you somewhere fancy to wear that," Velar said, his eyes sparkling with promise. I smiled already imagining the possibilities.

The Jubilee library was our final destination in the square, a haven that never failed to enchant me. As I wandered through the shelves, my fingers trailing over the spines of the books, my mind drifted back to the enigmatic goblin from the ball. "I wish I could live in a book!" I exclaimed, lost in the fantasy.

Velar's response was immediate and profound. "You already live in a fairy tale." I laughed, dismissing the notion, but his words lingered, resonating deep within me. As Velar settled into an oversized chair, looking like a king claiming his throne, I continued my exploration, disappearing into the fiction section, surrounded by the stories and worlds that had always captivated me.

As I delved deeper into the shelves, every book title I read tantalized me, leaving me eager for more. Before long, my arms were laden with a stack of books, each one promising a new adventure. Returning to the chair, I found Velar engrossed in his own reading material. I playfully plopped my books down on the table, and he asked, without looking up, "Are you sure you have enough?"

I waited for him to meet my gaze, and when his emerald eyes finally locked onto mine, I asked, "What are you reading?" His eyes dropped back down to the page, and he recited,

"And neither the angels in Heaven above, Nor the demons down under the sea, Can ever dissever my soul from the soul, Of the beautiful Annabel Lee."

His voice was low and hypnotic, and I recognized the familiar lines of Edgar Allan Poe's haunting poem. Velar's love for Poe's work was well-known to me, and I shared his passion.

In fact, Poe had been a friend to Velar, even visiting the circus in the past. This wasn't the first time Velar had read to me, and I cherished the memory of those moments. His voice brought me back to a time when life was simpler, and I was grateful for this small reminder of our past life together.

As we strolled back towards Casmira, our delightful day in the square coming to a close, we were suddenly beset by a flurry of energy. Lucca and the Bally twins burst into our tranquil scene, their faces alight with excitement. Lucca's eyes widened in astonishment as he took in the impressive stack of books Velar carried. "Are you going to read all of those?" he asked, his tone incredulous, his gaze darting to me as if seeking confirmation. I smiled, assuring him, "Yep." The twins, ever curious, looked at us with interest, and I posed a question, "What are you guys up to?" My subtle warning was not lost on them, and they understood that any mischief would need to be kept in check.

"Don't worry, we're just taking him into the woods, Mrs. Darlington," Pixie or Poppy said their voices were indistinguishable. I turned my attention to Lucca, my eyes locking onto his enthusiastic face. "And what are you doing in the woods, Lucca?" I asked, my tone gentle. His response was immediate, "We're looking for gnomes!"

His smile was infectious, and I couldn't help but feel a pang of nostalgia. I glanced past him at the twins, who were now giggling into each other's faces. I knew they were leading him on a wild goose chase, but Lucca's excitement was so genuine, so full of wonder, that I couldn't bear to disillusion him. The Emberlynn Forest held many secrets, but gnomes weren't among them. I kept my silence, allowing him to revel in the thrill of the adventure, his eyes shining with an innocence that tugged at my heart.

Instead, I adopted a serious tone, "Well, be very careful on your hunt, and Pixie, Poppy, make sure you stay with Lucca until you find one." The twins' giggles abruptly ceased, and they exchanged a guilty glance, realizing they'd been caught out. I knew Lucca would spend the entire day searching for the nonexistent gnomes, and the twins would be stuck with him, their prank backfiring.

Lucca, oblivious to the truth, jumped up and down with excitement, "C'mon girls, let's go!" he shouted, already racing towards the forest. I couldn't help but smile at the twins' predicament before they reluctantly followed after Lucca. Velar and I watched them disappear into the trees, and he chuckled, "That was brutal." I nodded in agreement, "I'm sick of them always teasing Lucca. Maybe this will teach them a lesson." Maybe the twins would finally experience a taste of their own medicine.

Upon returning to the house, Velar deposited the books on the library table, and my attention was drawn to the savory aromas wafting from the kitchen. I made my way to investigate, and my eyes landed on a cookie sheet bearing two steaming bowls of French onion soup. The cheese melted to perfection, forming a golden- brown crust that seemed to beckon me. "That looks amazing, I wish I could eat food." Velar remarked, his voice low and appreciative, as he appeared beside me. We sat down at the kitchen table; my first spoonful of the soup was like a symphony of flavors on my tongue. I devoured my lunch as Velar watched.

Later that evening, I packed a small bag and slipped out of the house with the stealth of a mischievous schoolgirl. I left a note for Lucca just in case he woke up and found me gone, but I knew him too well, he'd sleep soundly till morning.

With a thrill of excitement, I made my way through the woods, the path familiar beneath my feet. The trees parted, and I emerged into the town square, where Velar waited for me, his eyes glinting in the moonlight. The night air was alive with possibility, and I felt a sense of freedom, like I was escaping the ordinary and stepping into a world of wonder.

We savored every moment of our day together, indulging in a delightful array of activities. We strolled through the shops, lingered over lunch, engaged in a strategic game of chess, and immersed ourselves in the pages of our new books from the library. The only brief separation came at dinner, when I joined Lucca for a warm meal together before he retired to his room to prepare for bed. That's when I seized the opportunity to pack my overnight bag, my heart racing with anticipation. A mix of nerves and excitement coursed through my veins as I prepared to slip away into the night, the thrill of the unknown awaiting me.

Velar took my bag from me and then gently grasped my hand, leading me towards his home in the Emberlynn Forest. We navigated the steep hills of Jubilee, our footsteps steady and sure, until we finally reached the forest's edge. The woods here were different from those surrounding Casmira. It was denser, darker, and more mysterious. I drew closer to Velar, feeling a sense of security in his presence, as we followed a winding path that twisted and turned through the trees.

The town square's lampposts had guided us with a warm, golden glow, but the woods were a different story. The darkness was almost a thick veil that wrapped around us like a shroud. I used this as an excuse to draw closer to Velar, my hand nestled comfortably in his.

I knew that in Jubilee, the safest place in the world, there was nothing to fear in the darkness. And yet, the woods seemed to whisper secrets in the wind. Ahead, Velar's cottage beckoned, its windows aglow with a soft, inviting light. The thatched roof and half-timbered walls seemed to glow with a warm, honey-colored light, like a haven from the darkness. It was a charming, quaint sanctuary, and I felt my heart fill with anticipation as we drew nearer.

As we entered the cottage, I was struck by the familiar simplicity of Velar's home, reminiscent of his humble abode in Barrow. The space was small, yet cozy, with a warmth that belied its bareness. My eyes wandered to the fridge, where a photo of us together in our past life smiled back at me, filling me with a sense of specialness. But my gaze also fell upon a picture of Velar with Eve and Bellamy, a poignant reminder of the complexities of his past.

Velar caught me taking in the details of his home and chuckled, "It's no Casmira," he said. I smiled, "Nothing is," I replied. He led me to the brown leather couch, where I settled in, feeling the softness envelop me. "I'll be right back," Velar said, disappearing into the tiny kitchen, leaving me to absorb the warmth and comfort of his sanctuary.

When Velar returned, he carried a bottle of wine and a glass, which he handed to me with a gentle smile. "Thank you," I said, accepting the offering. He poured the glass more than halfway full, and I took a generous sip, feeling the rich, velvety texture of the merlot on my tongue. "That's good," I said, my eyes closing in appreciation.

As Velar began to kindle a fire, I watched, mesmerized by the flickering flames, my mind wandering to the differences between him and Bellamy. While Bellamy's magic was a powerful force, Velar's strength lay in his quiet, steadfast presence. And in that moment, I felt a pang of sympathy for him, a sense of regret that he didn't possess the same gifts as his friend.

I couldn't help but ogle Velar's tattooed arms, glistening in the firelight, his muscles rippling beneath his skin. His age and ruggedness were a potent aphrodisiac, his salt-and-pepper hair and piercing emerald eyes only adding to his allure. Compared to Bellamy's youthful appearance, Velar exuded a seasoned charm, his weathered look making him seem like a man who had lived a lifetime.

Though I knew he wasn't older than Bellamy, his mature presence made my heart race. Being near him accentuated my youth, making me feel delicate and vulnerable, yet drawn to him like a magnet. His rugged, battle-hardened air made me feel like a bloom in the presence of a seasoned warrior.

As the flames crackled to life, Velar sauntered towards me, his movements fluid and graceful. He stood before me, his waist inches from my face, his lean physique towering over me as he reached for the curtains. With a gentle tug, he drew them open, revealing the night sky's vast expanse. Then, he settled beside me, his thigh brushing against mine. The proximity of our bodies, combined with the warmth of the fire and the darkness outside, created an intimate atmosphere, making my heart race with anticipation.

I raised an eyebrow, curiosity getting the better of me. "Why did you open the curtains?" I asked, but Velar just smiled enigmatically, his eyes glinting with amusement. "You'll see," he said, his tone playful, but also hinting at a secret he wasn't ready to share. I shook my head, knowing that pushing him further would be futile.

Instead, I changed the subject. "Today was amazing, I loved spending time with you," I said, my cheeks flushing at the admission. Velar's smile grew wider, his eyes sparkling with delight. "I must say, I enjoyed it too," he said. "But tell me, why did you ask Bellamy if you could be with me?" he asked, as if seeking more than just a straightforward answer.

I rolled my eyes, playing coy. "Rules are rules, remember?" I said with sarcasm. Velar chuckled as he inched closer to me on the couch. My heart skipped a beat, anticipation building. He leaned in, his lips brushing against mine in a soft, gentle kiss. I had been longing for that moment all day. As I closed my eyes, savoring the sensation, I felt like time had stopped. But when I opened them again, I was struck by the magical sight outside the bay window. Delicate snowflakes dancing in the air, casting a serene silence over the forest.

"It's snowing!" I exclaimed with excitement. I leapt up from the couch, rushing to the window to gaze out at the wonderland unfolding before my eyes. The snowflakes danced and twirled, casting a spell of enchantment over the forest.

When I turned back to Velar, I found him still seated, his eyes fixed on me with a warm, knowing smile. "Did you ask

Bellamy to do this?" I asked, my curiosity getting the better of me. Velar's smile broadened, and he nodded his head in a gentle, affirming motion. In that moment, I realized that he had remembered my deep love for snow and had gone to great lengths to create this magical moment just for me.

He carefully set my glass down on the table, his eyes never leaving mine, the intensity in them burning brighter with every passing moment. Then, he claimed my lips with a passionate kiss, the anticipation and longing of the day finally unleashed.

I melted into his embrace, our desires aligning like the stars in the night sky. "I couldn't wait to just have you for a night," he whispered. "I needed to be with you all day." I felt the same desperation, the same craving. I kissed him back with equal fervor, our lips moving in perfect sync. He pulled me onto his lap, his arms wrapping around me like a warm embrace, and I knew in that moment, I was exactly where I belonged.

I straddled him, our lips locked in a fierce kiss, as his hands roamed my body with a hunger that couldn't be satisfied. This moment was different from the threesome with Bellamy, where we were mere puppets under his control. Velar's passion was unbridled, his desire for me was animalistic. He tore my clothes with such ferocity. I waited for his bite, but it didn't come.

As he teased my nipples with his tongue, I threaded my fingers through his hair, pulling him closer. Our eyes met, and the intensity of his emerald gaze sent shivers down my body. I could feel the hunger in his eyes, the urgent need to claim me. Without a word, he scooped me up and carried me to his bedroom, the darkness illuminated by the soft twinkle of Christmas lights strung above the bed. The atmosphere was electric, the air thick with anticipation. I knew at that moment, I was his.

As he laid me down, I watched as he mounted me. His naked body covered in tattoos, aroused me. I was exploring his body when his mouth found mine again. I breathed in his scent of pine and leather. I spread my legs wide for him to enter me.

I arched my back as he pushed himself deep inside me. I forgot his size and had to swiftly adjust. Oh, how I missed him. "Velar," I moaned. My moans only made him fuck me harder. I noticed he was looking at my neck and I gave him a nod of approval. He bit into my neck as he thrust himself inside me at the same time. Cries and moans escaped my mouth as I fell into a euphoric state.

Sometime during the wee hours, I nudged Velar awake, whispering "I'm starving!" He was half asleep and just groaned. I tried going to sleep, but I couldn't. I wandered out into his kitchen checking the cabinets and refrigerator. Other than a few containers containing blood it was empty. Nothing for me. *Damn vampire.*

After hearing Velar snoring away, I decided to go back to Casmira. As I walked through the snow-covered forest, the only sound being the crunch of my footsteps, I felt a sense of wonder and magic. The snowflakes danced around me, their gentle touch on my skin a reminder of the beauty and joy that Bellamy and Velar had brought into my life. I felt grateful for their thoughtfulness and love, and my heart swelled with appreciation for these two special beings who had gone to so much trouble to create this winter wonderland just for me.

I was taking my time walking back down the hill from the forest in the snow. It was cold, but not freezing. It felt good, almost rejuvenating. The enchanted snowfall made the town square look like a beautiful painting.

The snow-covered buildings seemed to glow with a soft, ethereal light, and the streets were empty and silent, as if the town itself was slumbering under a blanket of white. I felt like I had stumbled into a fairy tale, one that was mine alone to enjoy. As I walked past the square, the snowflakes continued to fall around me, their gentle touch on my skin a reminder of the magic that surrounded me. I felt alive, connected to the world in a way that was both peaceful and exhilarating.

As I walked into Casmira, the aroma of something delicious wafted from the oven, and my stomach growled. Casmira knew I was famished and had prepared a savory cottage pie, complete with tender onions, rich broth, and fluffy mashed potatoes. I dug in with gusto, savoring each bite and ignoring the gravy dripping down my chin.

I heard snickering and looked up from my meal. Lucca burst into laughter at the sight of me. "What's so funny?" I asked, wiping my mouth with the back of my hand. "You're covered in gravy!" he teased, approaching me. "What's that amazing smell?" His gaze landed on my plate, and his eyes widened. "Cottage pie? You're killing me!"

He grabbed a fork and dug in, closing his eyes in rapture. "Mmm, this is heavenly!" We sat there, savoring the warm comfort food and each other's company, our late-night snack turning into a cozy, laughter-filled moment.

As Lucca savored each bite, his eyes closed in delight, I couldn't help but smile. "Casmira culinary magic never fails," I said, feeling grateful. The cottage pie was exactly what I needed, and I loved that we shared this connection. My mind wandered, wondering what Casmira was like when I wasn't here. Did she cook for others, or was her kitchen a solo haven? The questions lingered, but for now, I was content to enjoy the warmth and comfort of this moment, with Lucca and the delicious food.

Lucca's casual question caught me off guard, and I paused, unsure how to respond. "When I die, will I come back here?" he asked, his eyes fixed on his empty plate. I struggled to find the right words, not wanting to alarm him. "That's something I'll discuss with Bellamy, okay? I'm not sure about the details," I said, trying to sound reassuring.

Lucca's gaze remained downcast, his voice barely above a whisper. "I hope so." My heart went out to him, and I felt a pang of sadness. I pushed aside my own fears and focused on offering comfort. "We'll be safe in Jubilee, all of us," I said, forcing a smile. "And we'll enjoy more of Casmira's amazing cooking, deal?" Lucca nodded, a small smile creeping onto his face, and I felt relieved.

Later I tucked my brother back into bed and I settled into my third-floor bedroom. I reflected on the day's joys, the adventure with Velar, the heartwarming dinner with Lucca, and the promise of tomorrow's reunion with Bellamy. Gratitude filled my heart as I snuggled into bed, feeling blessed and content. With a serene smile, I surrendered to slumber, the night's magic enveloping me in its soothing embrace.

The sound of the front door opening at Casmira's roused me from sleep. I lay in bed, listening as footsteps ascended the stairs, growing louder until Bellamy's familiar voice called out, "Are you alone?" I responded, "Yes, Daddy." He poked his head in, ensuring I was indeed alone, before entering the room. "I'm preparing to jump soon, but I wanted to check on you first. How was your evening?" He questioned, sounding curious.

I smiled, "It was nice." Bellamy's eyes sparkled with encouragement, as if urging me to share more. I obliged, my gratitude sincere, "Thank you, Daddy." His face lit up with a warm smile before he disappeared from the room, leaving me to settle back into bed. Shortly after, the familiar vibration of the jump vibrated through the land, signaling our new destination.

CHAPTER
TWENTY-TWO

Six long months had dragged on, and we were still seeking refuge in Jubilee. Lucca and I strolled along the familiar path, returning to Casmira from our excursion to the waterfall. With the circus still on hold. Bellamy's magic had transformed the hidden waterfall into a breathtaking spectacle, making it seem as though the enchanted sky itself was pouring forth a torrent of crystal-clear water.

The falls cascaded into a deep, clear pool, surrounded by rugged cliffs perfect for daring jumps. Bellamy's tireless efforts had also upgraded the homes and shops around the town square, adding charming gas-powered lanterns throughout Jubilee, a thoughtful precaution in case their magic ever faltered again.

As Lucca and I entered through the conservatory, the sounds of voices carried from the main room, growing louder with each step. "Lucca, why don't you go get ready for bed?" I suggested, and without a word, he headed upstairs to his bathroom. I rounded the corner into the main room, finding Sage, Ambrette, and Mesidor seated on the couch, their conversation halted as they turned their attention to me. Bellamy stood facing them, his eyes now fixed on me as well. "I don't mean to interrupt," I said, meeting Bellamy's eyes.

Bellamy's inviting gesture encouraged me to join the gathering, and I approached with a sense of trepidation. "What's going on?" I asked, standing beside him. The witches on the couch exchanged meaningful glances, their eyes sparkling with a mix of excitement and apprehension. Bellamy turned to face me, his eyes shining with determination. "After much deliberation," he announced, his voice filled with conviction, "we have decided to open the circus." The room seemed to hold its breath, awaiting my reaction to this unexpected news.

My mouth agape, I turned to gaze at the witches, seeking their input. Ambrette's encouraging smile and Mesidor's nod of approval bolstered my confidence. But Sage's enigmatic expression, her eyes fixed intently on mine, left me wondering. Bellamy's reassuring words broke the silence, "We're confident in our safety. With the elders' location in our sights, we'll have the upper hand. We'll jump more often, only open half days, minimizing our exposure." His words painted a vivid picture of their carefully thought-out plan.

As the plan unfolded, my surprise gave way to excitement. The prospect of performing again and restoring a sense of normalcy to Jubilee's residents was exhilarating. Mesidor's voice drew my attention to the map spread out on the coffee table. He traced a path with his finger, his eyes locked on the route. "This is where the elders are currently," he said, his finger circling a location in Rome. Then, he dragged his finger across the map, stopping at a point in Argentina. "And this is where we are." The distance between the two points seemed vast, but with the circus's unique abilities, it was a journey we could undertake in the blink of an eye.

As Mesidor traced the distance between our location and the elders', my apprehensions began to fade. Bellamy's reassuring words further bolstered my confidence. "Mesidor will navigate the map, and Ambrette's connection to me at the circus will serve as a safety net, allowing us to evacuate and jump if needed." Ambrette's warm smile and Sage's calm demeanor made my fears begin to dissipate. With a newfound sense of determination, I exclaimed, "Ok!" My voice was filled with excitement, and I was ready to embrace the plan and the promise of our circus's revival.

As the witches departed, Bellamy returned with Eve and Velar in tow, their faces beaming with excitement. "I shared the news with them!" Bellamy announced, his voice filled with enthusiasm, as they approached me with broad smiles. We were in this together, and the thrill of opening the circus was undeniable.

Velar plopped down beside me on the oversized chair, almost sending me tumbling off. "Now you can finally showcase that routine we've been honing for months!" Velar exclaimed. But before I could respond, Bellamy interjected, his tone firm but cautious. "No." My eyes narrowed, questioning his sudden objection. "What do you mean?" I asked, as Bellamy approached me with a deliberate stride.

Velar, sensing the tension, stood up and migrated to the fireplace, joining Eve, who watched the exchange with interest. "I don't want you to perform aerial stunts the first time around," Bellamy clarified, his eyes locked on mine, his expression a mix of concern and protectiveness.

My mouth dropped, I stared at Bellamy in disbelief. He wanted me to stay behind in Jubilee, but I couldn't bear the thought of being left behind. "I can't stay in Jubilee another day," I said, my voice calm and steady, my eyes locked on Bellamy's. I didn't raise my voice, but my determination was clear. "If it's safe enough to open the circus, then it's safe enough for me to perform one show."

I sat firmly in my chair, arms crossed, my resolve evident. Bellamy's displeasure was palpable, but Velar's intervention tipped the scales. "I'll watch over her, Bell. One show, and then she's back in Jubilee." Bellamy's resistance finally weakened and gave in.

As night fell, Bellamy's announcement echoed through the streets, and the town square erupted in cheers. "Sounds like the whole town is thrilled," Eve remarked, handing me a glass of wine as we lounged on Casmira's front porch, basking in the enchanted sunset's warm glow.

Our conversation turned to my upcoming performance, with Eve reminding me to return straight to Jubilee once I finished my act. "Rules are rules," Velar teased, playfully jabbing at Bellamy's strictness. Bellamy responded with a lighthearted middle finger, and Velar chuckled, the tension dissipating into laughter and camaraderie.

The next morning, I donned my dazzling blue trapeze costume, perfectly matching Eve's outfit. Over a serene breakfast, Bellamy, Lucca, and I savored a quiet moment together before the excitement of the day ahead. As we prepared to depart, I reminded Lucca, "Remember, you stay here, okay?"

He nodded obediently, then asked with a hint of hope, "Can I come tomorrow?" I glanced at Bellamy, who responded with a gentle "We shall see." Lucca nodded again, and I couldn't help but chuckle as he carefully placed his dish in the sink.

"What?" Lucca asked. I finished my last bite, then pushed my plate away. Luccas's gaze followed mine. My eyes fixed on it until it completely vanished. Lucca's expression turned to amazement. I met his gaze and we both burst into laughter. "It's a habit," he explained, sheepishly.

"It's showtime, Daddy!" I exclaimed, strutting ahead of Bellamy as we departed Casmira to join the others at the willow tree. He gave me a playful slap on the backside, and I sashayed away, grinning. Once we assembled, Bellamy instructed the group to wait in Jubilee while he and Velar scouted ahead.

As we waited for them, we chatted excitedly, discussing performances, tricks, food, and setup details. The performers looked fantastic, even the clowns were already in full makeup. Before long, Bellamy reappeared at the willow tree entrance, his voice booming through the enchanted speakers, "We are back in business!" The crowd erupted in cheers, and we all rushed towards him, me included, eager to get the show underway!

As we approached the willow tree, its branches parted wider than usual, allowing easy access for the eager crowd. Bellamy waited for me, and together we ascended the steps. When we reached the circus entrance, I paused, drinking in the familiar sights and sounds.

Six months felt like an eternity to be stuck in one place. I smiled, feeling a sense of freedom, but my curiosity yearned for more. I wanted to see beyond the circus boundaries, to gaze upon the real world outside. "Daddy," I asked, turning to Bellamy, my eyes pleading for permission, "may I go look beyond the gate?" My heart longed to behold the Argentine landscape, to witness the world beyond our enchanted realm.

I knew Bellamy had a ton of work to tackle, getting the circus up and running after our long hiatus, so I anticipated a denial. But to my surprise, he nodded, "As you wish." I took off running towards the entrance, my excitement building. At the front gate, I found lot-lice eagerly lining up to enter the magical circus.

Meanwhile, back inside, I knew Bellamy and the crew were scrambling to get everything ready, from setting up the big top to rehearsing performances. It was a Herculean task, but they were happily working to bring the circus back to life. I gazed beyond the crowd and took in the vibrant colors of the suburban homes, a stark contrast to the poverty that seemed to weigh heavily on the area.

Admiring the views, I was startled by Bellamy's presence behind me. "It's beautiful, isn't it?" he asked, his words puzzling me. I hesitated, not wanting to disappoint him, "It looks… sad" I ventured, confusion etched on my face. "Why did you choose this place?" I asked.

Bellamy joined me at the fence, his hands grasping the railing as we gazed out together. "Darlington Circus is an escape from reality for everyone," he said with conviction. "Who is more deserving of that escape than those who can't afford to flee their hardships?"

He turned to me, his piercing blue eyes holding mine, their charm and intensity captivating. "After being surrounded by magic for so long, it's easy to forget the struggles of the mortal world," he continued, his sad tone I didn't recognize. "You, too, have known that struggle, remember your lives before you returned to us? I once knew it as well."

I nodded, unsure how to respond, as Bellamy's words struck a chord deep within me. "We travel far and wide, bringing wonder to all, and I hope that in some small way, we can offer people a reprieve from their struggles, a chance to forget their troubles," he said, his voice tinged with sorrow.

I was surprised, having never heard Bellamy speak of the circus's purpose with such vulnerability and emotion. His words revealed a depth to our mission that I had never fully considered, and I felt a surge of appreciation for the impact we had on the lives of others.

As we gazed out at the crowd, more people gathered, eager to catch a glimpse of the magical circus. It was clear that our reputation had preceded us. "This is one of the poorest areas in Argentina," Bellamy said, his voice filled with a mix of sadness and determination.

I turned to him, curiosity getting the better of me, "Is that why you chose to come here?" I asked. When he turned back to me, a warm smile spread across his face, and I took that as a resounding yes. I smiled back, feeling a sense of pride and purpose in bringing joy to those who needed it most.

Bellamy took my hand, leading me back to the tent where I would soon mesmerize the crowd with Eve. He pressed a gentle kiss to my cheek, his eyes shining with pride and affection. As I walked away from him, I felt his gaze follow me until I reached Velar's side.

Just as I was about to disappear into the tent, Bellamy's voice rang out, "Remember, straight back to Jubilee after your performance!" I raised my hand in a silent acknowledgement, not turning back, but feeling his watchful eyes upon me until I vanished into the tent's folds.

When it was time to open the circus a sea of eager faces flooded in. Yet, I couldn't shake off a nagging sense of unease, its source elusive. The performers around me were beaming with joy, their enthusiasm infectious.

Everyone was dressed to impress, ready to dazzle the audience with their honed skills. I was set to perform a trapeze act with Eve, a routine we had rehearsed countless times, to the point where I could execute it flawlessly even in my dreams.

The thrill of performing for a crowd of enthusiastic fans is always electrifying! I dusted my hands with powder, wishing I had more to calm my nerves. "Ok, ladies, take your places!" Velar called out, approaching us with a confident stride.

I nodded and began ascending my ladder, Eve doing the same. As I climbed higher, I gazed out at the crowd, the stands filling with eager spectators. Suddenly, the ladder wobbled beneath me, and I froze, my heart skipping a beat, but before I could react, Velar sprang into action, steadying the ladder with a firm grip, ensuring my safe passage to the platform above.

As I stood atop the platform, my nerves reached a fever pitch. I looked at the faces below, then my eyes locked onto Eve. She was shining across from me, our matching outfits glinting in the light. Velar's concerned expression caught my attention, his eyes fixed on me with a mix of apprehension and focus from below.

I wondered if his nerves were due to my mortality, the risk of a fatal fall, or if he doubted my ability to recall the routine. Whatever the reason, it was time to push aside my fears and perform. I took a deep breath, the familiar rhythm of the music beginning to pulse through my veins and prepared to take the leap of faith.

I waited for Eve, ready to follow her lead. Our trapeze routine, honed over years of practice, was a finely choreographed dance. We'd added new flourishes and tricks, but the core remained the same. As the lights dimmed and the music swelled, the audience scurried to their seats.

I waited for Eve's nod, then launched myself into the air, arms outstretched. Her arms enveloped me, and we soared through the air, the crowd gasping in shock. We swung back in the opposite direction, Eve's strength propelling me upward.

I grasped the trapeze bar hurtling towards me, landing gracefully on the opposite platform. The lights shifted, and Eve nodded again. This time, we ran towards each other, and I executed a flip in mid-air before Eve caught me. We swung back, and she launched me into a split in the air, the crowd erupting into cheers and applause.

We landed gracefully on the opposite platforms, our routine unfolding with precision. The lights shifted, and Eve nodded again, cueing our next move. We sprinted towards each other, and I executed a flip, Eve catching me effortlessly. We swung back, and she launched me into a split, the crowd's cheers intensifying. We performed a total of ten thrilling trapeze tricks, each one more breathtaking than the last.

As the finale approached, the silk ropes descended from the tent ceiling, and two additional performers joined us. In perfect sync, we ran towards the ropes, which lifted us skyward. We secured ourselves in the ropes and took turns performing dazzling magic tricks, one by one, our movements choreographed to perfection. The audience gasped in wonder, our grand finale a truly unforgettable spectacle.

The crowd was amazed, applauding wildly after each trick. Eve wrapped herself in a silk rope and executed a breathtaking corkscrew flip, soaring through the air to land gracefully on the opposite rope. The tent erupted into more cheers, and Eve looked up at me, nodding her head. It was my turn, the final trick of our performance.

I wrapped the aerial rope around me, climbing higher and higher until I reached the peak of the circus tent. I paused for a moment, letting the anticipation build, the crowd holding its collective breath. And then, I let myself go.

I plummeted towards the ground at a heart-stopping velocity, the audience holding its collective breath as I hurtled earthward. Just inches from impact, I halted my descent, suspended in mid-air. The crowd exploded into a frenzy of claps and cheers, their relief and amazement palpable. I grinned, triumphant, and joined my fellow performers in a graceful bow. Together, we savored the thunderous ovation, our smiles beaming with pride and exhilaration. Then, with a final flourish, we dashed offstage.

As soon as our act ended, Eve rushed off to prepare for her next performance, but I raced into Velar's waiting arms. "You were amazing!" he exclaimed, sweeping me up in a warm embrace and lifting me off the ground. He spun me around in a circle, my feet dangling in mid-air, before gently setting me back down.

The next act was already entrancing the audience as we exited the tent. "I'd love to escort you back to Jubilee," Velar said, "but I need to assist the Risley family with their act." I smiled, still basking in the afterglow of our performance. "No worries!" I said, skipping joyfully down the path towards the willow tree, my heart full of joy and my spirit soaring.

I had barely reached the willow tree when a sudden commotion erupted, shattering the joyful atmosphere. Smiles and laughter turned to screams and chaos as the crowd near the front gate scattered in all directions in a panic. I pushed my way through the frantic mass, my heart racing, and reached the entrance gate. That's when I saw them, the elders, their dark hoods a horrifying sight.

Without hesitation, I sprinted back towards Velar and Eve, my warning cry lost in the chaos. Velar's eyes locked onto mine, and he hastened towards me, Eve close behind. "They found us!" Eve exclaimed, her voice laced with fear, as we converged in a tight knot, our minds racing.

"We need to get to Bellamy, now!" I urged, knowing he'd already be battling the elders. We plunged into the chaotic crowd, fighting our way through the sea of panicked bodies. Velar grasped my hand tightly, ensuring we didn't get separated in the mayhem. As we drew closer to the entrance, I saw Bellamy unleashing his magic to hold the elders at bay, his powers conjuring a shimmering barrier to protect the circus.

Mesidor, Ambrette, and Sage stood bravely at the forefront, their magic swirling in a fierce dance as they clashed with the elders. The air was electric with the sound of crackling energy and the scent of ozone hung heavy.

The elders hovered on broomsticks above the entrance gate, their dark evil presence was a stark contrast to the whimsy of the circus. Though they couldn't breach the protective spell that shielded the grounds, they persisted in their attempts, their dark magic swirling around them like a shroud.

My eyes locked onto a familiar figure among them, Petri, her eyes blazing with malice. With a flick of her wand, she began to manipulate the enchanted sky above the circus, the once-clear blue giving way to a dark gloom, the clouds darkening as if reflecting the evil that had descended upon our haven.

The moment Petri's magic darkened the sky, Velar bellowed "Sunlight!" Bellamy's voice rang out above the chaos, urging Velar to retreat, "Get back to Jubilee, now!" Velar didn't hesitate, turning to sprint back to the safety of Jubilee alongside the other vampires, seeking refuge from the impending sunlight. I instinctively moved to follow him, but a sudden blast of magic struck a nearby tent, sending me diving for cover. I hid behind the crumbling canvas, my heart racing, as the world around me descended into chaos.

I peeked out from my hiding spot to see Sage unleashing her potent magic, her spells striking the elder witches with precision. One by one, they tumbled from their brooms, plummeting to the ground where Ambrette and Mesidor stood ready, their own magic at the forefront.

The elders didn't stand a chance, and soon they fled in disarray. The circus crew and performers rallied together, united in our determination to protect our home. We stood firm, a formidable force against the darkness that had threatened to consume us. Meanwhile, the attendees scrambled for safety, some hiding in terror while others desperately sought escape routes.

As the elders fled on their brooms, I emerged from my hiding spot, still in shock. Bellamy rushed towards me, his eyes scanning me frantically. Instead of scolding me for not seeking safety in Jubilee, he asked with genuine concern, "Are you okay?"

His hands gently probed my face and body, searching for any signs of harm. I assured him I was fine, just a bit disheveled from the debris. Once he was convinced, we surveyed the circus grounds, taking in the devastation. The tents were torn and tattered, our enchanted sky now marred by a massive tear.

Bellamy swiftly issued instructions to the crew, prioritizing the evacuation of our visitors. Within minutes, the crowd began to disperse, their faces etched with worry and confusion. I knew this incident would spark a public relations crisis, and my mind raced with the challenge of containing the story and mitigating the damage to our reputation.

Just as I was about to head back to check on Velar, I heard Luccas's voice calling out to me. "Nicole!" he shouted, his footsteps pounding the ground as he sprinted towards me. I turned to face him, a mix of relief and annoyance washing over me. He had emerged from a nearby tent. I was about to scold him for leaving the safety of Jubilee, where he was supposed to be waiting, but my words died on my lips.

A dark shadow loomed over me, and I squinted against the sudden contrast. In an instant, an elder descended on her broomstick, her eyes fixed on Lucca. My heart raced in horror as she reached down and snatched him up, his tiny form dangling in mid- air.

Before I could even cry out, she soared back through the tear in the enchanted sky, vanishing into the darkness above. In the blink of an eye, my little brother was gone.

CHAPTER
TWENTY-THREE

"Lucca!" I screamed at the top of my lungs, my voice shredding the air. Bellamy's arms shot up towards the sky, but it was too late. In the blink of an eye, they were gone. My entire world came crashing down around me.

Bellamy rushed to my side; his face etched with determination. "We will get him back," he vowed, as I collapsed to my knees, overcome with grief. Bellamy knelt beside me, wrapping his arms around me as I sobbed uncontrollably. "They took Lucca, they took him," I repeated frantically, my words tumbling out in a desperate plea.

Tears streamed down my face, and I felt like I was suffocating. My heart was shattering into a million pieces, and I was powerless to stop it. "They're going to kill him; I know they are!" I wailed, my body shaking with anguish. I was consumed by self-loathing, blaming myself for bringing Lucca to the circus.

Bellamy held me close, trying to comfort me, but his words of reassurance felt hollow. "We will get him back," he repeated, but I couldn't bear to believe him. I wept uncontrollably as the crowd filed out of the circus, their faces a blur. Bellamy scooped me up, cradling me in his arms, and carried me back to Jubilee, my tears soaking into his chest.

As we made our way back to Jubilee, the news of Lucca's abduction spread like wildfire. I knew Bellamy was eager to jump, but I refused to leave without my brother. "We can't jump, they have Lucca! We have to get him back now!" I exclaimed, my voice hoarse from crying.

When we arrived at Jubilee, Velar was waiting anxiously at the entrance. "What happened?" he asked, his eyes wide with concern. I was too distraught to speak, so Bellamy filled him in. "The elders took Lucca." Velar's hands flew to his mouth in shock. "Oh my God, Nic, I'm so sorry."

He turned to Bellamy; his expression determined. "We will get him back, right?" Bellamy nodded grimly. "We need to jump right away." But Velar hesitated, his eyes clouding with uncertainty. "Shouldn't we go after them?" he asked, his voice laced with doubt. Bellamy didn't respond, instead, he continued walking into Casmira, carrying me in his arms, his jaw set in determination.

Velar trailed behind us, his persistence evident in his voice. "Are we going to go after them? We have to get Lucca back now!" Bellamy's stride suddenly halted, and he spun around to face Velar, his eyes blazing with frustration. "And how exactly do you propose we do that, Velar? Can you walk in sunlight? Do you possess powers that I'm not aware of, powers that could possibly defeat the elders?" Bellamy's tone was biting. Velar's eyes dropped, his head bowing in defeat, as he realized the futility of their situation.

Bellamy strode into the house, depositing me in one of the plush chairs before turning to leave again. I sprang up, desperate to stop him, but Velar caught me in his arms, holding me back.

"No, we can't leave him!" I wailed, struggling against Velar's grip. He held me firm, his arms a comforting embrace as I sobbed uncontrollably. The familiar sensation of the vibration only made me cry harder, my body shaking with grief. Eve burst into the room, her face pale and worried, and rushed to my side. She wrapped her arms around me, tears streaming down her face. "We will get him back," Velar whispered, his voice a gentle reassurance as I continued to weep.

When Bellamy re-entered the house, he approached me with caution, his eyes filled with concern. But I was too consumed by anger and grief to care. I was still being held by Velar, with Eve rubbing my back in a soothing motion. Bellamy reached out to me, but I shoved him away, my palms against his chest. "Go away!" I yelled, my eyes refusing to meet his. Velar's shoulders rose in a helpless shrug beside me, and Bellamy's face fell. He turned and walked away, leaving me to my sorrow and frustration.

My eyes felt swollen and heavy, my mind reeling with exhaustion, but my thoughts raced with a singular focus, how to rescue Lucca. I managed to stem the flow of tears, but my body shook with anguish, my mind consumed by guilt and regret. "He's mortal, they'll kill him," I moaned, burying my face in Velar's chest once more.

Bellamy's eyes met mine, filled with understanding and remorse, knowing I blamed him for leaving Lucca behind. He gestured to Velar, who quickly rose from his seat and motioned for Eve to take over. I watched through tear-blurred eyes as the two of them stepped out onto the porch.

"They'll figure out a plan, don't worry, we'll get him back," she whispered reassuringly. I couldn't fathom how she remained so calm in the face of such chaos. My emotions see-sawed between anger and sorrow; my mind consumed by visions of exacting revenge on the elders.

Eve handed me a warm cup of tea, encouraging me to take a sip. The moment the liquid touched my lips, a strange calm washed over me, as if the tea contained a soothing magic. My thoughts cleared, and I could finally engage in conversation, albeit in a numb, detached state.

Time became a blur, and I felt like an observer in my own life, aware of my surroundings but disconnected from my emotions. The sadness and pain were still present, but they lurked in the background, muted by the tea's calming effects. We waited in silence for what felt like an eternity, until the front door finally creaked open, and Velar and Bellamy returned, their expressions somber and determined.

As the door opened, Bellamy and Velar returned, accompanied by Mesidor, Ambrette, and Sage. The group's somber expressions reflected the gravity of our situation. Bellamy's eyes locked onto mine, and he hastened towards us, his face etched with concern. Ambrette approached me, her eyes brimming with tears. "I'm deeply sorry about Lucca," she whispered, her voice trembling. "We're here to help." I nodded, my own eyes welling up in response. Fear gripped my heart, not just for Lucca's mortal life, but for all of us.

Bellamy approached me cautiously. "I was hoping they could work here, in your conservatory," he said, his voice low and gentle. I rose to my feet, wiping away the tears that still lingered on my cheeks. Leading the way to the back of the house, I pushed open the door to the conservatory, revealing the vast collection of herbs and plants within. "Use anything you'd like," I offered, my tone numb.

As I turned to leave, I couldn't help but ask the question that burned within me, "Can you please find my brother?" Ambrette's eyes met mine, filled with sincerity and compassion. "We will, my dear." Sage, meanwhile, was already exploring the conservatory, her eyes widening in wonder as she took in the vast array of herbs. "You have everything here," she breathed. "Herbs from parts of the world that are hard to come by." She turned to Ambrette, a mischievous glint in her eye. "Sister, it appears we have been working in the wrong kitchen."

Ambrette's eyes widened as she surveyed the conservatory, her gaze lingering on the diverse array of herbs and plants. "I am impressed, Nicole," she said, her voice filled with genuine admiration. "How did you manage to gather all these?"

Bellamy intervened, a soft smile playing on his lips. "Nicole has a touch of the green witch within her," he explained. "And Casmira is attuned to her thoughts, providing her with everything she needs. It's as if the house reads her mind and manifests her desires." His smile grew slightly wider as he continued, "This connection has been present since I created Casmira. Even when Nicole is physically absent, her spirit remains, infusing the house with her essence."

"May we stay and work here?" Ambrette asked. I nodded, turning to leave, but my attention was swiftly drawn back by Sage's sudden gasp. I turned, along with the others, to find Sage holding an orange flower, her gaze fixed upon it with an expression of awe. "What's so remarkable about a Marigold?" Ambrette questioned her sister.

Sage's eyes widened, as if we were all missing something obvious. "This is the flower of the dead," she declared, her voice filled with wonder. Ambrette's eyes narrowed, her steps slow and deliberate as she approached her sister. "And...?" she prompted. Sage's eyes rolled in exasperation. "It isn't the living we should be searching for, it's the dead."

Ambrette and Mesidor exchanged a glance, their faces set with determination. I, however, was still perplexed, and my curiosity drove me to listen intently to their conversation.

"Do you think we can establish contact with an original elder, one of those who were crucified?" Ambrette asked Sage. Sage's gaze remained fixed on the marigold; her eyes gleaming with an unsettling intensity. "We'll need a lot more of these."

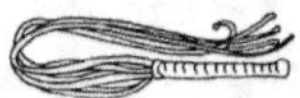

THE DAYS PASSED, AND THE CONSERVATORY WAS TRANS-formed into a sea of Marigolds, their pungent aroma permeating every corner of Casmira. The once-welcoming house now smelled like a funeral home.

Bellamy kept us hidden away, shielding us from the outside world until we were ready to face the elders. My impatience grew, but I knew the others were working tirelessly to prepare for the confrontation. I spent most of my days secluded in my bedroom, unable to face anyone, my grief and anxiety threatening to consume me.

One afternoon I ventured downstairs to see the progress for myself. The stairway was transformed into a vibrant orange carpet, with Marigolds lining every step. I carefully made my way down, mindful not to crush any of the delicate flowers. The soft rustling and murmurs grew louder, guiding me towards the conservatory. I followed the sounds, my heart beating with anticipation, and pushed open the door.

As I appeared in the doorway, Ambrette's eyes lit up, and she hastily rose from her chair, rushing towards me with a warm smile. Perhaps she was relieved to see me emerge from my self-imposed isolation. "We've found Lucca," she announced, her voice filled with optimism.

My heart swelled as I processed her words, initial relief washing over me. But it was short-lived, as dark thoughts crept in, my mind racing with the sinister possibilities. What had the elders done to my innocent brother? The uncertainty was suffocating, and my anxiety spiked once more.

I was aware that immortals would be joining our cause, as Bellamy had been referring to the upcoming conflict as a 'war for magic'. The very notion of war made me uneasy. Even with immortal allies, the prospect of battling elder witches was daunting. I couldn't shake the fear that my loved ones would be harmed, or worse, if our magic was stolen. The uncertainty of our future was a constant source of anxiety, keeping me awake at night as my mind raced with worst-case scenarios.

Despite the overwhelming despair that threatened to engulf me, I clung to the glimmer of hope that Lucca would be back with us soon. This fragile thread of optimism motivated me to assist Casmira in preparing lunch for the townspeople who had rallied behind our cause. The community's support was a beacon of light in the darkness, as they joined us in our quest to rescue Lucca and defeat the elder witches. Their determination and solidarity revitalized my spirit, and together, we worked towards a common goal, the safe return of my brother and the preservation of our magical world.

As the days passed, the community's support and determination only grew stronger. Velar and Bellamy led training sessions in the Emberlynn Forest, while Mesidor shared his expertise on spells, potions, and tonics with the residents. I put on a brave face, but the facade crumbled at night, and I'd sob uncontrollably in Bellamy's arms.

He'd hold me close, stroking my hair as I struggled with the overwhelming emotions. His magic was the only thing that kept me from wasting away, as I'd often find myself unable to keep food down. Each day felt like an eternity, my hope dwindling with every passing moment. I became withdrawn, avoiding the world outside my doorstep. I longed for my brother's return, and the wait was suffocating me. Every day, I'd wait for Bellamy's signal to march into battle, but it never came. The disappointment was crushing, leaving me feeling numb and trapped in a never-ending cycle of despair.

One night, I was jolted awake by a loud voice downstairs. I leapt out of bed, throwing open my bedroom door. Bellamy was right behind me, rubbing the sleep from his eyes. I couldn't wait for him to catch up, I had to know what was happening. I hastily wrapped my robe around me and rushed down the stairs, calling out, "What's going on?" as I went.

When I burst into the conservatory, Sage's wicked grin greeted me. "We've made contact with the spirit of an original ancestor witch," she announced, her eyes gleaming with triumph.

My jaw dropped in relief and amazement. Bellamy skidded to a stop behind me, grabbing the doorframe to steady himself. "Will they help us?" he asked, his voice urgent. I turned to Sage, my eyes fixed on hers, awaiting her response. She nodded slowly; her gaze locked on Bellamy. "I need you to speak with her," she said, her voice low and mysterious.

CHAPTER
TWENTY-FOUR

Bellamy eagerly agreed to work with Sage, and I refused to leave his side. I settled into a chair in the conservatory, watching intently as Sage worked tirelessly to reestablish contact. The hours dragged on, and I found myself drifting in and out of sleep, my exhaustion threatening to overwhelm me.

The atmosphere in the room grew increasingly tense as our efforts yielded nothing. Bellamy and I remained steadfast, refusing to give up, even as the sun began to rise the next day. Sage's determination was unwavering, despite her visible frustration. I repeatedly expressed my gratitude for her persistence, trying to bolster her spirits. Her resolve was unshakeable, and I drew strength from her unwavering commitment to our cause.

Just as the sun was about to rise, Ambrette suggested we take a break and resume our efforts later that night. "The witching hour is the optimal time for communing with the dead," she explained, "when the veil between our world and the spiritual realm is at its thinnest." Only when Sage finally agreed to take a break, Bellamy agreed.

We retired to our bedroom, exhausted. Once alone, I turned to Bellamy, seeking reassurance. "Did Sage really make contact?" I asked, my eyes searching for him. "I believe she did, and she will again," he replied, his voice confident. "Sage knows what she's doing." His words soothed my doubts, and I fell asleep, my mind and body rejuvenated by his unwavering faith in Sage's abilities.

When I awoke later that afternoon, the sound of Eve and Velar's voices drifted from downstairs, a gentle welcome back to the world of the living. I wasn't surprised to find myself alone in bed; Bellamy's responsibilities were many, and I'd have been more surprised if he'd still been lounging beside me. In the closet, I discovered an outfit thoughtfully laid out for me. A bright yellow ensemble that seemed to scream "sunshine."

I suspected Bellamy had grown tired of my monotonous black attire and was attempting to inject some color into my life. I donned the outfit to appease him, feeling a slight lift in my spirits. Upon reaching the downstairs area, I spotted Bellamy already immersed in his work with Sage in the conservatory, their focus intense. I didn't want to disturb them, so I simply observed from a distance, grateful for their dedication.

As I entered the kitchen, Eve greeted me with a warm smile. "Hey, I heard the good news," she said. I nodded, knowing she was referring to our successful contact with the ancestor witch. Velar approached me, carrying a steaming mug of black coffee, which he handed to me with a gentle smile. "Thank you," I said, appreciating the thoughtful gesture. The aroma of the coffee was inviting, and I took a sip, feeling the rich flavors revitalize my senses.

As the day wore on, the three of us waited anxiously for a positive update from the conservatory, but the silence was deafening. I grew increasingly worried that Bellamy and Sage's efforts might be in vain. We deliberately kept our distance, not wanting to disrupt their concentration or hinder their progress. Yet, as the hours ticked by, my restlessness grew. Velar and Eve exchanged knowing glances, aware of my mounting impatience. The wait was becoming unbearable, and I could feel my hope beginning to wane.

Despite their efforts to distract me with board games and books, my mind remained preoccupied with Lucca's rescue. I'd sit with Velar and Eve, physically present but mentally absent, my thoughts consumed by visions of my brother's return. As we sat by the fire in the main room, a knock at the front door broke the spell.

I rose swiftly, reaching the door before Velar or Eve could react. I flung it open, and to my surprise I beheld a sea of familiar faces on the porch. The witches of Jubilee, all gathered before me. Before I could utter a word, Ambrette emerged from the conservatory. "I hope you don't mind," she said, "but I thought they could lend us their assistance."

I swung the door wide open, welcoming the witches of Jubilee into Casmira with gratitude and relief. As they filed in, one by one, I stood at the door, greeting each familiar face with a smile. "Hello, Mrs. Darlington," they said, their voices warm and reassuring, as they made their way to the conservatory. I knew every single one of them, and my heart swelled with appreciation for their support. I felt a pang of guilt for my earlier despair, knowing that these kind and powerful women were rallying around me to help bring Lucca home.

Velar and Eve joined me, and together we thanked the witches for their support. Eve's eyes shone with optimism as she said, "They will definitely be able to connect now." I shared her hope, feeling a sense of relief wash over me.

As the last of the witches disappeared into the conservatory, Velar wrapped me in a warm embrace. I hadn't realized how much I needed it until his arms were around me, offering comfort and strength. I held on tight, savoring the warmth and security of his hug, and let my guard down for a moment, allowing myself to feel the emotional weight of the past few days.

The three of us returned to the main room, our wait tinged with anticipation. As the hours dragged on, Casmira silently appeared with three wine goblets filled with rich, red wine. "It must be five o'clock," Velar remarked, handing Eve and me our respective glasses. Eve quipped, "Does it even matter? In this situation, wine is for survival." Velar playfully rolled his eyes at her comment, then turned to me with a warm smile.

As the night wore on, I stirred awake on the couch, finding myself surrounded by the gentle snores of my companions. We had apparently dozed off during the movie. I glanced at Velar's watch, which read 12:47 AM. I nudged Eve awake. "Hey, we should sneak a peek into the conservatory," I whispered, my eyes fixed on the door.

Eve rubbed the sleep from her eyes, but I could see the intrigue in her gaze. Without a word, she agreed, and we both quietly got up. As we stepped out of the main room, the lights in Casmira began to flicker ominously, casting eerie shadows on the walls. We exchanged a knowing glance, and I could feel the anticipation building. The air was charged with an otherworldly energy as we made our way to the conservatory, the flickering lights casting an eerie glow on our path.

Eve and I clung to each other. As we approached the conservatory, the witches' chanting grew louder, their voices weaving a hypnotic spell. I peeked inside, and my eyes widened as I took in the scene. The witches had formed a complete circle around Bellamy and Sage, who sat at a small table, surrounded by candles, herbs, and a mirror. Bellamy's gaze was fixed intently on the mirror, while Sage and the others chanted in unison, their voices rising and falling in a haunting cadence.

Eve and I stood transfixed in the doorway, witnessing the witches' divination magic unfold. The lights continued to flicker, casting an eerie glow on the scene. Sage's voice rose and fell, her words weaving a spell, "Come to us, ancestor, we need your help." The witches' chanting grew louder, their voices building in intensity.

Suddenly, a cold gust of wind swept through the conservatory, sending gasps among everyone. I instinctively wrapped my arms around myself, searching for the source of the draft, but there were no open windows. Sage's eyes met mine, as if she knew my thoughts. "It came from the spirit world," she shouted, her voice barely audible over the chanting. Then, Bellamy's sharp gasp drew my attention. His eyes were fixed on the mirror, his face pale and frozen in a look of utter shock, as if he had indeed seen a ghost.

Sage's eyes locked onto Bellamy's frozen expression, and she declared, "She's here." The chanting ceased abruptly, and the room plunged into silence. Sage nodded to Bellamy, urging him to speak to the ancestor witch in the mirror. Bellamy hesitated for a moment before beginning.

"Uh, Hi there... I am Bellamy Darlington. Years ago, you gifted me with some of your magic... and now, elder witches are trying to steal it. We've contacted you for your help. They've taken a member of my circus, and we need to get him back. Can you please help us?" Bellamy's voice trailed off, and he waited anxiously for the ancestor's response.

The silence was oppressive, but Bellamy's nods portrayed a silent conversation. His eyes remained fixed on the mirror, as if he could hear the ancestor's whispers. The flickering lights grew more intense. The silence stretched out, heavy with anticipation. Finally, Bellamy turned to Sage, a look of confusion etched on his face. "You couldn't hear her?" he asked, as if it was inconceivable that others hadn't shared in the conversation.

Sage's expression turned annoyed; her voice laced with a hint of frustration. "No, Bellamy, only you could hear her." I nodded in agreement, my eyes locked on Bellamy's, sharing Sage's perplexity. The mystery deepened, leaving us all wondering what secrets the ancestor had shared with Bellamy alone.

"She's agreed to help us!" Bellamy exclaimed, his face alight with hope. "We just need to contact her again when we're ready." He turned to Sage, his gratitude evident. "Thank you so much, Sage. This means everything to me." He then turned to the witches, his thanks echoing through the conservatory.

He said in excitement, "She remembered me, knew my name... it was like no time had passed at all." A soft smile played on his lips, tinged with a hint of wonder. "It was... surreal, seeing her again." Bellamy's eyes seemed to glaze over, as if the weight of the encounter was still sinking in. The experience had left him shaken, yet hopeful.

I pressed Bellamy for more information about the ancestor witch, but he looked drained, his eyes haunted by the weight of their conversation. We bid farewell to the witches, thanking them for their assistance, and I embraced each of them warmly. For the first time, Sage, Ambrette, and Mesidor returned to their cottage, leaving only the four of us, Bellamy, Eve, Velar, and myself, to ponder the night's events.

Bellamy's gaze was distant, his mind still reeling from the encounter. "The ancestor witch has agreed to help us," he repeated, "however I fear it won't be enough. We need the Undying Council." His words were heavy as we realized the gravity of the challenges ahead.

The next morning, Bellamy set out early for the witches' cottage, determined to use their cheval glass to go to President Olivia and rally support from the Undying Council. I waited anxiously in Casmira, my mind fixed on the impending battle and the rescue of my little brother.

As the day wore on and Bellamy failed to return, Velar offered to stay the night. Though he tried to charm me into a distraction, my heart wasn't in it. I couldn't muster the energy to even kiss him, my every thought consumed by the mission to save Lucca. Velar understood, his expression softening in understanding, and we spent the night in a comfortable silence, each lost in our own thoughts.

Velar gently coaxed me to bed early, Casmira's soothing tea in hand. He attempted to pamper me further with a warm bath, but I politely declined. Casmira, sensing my resistance, intervened by shutting off the water as soon as Velar turned it on. It took him a moment to grasp the house's subtle hint, but eventually, he smiled knowingly and bid me goodnight, leaving me to my thoughts. The silence and darkness of my room wrapped around me like a comforting embrace, allowing me to surrender to my exhaustion.

Somewhere in the darkness of night, the sound of Bellamy's return pierced my slumber. I sprang out of bed, my heart racing, and flung open the bedroom door just as he reached the top of the stairs. "Daddy!" I exclaimed, throwing my arms around his neck and holding him in a tight embrace. The intensity of my grip surprised even myself, revealing a depth of longing I hadn't realized I felt.

As I clung to Bellamy, Velar slipped past us pulling his shirt over his head. I had forgotten he was still in the house, and his sudden departure left me wondering if he was leaving now that Bellamy had returned. But Bellamy's warm embrace and reassuring words distracted me from Velar's exit. "The Undying Council has agreed to help us," he said. "We'll be hosting many more immortals here in Jubilee soon."

I expected him to be anxious about the influx of new guests, but instead, he seemed eager to gather our allies. My heart swelled with gratitude and relief, and I surrendered to the moment, lost in the love and comfort of our embrace. Our reunion turned into an enthusiastic celebration, our love a beacon of hope in the face of uncertainty.

As the first light of dawn crept into our room, our loving embrace finally came to an end. I snuggled into the warmth of our bed, my mind racing with renewed hope. The promise of the Undying Council's aid and the impending arrival of our immortal allies filled me with determination.

Tomorrow, we would relocate to a secret location, a temporary haven for our gathering forces. From there, we would strategize and prepare for the battle ahead, our united strength focused on defeating the elders and bringing Lucca home.

As the day began, Velar and Eve joined us at Casmira, eager to receive their assignments. Bellamy and Velar were tasked with heading to the circus to welcome our new allies, while Eve positioned herself by the weeping willow tree, ready to escort them down to Jubilee. I would be waiting at the heart of our sanctuary, prepared to greet these esteemed guests.

This moment marked a significant milestone for our little community, the first time we had ever opened our doors to other immortals. Jubilee had long been a hidden gem, a secret treasure unknown to most. Today, we took a bold step towards building a stronger, united front against our enemies.

I had initial doubts, but Bellamy's reassuring words echoed in my mind, "It's a chance we have to take." He was right, as always. Some of these immortals had experienced the wonder of the Circus, but none had ever set foot in Jubilee. We were willing to take this risk, to get Lucca back.

As the minutes ticked by, the immortals began to arrive, descending the stairs one by one. I stood ready, extending a warm welcome to each new face, "Welcome to Jubilee." The words became a gentle refrain, repeated with sincerity as our gathering grew. Time was of the essence, they had only a brief window to arrive before we would need to jump again. And yet, despite the urgency, each immortal's eyes widened in awe as they stepped into our sanctuary, drinking in the beauty and magic of Jubilee. The same wonder, the same sense of discovery, played out on every face.

As Miss Poppet and Ambrette escorted groups of immortals around the town square, I was delighted to see Atlas emerge from the willow tree entrance. "Hello, Atlas," I said with a smile, watching as he ducked gracefully to avoid bumping his head on the tree's low-hanging branches. His eyes roamed the landscape, taking in the whimsical beauty of Jubilee.

"Of course, Bellamy Darlington would live somewhere like this," he said, his voice filled with amusement, as if he'd expected nothing less from his dear friend. Atlas's gaze lingered on the vibrant flowers, the shimmering fountains, and the charming cottages, drinking in the magic of our little world.

From the landing of the spiral stairs, I recognized the warm tones of Eve's voice, accompanied by a familiar cadence that stirred my curiosity. Reaching the top, I found Eve in conversation with none other than Draven. His eyes met mine, and he offered a gallant smile. "Mrs. Darlington, a pleasure to see you again, despite the dire circumstances. I hope I can be of help in rescuing your brother."

I interjected, my feet halting on the stairs. "Please, Draven, call me Nicole," I said. Thanking him, I hastened back down into Jubilee, aware that more guests were arriving. Draven remained beside Eve, helping to greet the newcomers before sending them down to me, his presence a welcome addition to our gathering.

Next to appear was Killian, accompanied by a trio of Fae strangers. "Hello again, Nicole," he said with a warm smile, before gesturing to his companions. "May I introduce Vara, Benson, and Alaric?" The three bowed their heads in unison, their graceful movements showing their Fae heritage.

I couldn't quite place them, unsure if we had crossed paths during my time in Barrow. Yet, their striking features, the pointed ears, the radiant complexions, left no doubt about their supernatural lineage. I welcomed them with a smile. I was left intrigued by the diverse assembly gathering in our little world of Jubilee.

As President Olivia's influence reached far and wide, witches from every corner of the globe flocked to our aid. One by one, they emerged from a shimmering portal. Each introduced themselves with a nod or a smile, their names and faces blurring together in my mind. But Sage, it seemed, was well-acquainted with many of them. She flitted from one group to the next, exchanging warm greetings.

As I stood at the entrance, awestruck by the sheer number of arrivals, Bellamy emerged from the tree alongside Eve, Velar, and Draven. "Quite the turnout, isn't it?" he said with a knowing smile. I shook my head in disbelief, my gratitude overflowing. "I can't believe they all came to help us." Bellamy's hand rose to the enchanted sky, and as the vibrations resonated through Jubilee, the reactions were priceless.

Eve turned to Draven with a mischievous grin, "Now we're in another part of the world." Draven's jaw dropped; his eyes wide with wonder. We all laughed, remembering our own initial bewilderment. In that moment, I felt a deep appreciation for this extraordinary life, surrounded by magic, friends, and allies from far and wide, all united in our quest.

As the crowd of allies swelled in Jubilee, Bellamy realized the need for more room. He unleashed his magic, and the air came alive with the sweet scent of creation. The gathered onlookers watched in wonder as a stunning white hotel materialized before their eyes, its walls rising with grace and precision.

The hotel's facade was adorned with numerous windows and balconies, each one offering a breathtaking view of the shimmering Opal Sea. The structure seemed to blend seamlessly into the landscape, as if it had always been a part of Jubilee's charm. The crowd erupted in applause and cheers, awed by Bellamy's mastery and the hotel's beauty.

As the crowd's applause and cheers filled the air, Bellamy's exhaustion finally caught up with him. He crumpled to the ground, his body limp with fatigue. I rushed to his side; concern etched on my face. "I'm fine, I'm fine," he protested, his voice weak but reassuring. I sat beside him; my eyes fixed on his drained expression.

Together, we watched as the immortals and other guests made their way into the magnificent hotel, their faces filled with wonder and gratitude. Bellamy's hand found mine, his fingers intertwined with mine in a gentle squeeze. I knew he was drained, but I also knew he was happy to have created a sanctuary for our new friends. As we sat there, I couldn't help but feel a sense of pride and love for this remarkable man, who poured his heart and soul into everything he did.

As the day wore on, the townspeople of Jubilee sprang into action, ensuring our guests felt welcomed and comfortable in their new surroundings. We were determined to make their stay as enjoyable as possible, knowing that their presence was crucial to our survival.

Once Bellamy had recovered his strength, we made our way back to Casmira, taking in the vibrant scene in the town square. The once-quaint streets were now abuzz with activity, as shops and restaurants bustled with customers.

As the evening unfolded, we gathered around the dinner table at Casmira, surrounded by the warmth and laughter of dear friends. Eve and Draven, Velar and Killian joined us, and I was eager to learn more about the enigmatic Draven. His refined demeanor and charming smile made it difficult to reconcile with the fact that he was a werewolf.

As I gazed across the table at him, I couldn't help but wonder about the secrets he kept. Despite Velar and Bellamy's playful teasing, it was clear they held Draven in high esteem. And Eve, her eyes shining with admiration, was unmistakably captivated by his presence. The atmosphere was filled with the joy of newfound connections and the promise of deepening friendships.

As the night drew to a close, I felt exhausted, ready to surrender to my bed. The day's events had been a whirlwind, and despite the help of our wonderful community, the weight of responsibility for our large gathering still lingered. But then, Bellamy's voice boomed through Jubilee's invisible speakers, his words echoing in every corner of our magical town.

"Welcome to Jubilee. Thank you all again for coming to help fight this war for magic. We greatly appreciate your help in this fight. Training begins tomorrow morning at nine am. Sleep well and have a magical night." His announcement was met with awe by Draven and Killian, their eyes wide with wonder. "That was incredible!" Killian exclaimed, as Draven added, "Bellamy, you've created a truly remarkable sanctuary here in Jubilee. I'm proud to stand alongside you in this fight."

As we bid our guests farewell, we gathered on Casmira's porch, watching as they vanished into the trees. Bellamy's arm encircled my waist, pulling me close as we stood together, savoring the magic of the night.

As I woke up to an empty bed, I reached for Bellamy's note on his pillow. "Training immortals today," it read. I smiled, recalling the previous night's conversations. Velar would be leading the vampires on a hunting expedition in the woods, while Sage and the witches would be brewing potions and tonics in the forest.

Eve, I knew, would be honing her skills alongside Draven and the pack of werewolves. And Bellamy, with his Fae warriors, would be perfecting their combat techniques. The thought of our diverse group coming together, each contributing their unique abilities.

As the others trained tirelessly, their determination to defeat the elders, I felt a sense of restlessness. My desire to rescue my brother was overwhelming, but Bellamy's words of caution echoed in my mind. I knew I had to be patient, but it was hard to wait. Seeking a moment of solace, I wandered down to the sea, the sound of the waves crashing against the shore a soothing balm for my frustration.

Sitting on a weathered piece of driftwood, I gazed out at the enchanted waters, lost in thought. Suddenly, I heard footsteps behind me. Atlas, the ogre, emerged from the dunes, his massive frame a gentle giant on the shore. "Sorry, I didn't know anyone was here," he said, turning to leave. But I called out, "Wait," He turned back to me, his eyes curious. "Please stay," I said, my words sincere. "I can leave if you'd like." I hoped he would remain, his presence a comforting respite from my worries.

Atlas hesitated, then ambled towards the water's edge, his massive frame shaking the ground. "I wanted to experience the enchanted Sea for myself," he said, a hint of curiosity in his voice. I smiled, understanding his desire. The sea's magic was renowned, and I'd witnessed its wonders myself.

As Atlas waded into the water, his shirt billowed behind him. Instead of swimming or playing in the waves, he suddenly vanished beneath the surface. I waited for him to resurface, my eyes scanning the water, but he didn't reappear. My initial calm gave way to concern, then panic. I hastened to the water's edge, peering into the depths, my heart racing with worry. Where had he gone?

Just as my anxiety was about to get the better of me, Atlas burst out of the sea. "Oh my God, I thought you drowned!" I exclaimed, relief washing over me. He chuckled, his eyes twinkling with delight, and then dove back into the waves, leaving me feeling a mix of amusement and annoyance. I settled back onto the driftwood, shaking my head in wonder. *Only an ogre would find joy in terrifying someone*, I thought, a smile playing on my lips. I watched as Atlas continued to frolic in the sea, his joy infectious, and my worries forgotten.

After what felt like an eternity Atlas lumbered up the shore, his eyes fixed on me with a serious expression. "So, the elders have taken your little brother?" he asked, his deep voice filled with concern. I nodded, feeling a pang of sadness. "Yes." His face set in determination. "I'm going to help you get him back."

"Thank you," I said, gratitude welling up inside me. With a nod, Atlas turned and headed back towards the hotel, leaving me to sit and ponder the vast expanse of the enchanted sea, its waves crashing against the shore in a soothing rhythm.

As night descended, I made my way back to Casmira, the darkness surrounding me like a shroud. I knew Bellamy would be worried, and sure enough, he was waiting for me on the porch, his eyes scanning me with concern. "I've been looking for you," he said, his voice laced with relief. I briefly mentioned my trip to the beach, and he nodded understandingly, not pressing for details.

Instead, he led me to the kitchen, his hands wrapping around mine in a warm grasp. His eyes, wise and knowing, held mine, and I sensed a gravity in his tone. "We go to war in two days," he declared, his words striking like a thunderbolt, sending shockwaves coursing through my veins.

CHAPTER
TWENTY-FIVE

As I hovered over the toilet bowl, my body wracked with dry heaves, I couldn't shake off the overwhelming fear and anxiety that gripped me. Tomorrow, my immortal family would be facing off against the elders to rescue Lucca, while I'd likely be stuck in this bathroom, my stomach in knots. The thought of what those cruel elders might be doing to my little brother was unbearable. My heart ached with longing and worry, and the mere possibility of losing him was enough to send me into another fit of nausea.

As I finally stood up, my legs shaky from the ordeal, I caught a glimpse of myself in the vanity mirror. My long brown hair cascaded down my pale face, framing a complexion that seemed almost ghostly. For a fleeting moment, the girl staring back at me appeared to be a stranger, a relic from a bygone era.

I gazed at my reflection, wondering if this was really what I looked like, a fragile, vulnerable version of myself. But my attention was soon diverted to the commotion outside. I wandered to the window, my eyes scanning the gathering of immortals below. They were arriving already, their numbers swelling by the minute. The impending battle was drawing near, and my heart raced with a mix of fear and determination.

Bellamy had decided to host a dinner party in Jubilee, a gesture of appreciation for our allies who had traveled far and wide to join us in the fight against the elders. Despite my reservations and lingering nausea, I knew I had to put on a brave face and play the hostess. I hastily applied some makeup, adding a swipe of mascara to brighten my dull eyes, and slipped into a stunning evening gown that cascaded down my ankles. The fabric hugged my body in all the right places, giving me a semblance of confidence and elegance. With a deep breath, I descended the stairs, ready to face our guests with a smile.

Velar awaited me at the bottom, his eyes fixed on mine with an intensity that made me wonder if he'd overheard my earlier struggles or sensed my trepidation about the impending battle. "How are you?" he asked, his voice low and concerned. I forced a smile, hiding my true state. "I'm fine," I lied, trying to sound convincing. I reciprocated the question, "How are you?" Velar's response was subtle, a smile with his fang flashing in the light before he shook his head.

Velar gently took my arm, entwining it with his, and together we strolled out of Casmira into the adjacent field, where the tables were beautifully set. The enchanted sun still shone brightly, its soft glow illuminating the scene despite the late hour. As we emerged into the open space, the gathering crowd grew larger, and for a moment, I worried that we might not have enough room to accommodate everyone.

Just as I worried about the space, gasps of amazement erupted from the crowd. I turned to see what had caused the commotion, and my eyes widened as two additional giant tables materialized alongside the original two.

The newcomers cheered and applauded, thrilled by the sudden appearance of more seating. Everyone adored magic, and Bellamy's skillful mastery of it was a wonder to behold. With a graceful wave of his hand, he had effortlessly conjured more space, his magic woven seamlessly into the fabric of the evening.

As the guests took their seats, Velar led me to my usual place at the head of the first table, directly across from Bellamy. "Thank you," I said, feeling a touch of special treatment as he gallantly pushed my chair in for me. But my moment of pampered indulgence was short-lived, as I soon noticed Velar repeating the same courteous gesture for Sage, his chivalry extending to her as well.

As the enchanted sun dipped below the horizon, a radiant magical moon ascended, suspended above us like a luminous canopy. Its silvery light bathed us in an ethereal glow, and I felt its gentle healing energy coursing through my veins.

The murmurs of wonder and gratitude from the assembly only reinforced my own awe, and I couldn't imagine a life without Bellamy's extraordinary magic. Entranced by the celestial spectacle, I was oblivious to Eve's approach until she suddenly appeared beside me, her presence startling me out of my moonlit reverie.

Eve suddenly whispered in my ear, "Draven wants to stay in Jubilee and join the circus with us after the war." She flashed a mischievous grin before darting off to rejoin Draven, leaving me with a secret that felt like a ticking time bomb. I knew Bellamy would never agree to such a plan, and now was not the time to broach the subject. Shoving the thought aside, I focused on the present moment as Bellamy approached me, his eyes shining with a warm smile that made my heart skip a beat.

As the room fell silent in anticipation of the meal, I rose beside my husband, and he began to speak, his words full of gratitude and humor. The crowd hung on his every phrase, and I couldn't help but feel a surge of pride and love for him.

As I scanned the sea of faces, a sudden urge to express my own thoughts and feelings overwhelmed me. I turned to Bellamy, my voice barely above a whisper, "May I say something?" He nodded graciously, and to my surprise, my words were magically amplified, resonating across the expanse of Jubilee, filling every corner of the enchanted land.

As I stood before the crowd, my nerves threatened to overwhelm me. Public speaking had never been my forte, but in this moment, I felt a surge of gratitude and determination. I gazed out at the sea of faces, my eyes locking onto the encouraging gazes of our allies.

My voice began to tremble, but I pushed on, my words spilling out from the heart. "Thank you all for gathering here to support us in this crucial battle. Your presence means the world to me, not only because we fight to preserve Bellamy's magic, but also to rescue my brother Lucca from the elders." My eyes swept across the crowd, and I was met with attentive listeners, their focus intensifying my nervousness, yet fueling my resolve to continue.

"All of you know my story, how I'm a mortal soul reborn to reunite with my immortal family. But Lucca, my dear brother, is different. He's from this lifetime, just a child of ten, and I brought him into this world. My immortal family has embraced him with open arms, making him one of their own. I'm eternally grateful for that."

My voice cracked as emotions overwhelmed me, and I hastily concluded, "Thank you all so much." I nodded to Bellamy, and in an instant, the magical amplification of my voice ceased, and I felt a wave of relief wash over me, grateful to have shared my heartfelt words without succumbing to tears.

As we gazed in wonder, Casmira's magic unfolded before our eyes. Plates bursting with a sumptuous southern feast emerged from the windows, hovering briefly before gently landing in front of each guest.

The tables were soon laden with an array of delectable dishes, crispy fried chicken, steak, and catfish, accompanied by fluffy mashed and fingerling potatoes, rich gravies, flaky biscuits, and creamy grits. The spread also included macaroni and cheese, collard greens, black-eyed peas, and cornbread, a true celebration of southern cuisine. The collective 'oohs' and 'aahs' of delight filled the night air as we eagerly anticipated our first bites.

As I gazed at the magically served feast, memories of Lucca's wide-eyed wonder flooded my mind. His innocent excitement from the first time he witnessed this spectacle still melted my heart. I fought to hold back tears, my eyes welling up with emotion. I pasted on a bright smile, hiding my true feelings from the others.

Throughout dinner, I engaged in lively conversations with the charming witches, Henrietta and Lucia, from a nearby coven, and the delightful Miss Poppet and Clove, seated on my other side. Mercifully, no one mentioned Lucca's name, sparing me from unraveling completely.

Following dinner, the gathering dispersed, with everyone retiring to their respective quarters. Velar remained at Casmira, generously offering his home to his vampire friends. As we prepared to face the elders the next day, a sense of anticipation and determination buzzed through the air.

While others seemed eager for the battle ahead, my anxiety spiraled out of control. The uncertainty surrounding Lucca's fate consumed my thoughts, rendering sleep impossible. Tossing and turning, my mind raced with worst-case scenarios, my heart heavy with worry.

At the first light of dawn, Bellamy's gentle whisper roused me, "It's time." We dressed swiftly and silently. Downstairs, Eve and Velar awaited us, clad in supple leather armor that seemed to have appeared magically. I didn't query the origin of their battle gear, merely felt a surge of relief that they had some protection.

Eve and Velar were pumped up, their banter and laughter filling the air as they psyched themselves up for the battle ahead. Meanwhile, Bellamy poured me a steaming cup of coffee, our exchange a quiet moment of intimacy amidst the chaos. "Thank you, Daddy," I said, my voice soft. "You're welcome, baby girl," he replied.

Eve and Velar, fueled by Casmira's special concoction, were like two warriors ready to charge into battle. Bellamy, on the other hand, was calm and collected. His mind was razor-sharp, strategizing and planning, a quiet storm brewing beneath his tranquil surface.

With our coffee cups still half full, Bellamy reiterated the plan, his voice low and steady. "Sage will provide the elders' location, we'll jump there and prepare to defend ourselves when they attack." His gaze then shifted to me; his eyes serious. "You'll remain in Jubilee." I felt a surge of frustration, yearning to contribute to the battle, but I knew my limitations. I nodded silently, understanding his words. My presence would only put others at risk, and I couldn't bear the thought of hindering our chances of success.

My anxiety was spiraling out of control, baffled by the calm demeanor of everyone around me. I felt like I was on the verge of collapse, my stomach churning with worry. I wasn't even going to be in the battle, yet I was a nervous wreck. I struggled to keep my fears hidden, plastering a fake smile on my face. Just then, Ambrette and Sage emerged from the conservatory, their quiet presence almost forgotten.

Bellamy greeted them with a bold smile, attempting to lighten the mood. "Where are we off to today, ladies?" he asked, his tone enthusiastic. Ambrette's somber gaze flicked to me before returning to Bellamy, her voice steady. "Blue Ridge, Georgia."

Bellamy clapped his hands together, trying to maintain the momentum. "The mountains are a good place to hide," Eve remarked. Bellamy nodded in agreement, "We won't have to worry about civilian involvement, that's for sure." I felt a slight sense of relief wash over me, until Sage's bold statement pierced the air,

"Nothing good ever happens in the south." Ambrette shot her sister a withering look, but the others seemed to ignore the comment.

The sisters retreated to the conservatory, leaving the rest of us to our goodbyes. As I wrapped my arms around Bellamy, our lips met in a long, passionate kiss. I savored the moment, breathing in his salty sea scent, committing it to memory. Time stood still as we cherished our farewell, the uncertainty of the future lingering in the background.

Our lips parted, but our embrace lingered, a tender moment that spoke volumes. Bellamy's kiss had mirrored my passion, but I sensed a hint of trepidation beneath his brave facade. He would never admit it, but I felt the faint tremor of uncertainty in his arms. As we hugged, I held on longer than usual, savoring the warmth of his embrace. It was a goodbye that spoke of the unknown, a farewell that my soul urged him to return safely, to come back to me.

Eve gave me a quick hug, not showing any weakness, a reminder that her immortality had honed her into a formidable force. "We're going to kick some elder ass!" She declared; her confidence inspiring. Bellamy nodded in agreement.

Then, Velar approached me, his massive arms opening wide. He wrapped me in a crushing hug, his leather and pine scent filling my senses. As my head rested on his chest, I felt a deep connection, a sense of longing for more moments like these. "Please be careful," I whispered, my gaze meeting his piercing emerald eyes.

I felt a pang of regret for not spending more time with him. When he finally released me, I breathed a sigh of relief, my lungs grateful for the reprieve. Velar's gentle kiss on my forehead was a tender gesture. As he joined Eve on the porch, I felt a knot form in my stomach.

As Bellamy reached the front door, he hesitated, turning back to me with a stern expression. "Stay here," he commanded, his voice firm. Before departing, he opened his fist, revealing the witch's knot I had crafted for his previous encounter with the elders. I hoped the spell still resonated within its threads.

The moment the door closed behind him, I sprinted up to the third-floor balcony, my heart racing. From this vantage point, I watched in anguish as the three people I held dearest in the world venture into the unknown, their figures growing smaller as they disappeared into the distance.

From my balcony, I watched with bated breath as our trio joined the assembled immortal force. As soon as everyone was in position, Bellamy's magic burst forth, and I felt the familiar hum of his power. The vibrations coursed through me, and in an instant, I knew we were near the elders and near Lucca. I could feel him.

CHAPTER
TWENTY-SIX

The floorboards creaked in protest as I paced restlessly. It wasn't until Casmira's plaintive whine from the floor once more that I finally halted my frantic stride. As I descended the stairs, my feet seemed to move of their own accord, drawing me to the second floor, a place I had studiously avoided since Lucca's abduction. The pain of seeing his bedroom had been too much to bear, a constant reminder of his absence. Yet, now, I felt an overwhelming need to be near his space.

I stepped into Lucca's bedroom, and my heart wrenched at the familiar sight. The Star Wars theme stared back at me, a reminder of his passion and the memories we shared in this very room. Everything remained frozen in time, unchanged since that fateful day he was taken. Tears pricked at the corners of my eyes as I felt an overwhelming sense of his presence. I knew I was close to him, and my determination to rescue him surged.

I swiftly brushed away my tears and raced downstairs to the conservatory, where Mesidor sat waiting. I had momentarily forgotten that he was tasked with conjuring the ancestor witch when the time came. My eyes landed on the map spread out on the table, and my heart raced with anticipation.

A black circle, crafted from candle wax, dominated the center of the map. I pointed to it; my voice laced with urgency. "Is this where Lucca is?" Mesidor hesitated. "If he's alive, he'll be there...I'm almost certain." His words trailed off, and I felt a knot in my stomach as I refused to entertain the possibility that Lucca might not be alive. Mesidor's eyes reflected his embarrassment at his own uncertainty, but I knew his words were spoken with the best of intentions.

I hastened out of the conservatory, driven by a sense of urgency and determination to rescue Lucca. "I'll be back," I called out, already moving towards the kitchen. As I passed through, a teapot on the stove began to whistle, and I saw that Casmira had prepared a brew. I wondered if it was the same concoction that Velar and Eve had consumed earlier that morning. Without hesitation, I poured myself a cup and took a sip, hoping to find some semblance of courage or clarity in its contents.

The brew was exquisite, its silky-smooth texture and warm chocolate flavor enveloping my senses. "Thank you, Casmira!" I called out in genuine appreciation. I reached for a refill, but the teapot was already empty, and to my surprise, spotlessly clean. A faint sense of unease tickled the back of my mind, but exhaustion suddenly overwhelmed me. As I entered the main room, a fire roared to life, and I felt an inexplicable pull towards the couch. I wrapped myself in a blanket, and before I could resist, my eyelids drooped, and I succumbed to a deep sleep.

"Casmira!" I bellowed, my anger echoing throughout the house. As I sprang up from the couch, I realized that I had been drugged. My own home had been used against me. I raced towards the conservatory, panic coursing through my veins. Mesidor's knowing smile greeted me, and I scowled at him. "Why didn't you wake me?" I demanded. Mesidor's chuckle was infuriating. "I promised Bellamy," he said, his eyes gleaming with amusement.

My jaw dropped in shock, but I shouldn't have been surprised. Despite my annoyance, I needed to know what had transpired. I glanced at the standing tree clock in the conservatory, and my heart sank. I had been asleep for nearly two hours. Anything could have happened in that time.

"The witches haven't attacked yet," Mesidor said, noticing my concern. "They might be aware of our trap and too cautious to come after us. Perhaps the elders are even intimidated by our immortal army." I raised an eyebrow, skeptical. How could they know about our army? Mesidor simply shrugged and returned to his book, leaving me to my worries.

The possibility of not rescuing Lucca began to haunt me. If the elders don't attack, how will we retrieve him? What if Bellamy jumps again without him? What if they attack and steal Bellamy's magic? My mind raced with worst-case scenarios. If they leave this location, they'll surely take Lucca with them. I couldn't let that happen. I had to think of a new plan, and fast.

I paced back and forth, racking my brain for a plan, but my mind was a blank slate. Just as I was about to give up, I heard Mesidor mutter something. I rushed back to the conservatory, eager to ask him what he said, but as I turned the corner, we collided, and he dropped the items he was holding. I quickly bent down to pick up the books of spells, a mirror, and candles that had fallen to the floor. "They've attacked!" Mesidor exclaimed, his eyes wide with surprise, as he took the items from me.

He looked shaken, and I helped him gather his belongings. "I need to get to Ambrette," he said hastily, already heading towards the front door. "Please stay here, Mrs. Darlington." I nodded, watching as he rushed out the door.

The moment of truth had finally arrived. They had attacked, but my initial excitement was quickly replaced with uncertainty. We had been waiting for this, but now that it was happening, I wasn't sure if we were ready. I returned to the conservatory; my eyes fixed on the map that Mesidor had been studying. Our new location was marked with a DC, and another circle indicated the elders' location, and likely, Lucca.

It was only a mile away, too close to ignore. I couldn't just sit back and wait anymore. I had to act. I dashed upstairs, rummaging through my closet, tossing dresses aside until I found a pair of black leggings, a tank top, and my trusty sneakers. I had a plan forming in my mind, and I was determined to see it through. I was going to get Lucca back, no matter what it took.

I sprinted down the stairs, my heart racing. I grabbed the doorknob and pulled the front door open, but it slammed shut with a force that jerked my hand forward. Confused, I tried again, only to hear the distinct 'Click' of the lock engaging. I turned the lock, but as I reached for the doorknob, it clicked again, refusing to budge.

Realizing what was happening, I quickly unlocked the door and yanked it open before it could lock itself again. But just as I managed to pry it open a few inches, it slammed shut once more. "CASMIRA!" I shouted in frustration, aware that she was behind this magical obstruction.

I realized that Bellamy must have instructed Casmira to keep me confined. But I was resolute in my determination to escape. I paused, adjusted my stance, and bellowed at the top of my lungs, "CASMIRA!" The front door creaked open a crack, as if defeated, and I sneered, "Thank you." I turned the knob once more, and to my relief, the door swung open, no longer enchanted to keep me captive.

Before I knew it, I was already standing at the base of the willow tree, my mind a blur as to whether I had walked or run there. As I began to ascend the stairs to reach the circus, a deafening explosion rocked the tree, leaving me frozen in fear.

The stairs creaked beneath my feet as the tree trembled, and I hesitated, half-tempted to retreat back to the safety of Jubilee. I took another step up, only to be met with an even louder blast, like a hundred fireworks detonating simultaneously. The tree shook violently, and I couldn't tell if it was the tremors or my own fear that had me trembling. When the dust finally settled, I took a deep breath and stepped out into the chaos of Darlington Circus.

Through the delicate, weeping branches of the willow tree, I gazed out in disbelief at the destruction before me. Clinging to the tree for support, I stared aghast at the ruins of my beloved circus. Tents lay tattered and torn, their once immaculate fabric now dulled and shredded.

Shattered equipment littered the ground, and the once-familiar scent of kettle corn and baked apples had given way to the acrid smell of smoke and magic. The air reeked of decay and rot, a stark contrast to the vibrant, thriving circus I knew. My eyes widened in horror as I took in the devastation, my mind struggling to comprehend the extent of the destruction.

Summoning my courage, I released my grip on the tree and ventured towards the entrance, where the chaos and fighting intensified. The cacophony of yelling, shouting, and explosions grew louder with each step, and I approached the billowing smoke with trepidation.

As I drew closer, it became starkly clear that this assault was far more brutal and devastating than the elders' previous attack. My heart raced with fear and apprehension, but I pressed on, determined to face whatever lay ahead.

Another explosion sent me tumbling to the ground, my body shaking with fear. I gazed in horror as a thick, impenetrable cloud of black smoke engulfed the entrance, obscuring my view of the battle raging within. My heart raced with worry for Bellamy, Velar, Eve, and the countless others fighting for their lives. I prayed they were safe, but the dense smoke choked my vision, leaving me blind and helpless. The magic in the air seared my lungs, and I coughed, my eyes streaming with tears as I desperately scanned the darkness for any sign of my friends.

I slowly rose to my feet, ready to retreat back to the safety of Jubilee, but then I heard the voices. I froze, realizing I was dangerously close to the battle. Bellamy and Velar would be furious if they saw me here.

Just then, a fireball whizzed past me, narrowly missing its mark. My heart racing, I sprinted towards a nearby ice cream stand that had been overturned and dove behind it for cover. Another loud crack resounded, and I curled into a ball, holding my legs tight against my body. I was shaking like a leaf, my fear overwhelming me. *What had I been thinking?*

I took a deep breath, peeked out from behind the broken ice cream stand, and my heart sank. Through the thick smoke, I saw a terrifying sight in the distance. Elders on broomsticks hovered above the entrance, their faces twisted with malevolence as they unleashed powerful magic.

Their spells cracked the enchanted sky, creating a rift that seemed to pulse with dark energy. With wicked precision, they hurled fireballs and lightning bolts from their fingertips, striking the ground with deafening crashes. The sheer force of their magic sent me into a panic, and I knew I had to get out of there fast.

The sight of the elder witches hovering above the entrance, their magic wreaking havoc, was paralyzing. My stomach churned with anxiety, my worry for my immortal family rendering me immobile. But as I continued to watch, a glimmer of hope emerged. Ambrette and Sage, fighting in tandem, unleashed a powerful blast of lightning that struck an elder with precision, sending her tumbling off her broom to the ground.

As I watched, a surge of pride swelled within me. The devoted witches of Darlington were fighting back with all their might, their magic crackling with intensity. I silently cheered as Sage blasted another elder off her broom, sending her crashing to the ground just outside the gate. The witches continued to strike back, "Yes!" I breathed, my excitement building as Sage took down several elders at once. But my joy was short-lived, as I spotted an elder slipping through the torn enchanted sky. She swooped into the circus; her eyes fixed on the immortals below. With a cruel smile, she raised her hand, conjuring a fireball that seemed to mock my friends. My heart raced as I longed to warn them, my voice caught in my throat.

I yearned to help but felt powerless. I darted from one vendor stand to the next, inching closer to the battle without being noticed. If only I could reach Bellamy, he could take down the elder. I gazed up to see her expertly dodging Ambrette's spells, tauntingly displaying the growing fireball in her hand. I ducked behind a pile of rubble, my heart racing. The elder was positioning herself to unleash the fireball, and I couldn't bear to watch. Just as I was about to turn away, a blur of motion caught my eye. Atlas came sprinting out of nowhere.

The elder witch was oblivious to the danger lurking behind her. Atlas seized the opportunity, moving with lightning speed and stealth. He sprang into the air, grasping the broom and using his momentum to hurl the elder to the ground.

The impact was brutal, her body thudding against the cobblestones. In the blink of an eye, a vampire appeared, sinking their fangs into her throat and tearing it open. The swift and deadly teamwork left me breathless. I swallowed hard; my eyes fixed on the gruesome scene unfolding before me. The bloodstain spreading across the cobblestones seemed to pulse with a life of its own.

I spotted Petri soaring above, her broomstick precariously balanced as she gazed down at the carnage below. When she saw the vampire's brutal attack on her sister, her eyes blazed with fury.

Unleashing a deafening cry, she channeled her rage into her magic. The enchanted sky trembled under her wrath, as she blasted gaping holes and slashes that allowed even more sunlight to pour in. The vampires, forced to retreat from the intense light, scrambled to safety, some fleeing as far back as where I was hiding. The sudden turn of events left me awestruck, my heart racing with fear.

"Mrs. Darlington!" The urgent voice startled me, and I turned to face him. It was Henry, a vampire and a dear friend from the circus, his eyes blazed with concern. "What are you doing here?" he demanded, his tone laced with worry. Another explosion rocked the ground, and we ducked into a still-standing tent for cover. "You need to get back to Jubilee, now!" Henry yelled over the battle. I tried to protest, "I need to find my brother!" but my words were lost in the chaos. Henry grasped my arm, his grip firm, and began dragging me back towards Jubilee, determined to keep me safe.

"I'm getting my brother!" I shouted over the explosions, my determination evident. Henry's expression turned grim, "They'll kill you!" But I refused to listen, my stubbornness getting the better of me. I tried to turn back towards the entrance, but a faint tearing sound made me freeze.

Henry's eyes met mine, and we simultaneously looked up to see the enchanted sky cracking open, the rift slowly expanding. Panic set in as we realized the entire sky was on the verge of destruction. Henry's voice was laced with fear, "Please, come back with me to Jubilee. We just got you back, we can't lose you again! Bellamy can't lose you again!" His words struck a chord.

I knew Henry was right, and I needed his help to get back to Jubilee. I nodded, and we started running towards the willow tree, joining the other vampires in their retreat. We were almost there when a massive crack shook the entire circus, sending everyone crashing to the ground. The impact sent me flying, and I landed hard a few feet away. My ears rang, and my lungs were filled with dust. I couldn't open my eyes until the dust settled. As I lay there, I could hear screams and cries, the sounds of fighting continuing all around me. The chaos was far from over.

As the smoke and dust began to clear, I forced my eyes open, blinking away the grit. I looked around, trying to locate Henry, but the dust was still too thick to see more than a few feet in front of me. I groaned, my body aching as I struggled to my feet. But as the dust continued to settle, I started to make out the shapes of the vampires, fleeing back to the safety of Jubilee. My heart raced as I scanned the area, desperate to catch a glimpse of Henry's familiar face.

"Sunlight!" someone shouted, and I watched in horror as a vampire mere feet away from me burst into flames, consumed by the deadly rays. Panic set in as another vampire rushed past me, yelling, "We're going to jump! Bellamy wants everyone back at Jubilee!" My heart sank, my mind racing with the implications. We couldn't leave without Lucca! I had to find Bellamy, and fast. I scanned the area, desperate to locate Henry, knowing he would help me reach Bellamy. As the dust settled, I spotted Henry, motionless on the ground.

"Henry!" I yelled, sprinting towards him with a surge of adrenaline. I didn't wait for a response, instead using all my strength to lift the heavy debris that had been hurled on top of him by the explosion. I frantically cleared the rubble, my heart racing as the sky tore open above us, letting in more natural light. As I looked down at Henry's face, my heart sank. He wasn't responding, and I quickly scanned his body to see why. That's when I saw it, a giant piece of wood piercing out of his chest. I fell to my knees beside him, my mind reeling with shock and horror.

I felt like I'd been punched in the gut, unable to draw a breath. Everything around me became a blur as shock and grief overwhelmed me. I knew I was exposed and vulnerable, but my legs wouldn't budge.

More vampires fled to the safety of Jubilee, but I remained frozen in place. I vaguely heard my name being called out in the distance, but it was a distant echo, drowned out by the sound of my own heart shattering. My eyes refused to leave Henry's lifeless form, my mind struggling to accept the reality of what lay before me.

Velar knelt beside me, following my gaze to Henry's lifeless body. Another tear in the sky ripped open, and without a word, Velar scooped me up and sprinted towards Jubilee just as the enchanted sky collapsed. We reached the safety of the tree just in time. Velar shook my shoulders, trying to snap me out of my trance. "Why did you go up there?" he asked again, his voice firm but with concern.

I couldn't respond, my mind reeling in shock. Tears streamed down my face as I struggled to process what had just happened. Then, a fragmented memory surfaced, a vampire mentioning Bellamy's plan to jump us to safety. I grasped onto the thought, my voice shaking as I asked Velar, "Is Bellamy going to jump us?" Velar's grip on my shoulders tightened, his eyes locked onto mine.

I knew it was true by the look on Velar's face. "That's one of the plans," he admitted, his expression defeated. I felt a surge of protest and anguish. "We can't leave Lucca!" I exclaimed, tears streaming down my face. But Velar's attempt to comfort me with a hug only made me angry. I pushed away from him; my determination renewed. There was no way I could leave without Lucca.

The thought of abandoning him to certain death was unbearable. Velar knew better than to try and restrain me, and I took off sprinting towards the hills of Jubilee, driven by my desperation to save Lucca.

I sprinted towards the hills of Jubilee, my mind racing with a plan I knew he wouldn't approve of. I had to move fast, before he realized what I was up to. I paused at the hills to catch my breath, gazing back at the chaos below. The retreat into Jubilee was in full swing, with figures fleeing in droves. I spotted Velar, his arms waving wildly in my direction. He must have guessed my plan, and I knew I had to act quickly before he or anyone else could stop me.

I saw Velar charging towards me from afar, his realization of my plan written across his face. I took off in a sprint, dashing up the hill towards Mesidor and Ambrette's cottage. My heart raced with urgency, feeling Velar's pursuit mere seconds behind. I banged on the door, but it remained shut. No answer.

Time was running out. Velar was almost upon me. Without hesitation, I turned the knob and burst inside. I took the stairs two at a time, my feet pounding the wooden floorboards. I reached the attic, and there it was, the cheval glass, uncovered and waiting for me. Its eerie glow seemed to pulse with an otherworldly energy, beckoning me towards the unknown.

I recalled the address where Lucca was being held captive, Vintage Road, Blue Ridge GA. I stepped through the cheval glass, uttering the address aloud. A faint "NO" echoed from behind, but it was too late. I had already emerged on the other side, standing in front of a dilapidated cabin deep in the forest.

I quickly scanned my surroundings, trying to get my bearings. In the distance, above the treetops, a plume of heavy smoke rose into the partly cloudy sky. I stood still, my ears straining to pick up any sounds. Faint explosions echoed through the air; the war was still raging on. I needed time to find Lucca, and the ongoing chaos was my only hope.

I crept towards the cabin, my heart racing with fear and hope. I peeked through the windows, but the darkness inside revealed nothing. My mind raced with worst-case scenarios. I couldn't give up, I had to keep searching. I circled around the cabin, my feet crunching through the dry leaves that carpeted the ground.

My nerves were stretched taut, but I forced myself to move forward. And then, I saw a window left open, a sliver of hope in the abandoned cabin. I froze, my heart pounding in my chest. I cautiously approached the window, my eyes scanning the interior for any sign of movement. Seeing none, I reached up and pushed the heavy window open, my muscles trembling with anticipation.

With a surge of adrenaline, I pushed the window open, the loud "Clunk" echoing through the stillness. I froze, holding my breath, waiting for any sign of movement or response. But the silence was deafening. I hesitated for a moment, then peeked inside, my eyes scanning the abandoned room.

The emptiness and quiet made my heart instantly ache. I couldn't bear the thought of Lucca being gone. Impatience and fear got the better of me, and I called out in a loud whisper, "Lucca?" The silence that followed was crushing. Tears welled up in my eyes as I realized he wasn't there. The thought of losing him forever flashed through my mind, and I couldn't shake it off. Tears began to fall down my cheeks as I struggled to come to terms with the possibility that I might be too late.

I withdrew my head from the window, about to leave, when a faint "Clank" echoed from within the cabin. My heart skipped a beat as I froze, wondering if it was the elders or Lucca. I cautiously returned my gaze to the window, my ears perked up, waiting for another sound. And then, a faint "Thump" resonated from the basement.

Without hesitation, I widened the window opening and hoisted myself inside. I tried to tread silently, but the creaky floorboards betrayed my every step. I hastily opened door after door, searching for the stairs leading down. The darkness and dust seemed to swallow me whole, and my impatience grew with each room I entered. And then, I pushed open another door, and my eyes strained as I peered down into the darkness.

I stood frozen at the top of the stairs, my ears straining to pick up any sound. The silence was oppressive, heavy with foreboding. And then, a faint rustling echoed from below, sending my heart racing. I knew it was Lucca, I had to find him.

Fear gripped me, refusing to let go. I forced myself to move, my hand grasping the old railing like a lifeline. I descended into the darkness, my feet feeling their way through the void. I took a tentative step forward, my voice barely audible as I whispered, "Lucca..."

The response was muffled, but unmistakable. Lucca's voice, faint but defiant. My heart surged with hope and fear, I moved towards the sound, my hands outstretched like a blind person. Something was gagging him, I had to find him, had to free him.

I groped through the darkness, my hands outstretched like a blind person, desperate to find Lucca. My fingers finally made contact with his head, and I swiftly removed the bag covering his face. A cloth gag was tied around his mouth, and I frantically worked to untie it. "You came for me?" he gasped, his voice laced with relief and fear. "Of course," I replied, my voice trembling with urgency.

Lucca's words tumbled out in a panicked rush, "We have to leave, they'll be back soon!" My hands raced to untie his bonds, my fingers fumbling in the darkness. I reached down, and my heart sank as I felt the ropes binding his hands and body to the chair. Time was running out, and I knew we had to escape, now.

In the oppressive darkness, I struggled to untie the knots, my fingers stumbling over the ropes as tears of frustration and desperation streamed down my face. Lucca's words, meant to comfort, only broke my resolve, and I sobbed harder, my body shaking with the effort of trying to free him.

I gritted my teeth and attacked the knots with renewed ferocity, my fingers moving with a feverish intensity as I fought to undo the bindings and save him. Time was slipping away, but I wouldn't let it slip away from us. I would not fail Lucca now.

"I'm going to get you out of here," I vowed, my voice steady. This time, I targeted the chair itself, pulling at the wooden frame with all my might. The old wood creaked and groaned, protesting the force I applied. Lucca understanding my plan joined in, rocking the chair back and forth with a fierce intensity.

The wood snapped, the chair leg breaking off with a loud crash, taking the arm with it. The ropes binding Lucca loosened, and he wriggled out of them. "I'm free!" he exclaimed, his voice triumphant, as we both let out a sigh of relief and hope.

Lucca's small hand clutched my shirt, his fingers digging deep into the fabric as we stumbled through the darkness, our hearts racing with fear and hope. Finally, we saw the sunlight streaming down the stairs, and we sprinted towards it like escaping prisoners. We burst out of the cabin, not daring to look back, our feet pounding the earth as we dashed across the dirt road and into the safety of the woods.

Only when we stopped to catch our breath did I wrap my arms around Lucca, holding him so tightly I never wanted to let him go. Tears of joy and relief streamed down my face as I held my little brother close, feeling his warm breath on my neck. But as I finally released him from my embrace, my heart shattered into a million pieces.

His tiny body, once full of life and energy, was now a mere skeleton, starved and depleted of all vitality. His eyes, once bright and sparkling, were now sunken and haunted, with dark circles etched beneath them like a cruel mockery. His skin was dry and pale, his lips cracked and parched. He was a mere shadow of his former self, a tiny, fragile being who had been brutalized by the elders' cruelty.

My tears dried up, replaced by a burning rage that coursed through my veins like molten lava. Something primal and fierce awakened within me, a fierce determination to protect my brother at all costs. At that moment, I knew I would stop at nothing to make the elders pay for their atrocities. I would not rest until they faced justice, until they suffered as Lucca had suffered.

We huddled in the woods, our breathing synchronized with the pounding of our hearts. I scanned our surroundings, desperate to find a safe path back to the circus. Lucca's frail body swayed precariously, his eyes sunken with exhaustion. Every second counted; I knew he was running out of time.

The smoke in the distance was clearing, a grim sign that the battle was subsiding. "We have to move, now," I whispered, my voice laced with urgency. Lucca's gaze met mine, his eyes pleading for strength. I helped him up, his legs trembling like a newborn fawn's. My heart wrenched as he leaned on me, his tiny body wracked with pain. The healing grass at Jubilee's was our only hope. I grasped his hand, and we stumbled forward. The circus was our sanctuary, our haven. We had to make it back, no matter what.

"We're almost there!" I yelled, sprinting ahead of Lucca as the circus tents came into view. Our descent down the mountain was fraught with danger, the explosions growing louder and closer with each step. We ducked into the forest, our hearts racing, as I frantically scanned our options.

Bellamy would most likely be at the main entrance. Lucca's frail body couldn't handle the climb or jump over the fence. Our only hope was to find Bellamy, and fast. I motioned to Lucca, and he nodded, his eyes flashing with determination. The next blast shook the trees, and we knew we had to move. I grabbed Lucca's hand, and we made a break for the circus.

As we approached the entrance gate, I spotted Eve, Draven, and the werewolves, their eyes fixed on the chaos within. I gestured to Lucca, and we darted towards the gate, our bodies low to the ground, using the trees for cover. My heart raced with every explosion, blots of magic whizzing past us.

We reached the fence, our faces inches from the metal slats. We crawled our way along, my eyes fixed on the entrance gate. Finally, I reached the opening, my gaze locking onto Bellamy's. His expression was a mix of confusion and urgency, but he didn't know the full extent of our peril. He motioned for me to hurry, but I refused to budge, my eyes scanning the area for Lucca to catch up. I counted ten elders, their eyes scanning the grounds. My heart was a jackhammer in my chest, pounding out a rhythm of fear and adrenaline. *Where was Lucca?*

One of the elders crashed to the ground mere feet from me, her eyes locking onto mine with a malevolent glare. I froze, my body petrified with fear, as she began to rise, her wand trained on me. Bellamy appeared out of nowhere, his hand unleashing a bolt of magical lightning that sent her flying back to the ground. "What are you doing?!" he thundered, his voice shaking me out of my trance.

I stumbled backwards, my eyes fixed on the elder, as Bellamy grabbed my arm, his grip like a vice. "Lucca!" I stammered, my gaze frantically scanning the gate for my brother. And then, I saw him, stumbling through the entrance, his eyes wide with fear. But our relief was short-lived, as two more elder witches appeared, their wands raised, their eyes blazing with fury.

"RUN LUCCA! RUN!" I shrieked at the top of my lungs, my voice tearing through the chaos. I didn't wait for Bellamy's response, I launched myself towards my brother, my legs pumping furiously as I sprinted towards him with a speed, I never knew I possessed. My heart was pounding out a rhythm of terror.

I saw the elder raise her wand, her eyes blazing with malice, and a green flash shot out, hurtling towards Lucca like a deadly snake. "LUCCA!" I screamed, my voice cracking with fear, my legs burning as I pushed myself to run faster, my arms outstretched, desperate to reach him before it was too late.

A mysterious force field shielded Lucca, and I seized the opportunity to grab his hand, yanking him towards the circus. Sage and the ancestor witch stood before us, a faint glow emanating from the ancestor's spirit form. Her eyes locked onto mine, and I felt a surge of protection and strength. White light burst from her fingertips, repelling the elders and their dark magic. I didn't dare look back; my focus fixed on reaching safety. But a blast from another direction sent me flying, my body scraping against the ground, my arms bleeding, my vision blurring. "Lucca!" I screamed in terror.

Bellamy's magic roared to life, deflecting the attack, and clearing a path for us. I stumbled towards Lucca, my eyes fixed on his frail form, my heart pounding with fear. We stumbled into the circus, our bodies battered and bruised, but alive, thanks to the ancestor witch's protection.

As the dust finally settled, I gazed out upon a scene of utter devastation. The circus grounds were littered with the lifeless bodies of witches, vampires, werewolves, and Fae, their limbs twisted in unnatural poses. I frantically scoured the carnage for a glimpse of Lucca's fragile form.

Tears streamed down my face, my vision blurring as I pleaded with fate to spare my brother's life. I stumbled through the gruesome landscape, my feet trembling beneath me, my soul screaming in anguish. Every breath felt like an eternity as I searched for Lucca, my mind refusing to accept the possibility that he might be lost to me forever.

Bellamy raised his arms to the heavens, his eyes blazing with fury and magic. The sky responded, thunder booming and lightning crackling with energy. With a mighty cry, he brought his arms down, unleashing a torrent of lightning bolts that struck the three remaining elders with precision.

The air was filled with the acrid smell of ozone and burning flesh as the elders' bodies were incinerated, reduced to nothing but smoldering ash and the faint echoes of their evil screams. The ground trembled beneath our feet, and the wind howled in fury, as if the very elements themselves had risen up to exact justice upon our enemies.

My heart skipped a beat as I saw Lucca's fragile body hurled to the ground like a discarded toy. I held my breath, my eyes fixed on him, willing him to move, to live. And then, miraculously, he stirred, struggling to free himself from the debris that pinned him down. Without hesitation, I sprinted towards him.

The smoke swirled around me, obscuring my vision, but I pressed on, driven by a fierce determination to protect my brother. And then, an elder appeared, her eyes fixed on Lucca with evil intent. Bellamy's desperate cry echoed through the chaos, but I couldn't stop, wouldn't stop. The fear of losing Lucca was a burning fire that consumed me, a fear that eclipsed even my own mortality. I knew the elder's next move would be the final blow, and I would not let that happen, no matter the cost.

I sprinted with every ounce of strength I had, my legs pumping furiously as I desperately tried to reach Lucca before it was too late. The elder's wand was poised, her eyes flashing with malevolence, and I knew I was running out of time. With a flick of her wrist, a deep purple lightning bolt shot towards Lucca, its deadly trajectory unmistakable.

I launched myself at Lucca, my body stretching out to cover his, shielding him from the impending doom. I felt the weight of my sacrifice, the agony of my decision, but I knew it was the only way to save him. My own scream was drowned out by the crackling energy of the lightning bolt, and then, everything went white. The pain was a burning fire that consumed me, a torment that threatened to tear me apart.

I felt my body rupture, my internal organs shredding apart as the lightning bolt's energy coursed through me. I was flung off Lucca, my limbs splayed at unnatural angles, my vision blurring in and out of consciousness. Bellamy's voice was a distant scream, a despairing cry that echoed through the chaos, but his words were lost to my fading consciousness.

I lay there, my body paralyzed, my gaze fixed on the scene unfolding before me. The ancestor witch's spirit materialized, her ethereal form drifting towards Petri, the elder who had struck me down. Her eyes blazed with a fierce light, her presence crackling with ancient power. I knew she had come to exact justice, to avenge my sacrifice.

The elder unleashed a torrent of magic, bolt after bolt striking the ancestor witch with incredible force. But the ancestor witch stood firm, her spirit form unwavering, the magic passing harmlessly through her. The elders' eyes widened in disbelief, her face contorted in rage, as she realized her attacks were futile.

Finally, she collapsed to her knees, exhausted and defeated. The ancestor witch loomed over her; her hands raised in a gesture of judgment. I waited, expecting her to deliver the final blow, to exact justice for the evil that had been done. But instead, she spoke in a voice that resonated through the air, a voice that was both ancient and eternal. "Ego magicae tergum meum." Everyone could hear the ancestor spirit now.

The ancestor witch's palms faced upwards, and instead of radiating light, they seemed to be drawing it in. The elder watched in horror as her own magic was siphoned from her body, her light essence pouring into the ancestor's hands like sand in an hourglass. The elder's face contorted in a silent scream, her body crumbling to ash as her magic was depleted.

I lay paralyzed, my gaze frantically scanning the chaos for a glimpse of Lucca. My vision blurred, my eyes struggling to stay open as blood poured from my wounds. Bellamy's voice was a distant murmur, his words indistinguishable from the ringing in my ears. I forced my eyes to stay open, my vision tunneling as I searched for my brother. *Where was he? Was he safe?* The thought was my only anchor to consciousness, my only reason to keep fighting against the darkness that threatened to consume me.

My eyes fluttered open, and I was met with Velar's anguished face, tears streaming down his cheeks as he cradled me in his arms. He held me close, rocking me back and forth, his body shuddering with sobs. I tried to speak, to call out for Lucca, but my voice was lost in the void. Bellamy's face appeared above us, his eyes red-rimmed, his tears falling like rain. Eve's voice was faint, her words barely registering in my haze-filled mind.

But I didn't need to hear her words, I needed to see Lucca. My eyes scanned the chaos, my vision fading in and out of focus. And then, I saw him. Lucca stood tall, unharmed, alive.

My heart swelled with relief; my final thought a prayer of gratitude. As my eyes drifted closed, Velar's sobs grew louder, his body trembling with grief. I knew I was leaving him, leaving them all, but I was at peace knowing I would return. *Lucca was safe*. And with that thought, I surrendered into darkness.

Until next time...

Stay tuned for more Darlington Circus adventures.

ABOUT THE AUTHOR

SK HINKLEY, A SEASONED MEDIA PROFESSIONAL WITH A passion for storytelling was born and raised in Lancaster, Pennsylvania. She made the bold move to New York City, at the age of 20, to pursue her dreams in broadcast media.

SK has worked with some of the biggest names in the industry, including NBC, MLB, CNN, Aljazeera America and Court TV.

When she's not behind the camera or creating engaging media content, she can be found exploring the great outdoors with her husband and children in her home state of Georgia.

SK finds inspiration in nature and the beauty of the world around her. And that inspiring love of adventure shines through her writing making her a compelling voice in the world of fiction.

You're invited to come on in and find a seat... It's Showtime!